FILTHY ROMANCE

An Instalove Novella Collection

LOGAN CHANCE

Copyright © 2022 by Logan Chance

All rights reserved.

No part of this book may be reproduced in any form or by any electronic or mechanical means, including information storage and retrieval systems, without written permission from the author, except for the use of brief quotations in a book review.

Cover By: Susana Mohel

Editing by: Paula Dawn with Lilypad Lit

For all those who love to read about dirty-talking heroes.

Sold To The Hitman

Chapter 1

Titan

"Look, Titan, you can garden your ass off after this job. Make your little spice blend and let out your demons. Hell, you can rub spices on my ass for all I care… as long as you say yes."

I chuckle a little, spraying pods of glossy red pepper plants with a stream of water. "I'm not sure your ass could handle my *Killer Spice Blend*."

"My ass can handle anything." True enough. Rogue is one tough bastard. He's a surly old man who has seen his fair share of crime, but he's also one of my best friends, so it's hard to say no to him.

He leans against the trunk of an oak with inked arms crossed, dark eyes narrowed on me. "One last job, one last hit, that's all I'm asking."

"I'm retiring from Ruthless Corp. at the end of this month, remember?"

"You're only thirty-five."

"And?" His gaze sears my skin as I mosey down the neat

garden rows in my backyard, checking the onions and saffron, basil and mustard, giving anything that looks thirsty a drink of water.

"Listen… I can't ask just anyone to do this, Titan." He follows hot on my heels as I cross the yard to the patio and coil the hose around its metal holder. "It's hush-hush, and I need the best man on this one."

I snag my still chilly beer off the patio table and knock it back, eyeing him over the bottle. "Well, I am the best," I say, tossing the empty in the recycle can, making Rogue grin. "I don't think anyone would dispute that."

Our casual conversation about murder might seem shocking to ordinary people who work mundane day jobs and then drive home to a loving family where they cook and eat a meal together around a dining room table.

I'm not ordinary. I wasn't brought up that way.

Killing is in my blood.

I detest bragging, but I'm damn good at being a hitman. In and out. Job completed before the mark blinks. I've made more money than I can spend, but I want out. In the beginning, it was thrilling. There was so much action-packed adventure, I couldn't stop even if I tried. Yet, that adrenaline rush finally crashed and burned. After working for Rogue for many years, I realized there had to be more to life than ending someone else's. Even if they were evil fucks and the world is safer without them in it. I prefer to stop and smell the roses, as they say. Or lavender. It smells fucking amazing.

"Don't go getting a massive head on me or anything." The corners of Rogue's eyes crinkle as he grins. "You said if I ever had a job I needed dealt with, I could call on you. I'm calling on you, bud."

Rogue doesn't appreciate hearing the word no, something I learned working for him for many years. "Fine, what do I need to do?"

"It's easy." He plucks a piece of paper from the pocket of

his jeans. "Just go to this address tonight and check the place out. You'll see a man named Steele. Big motherfucker with a tattoo of a rose on his neck. Steele is a buyer. The man he's buying from is coming into town to meet with him. The hit is the man running the whole show."

"What's the mark's name?" I ask as I accept the piece of paper from his hand.

"Don't know." Rogue shrugs. "It's why you need to find Steele and let him lead you to the man calling all the shots."

I nod, understanding completely. "I'll call you once I've got something."

He clasps my shoulder. "Be careful."

I smirk. "Always."

IT'S LATE, and the moon is high in the sky when I hop in my truck. The streets are deserted as I head across town, but this is the time of night when evil lurks, so I don't let my guard down. I locate the nondescript building Rogue sent me to and pull my truck around to the rear and park amidst the rows of fancy cars. I'm not sure what to expect when I walk inside this abandoned warehouse-looking place, but I'm always ready to attack when the need arises.

The military ingrained that into me. Ex-military, ex-hitman, it's been an adventure, but I crave the simple life.

I stride up to a red door and knock twice. A short window slides open and a man sticks half his face out. One blue eye peers at me.

"Name?"

I swear if he asks for a password, I may just kick his ass. "Rogue sent me."

No one wants to cross Rogue in this town, so the door opens without further questions and I'm ushered inside a dimly-lit entryway.

"In the back," the bald man says. "Through there." He points toward a black curtain and as I walk past, the man looks at my boots. Not your typical cowboy boots; steel-toed shit kickers, so if I get into a jam, I can kick my way out of it. They're also a terrific place to tuck away a piece, and my Glock-43 fits perfectly there. But my Colt-45 is nestled securely by my side in its holster. It's always good to be prepared.

Through the drapery, I enter a broad hallway and continue moving until I come to a door which reveals another passageway. This is a damn maze. Finally, I reach the end when I open a steel door. The place opens into a nightclub with flashing lights, techno beats, and a bar off in the distance. In the room's front is a rectangular stage, and I see a few women lined up along the back.

"Find a seat, everyone," a voice booms into the vast space. "The auction is about to start."

I follow the herd of men and turn my attention to the high rollers.

You can always tell who they are at any club. They're the ones with girls hanging around like accessories, sitting at a secluded table, protected by a swarm of security. They're usually drinking a bottle of expensive booze, and being boisterous about how much fun they're having. Right away, I spot a group doing just that. I keep them in my crosshairs as I head to the bar to grab a beer and blend in with the crowd. If I want to find Steele, then the fellow behind the bar is my best bet, because the person with the most information is always the bartender.

"Take a Heineken," I say to the bearded guy polishing glassware.

He nods, turning to the cooler behind him to get my beer.

"Thanks," I say as he hands me the green bottle. "Busy tonight. What's going on up there?"

He stares at me for a moment, taking in my black henley

and jeans, and I can see the cogs spinning in his mind, most likely wondering if I'm a cop or not. Once he's convinced I'm not a threat of the legal aspect, he says, "They're selling off the new batch."

"Batch of what?" I ask. "Cookies?"

"Women. Each month they have a new batch come through here."

I take a pull from my beer, thinking what to say next, because what the fuck? "Steele here?"

He nods toward the men I noticed earlier. "Man in all black. With the neck tat."

I study Steele for a quick second, sizing him up while he motions to a server near the table. He's tall, around the same height as me, but I've got about a million more muscles. He may not be a physical threat, but he's packing enough firepower on the security team standing in the shadows behind him to do some major damage to my sweet ass.

"Thanks, man."

I leave the bar, heading toward the stage as a man with a microphone tries to get everyone's attention.

These fuckers are actually going to bid on women. I never in my life thought I'd be at a place like this, but the women for sale aren't what I'm here for. I'm here to gather intel on Steele and his people, not get a conscience.

I move near the stage and pull out my phone, pretending I'm looking at a message as I snap a few photos of the group of men focused on the announcer.

"The first woman up for bid is from Romania. She can cook and clean, among other things," the announcer says, like he's selling a car and not a person.

A spotlight lands on a blonde in a tight, black dress, and the crowd cheers like they've never seen a pretty face or been laid in this century.

The bidding starts, and it's lightning fast. The woman goes for five grand and I'm so disgusted I nearly spit out my beer.

The next woman ambles closer to the announcer, and big blue eyes stare out into the throng like she's searching for someone. They settle on me for a moment, and a zap of charged energy ricochets between us.

She's exquisite, long legs, full curves, and brown hair that spills in waves past her shoulders.

The bidding starts, and within seconds, Steele bids on her. Fucker thinks she's only worth a grand? White-hot heat warms my veins that he thinks she's only worth a thousand dollars. The woman on stage has caught my attention and a protective force overtakes me. I don't know what possesses me, but…

I need more time with this beauty.

I need these assholes not to have her.

I need to make certain this woman is safe.

I place a bid.

Chapter 2

Blue

Journalism 101: Always pay attention to the five W's.

Who—a towering, strapping, gorgeous guy with spectacular hair.

What—driving my price up and spoiling everything.

When—now.

Where—sex-trafficking auction.

Why—I don't know. Because life sucks?

This is bad. Numbers fly around me, five, ten, fifteen thousand, and I watch my entire plan go up in flames, the match lit by Mr. Sexy. Steele goes higher with his bid, merely to be prevented again from winning me when the guy with piercing dark eyes offers twenty thousand. Wow.

Steele goes to raise his hand to bid more, but one of his henchmen whispers in his ear and he turns toward the exit door. In a rush they leave, and I'm screwed. With long strides, Mr. Mysterious marches to the stage to claim his bounty while I gawk at him in disbelief.

"I know. I can't believe it either, sweetheart," he says to me.

We're hustled off stage to a claustrophobic office where he pays the twenty thousand dollars before whisking me down a series of hallways and outside where I finally catch my breath.

"Nice to meet you," he says in one of the sexiest sounding voices I've ever heard.

And that I am even thinking about his voice makes it all the more annoying he side-tracked my plan. "Why the hell did you buy me?"

"Excuse me?"

I park a hand on my hip. "Why did you buy me?"

Ugh. I should have planned for the risk someone else could outbid Steele, but I really didn't think anyone had a giant set of balls to do such a thing. This guy must have Mt. Everest-sized balls.

Steele Wentworth is *the* man around these parts, and no one, I mean *no one*, crosses him. It was all set up perfectly. My girl on the outside guaranteed if I looked lost and innocent that Steele would go for my bait—hook, line, and sinker.

And he did until the guy staring at me like I have two-heads ruined months of planning.

"Why do you think?" he finally says. "You can't tell me I'm not your best option from what was in there. Can you? Think about it. I'll wait. Let you study the goods like the people in that building did you."

He's got a valid point. "You know what, I *am* going to study you. As revenge for all the women being ogled everywhere."

He holds his arms out as if to say 'enjoy the view' and warmth spreads across my cheeks as I peruse his sculpted body, starting with his booted feet, traveling up his long legs, past his lean hips, lingering on his broad chest before stopping at his handsome face. A smirk graces his sensual lips as I scan the angles of his cheekbones, across his scruffy jaw, over the dark hair cut close to his head and end by meeting his even darker eyes.

"How was the tour?" he asks. "Satisfied with me?"

I mean, yeah. There's no denying if you're going to be bought by someone, you would want him as the buyer. He's even got colorful tattoos peeking out of his t-shirt, and if the situation were different, I'd love to see them.

"I said," I draw out, "that you should have let Steele pay for me. You ruined everything." I step away from him, heading toward the parking lot.

"Wait a minute," the man says. "I bought you to protect you. Do you know Steele?"

I stop, turning around. "Do *you* know Steele?"

"No, not really."

"What does that mean? So, you *do* know him?"

"I said no, ok?"

I spin back around, heading toward the cars again, and say over my shoulder, "Then why do you think I need protection?"

"I didn't say you did. Hold on, can you please stop?" He walks behind me, catching up quickly.

The only reason I stop is because he said please. "What?" I ask, tapping my foot.

"Let's start over. I'm Titan. And you are?"

"Blue. I need to know where Steele went."

His eyes narrow. "You his girl or something?"

"Yeah, something like that." I don't trust this man to reveal the truth, and I want to get to Steele before I lose him. Maybe he's still here, somewhere in the parking lot. Maybe I can still catch him.

Maybe I can convince him to take me anyway.

"So, you wanted Steele to buy you or something?"

"Or something."

"But if you're his girl, why do you need him to buy you?"

I blink. I still can't believe I made it this far undercover in the sex trafficking ring to have everything ruined by this... what did he say his name was? Titan? "Listen, thank you for buying me, but I have to go." I dash away from him but he follows.

"Wait, I bought you."

I stop. I was scared of this happening. Here's the thing... I am a woman. I am my own independent person. I am not a piece of property to be purchased and sold against my free will. I'm a journalist struggling to stop what law enforcement won't. Frank, my boss, and I came up with this plan to work undercover and expose the whole operation. Six months I've been working on this assignment. And now Titan has wrecked it in less than an hour.

"What's your last name?"

"Titan Henry."

"Well, Titan Henry, I'm not a woman who is for sale. I can't be purchased. Maybe they'll give you a refund if you say I ran off."

His eyes blaze into mine. "Look, I'll level with you. I didn't buy you for any of the reasons men buy women. I bought you because you looked like you needed help."

I laugh a little, but feel a pang in the center of my chest that he wanted to rescue me. "Well, I don't need help. Thank you, though."

And I walk away, hoping like hell he doesn't follow.

Chapter 3

Titan

Fucking shit. This woman is a bit of a handful. But I love a satisfying challenge.

"Um, Blue," I say as she weaves between cars.

Headlights blind me when an SUV pulls out of a spot and cuts off my path. By the time it's out of my way, Blue is nowhere to be found.

I glance around, searching for movement, but it's too dark with the streetlight out to see where she went.

"Blue, where are you?" I call out into the emptiness.

"Shh, you're going to get us both killed." She's kneeling next to a Range Rover about ten feet away and I bound over there, dropping myself beside her.

I follow the direction of where she's watching and spot Steele, in the back edge of the lot, on the phone, pacing back and forth, squawking into the phone like he's going to destroy whoever is on the other end. And who knows, this is the kind of guy who just might do it.

"You're not planning on following him, are you?" I whisper.

Blue looks up at me with those gorgeous baby blues. "I do." She plants a fingertip on my lips to avoid what I'm about to say. "Listen, I'm undercover, ok?" My brow lifts. "I need to discover who he's buying from. I need to expose this operation."

She withdraws her finger from my mouth when she's stopped speaking. It's adorable.

"You're a cop?" I feel a little better about letting her charge off to pursue Steele. Only a little better, though.

She shakes her head. "No, an undercover reporter."

"Ah, I see."

"So, you can understand why I'm so agitated you ruined everything by buying me. Now, if you'll excuse me."

"I can't let you go after him."

Steele hangs up his phone, shifting closer to a black BMW SUV.

"And why's that?" Blue asks, easing up from her stooped position, ready to make her move.

I lay a hand on her arm, gripping lightly and say something I never imagined when I left my house tonight. "Because I own you, remember?"

Blue's eyes enlarge to saucers. "You did *not* just say that to me."

I'd laugh if this weren't a dangerous situation because her reaction is priceless. "Take notice of what I'm saying. You're a smart girl. You can't just go wandering after a bad guy. What's your plan? Do you have a plan?" She remains silent. "Always have a plan and a back-up plan."

"I'll have you know, I do have a plan. And maybe a back-up back-up plan. What is your plan? To steal my plan?"

My lips twitch, trying not to laugh at her cuteness. "How were you planning on getting away if he bought you?"

She explains how her 'partner' in this madness planned to use a contact of his to get her out safely.

"That's a bullshit plan," I tell her.

I can see I'm making her upset by the way her upper lip curls and her breathing becomes heavier. She rises, wriggling out of my grasp, and advances toward Steele. I accompany her, whether or not she wants it. I'm guessing it's a not, by the daggers she flings over her shoulder at me. She can throw me all the dirty looks she wants, I'm making certain nothing happens to this beauty.

"Well, hello," Steele says in the most revolting way when he sees her approaching him.

I hold my breath, ready to draw my Colt out.

"Hi. I was heartbroken to see you didn't go any higher in the bidding. Maybe you two could work something out?" Blue says, motioning her hand to me.

Steele's lip curls up into a sinister smile. "Oh, really?"

Blue moves closer, wiggling her body in some sort of sexy move to walk, her hips swaying like a pendulum. "I was kind of hoping you'd win." She giggles, and I can tell it's fake as fuck.

Hopefully, Steele doesn't detect her bad acting.

"Oh, yeah?" Steele's dark eyes find mine. "You need to keep a stronger handle on your property."

And then my world goes black.

Chapter 4

Blue

I'm really struggling with the five W's right now.

Who—Titan.

What—Hit over the head by one of Steele's men.

When—Just now.

Where—Right before my eyes.

Why—I don't know.

I can't believe this just happened. One of Steele's men struck Titan over the head with the butt of a gun, and he crashed to the ground like a fallen oak tree. With a yelp, I rush to Titan's side. Steele and his men hop into their SUV and peel out of the parking lot.

"Are you ok?" I ask, but he gives me nothing except disturbing silence.

I check for a pulse and breathe a sigh of relief when I feel the steady thump in his neck. Please, be ok.

"Titan, can you hear me?" I try to shake him awake, but he's out cold.

He doesn't even budge when I push against him.

This is not in the plan. What do I do? I don't have my car, phone, or any of my things, because I needed to blend in to avoid blowing my cover.

I tap at his cheek, staring down at him. "Hello, Titan?" I tap a little harder. "Please, wake up."

He stirs, and I lift his head to rest it on my lap. "What happened?" he mumbles.

"One of Steele's men came from behind and hit you." He tries to sit up, but I stop him. "No, don't move. I'm sure you have a concussion or something. Take a minute."

"Did they hurt you?"

I smile, liking the way he's worried about me, even though he's the one who's hurt. "No, I'm ok. They hit you and drove off."

Titan lifts a muscular arm to rub the back of his head with his hand. "That's weird. They did nothing else?"

"Nope." I shake my head. "They just left."

He tries once more to sit up, and this time I let him. "He must have had somewhere else more important to be."

"I guess." I move from beside him. "Do you want to stand?" He nods, and I help him to his feet, wrapping an arm around his waist until he finds his footing. "Let me use your phone to call an Uber. I'll take you back to my place. I don't live far from here."

"My truck is around back," he mumbles, swaying a bit and pulling his keys from his pocket.

Somehow, we make it to his massive truck without him toppling over and taking me down with him. Once he's settled in the passenger seat, I shut the door and round the hood to the driver's side and climb in.

"I'll have you all better in no time."

Under the interior light, I see he's got a nasty gash that's bleeding on the back of his head, and I start the engine to speed to my house.

"Thank you. But I feel fine."

"You have a head injury."

"I feel fine," he gruffs out. "I've had worse injuries."

"Big, strong man. I'm fine. Like caveman." I make the caveman deep voice, and pound on my chest before I back out of the space and zoom away.

"Tarzan pounds on his chest, not cavemen," Titan says as I make a right onto the street.

I shrug. "Same thing."

"Um, not even a little bit the same thing."

"Sure it is." I glance over at him. "Tarzan was a simple man who didn't know the way of the modern world. Just like cavemen."

Titan rubs at his head as I zip through the empty roads. "But they existed at completely different times."

I shrug again. "You say tomato."

He laughs, rich and deep, and I really like the sound of it. "Whatever you say."

I pull up to my one-bedroom house and park. "We're here," I say.

"What is that?" Titan asks, leaning forward, peering through the windshield.

"It's my house."

"Yeah, but I mean, what is that?"

I laugh a little at his reaction. "It's a glass home. Ever heard of them? All the walls are made of glass."

Titan shakes his head as he gets out of my car. "Nope, never have. What would possess someone to buy a glass house?"

"The views are spectacular."

He looks over at me. "I'm sure it is." The way he says it makes me think he doesn't mean the view of the woods surrounding us. "Hope you didn't spend too much on this, though."

"You really shouldn't throw stones at people who live in glass houses."

"I think you got that saying backwards." He grins, and I help him to my front door and inside.

"Does it really matter? Either way, the glass will break. Besides, they're the same price as a regular house."

"You've got to be fucking kidding me." Titan stands in the living room, glancing around at the open floor plan surrounded by glass walls. "It's got character, kind of like you. So, do I own this place now because I own you?"

"Ha-ha. Don't get any ideas." We still haven't discussed the fact they sold me to him or that he spent a lot of money on me. Should I offer to pay him back? "Have a seat."

Titan drops down on a lemon-yellow wingback chair and massages his temples. "My head is killing me. I'd like to see that fucker try that again. Normally, I'm sharp as a razor on my feet," he glances up at me, "but I was preoccupied by your hips."

"I'm sorry." I pretend he didn't just say he was watching my hips and move closer to his head, assessing the gash on the back with gentle fingers. It's not as bad as I thought. Luckily, he won't need stitches. "What do you do for a living?"

Titan inhales a deep breath and lets it out slowly. "Retiring hitman."

My fingers pause in his hair. "Oh, ok," I say with a little laugh. I cross to the kitchen and snatch a clean towel from the drawer by the sink. "What do you really do?"

"I'm serious," he says as I turn on the faucet, wetting the rag with warm water.

I stop moving, knowing that a man who visits a place like the one I was in tonight is probably not joking about being a hitman. "Oh."

Once I'm sure I won't pass out from what he just told me, I return to clean his wound. He grabs a hold of my hand on its way to his head. "I won't hurt you. I'd never hurt someone like you."

"Like me?"

"Yeah, like you."

I half-laugh because I don't know what else to do right now. "Wow, does this work on other women?"

The corners of his lips turn upwards. It's breathtaking and nearly knocks me off my feet when I see a slight dimple peek out at me. "I don't know. I've never used it on any other women."

I narrow my eyes on him. Hitman or not, this man is beyond gorgeous. I'm sure women line up to date him all the time.

"So… you've killed people?" I ask, changing the subject back to what's important.

"Only really bad people. People who have no soul and do things you couldn't imagine." His dark eyes capture mine, making my body feel like I'm in a sauna. "People like Steele and the man he buys from."

"Do you know who that is? Is that why you were in the club tonight?"

"Yes, that's why I was there. I don't usually partake in buying women. And no, I don't know who it is. I need to find him."

"Is that why you bought me? Because Steele wanted me?"

Titan rakes pearly whites across his full bottom lip, like he's stalling to answer my question.

"Actually, no. I bought you because there was just something about you. I knew I had to have you."

My heart rate kicks up, and I don't really know how to process the knowledge that he bought me because he wanted me.

"I know you're not really mine, but I want to help you. We're both after the same enemy. We can team up and work together."

"Oh, I don't know." I move behind him, so I don't have to feel his penetrating stare and dab at his wound, cleaning the blood out of his hair. "I kind of like working alone."

Titan stops me from tending to his gash. "Well, you're gonna just have to deal with me tagging along, keeping you safe. Because you're not gonna be able to get rid of me."

Chapter 5

Titan

I know this woman thinks she can handle Steele on her own, but she's crazy. I can't let her traipse around in dark alleys and dangerous places looking for a man who could kill her with one bullet to her head.

Nope.

I won't let that happen.

I won't let anyone hurt her.

Now that I've met her, I can't ever let her go. This sort of possessive thing has never happened to me before, but my gut tells me this is fate. That she's my woman. I've never had this primal urge I can't ignore.

"What's your last name?" I ask, wondering if she's even given me a real name.

"Payton. Blue Payton. And yes it's my real name."

I laugh a little at her reading my mind. "I guess your parents named you after those striking eyes of yours?"

She moves in front of me and shrugs a little, in a cute as

hell way. "Yeah, they said they were the bluest eyes they'd ever seen."

I'm right at her plump breasts. I look up at her, licking my lips.

Her gaze drops to my mouth and then darts to the cloth in her hand. "You're all clean." She skitters away to toss the towel in the washer that's off to the side of the kitchen.

"So, how do you think we can work together?"

"What do you mean?"

"Like, do you have a plan?"

"I've always got a plan." This is a big fat lie, but I like to pretend I have a plan most days. Usually, I just go in places and fuck people up, no plan needed. But I can tell that Blue is a planner. "I suppose you like to plan?"

She beams, jabbing a thumb over her right shoulder toward the opposite end of the house. "I have three planners in my bedroom."

Not shocked. Anyone who has a calendar on their refrigerator with post-it notes and stickers all over it is a person who doesn't just wing it. After spotting that thing when she fled to grab a towel, I knew. Based on the amount of things on it, she appears to be the busiest person on the planet. And the sexiest.

At the mention of her bedroom, my body heats. I wish I could take her back there and get a feel for her bed, with her in it. We could plan how I'm going to slide my dick inside her and claim her as mine.

"Ok, as of right now, I have no plan," I confess. "But I'm confident we can think of something."

Blue nods. "I'm sure we can. Maybe we should get a good night's sleep and start first thing in the morning?"

I peek over at the navy sofa covered in daisy print pillows. "I guess I'll take the couch?"

"You would guess right," she says with a wink, gliding across the tiled floor, past the kitchen. She disappears for a few minutes and comes back with a blanket and pillow. "You'll love this faux fur blanket." She spreads it out on the cushions with a whoosh, and tucks it in, giving me a prime view of her delectable ass. "Got it on sale at QVC. It was a steal."

Her chatter makes me grin. "Thanks."

"You shouldn't fall asleep or use any electronics. Concussions are a big deal."

I rub my head, feeling the bump there. "Yeah, I know."

Once she's gone to bed, I make a call to Rogue, filling him in on everything. I know I shouldn't go to sleep just yet, in case I really do have a concussion, so I stare out at the vast woods outside her home. It really is quite peaceful.

I think about the woman I just met tonight. Behind my eyelids is a vision of long brown hair flowing in the wind when I took her outside. A few strands swept across the porcelain skin of her face and I wanted to brush it behind her ear like I've seen done in movies when the hero saves the girl.

I roll over and plump the pillow, unable to get her out of my mind. Her eyes are possibly her best feature. Sky blue like a cloudless day. She's the type of woman when you see her, you keep staring just to take it all in, just to keep your breath from escaping your lungs too fast.

She's the type of woman you can't wait to get home to every day. The kind you don't like leaving.

I toss and turn, trying my best to stop thinking about Blue and everything she has to offer.

OPPOSITES ATTRACT, I guess. Blue is a morning person, and I'm definitely not, even more so because she woke me up every few hours to make sure I wasn't in a coma. I jolt when she kicks the side of the couch.

"Time to get up. We have bad guys to catch." She's bright

and chipper, and I cover my eyes against the rays of sun pouring in from all the glass.

"Go away."

"Oh, no you don't. It's time to get to work. Isn't this how you get things done?"

I groan louder.

"Well, sorry, I guess hitmen only work at night? In the shadows?"

I pop one eye open, staring at her.

She lifts her arms, palms facing me, like she's surrendering. "Ok, ok. I guess hitmen don't like to be bothered in the mornings. I'll make a note of it, in case I ever cross any other's path."

I think about the brothers I work with at Ruthless Corp. "You'll never meet another hitman."

Blue's eyes fill with questions. "I won't? Why not?"

"Hitmen just don't go places. They don't go to bars and meet pretty girls."

"They just buy them?"

I sit up, removing the blanket she gave me to use last night from my body. "You sure ask a lot of questions for this early in the morning."

She rolls her eyes. "Want some coffee?"

My ears perk at the mention of a nice hot cup of joe. "Yes, now that sounds great."

"Wonderful. I have a Keurig, so you can have any flavor you prefer. I have caramel mocha, creme brulee," she taps on her fingers as she names each flavor, "pumpkin spice, glazed donut, hazel—"

"Do you have any coffee-flavored coffee?" I interrupt.

She laughs, and it's the cutest sound. It lilts and sails in the air, making my heart thump. "Of course, I do, silly." She praddles off into the kitchen, and I'm not ashamed that I check out the sway of her hips as she saunters away.

I follow her into the kitchen. "I need to get home and tend to some things there."

Blue's gaze catches mine, one brow raising. "Ok, I can take you to your place and you can pick up some clothes and manly items."

"What are you talking about?" I prop against the counter.

"Well, I figured you'd stay here until we catch this guy."

"I will?"

Blue diverts her attention back to the cupboard and searches around in it, rising on her tiptoes. "Actually," she says as she whirls around to face me, "it looks like I don't have any coffee-flavored coffee." Her eyes sparkle as she smiles, and I'd much rather have that than coffee.

"I'll just take whatever you're having."

She pulls down two red mugs from a cabinet. "Chocolate mocha it is then."

"Now, why do I need to stay here?"

"Well, honestly, I'm kind of afraid after last night I may have blown my cover."

My muscles tighten at the notion of Blue in trouble. "Then you can stay with me. I need to stick around at my place anyway."

She places a pod into the Keurig and turns it on. "Oh god, I never even asked if you have a pet or a girlfriend."

I shake my head. "No girlfriend. No pet either."

"Phew, you were about to make me feel lousy for holding you prisoner last night."

I smirk, my mind heading into perilous territory at the thought of being trapped with her all night, her my prisoner. "No, but I need to go home. I've been away for too long already. There's something there I need to take care of."

"Right, ok." Blue is all business now as she immerses herself with preparing the coffee and bringing the mug to me.

I take a sip and nearly spit it out for fear of becoming diabetic. "That's very sweet."

Blue has a sip and sighs. "I love it."

I love watching her drink it. Her pink lips form an o as she blows on the hot drink and I can barely tear my gaze from the sensual action. We eye each other over the rims of our cups until she moves away to check email. After she's drunk her coffee and I've pretended to drink mine, she packs a bag and then I drive her to my place.

I pull into my driveway and shut off the engine.

She gawks at my sprawling stone house. "Wow, this place is massive."

"Yeah," I shrug, "it's home."

"Well, in your line of work I guess you have the luxury to afford nice things."

I give her a sly smile. "I work hard for it. Come on inside."

"Right, you have something mysterious that demands your utmost attention." She raises a hand to her mouth. "You don't have a prisoner in your basement, do you?"

"A what?" I lean closer to her as I open my truck door. "You watch too many movies. Besides, I'm retiring, remember?"

She opens her door. "Well, what's the rush to get home?"

"My garden."

Blue nearly slams the door on her leg, whipping her head to me. "Garden?"

"Yeah." I get out of the truck. "My garden needs tending."

"You're not joking, are you?"

"Come on, I'll show you."

Inside, I lead her on a mini tour of the house. She moves throughout my living room, staring wide-eyed at the vaulted ceilings and the artwork on the wall. Rogue collects extravagant artwork and kind of got me interested in collecting a few pieces for my own home.

I show her my favorite pieces of art. Mainly the Salvador Dali original hanging over my black-leather sofa. I show her my kitchen, where I love to cook using my own spice blends, and the spacious patio. We walk across the back yard to my favorite place.

"This is my garden." I show her my tomato plants and other vegetables. She marvels at my green thumb while I explain I'm growing basil and a host of other spices and herbs.

"Wow, I would have never pictured you as a gardener."

I bend down on one knee to pick a few weeds near the cabbage. "When I decided to leave Ruthless Corp., I had a lot of stress and madness going on in my head. People suggested therapy, and I thought I'd give it a try. One therapist suggested I take up gardening." I laugh a little. "I thought she was insane at the time and didn't want to deal with a garden. But I finally did it."

"Oh," she says, staring at all the basil plants lined in neat little rows. "So, this is what you're retiring to do?"

My chest puffs out with pride. "I am. I'm going to start my own spice blend company."

Blue's bright eyes light up. "I love it."

"It's called *Killer Spice Blend*."

Blue gives me a cheesy grin. "Oh, I get it. Very clever."

Is it weird that I already feel very comfortable around this woman? No one I've ever brought home has ever known what I do for a living, but with Blue it's a non-issue. "Besides, the gardening has helped me in so many ways."

"Helped how?"

"To quiet the demons."

Chapter 6

Blue

I suck in a sharp breath at his words, because I can't imagine a life of crime and murder. A life hiding in the depths of the dark underbelly in this cold, hard world.

Titan lived there. He dwelled in a life with mayhem and always watching your back for so long I can only imagine what it must have been like to stop.

"When you decided to quit, did you do it cold turkey, so to say?"

He nods, still down on bended knee. "Yeah. One day a job went sideways, and I told my boss I just couldn't do it anymore."

"I'm surprised he agreed. I always heard you're a hitman until you're dead."

Titan laughs a little under his breath. And it's the sexiest sound I've ever heard. "Where'd you hear that?"

"John Wick." I shrug.

He laughs again. "You watch too many movies." He

stands and holds out his hand. "Let's go inside. I need to get on my secure line to make a few calls to see where we can find this Steele guy."

I take his hand and ignore the sudden tingles in my fingers as we walk toward the house.

He sets me up in his gourmet kitchen with a glass of ice water, with leaves of fresh mint from his garden, and excuses himself to head to his office. I glance around when he's gone. Stainless-steel appliances and dark granite countertops sparkle, surrounded by dark oak cabinets that have no blemishes. Everything is so clean.

Does anyone even live here?

I move from the kitchen into the living area. Same thing in here.

No mess.

No lived-in love.

It's like a showroom in a furniture gallery. The leather couch is perfectly perfect with red throw pillows strategically placed in the right spots. Even the floors have no scuff marks.

I don't touch anything.

I continue walking, wondering if the whole house is like this.

I cross into a hallway, checking out each room as I pass by the open doors and stop at what appears to be a library.

Wow.

I nearly leap into the room, admiring all the neatly lined books on the built-in shelves. "I'm in heaven," I murmur to myself.

Based on Titan's immense collection, he's a well-read man who enjoys mystery. He's got two complete shelves dedicated to Sherlock Holmes.

"There you are." Titan's voice booms from behind me.

I jump, spinning around, caught completely off guard. "I wasn't drooling."

He cracks a grin, plunging his hands into the pockets of his jeans. "Drooling?"

I jab a thumb over my shoulder. "I love books."

"Ah, me too." He steps past me. "This is my favorite." He pulls a gardening book off the shelf and I grin.

"No, it's not."

"Ok, maybe it's not." He sets the book back and rests his shoulder against the bookcase. "So, I found out that Steele will be meeting with the man who's selling the women tonight."

"Ah, where's that?"

"A private party."

AFTER GETTING my bags unpacked and everything settled to stay at Titan's place, we both get ready for the party.

When I step into the living room, he lets out a low whistle. "Is this ok?" I ask, making certain my red dress isn't too short.

"Wow," he says, his eyes doing a lingering sweep of my body. "You look perfect." He walks closer, bringing the heat with him. "Completely perfect."

I tug at the hem of the dress, struggling to make it longer. "It's not too short, is it?"

Titan's eyes roam over me. "Blue, it's perfect."

"Ok." My pulse races at the sight of him. "You look perfect, too."

He looks like sin and money dressed in a black-on-black suit, and I want to gamble with it all.

I'm not this type of girl.

I'm safe.

I date safe guys. I go on safe dates. And I lead a very safe and rather boring life. So, this is all new to me.

When Frank gave me the assignment to go undercover as a sex-trafficked woman, I had anxiety attacks every night, not sure if I could play the part. But then I remembered why I got into journalism and knew there was a story here. And I needed to expose the truth. And that's what I remind myself as we drive to the party.

I feel safe on Titan's muscular arm as we enter the venue where tons of party people mill about, chatting and eating hors d'oeuvres.

I notice a few older gentlemen near the bar and do a double take once I realize where I know them from.

"Is that the mayor and chief of police?" I whisper to Titan.

"Yeah, everyone here is either government, police, or mob."

"All at the same place?" I don't pretend to be naive about crooked politicians and police officers, but the mayor and chief of police? That's way too high up.

We make our way to an opposite bar on the other side of the room. Titan orders me a glass of champagne and himself a bourbon neat.

He swallows it in one gulp and asks the bartender for another as I sip on my champagne. Titan's second drink is drained from the tumbler just as rapidly as the first.

"Let's dance," he says to me.

I nod, setting my glass on the bar.

He leads me onto the dance floor and holds me close to his body. I lean in, casually sniffing him so he doesn't notice.

"Did you just sniff me?"

Oh, oops.

"Maybe a little." I peek up at him.

He stares at me, not uttering a single word. And then he leans in and presses his lips over mine, sending shock currents across my mouth. To hell with it. I kiss him back, opening my mouth to let his tongue swirl around mine.

The kiss deepens, and Titan's hands grip me tighter.

Should I care that we're engaged in a passionate kiss here on the dance floor? I don't.

I don't care one bit.

Because being here in Titan's arms is the best place I've ever been. My heart races as his hand lowers down my back.

He breaks the kiss, wrenching his lips from mine. "I forgot where we were for a minute."

"I didn't mind."

He makes some growly sound in his throat, and I pull myself together. "Let's find Steele."

We leave the dance floor and mingle with people we don't know. Titan stops cold when he spies Steele across the room talking to another man with salt-and-pepper hair. He's as tall as a skyscraper with bulky muscles and a hard jaw set in stone.

"We need to leave." He takes my hand and leads me back the way we came.

"Why are we leaving?" My heels click trying to keep pace with his long strides. "We just found Steele."

"We just need to go."

"Do you know that man he's talking to? Is that who's running the trafficking operation?" It's the only thing that makes sense in my head.

"Yeah, I know him." He leads me out into the parking lot. "And yes, that's him."

"How do you know?"

"Because he's got the most security in this whole goddamn place. Plus, Steele looks at him like he's a God." Titan opens the passenger door of his truck for me. "I used to look at him like that too. Like he was a master of all things."

Chapter 7

Titan

Son of a bitch. I help Blue into the truck and stalk around the hood to hop into the driver's side.

"What's going on? Who was that man?"

"I'll explain everything once we're gone."

I drive us back toward my place. I need to call Rogue on a secure line and see who hired him for this hit.

I'm seething. Because this shot my plans for the evening. Every part of me wants to be taking Blue home to explore her sweet body instead of dealing with this shit.

I didn't plan on kissing Blue on the dance floor, but after she sniffed me, and her eyes… she was just too damn sexy to not lay my lips all over hers. And the moment our mouths met, I forgot my own name.

I forgot about the mission.

I forgot where we were. All I could think about was getting myself closer to her. And now here I am, trying to tame an angry beast of a hard on so I can deal with this madness.

Gunner Marble.

That's who Steele was talking to at the party.

Gunner Marble, the man who taught me everything about being a hitman. He was the first person I met when I started with Ruthless Corp. many years ago.

He took me under his wing, teaching me everything about the business. Hell, I considered him a friend… until one day he just disappeared.

I tried searching for him for a short time but gave up when I couldn't get any leads.

I still can't believe he's the man I'm supposed to kill.

I left the party because I couldn't risk the chance of him seeing me, and I couldn't let Steele tell him I bought a woman because Gunner knows me better than that.

He knows I'd never buy a woman.

But I did.

Because I couldn't let this one get away. Have I lost my mind?

I turn my head to stare at Blue as I wait for a red light to turn green.

"Who was that man?" she asks again.

I shake my head, not ready to go down this path with her.

"You can talk to me, Titan." She wraps her hand around my bicep, gently rubbing my arm.

I push on the accelerator as the light turns green. "I guess you can say he was my mentor."

"Ah." She leans back in her seat, waiting for me to finish my story.

"I trusted him for many years and then one day he went away."

"Poof, gone."

"Exactly," I reply. "I could never understand how he could leave me like he did. We were like family."

"I'm so sorry."

Pity is not what I want from Blue. She strokes my bicep

and maybe I do want her pity. Silent, I speed down the street, making it to my home in the Hills in record time. I pull into the driveway and shut off the engine, wanting to forget about Gunner Marble for a while.

That won't happen, because I need to let Rogue know I've spotted Gunner. Find out who wants the hit on him. Because… this is a hit I might not be able to fulfill. And that's never happened to me before. I've always been able to take care of any job that's come my way. Always.

I try to picture it. A gun in my hand. Me aiming it at Gunner. Would I really be able to pull the trigger?

"Are you ok?" Blue asks as I open her door.

"Yeah, I just need to talk to my boss, Rogue."

"Ok, I can Uber back to my place and give you some time alone."

"Not a chance in hell."

"I'm not in any danger. No one even knows we're onto them."

I inch closer. "I'm not taking any chances."

"Ok."

She follows me into the house, and I make sure she knows to make herself at home before I head into my office, shutting the door behind me.

On a sigh, I dial Rogue's number.

"Hey," I say when he answers. "You alone?"

"Yeah, man. What's up?"

"You'll never believe who Steele is buying from."

"Who?" Rogue asks in a hurry.

"Gunner."

There's silence on the other end of the line, and I know Rogue is trying to process what this all means. "Gunner Marble?"

"The one and only."

"That makes no sense."

"Who hired you? Who put the hit out on him?"

"You know I don't have that information." He curses under his breath. "You know the hits come in through an encrypted messaging system, and the money is untraceable."

"Think we should bail?"

"Ok, here's what we're gonna do," Rogue says, taking charge. "You're going to keep digging. Find out what you can. And I'm going to do some investigating on my end. See if I can figure out who paid for the hit."

"I'll keep you updated." Before I can say anything else, I hear my truck start in the driveway. "Fucking shit. I gotta go, Rogue." I slam the phone in its cradle and rush through the house, straight out into the driveway.

I'm too late. She's gone. I watch the back tail lights disappear into the night.

Well, this just won't do. I race back inside to grab my keys to my motorcycle in the garage. I need to catch her. I hop on my Harley and race after her.

Shit just got too serious for her to think she can do this all on her own.

Chapter 8

Blue

Basic rule of journalism: once something is off the record, keep it there. The things Titan told me were not off the record, so I have to get a call into Frank and tell him Steele is working with a man by the name of Gunner Marble. We need to run a search on the name. Find out who he is.

All I know is he used to be a hitman who trained Titan in the art of the kill.

As I speed down the street so I can't be followed, I grab my cell, pulling up Frank's contact info. I hit send and put the phone up to my ear. "Frank, meet me at the station. I have some information."

"I'll be there in twenty."

A single headlight in my rearview grabs my attention. Dammit, Titan.

I'm no racecar driver, and kind of don't want to break the law, but I try my best to outrun him. It's no use. He's gaining on me, so I pull into a gas station and get out of his truck.

"What are you trying to do?" I yell. "Are you trying to get yourself killed?"

He slides off his bike, and it's really sexy and really inappropriate for me to think that right now. "Where are you going in *my* truck?"

I park a hand on my hip. "You don't own me, ya know?"

He crosses his arms. "Actually, I kind of do. I paid twenty grand for you."

My mouth drops open. "I can't believe you just said that to me."

He steps forward, wrapping an arm around my waist. "Believe it, sweetheart. You belong to me, and there's no way I'm gonna let anything happen to you."

He can't possibly think he really owns me. Can he? "I appreciate the sentiment, but I'm fine." I square my shoulders and raise my chin so he knows I've got this.

"Better safe than sorry." He stares down the road. "Where are you going? This isn't the way to your house."

I bite my lower lip. "I was headed to the station to talk with my boss Frank."

"About Steele? About Gunner? About me?"

"Listen," I place my hand on his chest, "we have databases where we can search for Gunner. Find him. Instead of continuing to go to low-end bars and hoping he shows up."

Titan purses his lips, tilting his head, as he considers my words. "Blue, you think he will find something *we* can't. You don't think we have the best databases at Ruthless Corp?"

"Don't database shame me, ok?"

"Don't what?"

"Just humor me, ok? Let's see if Frank can find something out."

"I still don't like the fact you ran off."

"Let's go meet with Frank, and then we can go back to your place and I will behave." Saying the word behave isn't the word I was going for, but it makes Titan's jaw tick. Like he enjoyed hearing that word fall from my lips.

"And just how are you going to behave for me?"

I trace my fingers up his t-shirt, willing to play with fire. "Any way you want me to."

Chapter 9

Titan

The thought of Blue behaving for me any way I want makes my dick swell with excitement. Makes me want to do whatever she says.

But I am not on board for meeting up with her boss at the station and giving up any info on my old pal, Gunner.

Yet, I'm running out of options here. I can't very well walk up to Gunner next time I see him and shake his hand. Someone wants him dead.

Someone hired Ruthless Corp to do it.

I need answers. And if this guy Frank can search some secret database to find them, then so be it. I've already got Rogue searching as well, what's one more guy looking gonna hurt?

"Ok, I'm in." I park my bike in a spot by the station, making a note to pick it up on our way back home, and hop behind the driver's side of my truck. I still can't believe she stole my vehicle.

Ten minutes later, we arrive at her work complex and I pull next to an old beat-up Chevy in the parking lot. A man wearing a ball cap pulled low, shading his face, looks over at us.

"That's Frank," Blue says, opening the truck door. "I'll be right back."

I grab her wrist. "Do you trust this guy?"

She smiles. "I'll be fine."

I stalk her with my eyes as she crosses to his door and speaks to this Frank guy through his rolled-down window. I crack my neck from side to side as I continue to watch them.

I have an uneasy feeling about this situation.

I can't see his face. It pisses me off and right when I'm about to step out of my truck, she's back, hopping into the passenger's side.

"Ok, Frank will check into it."

Frank's already driven away before I can get a good look at him. Fucking bastard.

"I still don't know if that was our best move."

"It will be, trust me."

"Trust you?"

She leans closer to me. "Yes, trust me."

We make a detour to grab my bike before we head back to my place. My anger's still brimming near the top and ready to bubble over when we arrive home. My brain still can't wrap around the fact I saw Gunner Marble. Where has he been for years?

Did he just walk away to join the dark side?

Did he get a better offer?

"Penny for your thoughts?" Blue asks me, emerging from the guest room looking just as beautiful in a pink tank top and black yoga pants as she did in the red dress.

"I'm just wondering what's going on." I move closer to Blue, my heart hammering inside my chest. "I'm wondering how you and Frank got mixed up in all of this."

"We're on a story. We want to find out who's behind the sex trafficking."

I nod. "I get that. How did Frank hear about it all?"

Blue shrugs and the light overhead showcases the graceful slope of her shoulders. "I don't know."

I take a seat on the couch, hoping she'll join me here. "I'll do anything to protect you."

"Maybe I don't need protection," she says as she sits down next to me.

"I think you do."

She says nothing, just gazes into my eyes and I nearly get lost in hers. "I'm fine. You don't owe me anything."

I laugh a little. "Owe you anything?"

"Well, it's not your duty to protect me. I just don't want you thinking I'm yours or something because you bought me."

I laugh again but there's no humor behind it. "I do own you."

She bounds off the couch. "Um, no, you do not."

I stand. "Yes, I do. You're mine, and that means it's my job to keep you safe from everyone. Even yourself."

She crosses her arms. "Listen, we'll get you your money back when we take down the whole operation."

"I don't want some sort of refund." Hell, I'd pay the same money again if it means I get to spend any time with her.

She stands in front of the floor-to-ceiling window, and moonlight pours into the room, highlighting all her arousing features.

Her perky tits hiding behind her tank top.

Her long legs leading up to her sweet ass.

And her long brown hair, falling in waves over her shoulders.

I step closer, wanting more than anything to touch her.

"Well, you didn't *technically* buy me," she says, doing the air quotes with her fingers.

"It doesn't matter. I still owe it to myself to keep you safe at all costs. And I don't trust Frank."

"Well, I think he'll be able to help us."

I step even closer. "I don't think so. I think we need to take matters into our own hands."

Blue purses her lips, her gaze connecting with mine. "I think you're a big bear and don't like trusting many people."

"A bear?" I laugh at her assessment.

"Yes, a bear. All grizzly and growly when you have to trust anyone who isn't you."

"Listen, this conversation is going nowhere, and we have real problems happening."

"That's why we need to wait for Frank to get back to us."

I hate that she's right.

I hate that my heart beats double time when she smiles, knowing I've realized she's right.

I hate it.

I hate that my cock is hardening at the thought of the kiss we shared.

I want more of it.

I lean closer to her, brushing my lips against hers.

Her body presses against me and I growl out a bit, just like the bear she's pegged me as.

"I need you," I say when I break the kiss.

Her blue eyes stare into mine and she nods. "Yes, I need you, too."

I waste no time getting her into my master suite and place her on the king-sized bed. Her creamy skin looks delectable against the navy blue sheets and comforter.

I yank my shirt off and she gasps.

"Wow," she says, her big blue eyes even bigger. "I've never seen so many muscles all at once before."

Involuntarily, I flex a little, moving closer, my dick already swelling. "I've got something else to show you too."

She condones my corniness, and I kick off my shoes and socks.

"Take off your top," I tell her.

She does as I say, and her black lacy bra is the prettiest I've ever seen. There's a pink bow in the center, and I know I need to get a closer look at it before she removes the bra completely. She's got a magnificent set of tits, and I can't wait to play with them, but I want to take my time with her.

The bed dips as I climb onto it. I kiss her neck, trailing my lips along her collarbone.

She moans, obviously enjoying the way I touch her.

I lay her back and hover over her. "I've thought about doing this with you since I first laid eyes on you. I couldn't let that asshole take you home. I had to do something." I capture her lips with mine and my cock presses against the zipper of my jeans.

I need this woman.

And I need her now.

"I wanted you too, even if I acted like I didn't." She holds onto me for dear life.

I keep kissing her, and then I make my way down the column of her throat to the swell of her breasts, to the little bow at the center of her bra.

I run my teeth over it, plucking it between my lips. "I want to be the only one ever to see you in this."

"You are."

"I mean it, Blue. No one else, ever. You're mine."

She closes her eyes at my words, and I reach around her back to unsnap her bra. I remove it in one effortless movement, and pink, hard nipples point toward me as I lower my mouth over one and then the other.

I nibble on the hardened peak, running my teeth lightly over her skin.

She moans even louder. And I know my girl likes this. And

yes, she *is* my girl. I keep going, not letting up as her moans increase.

I move down her stomach, all the way to her pants, which I remove and toss over my shoulder.

Damn, she's got a matching set. Black panties with a little pink bow at the top.

I play with the bow between my teeth, rubbing my hand over her hot center. "Did you wear these for me?"

She nods. "I did."

That thought turns me on, knowing she has thought about this like I have.

I slide her panties down her tanned legs, tossing them onto the pile of clothes on the floor.

She arches her back as I move further south, spreading her legs before me.

Is this heaven? Because it sure feels like I've just died and gone there.

Chapter 10

Blue

The way Titan stares at me makes me self-conscious for one moment. But when I hear him growl, and see the tiny smile playing on his lips, I know he's enjoying himself.

I've done nothing like this before tonight.

Sex with my ex was always methodical. Not good at all. But I can tell with Titan he's driven by the fact he wants me, not just some meaningless action.

He swipes his tongue over my wetness, ending at my clit.

I lean back, squeezing my eyes shut.

"Oh god, Titan."

He hums against my skin. "I'm just getting started, Blue."

My skin prickles at his words, ready and eager for what he has planned for me. My heart beat ramps up to super speeds, wanting to feel more and more of him.

He swipes his tongue over my heated skin, getting closer each time until there is no room between his face and my most private part.

He has a rhythm I find intoxicating, and then he uses his fingers on me. I can barely hang on, and I grab hold of the sheets, fisting them as he sticks one finger in, and then another, until he's reached a spot deep inside me and I'm screaming out his name.

"Oh god, Titan. Titan," I yell.

He keeps going and my body builds and builds as he fucks me with his tongue. It feels so good, and I'm edging toward my orgasm at an alarming speed.

And I don't want this to ever end.

"Titan, please don't stop."

He doesn't.

In fact, he goes even faster and faster, his lips humming along my clit as he shoves another finger deep inside me.

"Titan, I'm coming."

My body thrashes beneath him as stars explode behind my eyelids. My heart races, and I pant as I try to catch my breath.

"That was so fucking hot," Titan says as he leans on his elbow to stare into my eyes.

I caress his cheek. "You're hot."

A lazy smile spreads across his face, and he really is the most handsome man I've ever seen. Before I can even think about moving, my phone rings from the other room.

I know it's Frank because I've given him his own ringtone. *Flight of the Valkyries.*

"Frank. I should answer it."

Titan slides off the bed, repositioning his dick in his pants. "Get to it then."

I leap from the bed, grabbing my clothes as I race out of the room.

Earlier, when I spoke to Frank, he was confident he'd be able to find information on Gunner Marble. He was actually kind of excited I got a name for him.

Frank's an older man, no family, no anything really, so this is a big story for him too. He breathes the journalism life, trying to investigate everything that comes his way.

He's mainly been interested in the underbelly of Los Angeles more than anything else. He says he hates crime and hates the mafia and men who run the streets.

He's passionate about all he does.

"Hello," I say into the phone. "Frank?" I pull on my clothes as I wait for him to say something.

"Blue, can you meet me? I've got some info on this guy." He breathes into the phone like he's been running a marathon. "It'll be quick. Meet me at the 7-11 by your house."

"Ok, I'm on my way." I rush back to the bedroom, and Titan has hopped into the shower. I open the door to the bathroom, wondering if I have time to join him in there. The need to see Titan with no clothes and soap running down his broad muscles almost wins out, but I need to see what Frank's found.

"I'll be right back," I tell Titan, and then rush out of the house. He won't mind if I *borrow* his truck for a second time, will he?

Chapter 11

Titan

"Did you say something?" I pull back the shower curtain, but I'm alone in the bathroom. I figured I'd hop in the shower while Blue spoke with Frank, because I plan on rocking Blue's world all night long.

She doesn't answer, so I finish and sling a towel around my hips, exiting the bathroom.

"Blue?" I move out of the bedroom and toward the kitchen. Is she still on the phone?

I don't hear her talking, so I figure she's done with her call.

"Blue?" I enter the kitchen and don't see her anywhere. "Blue, where are you?"

Now I'm racing through my house, because I've got a bad feeling.

Where the fuck is she?

I check the driveway, and my truck is gone… again. Motherfucker.

I'm so pissed I can't think straight.

The only thing my mind has come up with is that asshole Frank asked to meet with her somewhere.

But where?

I hop on my Harley and head toward Blue's work.

It's the only place I can think of that they'd meet.

They're not there when I show up, and I drive around the lot.

Fuck.

I don't even have Blue's number to call her.

Instead, I call Rogue, telling him we need to meet. He instructs me to meet him at Poor Paul's, a local dive bar.

I turn my Harley in that direction and take off.

"SO, you didn't see this guy Frank at all?" Rogue asks from the corner booth in Poor Paul's. It's a secluded booth where the servers and any patrons know to leave us the fuck alone.

We want quiet while we discuss our plans.

"What do you think about Gunner resurfacing? Is he really selling off women?"

Rogue rubs at his chin, his gray hair catching the soft light hanging overhead. "I've contacted some people to find out who put the hit out on him."

I shake my head. "I still can't believe this is happening." I chug the rest of my beer. "I need to get back to my house in case Blue shows up."

"Ok. When I have more info for you, I'll call you."

"Can you do me a favor?" I ask.

"Anything."

"Look into this Frank guy. I don't trust him."

Rogue shakes my hand as I stand. "Sure thing, brother."

"Thanks."

I race back to my house, not caring about speed limits or

anything else. My mind has already conjured up the worst, but I know I'm overreacting.

My truck is parked safely in the driveway, and Blue's sitting on the steps of my porch. She stands when she sees me.

"Thank god, you're here."

"Of course, I am. I just—" Her words are cut off because I've already swept her into my arms, kissing her square on the lips as I walk her into the house and slam the door.

I take her right to the couch, unable to make it the extra steps to the bedroom because I need this woman right the fuck now.

I strip off her clothes, removing mine just as quickly. "I have to have you right now. I thought something bad had happened to you."

"I'm sorry I took your truck… again. But I found something out." Her blue eyes gaze into mine.

"I don't care about any of that right now." I cup her face with my hands, bringing my lips to meet hers. "I have to have you," I say once I've broken the kiss.

"I'm yours."

Fuck. Those two words do something inside my chest. I sit on the couch and move her to straddle me, kissing her full lips, memorizing every single detail about her.

She grinds her hips against me, and within minutes, I've got a condom wrapped around my cock and pushing into her tight heat.

Ah.

She feels so damn good.

Like sliding into home.

She's mine.

I thrust up into her as she runs her fingers through my hair. I never want this to end. She's right, I don't technically own her. No one can own another living human being. Or at least they shouldn't.

I make it a vow to help her bring down this sex trafficking operation. And once we do, we'll figure things out from there.

As long as she knows I'm not going anywhere.

She's my woman, and I won't let her go.

I groan a little, loving the way she rides my hard dick. She's so beautiful, with the glow of the moon cascading through the window. It makes me think thoughts like love, forever, marriage.

Things I'd never thought about before.

But after meeting her, I can see it now. I can see a future with her. Her writing. Me working in my garden so I can get my product to market.

"I want to share my life with you," I tell her, my cock slamming inside her.

"I want that too."

My heart hammers inside my ribcage as she keeps riding me. My body builds, my mind not wanting this to end too soon, because I want to keep feeling this woman forever and ever.

I push inside her a few more times as she crumbles around me, crying out through her orgasm. I follow shortly behind, whispering her name in her ear as I come.

Chapter 12

Blue

"So, what did Frank find out?" Titan asks after we've cleaned up from the best sex I've ever had in my lifetime. We're in the kitchen, both of us drinking a bottled water from the fridge.

"He wanted to know more about you."

"Me?" Titan glances around. "Want something stronger? Whiskey?"

"Sure."

"That's my girl." Titan opens another cupboard, looking for two glasses. "So, what did you tell Frank about me?"

"Not much. I don't really know much about you. I just said you're a silent guy who keeps to yourself."

"Did you tell him about what I do for a living?"

I shake my head, remembering my conversation with Frank and him asking me what Titan Henry does for work. "I told him you retired." And it's the truth. I told Frank that.

"What did he say about Steele and Gunner?"

"He said he found out Gunner owns a company by the name of GMM, Inc."

"What does that company do?" Titan asks, handing me a glass of whiskey.

I shrug. "It's obviously a front company. Something to hide his illegal activity."

Titan takes a sip of his drink. "Obviously. I just wish I knew how he got mixed up in all of this."

I set my glass down, not yet taking a sip. "We'll figure it out together."

Titan wraps his powerful arms around me. "I really like you a whole lot."

"I like you too." I kiss his chest as he holds me close.

"Blue," he leans me back so he can stare into my eyes, "I don't want to lose you."

Warmth rushes through my veins. "I don't want to lose you either."

"Let me text this info over to Rogue."

While he steps away to get his phone, I pick up my drink and take a tiny sip. I've never been one for whiskey.

I think about Titan.

About Titan owning me.

How did he feel when he bought me?

Those thoughts dissipate when Titan picks me up and tosses me over his shoulder. "I want to have my wicked way with you once more tonight before we go hunting Steele."

And he does. Over and over again.

MY SKIN IS CRAWLING, and not in the exquisite goosebump kind of way from earlier when we had sex. Titan and I are back in the club where we first met, and I spot the women on stage, waiting for someone to purchase them, wishing I could save them all.

Our story is Titan is looking to buy another woman. So far, it's working. No one's even questioned us as we walk into the dimly lit bar.

I try to act like a sex slave, being led around the place by my master, walking with my head down, following closely behind Titan.

He's so big and strong, I feel like he's my protector or something.

And I like feeling protected by him. Even though we haven't known each other that long, I can picture a life together.

A future.

Him in his garden.

Me writing the novel I've always wanted to write.

Us living together, enjoying each other every chance we get.

I yearn for the closeness of another human being. But not just anyone… him.

He reaches for my hand, and leads me to the bar. He orders me a vodka and soda, and we sit on the barstools, spinning them so we have a good view of the stage.

"Any sign of Steele or Marble?"

Titan looks around. "Not yet." His mesmerizing eyes land on me, and he gives me a soft smile.

There's something so irresistible about this man that I just can't take it anymore.

I want to take him to a back room and have my dirty way with him.

But I squeeze my thighs together, trying my best to let go of the insatiable need I have for him.

"What are you thinking about?" he asks me with a grin, like he can read my mind.

"You don't want to know."

He leans closer, his eyes darkening. "Oh, hell yes, I do."

I whisper in his ear. "Just about what we did earlier but doing it here instead."

His smile drops, his eyes growing serious. "I'd love nothing more than to take you into some broom closet and fuck you silly, but look," he nods toward the door, "Steele and Gunner just got here."

I pout, but it's for the best. We're here for a mission not to goof off in some random closet. "Are you going to talk to him?"

He nods. "Yes."

"Like a random meeting?"

He shakes his head. "He's never gonna buy the story I bought a girl, but I'm just gonna have to go with it."

"I agree. Because you really bought me knowing nothing."

His eyes rake over my body. "Exactly. And I've been thinking. If he's gone to the dark side, who's saying I haven't as well?"

"Very true."

"Can you stay here and out of trouble?"

"Yes, sir," I murmur.

"Good." He kisses me on the cheek. "I'll be right back."

He stalks toward Steele and Gunner with not a single worry in the world. That kind of confidence is so sexy to me.

I can't get enough of him.

Chapter 13

Titan

I move closer to Gunner and my heart nearly beats out of my chest. So many emotions rush through me all at the same time.

Confusion.

Sadness.

Worry.

And anger.

Why did he walk away all those years ago?

He scans the club, his eyes zeroing in on me and widening as they do. His face says it all. He's not expecting me here tonight.

"Titan, is that you?" He holds out his arm, extending his hand for me to shake. "How the hell are you?" He acts like nothing's wrong.

"Gunner." I shake his hand.

"This is Steele." Smart man. He doesn't offer up any reason they know each other.

"How'd you two meet?" Of course I'm going to ask.

Gunner smiles, his piercing grey eyes lighting up as he does. "He's a very good client of mine." He slaps Steele on his shoulder. "Isn't that right, Steele?"

Steele mumbles a 'yes' under his breath, as if he's not happy with the arrangement at all.

It makes me pause. Something's going on here. Something more than I'm seeing. "Can we talk alone?" I ask him. "Catch up on old times."

"Of course, I have a private room upstairs."

I glance back at Blue, not really wanting to leave her here alone. Especially with Steele nearby. "Can I bring my woman?"

Gunner nods. "Sure, the more the merrier."

I wave at Blue, gesturing for her to come with us. She gets off the bar stool, making her way across the floor.

She steps up next to me, and I wrap an arm around her and smack a kiss on her lips. It may be a little overboard, but I need to let this whole fucking place know she's mine.

We follow Gunner up the stairs to a private room. He gives me a look like he wants to speak freely without Blue's ears listening to the conversation.

"Wait right here," I tell her. "Knock if anyone comes up here." I give Blue a kiss on the forehead as she nods her acceptance.

I step into the room with Gunner, and he shuts the door. I'm not happy that I had to leave Blue behind, but it's better than leaving her downstairs with all the sharks. Besides there's a small window and I can watch her while inside.

"I'm sure you have a lot of questions," Gunner starts. "I have a lot of questions myself."

He's much older than when I last saw him. The years haven't been kind to my dear friend.

His dark hair looks grayer now, and the crow's feet crowning his eyes deepen as he smiles.

"I do have a lot of questions. Starting with, where the fuck have you been?"

He stuffs a hand into his suit jacket pocket and pulls out two cigars. "Something personal came up." He hands me a cigar and I take it.

"Personal?" I take the cutter from his hand and clip the tip.

He smirks like the Cheshire Cat, like everything is normal. Like he didn't vanish for over ten years. "Yeah, personal." He hands me the lighter after lighting his own cigar. "How've you been? Still working for Rogue?"

I shake my head as I light my cigar. "I'm retiring."

"Rogue must have hated that news."

I lift my shoulders in a slow shrug. "I guess. I'm trying to get my own thing going."

"What's that?"

"Herbs."

"Like marijuana?"

I crack a grin at his assumption. "No, like herbs. Ya know, for cooking and shit."

This makes Gunner nearly buckle over from laughter. "You always surprised me, Titan."

I don't laugh as I suck on the end of my cigar. "Why are you back?" I ask once he's done laughing and the room's gone quiet.

He puffs on his own cigar, stalling to answer. "I, too, started my own thing."

"I hope it's not selling women."

Gunner's piercing eyes sear into mine. He chuckles, like he's trying to hide the fact that I just hit the nail on the head. "Nah, nothing like that. Actually, it's complicated."

"Care to uncomplicate it for me?" Should I tell him someone ordered a hit on him?

Should I tell him that his life is in danger? From me.

"Titan, you know I would if I could." He stamps out his cigar in an ashtray on a nearby table. "It's compli…"

I cut him off before he can finish the word, "Complicated. I got it." But I have nothing.

Is he in trouble? Besides the obvious trouble of someone putting a hit out on him. "There's a hit out on you, man."

"Oh, yeah?" He smiles. "Who took the job?"

I don't answer, and puff on my cigar, rolling it in my fingers while I do.

"Is it you?" he asks.

"It is."

"Thought you were retiring."

I stamp out the cigar and then stuff my hands in my pockets. "I am."

He blinks at me, and it's a fucked-up situation. I can't even explain it.

"Who ordered the hit?"

I shake my head. "Rogue's looking into it."

Gunner stares at me with fire in his eyes. "Don't bother. I think I already know."

Chapter 14

Blue

One thing I hate more than creepy men in a nightclub staring at me is being left in the dark. Titan and Gunner have been in the private room talking for what feels like ages. I can't complain though because I was grateful he brought me upstairs with him. But the journalist in me is dying to get the scoop.

I lean against the wall and think about what Frank said about watching my back with Titan.

A part of me wonders how he even knew who Titan was. I didn't tell him much, but when he said to watch my back, my skin prickled. I'm sure Frank is just watching out for me, making sure I'm not getting myself into trouble.

I'm also sure the moment they sold me to someone other than Steele in the club, he checked out everything he could on the man who bought me.

My cell pings in my pocket and I check the incoming message from Frank.

"Come meet me outside of the club."

I told Frank to stay close but remain hidden. The fact he's right outside the club makes me worry. I hope no one sees him.

I glance at the closed door and step away from it, needing to make sure Frank isn't standing right outside in the view of any prying eyes. It could raise questions.

I rush down the stairs, ignoring all the stares from the other men employed by Steele and Gunner. The entrance to the club comes into view, and I cross the floor without anyone trying to stop me. I'm property. So as far as anyone knows, I'm Titan's, and he's the one who told me to go outside.

I rush through the doors and scan the parking lot.

A car in the distance blinks its headlights in my direction and I make my way over there with caution, wishing I had a weapon.

"Frank?" I ask as I head closer.

The hair at the back of my neck stands on end as I lean down to speak to the man behind the driver's wheel. Something doesn't feel right.

Why hasn't he rolled down his window?

In a second, an arm has wrapped around me and a hand covers my mouth. I try to scream. I try to kick.

But I'm lifted off the ground and shoved into the back of a nearby white van.

"Shut the fuck up," a voice calls out as the door slams shut.

The van pulls away, and I'm once again trying to scream. A piece of tape is slapped over my mouth, and a bag is put over my head to silence me. Someone ties my hands behind my back, so I'm really screwed.

My heart beats frantically as I try to remember everything I've ever learned about what to do in these types of situations.

I can't think of anything, and my body shakes from fear.

"What is she doing?" one of the three men in the back of the van says.

Hmm. I shake harder, like I'm having some sort of episode. Maybe they'll remove the sack. I thrash my body around on the back of the van floor, and the men do nothing at first.

"Is she dying?"

"Untie her hands."

They shout commands, and somebody finally unties me and removes the sack from my head.

I've got nothing to lose, so I rush at the biggest man, trying my best to scratch at his face with my nails. I kick and flail my limbs, trying my best to get to the door and out of the van. I don't even care if the van is in motion.

"Tie her back up," the bald man says to the other two.

The man behind the wheel slows down and turns around.

It's Frank.

My fight falters, my eyes going wider at the sight of him. I'm in trouble now, and I'm not sure what to do except keep trying to free myself from this van. We tussle more, but they gain control, tying my arms together. They leave the sack off my head, but it doesn't matter, I can't see anything out the tinted windows, anyway.

My phone is in my back pocket, but it's almost like these guys can read my mind because they grab it and toss it to the front of the van.

All hopes of getting a hold of Titan flies out the window.

I sit still, no sense trying to get away when I'm outnumbered. Yet, I keep my options open, trying my best to think of something that I can do to escape.

I'll always go down fighting.

I will not accept this as my fate.

The van takes a hard left, and I bang my head on the floorboard as I'm tossed around. Frank comes to an abrupt stop and I'm pushed forward as the door opens. I kick and flail as the men bring me into an abandoned warehouse. My hands may be tied but that doesn't mean I won't try to claw my way out of here. I kick at the men as they rush me into an open area with a wooden chair in the middle of the room.

Yes, it's just like in those movies where they torture the person in that chair.

I freak out a little, but they don't sit me in that chair. Instead, there's a large cage, the kind for a big dog, and they shove me inside and lock it.

I can barely move, and I realize they're using me as bait. But for who?

Titan?

Steele?

My mind rolls over the possibilities as the men set up the room for the main attraction. How can I get out of here?

What can I do?

Chapter 15

Titan

Ever get that feeling? That feeling that something isn't right? I've got this tingling traveling up my spine setting off alarms.

I glance through the small window.

"Where's Blue?" I ask, scanning the top floor of the club. She's no longer standing in the spot I left her in when I went to talk to Gunner.

"Is she downstairs?" Gunner hurries behind me as I race down the steps.

That feeling is back, moving up my spine and casting a dark shadow all around me.

I question the men on the first floor.

We talk to a few more men who said they saw her go outside. I rush out there, not even caring about anything, until I see the blue-eyed beauty standing safely before me.

But outside is empty. There's a chill in the air. And the quietness creeps closer. I search around, not ready to give up just yet.

"We'll find her," Gunner says. "Calm down."

"I can't be calm when some motherfucker could do something horrible to *my* girl."

Gunner puts a hand up, stopping me from moving further. "Wait a minute. Are you telling me you actually care about this woman?"

I nod. "Abso-fucking-lutely."

"A lot has changed since I've been gone."

"Yeah, funny how that works, huh?" I rub at the back of my neck.

"I have an idea who took her and where they are," he says, already moving toward a black SUV in the lot.

We hop in, and Gunner peels out of the lot. I'm not really sure how I feel about him helping me find Blue, but right now I'll take it.

I pull out my phone, calling Rogue. He answers on the first ring.

"I was just about to call you. I looked into that guy, Frank DiMaseo."

"What did you find out?" I ask in a rush.

"He's a ghost before he went to work at the station."

"What do you mean ghost?"

"I mean, there's nothing."

"Son of a bitch."

Gunner asks, "Who's a ghost?"

"Frank DiMaseo," I say, giving him a brief description of who he is.

"He's the one who gave me Blue."

"Yeah, it was an undercover sting operation to bring the whole thing down."

Gunner shakes his head, pulling up to a red light. He glances at me. "No, he's brought me women before. He's not who you think he is."

My hands ball into fists as anger overtakes me. I never trust many people, and Frank was someone I should've listened to my gut about. Why didn't he get out of the car to meet me that night they met in the parking lot? Why didn't he want to know the man who messed up their plans and bought the woman he coerced to run a sting operation?

What really makes my blood boil is the thought he probably intended for Steele to buy her, but not for their story. To really own her.

I see red as Gunner speeds through the streets until he pulls up to an abandoned warehouse. We pile out of the SUV. "Rogue, I'm sharing my location with you. Get here." I hang up the phone.

Gunner moves beside me, pulling out his gun.

"How do you know she's here?" I ask. A cold snap of air hits me dead in the spine when a car that was following us pulls up to where we stand.

Steele and three of his henchmen exit the car, pulling their guns on us.

"What are you doing here?" Gunner asks, moving away from Steele.

I've already got my gun drawn, but Steele points a gun in my face.

"Drop it," he says.

"Not a chance in hell." I'm prepared to die. I'm sure he isn't.

"Titan, let's not make this more messy than it needs to be. You were never supposed to be involved," Steele says, pointing a gun at Gunner.

It all falls into place. Steele and Frank are working against Gunner. This has all been about him. Blue and I are just pawns in a well-orchestrated plot to take him down. I'll make sure that doesn't happen or die doing it.

"I don't care what's happening here. All I care about is saving Blue." I say as I hand over the gun to Steele. I could easily bash his skull in as he steps closer to retrieve the gun, but not before they kill Gunner. And who knows what would happen to Blue if I made a hasty decision like that.

Steele keeps the gun pointed at my head as we're all led inside.

Fury rages through my body when I spot Blue sitting inside what appears to be a dog cage.

What the hell?

There's four other men in the room, and Frank.

"Let her go. You have who you want now. Let her go," I say, speaking directly to Frank.

They laugh.

"And why would we let her go? She's a little treat for after the key event," Steele says. "Besides, she was supposed to be *mine*."

The way he growls out the word *mine* makes my skin crawl.

"Ok, let's all calm down," Gunner says as Steele leads him to a chair in the middle of the room.

"Let's get down to business." Steele walks to the cage, looking at Blue with desire clear in his eyes.

I plan on shooting him first.

Chapter 16

Blue

The way Steele and his men stare at me like I'm some piece of property to be claimed makes my skin crawl. The sight of Frank holding a gun to Titan confuses me. I want to shout at him and ask him what he's doing, but I need to figure out what's going on first.

It's obvious I put my trust in the wrong man.

They plop Gunner down into the chair in the middle of the room, and my mind races. Why is Frank involved in this?

Steele circles the cage like a rabid beast waiting to be fed. "Let's get down to business," he pauses, "so I can have my pretty little plaything all to myself."

My eyes meet Titan's. It's almost like he's trying to tell me that won't happen.

"Gunner, I'm tired of buying women at a huge markup. I'd much rather run the operation all on my own," Steele says.

"Like you could. Where would you even get the women?"

Gunner asks as the nameless men who kidnapped me bind his hands behind his back.

Steele scoffs. "Frank's been bringing you women for years. And I just made him a better deal. That's why we devised this little plan to get you in our grasp."

Tears fill my eyes as I glance at Frank.

Titan pushes forward. "You asshole."

"Hold him back," Steele says to Frank. "You weren't supposed to be involved."

"Yeah, yeah, I know," Titan drawls out.

I'll most likely be dead by the time the sun rises tomorrow morning, and I can't help but want Titan to know that I've fallen for him. The thought of dying without Titan knowing how I feel is killing me slowly.

"Titan," I call out.

Steele kicks the cage, the pain from it silencing me. "Shut up, you bitch."

I want this all to end… quickly.

Titan mouths something to me. I concentrate on his lips, the contours of his mouth as he tries to communicate with me.

I shake my head, unable to make out what he's trying to say.

"So, it was you who ordered the hit on me?" Gunner asks Steele.

Steele laughs. "Yes, but when it was clear Titan wouldn't be fulfilling his duties, we decided to do the job ourselves."

"Give me a gun and I'll finish it right now," Titan shouts.

Always the hero. But this is not the time or place to be that hero. We need to figure out a way out of here, and so far, I've got nothing.

I can barely even move.

"Stop talking now, Titan. You're here to watch. I'm not stupid enough to give you a gun." Steele stares at him.

Titan shakes his head. "You're gonna have to kill me."

Steele laughs. "That's the plan."

"Titan, no. Let me handle this," Gunner's gruff voice booms from the office chair.

All eyes are on him as Frank moves closer to my cage. I guess he feels Titan would be an idiot to make a move right now with all these people around.

"You were fun to manipulate," Frank says with an evil snarl that makes my stomach churn with acid. "You believed every word I said."

"You make me sick," I spit out.

"If it weren't for that man over there, you would have been sold to Steele. And there wouldn't have been a damn thing you could have done about it." He laughs.

Steele laughs along with him. "I have to thank you, Titan. Now I get her for free."

Titan rushes forward, grabbing a knife from an ankle holster. He slices Frank's neck right before my eyes and an involuntary scream escapes me. Before anyone even knows what's going on, or can react to it, Titan's got a hold of Frank's gun and has already put two shots into Steele's chest.

Another man enters the room, taking out the other men. Bullets fly through the air and I close my eyes, holding onto myself to stay safe.

The room goes silent as the man steps further into the room. "All clear, Titan?" the man shouts.

"All clear," Titan says back, aiming his gun at Gunner, who is still tied to the chair in the center of the room.

"Listen," Gunner tries to shift in his seat, "take the girl. I won't say anything. You can live out your days with her."

"And you go back to trafficking women?"

"What do you care?"

"No. There's one thing you never got around to teaching me."

"What's that?" Gunner asks.

"Morals. There's no way we're letting you go."

"Rogue, Titan, I'll pay you."

The man must be Rogue, Titan's boss. Titan and Rogue laugh. "Money we've got," Rogue says. "I can't believe you went dirty."

Gunner stares at the older man. "I can't believe you think we're that much different."

Rogue steps closer to Gunner, leaning over to stare him directly in the eyes. "I'm nothing like you. I would never hurt an innocent soul."

Rogue grabs his phone, putting in a call to someone.

Titan holsters his gun and moves over to the cage I'm trapped in and fiddles with the lock, then turns to look for a key in Frank's pockets.

Titan kneels, unlocking the lock but glancing over his shoulder at Rogue. "What are you going to do with him?" He opens my cage and helps me out.

Rogue shrugs. "Not sure yet."

"I never thought I'd see you again." I wrap my arms around Titan's waist and squeeze him as tight as I can. "You saved me. Thank you."

His strong arms wrap around me in an instant, and he nearly lifts me off the floor. "I'd never let anything happen to you," he says against my ear.

"Take her home," Rogue says. "I'll call some men to help me clean up this mess."

"I've never been one to let someone clean up after me," Titan says.

"Go. Take her out of here. She doesn't need to see any more of this."

I stand on my feet, letting my arms fall to my sides. "What about all the women? All the women Gunner was selling?"

Rogue rubs a hand along the back of his neck. "I promise you, we will get to the bottom of it all." He tosses Titan a set of keys he grabbed from Gunner's pockets.

Titan nods, lifting me off the ground like a bride he's

about to carry over the threshold. Instead of carrying me over the threshold of a new home, he carries me out of the warehouse and into the back of an SUV.

"Whose car is this?" I ask.

"Gunner's. I'm sure he won't mind if we borrow it."

IT'S BEEN NEARLY a month since the night Titan saved me.

Since the night Titan saved us all. True to their word, Rogue and Titan got the information I needed to write up an article on the whole operation.

The station still can't believe they ever trusted a man like Frank. Many people from my work have come forward with stories about him abusing his power.

I feel like a naïve idiot. All the clues I found were ones he set me up to find. I thought I always had a keen eye for reading people, but Frank pulled one over on me, promising me fame and glory if the story ever broke. Well, that's one thing Frank didn't lie about during his scheme.

Since publishing the article, I've received some national media attention, and there's even mention of a book deal headed my way.

I have to thank Titan Henry, though. Without him, none of this would have ever been possible.

None of it.

"You home?" I ask as I shut the front door to Titan's house.

"Back here," he says.

I head in the direction of his voice, back near the kitchen where he's preparing something that smells fantastic. Basil floats through the air and garlic entices my nose in a way that has me salivating over the pungent smell.

"What are you making?"

"I'm trying a simple pasta sauce with my herbs from the

garden. I'm trying to get a good flavor profile for a new spice blend I'm working on." He kisses me on the top of my head as I stare into the pot on the stove. "I see the key worked."

I smile up at him. "Like a charm." Titan gave me a key to his place, pleading for me to move in with him.

Obviously I'll say yes, just haven't told him yet.

"Did you bring the wine? Rogue and some of the guys will be here shortly."

I hold up the bottle of Pinot Noir I spent a good thirty minutes searching the liquor store for because I'm nervous about having dinner with Titan's friends and old co-workers. Basically, dinner with a bunch of hitmen.

I feel like I will be one of the safest women on the planet tonight, but still my nerves are all over the place.

Not for fear of these men, but fear of them not accepting me. Or liking me. I want to make a good impression.

So, while Titan tends to the meal, I step outside and survey his lush garden, looking for fresh flowers. I spot a rose bush in the corner and bring the clippers from the side table that holds all of Titan's gardening supplies.

I snip off a few red buds and bring them inside.

"You didn't need to get me flowers," Titan says with a laugh.

"They're not for you. They're to spruce up the place."

Titan grabs a crystal vase from under his sink and fills it with water. He sets it on the counter, and after I stuff it with roses, I carry the arrangement into the dining room, placing it in the center of the dark table already set with white dinnerware and lit candles.

It's intimate and looks amazing.

The doorbell rings, and I smooth my hair in the mirror in the entryway, making sure I look presentable for the people I'm about to meet.

"You look perfect," Titan says with a kiss to the top of my head.

He opens the door and the first face I see is Rogue's. He has a wide smile, and enters with a kiss to my cheek. "How're you feeling?"

"I'm fine."

"This is Merrick and Cash." Titan introduces two men standing with Rogue.

"Hi, how are you?" I extend my hand for them to shake.

Cash, with the bluest eyes I've ever seen, takes my hand in his giant one. "Pleasure."

"Please, come inside." I lead them back to the living area as we wait for more men to arrive.

After a few more minutes, the house is filled with so much testosterone I can feel the effects wearing off on me as I drink my beer straight from the bottle. Normally, I'm not really a beer type of girl, but when bulky men hand you a beer, you take a beer.

Everyone has been so nice.

Everyone has been so normal.

"I like your friends," I tell Titan.

He smiles. "Yeah, they all like you too."

I beam with pride, knowing I've gained the approval of his friends. Not that Titan appears to be a man who cares about having their approval. But it helps.

We eat and drink. The men share stories about Titan, and I laugh the whole night away.

Later, when everyone has left, and it's just me and Titan, I snuggle up close to him. He kisses the top of my head, which I'm learning is one of his favorite things to do.

"I'd like to live with you," I tell him, giving him the answer he's been waiting for.

"Actually, you waited too long to answer so I've taken back my request."

I stare into his dark eyes. "Are you serious?"

"Yeah, now I want to know if you'll marry me?" He moves from the couch, kneeling before me, producing a black ring box from his pants pocket. He opens it and shows off the biggest blue diamond I've ever seen. "Blue, I'm in love with you. There's no point in trying to take things slowly when I know what I want. And what I want is you. As my wife."

I grin wide. "Yes."

"I mean, I paid a pretty penny for you. I guess you could say you kind of have to marry me."

I pretend like I'm shocked at his words. "Hey, you do *not* own me."

He smiles, his brow rising a bit. "I never got my refund, so I kind of think I do."

I slap his bicep playfully. "Well, what are you going to do with your property tonight?"

"Oh, I have lots of naughty ideas."

He stands and slides the ring on my finger.

I love the way it feels on my hand. He may not own me in a monetary sense, but he owns my heart and soul. I couldn't have written a better ending myself.

Journalism's first obligation is to the truth.

And the truth is—I love him.

Thank you so much for reading about Titan and Blue.

Step-Santa

Chapter 1

Winter

Elf you, world. I can't believe she eloped. What was she thinking? How could she not tell her daughter? Her own flesh and blood.

My mother isn't the spontaneous type who boards a plane and flies to the south of France to marry a man she just met, but that's what she did.

I didn't even know she was serious with Randall Snow, and now she's married? Three weeks into dating him?

"When you know, you just know, sweetheart," is what she told me over the phone.

So, of course, I rushed home to Jingle Hills, Colorado, to talk some sense into her.

Married.

As I travel up the snow-covered mountain pass to reach Jingle Hills, I slow my car, hoping I don't swerve on the icy roadway. Who gets married right before Christmas?

While others enjoy their peppermint mocha, I'll be talking some much-needed sense into my mother's Chanel earmuffs.

Married.

Sometimes I feel like the adult instead of the child. Sure, she and Dad didn't have the best marriage, and when it ended, I was happy to see them part, but she wasn't even single five years before remarrying.

What is she thinking?

And at her age.

I guess you could ask me the same question. Maybe if I hadn't let a curse word slip, I'd still have my job. I've vowed never to say another, but I don't know if my mother will vow to stop getting married.

I snail it down the two-lane road, when I spot a deer up ahead, meandering near the tall pine trees.

"Please, stay over there," I mumble.

The deer ignores me like I know Mom is going to do this week, and trots onto the snowy pavement, antlers held high. I slam the brakes, causing my blue Honda to swerve out of control.

Freddy Sparklepants, please, let me be ok.

My tires come to a screeching halt on the shoulder of the road.

The deer gives me a little smile as he prances away and down the mountain.

Asshole. I mean, Cookie McJingles.

My car sputters and stalls, and I try to turn over the engine.

Fuc— I mean Twinkle Figgybottoms. This is not my day.

Instead of cursing this year I plan on creating crazy elf names instead. It works. Call it a weird quirk, or call it insane, but it's me. Winter Joseph.

I rifle through my bag, looking for my phone, and relax once my fingers wrap around the familiar metal.

Yes. My savior.

My savior turns out to be a fake because the darn phone is dead, and the charger is the one thing I forgot to pack. This just went from ordinary bad luck to the start of a horror movie.

I try the engine once more with no luck.

Spanky Elf-droppings.

No problem. Everything is fine. This is a heavily traveled road, since it's the only path that leads into Jingle Hills, so help will arrive. The sun shines over the mountaintop, promising to stay with me for a few more hours, so at least I have some company.

The engine most likely needs a rest, that's all.

It's getting chilly without the heat on, so I grab my gingerbread-colored mittens from my Tory Burch bag and panic in the privacy of my car.

I'm stuck and no one will find me until morning after I've frozen to death.

This literally can't be my life right now.

Not only will wild animals maul me, I lost my manager's job at the Tory Burch store in the mall. It's not surprising. Deidre, my boss, always hated me.

As ludicrous as it sounds, my strawberry-blonde hair made her jealous.

From day one, she asked me, "What dye do you use on your hair?"

When I told her it was natural, she laughed and then mumbled under her breath, 'So are your tits.' They are, thank you very much. A week ago, just before Thanksgiving, Deidre announced a bun-only policy for me. My hair is a distraction to the customers, she said.

My response, "Are you fucking kidding me?" was probably not the professional way to address the problem, and ultimately got me canned. Hence, why I've taken to substituting crazy elf names in times of stress so it never happens again.

My best friend, Aspen, said I should take my dismissal to a

higher up, Tory Burch herself, and she would tell them my firing wasn't justified. It's just not worth it. She works there with me, but she's biased because we've been besties since we were five-years-old. Went to college together and everything. So yeah, pointless. She's coming home to Jingle Hills in a few days and will probably be the one to find my cold-dead body in a frozen block of ice in my car.

A tear trickles down my cheek at the thought of losing my job… and my life. I will not waste my last hours alive crying.

So my mother didn't invite me to her wedding. Big whoop.

So what, I lost my job. Double big whoop.

My car broke down in the mountains. Who cares?

My phone is dead, just like I'll be in a few hours.

How long does it take to freeze to death? I wish I could Google the answer.

As my thoughts run down a path of complete madness, the sound of tires crunching snow stops my mental breakdown.

A white Dodge Ram pulls up beside me, and a tall man wearing jeans and a navy coat hops down from the front seat. His long legs stride toward me.

"Oh, thank Ernie McSmartypants you came along," I say as I step out of the car. "I would have died out here."

The man with dark hair and a full beard to match smiles at me. "Ernie Mcwho?"

I swat away my nonsense. "Nevermind. Thank you so much for saving me. You're like my knight in shining armor."

The stranger focuses green eyes on me. "You're very lucky you didn't end up in that ravine." To emphasize the peril, he points to a deep crack in the earth just off the road.

I cringe. "I'm Winter. My car won't start."

His chiseled jaw ticks as his eyes roam over me from head to toe. "I'm Kane. Nice to meet you."

I stick out a mitten-covered hand for him to shake. "The pleasures all mine."

When does this ever happen to someone like me? A handsome, rugged savior comes to rescue me?

"I'll look under your hood."

A sublime tingle moves from my toes to the top of my head as I watch him finger the hood and pop it open. He caresses the cables while chattering away about the temperature dropping, and how the car probably flooded. I'm barely listening, because I'm memorizing the way his body bends over the mechanical gobbledygook like a man who knows what he's doing. Memorizing the tiny puffs of smoke wafting past his sensual lips as he talks about batteries and oil.

"You probably hit the gas too hard when you tried to start the engine," he says, snapping me back to the present.

"Right," I answer, like I paid attention.

He rises to his full height, towering over me. "Let me try."

I hand over my keys and watch as he sits in my driver's seat. Please, don't let it start. Thoughts of him driving me into town turn into climbing into his backseat so we can get it on.

No such luck. The car purrs to life under his manly hand.

He winks at me while showing off a gleaming set of straight teeth. "There." He says the word like he's the master of the universe, and an unexpected part of me wants him to be the master of mine.

"Wow, you're amazing," I blurt out.

He gives the steering wheel a loving pat before swinging his long legs out of the vehicle. "Will you be ok to make it into town?"

I nod. "Yes, I'm good."

"You sure? Make sure you keep it slow and don't brake too fast."

I don't want to tell him about the deer and instead slide into the driver's seat. "Thank you again, Kane."

He leans against the car frame, one arm slung over the door, staring down at me. "Don't mention it."

He shuts my door and, arms crossed, watches me drive away.

Franky Stripeytights. I should have asked for his number.

"MOTHER, you can't rush off to get married without telling your only daughter," I say, turning off the loud beat of the Black Eyed Peas, "Imma Be," blaring through the speakers as my mother sweats on her elliptical.

She stops pumping her legs and reaches for a huge jug of water. "Once you meet Randall, you'll understand."

"Is he made of candy canes?"

Everyone knows candy canes are my favorite, but I'm being sarcastic, obviously. I swear I don't recognize this woman standing before me. I mean, she's exercising.

"No, but he definitely tastes sweet."

"Mom, I don't want to hear that." I cover my ears, moving away and tossing myself onto the king-sized bed in her master bedroom.

She laughs at my reaction. "When you fall in love, you'll be just as corny as me."

"Not likely." I rest my back against the mountain of pillows to stare at my mother, taking in her new look of bleached-blonde hair and oh my god, has she gotten Botox?

She smiles. "You're coming to the annual event, right?"

I nod. "That's why I'm here."

Every Christmas, Mom organizes an event at her family's resort in the mountains of Jingle Hills to raise money for Toys For Tots. This year, my helper role has doubled—I'm creating a children's book to gift the children visiting Santa and also playing Santa's little elf. It's not like I have a job anymore, so I'll have plenty of time on my hands to finish The Adventures of Sparkly Figgybottom.

"Will Randall play Santa?" I ask. Last year, it was cousin Derrick, and let's just say he was not jolly playing the part.

"No, Randall will be too busy entertaining guests with me. His son will be Santa this year."

I tilt my head. "His son?"

"Yes, your new stepbrother."

"I have a new stepbrother?"

"Well, yes." She steps off the elliptical. "Your stepbrother is a tad older than you."

"Can you really call him that when I'm twenty-six years old?" This is weird. "I mean, it's not like we're all living together like the Brady Bunch. Any other siblings I need to know about?"

"No, just the one son who lives here in town."

"Great. And by a tad bit older, how old are we talking here, Mom?"

"He's thirty."

I climb off the bed. "How old is Randall?"

My mother crosses to the dresser and pulls open drawers, removing clothes. "Randall's a tad older too."

"Was it his idea to run off and get married?"

She turns to face me. "Yes, he thought it would be romantic."

"Did he think it would be romantic not to invite your kids?"

"Honey, I promise we will make it up to both of you this weekend. We'll do some real family things."

I roll my eyes. "Mom, I'm not looking to play family with your new husband and his son."

She pouts, knowing I can never say no to her. "Please?"

I sigh. "Fine."

She grins and kisses my cheek. Lovely. Now I get to pretend we're one big happy family at the charity event in a few weeks.

Chapter 2

Kane

"Explain to me again why you rushed off to marry this woman?" I ask my father the million-dollar question at the bar of our country club. "Are you sure she didn't just marry you for your money?"

Dad laughs, deepening the crow's feet at the corners of his eyes. "She has her own money, Kane."

I slump back in my seat, staring at my bourbon on the rocks, unhappy he married a woman he met mere weeks ago. "Then tell me why you did it, Dad?"

"Love," he says, as if that explains everything.

It's my turn to laugh. "Love is a myth. It doesn't exist."

My father's eyes widen to owlish proportions. "Who told you that lie?"

I take a sip of my drink. "You did."

"That was the old me. I'm a changed man. I love Crystal. You're still coming to the charity event, right? Please, say you are, Kane."

I set my crystal tumbler on the lacquered-oak bar. "Yes, Dad. I'm still going. And I'll play Santa." I roll my eyes because there's an infinite number of other ways I'd rather spend the holiday season.

Like finding Winter.

Why didn't I get her number? Or a last name. Or anything that could help me find out who she is. I have to say, when I played Good Samaritan and pulled over on the side of the road, I didn't expect a beauty to emerge from the car like a peppermint candy ready to be sucked.

Ok, I'm letting my thoughts run away from me here. Yet, that's what she reminded me of with the white knit hat on her strawberry hair that floated down her back in waves. Her ruby-red lips were kissable as fuck, and I'd love to know what was underneath the oversized parka on her petite frame.

Instead of organizing a statewide manhunt for the mysterious woman, I'll be playing Santa to a bunch of kids. Don't get me wrong, I love kids.

I'd just rather spend more time with the gorgeous redhead.

"You'll be meeting Crystal's family there too," my father says.

I motion to the bartender for another round and catch up with my father. I haven't seen him since he returned from his wedding honeymoon combo.

Crystal's a nice lady. I met her once, and my father appears smitten with her. I just don't understand why they felt the need to rush into a marriage.

I'm not a relationship-type of guy. I'm more of a go-on-a-few-dates-and-let-things-fizzle-out kind of guy.

It's easier.

Besides, I've never met a woman who can keep my attention.

"Are you staying for dinner?" my father asks as the bartender sets two fresh drinks in front of us.

"Sure, why not?"

"Crystal's bringing her daughter," he says just as I take another sip of bourbon.

I nearly choke. "Daughter? How old is she?"

"Mid-twenties. I don't know. You be nice to her."

"When am I not nice?"

He arches a brow at me. "Be nice. She'll be your helper elf, so it's good you meet now to avoid the awkwardness."

I roll my eyes. "I'm always nice."

As soon as I say that, I glance toward the front of the restaurant, and there she is.

The woman from earlier today. She's out of her oversized coat and has a body I can't stop drooling over.

Her strawberry-blonde hair hangs like silk past her shoulders. I'd love to wrap those tresses in my fists as I pound inside her from behind.

"Dad, I'll take a raincheck for dinner." I slide off the barstool, setting my glass on the bar, keeping my eyes locked on Winter.

"No, you said you'd stay." My father stands from his barstool. "Oh, there they are now." My father waves toward Winter, and that's when I spot Crystal standing right next to her.

It all happens in slow motion as the realization strikes me dead center: Winter is Crystal's daughter.

I'm definitely staying for dinner.

My feet move of their own accord until I come face to face with Winter.

"Shitson Humberdink," she whispers as her eyes meet mine.

I crack a smile. "What are those? Elf names?"

A pink blush tinges her cheeks. "I'm sorry. New habit."

The reaction I'm getting from Winter right now is a major turn-on. She clears her throat, glancing at Crystal. "It's nice to meet you, Kane Snow," she says, holding out her hand for me to shake.

This time it's not covered with a furry mitten, and I clasp my palm to hers, loving the warmth of her skin. "Nice to meet you too," I whisper, leaning in.

"One big happy family," Crystal says.

Fuck.

One big happy family?

That's not exactly what I had in mind.

My father leads us to a reserved table in the dining room, and suddenly the whole situation comes into full focus. Winter is now my new… I don't even know what to call it. Is she a stepsister?

Can someone really be a stepsister if we aren't living together? If it isn't even really a family at all?

"So, your stepbrother works in publishing. Isn't that lovely?" Crystal says to Winter, and then she turns her attention to me. "Winter is putting together a children's book for the charity event."

Have you ever wondered what it would feel like if you had your parents on a date with you? Well, this is it.

I can't focus on anything other than the beauty that's now related to me.

"That's fascinating," Winter says, her voice sounding like an angel.

I give a curt nod. "Thanks. Very cool about your book."

To block out my attraction for Winter, I raise the menu in front of my face while Crystal and Dad act like this is normal. I read the same word over and over and finally slam the leather-bound book down on the tabletop.

"Winter, what did you think about our parents' recent nuptials?" I ask, not playing Mr. Nice Guy like I promised my father.

But technically, he told me to be nice to Winter, which I am.

Winter fiddles with the white-linen napkin in front of her. "Well, it definitely was a surprise."

I have to give it to her for remaining impartial as she sits here with her new family. My father launches into the wedding spontaneity, and talks about how they wanted a new beginning.

If it were anyone else, I'd be on board. Hell, I'd be their biggest cheerleader. But this is my flighty father we're talking about here.

And I don't think he's seriously thought this through.

I hate to say it, but he's done things like this before. Never to this extreme though.

"Where will you live?" I ask. "Have you thought about this yet?"

"Um, well," he squirms in his seat, "we're planning on selling my place and I'll move in with Crystal."

I scoff. "You're selling your place?" News to me.

His lips press into a thin line. "Kane, can we talk about this later?"

"One big happy family here." I lean back in my seat. "Let's discuss it now."

"You're acting like a petulant child."

He's right. I stand from the table before I throw a bigger tantrum and stalk toward the glass doors leading to the balcony. The chilly breeze swirls around my rigid body when Winter steps up beside me.

"They're the children," she says.

I shove my hands in my pockets as we overlook the vast golf course covered in snow. "They don't think about how their decisions affect us."

"They'll have to learn from their own mistakes." She runs her hands over her bare arms. "If this is one."

"You're cold? Here, take my sweater." I pull the black cashmere over my head and hand it to Winter.

"No, it's ok. I can't take your sweater."

I shrug, wearing nothing but a plain white tee. But it must

provide more warmth than Winter's short red dress. She must be freezing, even indoors.

I'm thankful I get to see all her glorious, sun-kissed skin, but I push my sweater to her once more. "Please, put it on."

She rejects it with a brief shake of her head. "I'm going to head back inside. Are you coming?"

Her words toss my mind into the gutter momentarily, but when she smiles, I realize I'll follow her anywhere.

"Ready, little sis," I say, to remind myself she's off limits.

Starting anything with her would definitely land me on Santa's naughty list.

Chapter 3

Winter

Having a new stepbrother is all I could've ever wanted. Said no one ever. Especially not me.

My bones shake, but not because I'm freezing. Well, partly because I'm cold, but mainly because Kane walks to the dinner table at Mom's house super close to me. We arrived at the same time, and he opened my car door for me. I tried not to swoon at his gentlemanly behavior. Secretly, I wish he'd place his hand on the small of my back, but nope. And that's for the best.

Mom has attached us at the hip the last few weeks doing what she calls 'family' things, which basically comprise eating dinner at her house, and my attraction to him is otherworldly.

It was like a punch to the gut when he called me his little sister at the restaurant, because I know I will never think of this gorgeous man like a brother.

There's just no way I ever could.

Not only is he hotter than Hades, but he seems normal… and nice. He's attentive when I talk and has fascinating publishing stories.

Should you fantasize about a step-sibling? I don't think so.

Have I? Absolutely.

We arrive in the dining room to find our parents huddled together, canoodling. Yes, they're full-on canoodling at the table.

Kane clears his throat. "Can you please not do that in my presence?" He sits down next to his father.

"Kane, when you love someone, show them all the time," Mr. Snow says.

Kane's eyes meet mine as I sit, and like every time he looks in my direction, my nipples salute him.

For the next few minutes, we enjoy awkward small talk over ribeye steaks and baked potatoes. Well, I enjoy the food at least. Until the moment I've been dreading happens.

My mother peers at me over the rim of her wine glass. "How's the job?"

I shift in my seat, clearing my throat, struggling to think of something I can say to change the subject, so I don't have to face the disappointed eyes of my mother. "Um, actually…" My words fade away.

"It's going great. Isn't that what you were saying earlier?" Kane chimes in.

I nod, letting my mind catch up with my mouth. "That's right." I'll confess to my mother after Christmas. "Yes, it's going great." I plaster a fake smile on my face.

"Where do you work?" Mr. Snow asks.

"For Tory Burch."

Thankfully, Kane changes the subject, "I've been helping her with the children's book."

"Oh, yeah?" Randall cuts into his ribeye. "How so?"

"Yeah," I say. "I normally use Kinko's, but Kane offered

his printing service, so it's the real deal. It will have a cover and a spine and everything."

Kane grins at me, igniting that familiar fire in my veins that's been steadily burning for weeks.

My mom douses the smoldering in my belly by saying, "That's what family does, dear."

My gaze flits to Kane's before dropping to my plate. It's not good for me to look at his sexiness. He's all wrapped up in a green button-down shirt that matches his eyes, with the sleeves rolled back, exposing his arm porn. Mr. Snow brings Kane into a discussion about sports and I try not to stare at the way Kane rubs the pad of his index finger against his top lip.

Mom pats my hand. "I know I have upset you about missing the wedding, so we're going to have a party at the resort so everyone can celebrate our marriage with us."

I smile. "That's great." I feel like I've said 'that's great' more times than necessary these past weeks.

"Tomorrow, Randall and I will ride out together. We have to leave early to get there before anyone else. Kane, would you mind Winter riding with you?"

Kane glances at me before answering. "I don't mind. Is that ok with you?"

I nod. "Sure."

I breathe in deeply, letting it out in one long smooth, controlled breath. I can't believe we'll be alone for a whole car ride. The retreat is about a two-hour drive, and now I'm worried about being so close to him.

I'll bring books. And work on my resume while he drives. Yes, that's what I'll do.

"THANKS FOR SAVING me with my mother," I tell Kane fifteen minutes into our car ride to the resort.

At first, I tried to read, but my eyes wanted to admire Kane's muscular arm draped over the steering wheel. Then I tried to work on my resume, but couldn't focus on anything except the way Kane's thigh flexed each time his foot pressed down on the brake or moved to the accelerator.

To say this has been an unproductive trip so far is an understatement.

"No problem. Want to tell me what really happened? I could tell by your face you didn't want to discuss it."

Funny, in the short time we've known each other, he can read me so well. I blow out a deep breath. "They fired me." My lips turn downward as Kane merges in the traffic on the interstate.

"Why?"

"I cursed at my boss."

He almost looks amused as I give him the details.

"I'm sorry," he says. "Did you like working there?"

I let that question bounce around my mind for a few seconds. "Actually, no. It was just a job."

Kane smiles. "If you could have any job in the world, what would you want to do? Don't think too hard… and go."

"I'd love to illustrate more books."

"Why don't you?"

"Ha," I blurt out. He acts like it would be so easy to just think of things to write and draw. "It's a lot more complicated than that."

"Why?"

"You're full of questions."

He chuckles. "I just think you shouldn't discount your dreams because it sounds too hard for you to accomplish."

"I never said it was my dream." I'm getting a little frustrated with him for thinking life is so easy.

"Oh, sorry." He backs off from the interrogation, and I stare out the window.

Is it my dream?

Have I been working at Tory Burch all this time just to hide from my own dreams? Do I really want to write and illustrate children's books?

I have to admit, I've thought of some ideas. Sparkly Figgybottoms has a lot to teach kids.

Kane drives in silence, opting to turn on the radio after a few more miles of neither of us talking. I continue contemplating my life, wondering if I could really make a go of it. My attention drifts to Kane, wondering what type of dreams he has for his life. Is he living them? Is he happy?

If I hadn't snapped at him, I'd probably ask, but instead, I watch the passing trees and mountains.

"I think we should address the elephant in the room. Well, truck," Kane says.

I swivel in my seat to face him. "What do you mean?"

"It's obvious we're both attracted to each other, and…" he doesn't finish his sentence because I'm too busy laughing.

"Are you serious?" I ask through a snort.

It's true I'm attracted to this man, but what kind of guy just blurts it out and thinks they know it all? Have I been that obvious with my ogling? Or is he just cocky and thinks every woman likes him because they're in the same vicinity?

Probably all of that.

"Yes, I'm serious."

"What makes you think there's an attraction here?"

"I'm attracted to you, Winter. And if we weren't somewhat related, I'd pull this truck over and show you just how into you I am."

It's like he threw a match on gasoline. The flame simmering low in my belly spreads like wildfire.

I blink. "Oh."

I mean, what does someone say to those words?

I'd like to tell him to pull over right now. I'm half-tempted to yank the steering wheel to get us to the side of the road quicker.

But I don't.
Because I can't.
And won't.

Chapter 4

Kane

Am I coming on too strong? Probably. But I know what I want. And what I want is here in this truck, gaping at me.

I continue driving as Winter absorbs the words I've said to her, not really verifying anything. Did I read her all wrong?

Is she not into me like I am her?

Am I really misreading the vibe between us?

I don't think so.

"Ok, maybe I'm a little attracted to you," she finally says after a few minutes of silence.

I grin. "I knew it."

"You're kind of arrogant, aren't you?"

I shrug. "I know what I know."

"Please, stop. You sound like our parents. 'When you know you just know,'" she quotes them.

"Piddly Dimplesticks," I say, creating an elf name just like she likes to do.

She laughs. "What was that?"

"I'm doing what you do."

"Yeah, but, Piddly Dimplesticks isn't a real name."

"Sure, it is."

She shakes her head. "No, it's really not."

"Is there some comprehensive book of elf names you take from? I don't know the rules."

Her laughter fades away. "No, there's no book. I just make them up, but they have to be elf-like names."

"Mine's completely elf-like."

We laugh, and I like the vibe that fills the truck cabin. I could talk to this woman all day long.

"As you were saying before you ruined the elf name… It would be wrong of us to start anything. We're now sort of related," she says, turning her attention back to the passing trees lining the interstate.

"I agree." Even though I really don't. But I'll try my hardest to stay away from Winter while we're at this resort.

WE RIDE in silence until I pull into the picturesque Mountain Goat Resort high on the mountaintops. It's like a Christmas village surrounding a mammoth log building that's strung with Christmas lights.

The property is beautiful, and I remember Crystal said her family owns the place.

"You probably came here a lot growing up."

"Every year for Christmas," Winter says, staring at the sign reading, 'Mountain Goat Cabins.' "There's a ski section too."

"That sounds like fun."

While she gathers her things, I exit the truck and round the hood to open Winter's door.

Her mouth forms an o. She looks taken aback by my chivalry, before she hops out and rambles, "My cousin,

Graham Steele, has been running the place for the past few years. He just got married, and we attended his wedding. Zoe's awesome."

"I bet." I stride to the back and drop the tailgate to grab Winter's luggage. "Can't wait to meet them."

As we walk toward the resort lobby, Crystal rushes out the front doors. "There you two are. I've got your costumes." She hands Winter a red and green garment and me a Santa suit.

I smile. "Wonderful."

"Can we get settled in before we work?" Winter asks.

"Yes, there's an issue, though. There were no vacancies, and sweetie, I had to put you in a cabin with Kane. Don't worry, it's two-bedrooms. It'll be fun, bonding with your new brother," Crystal talks so fast I barely comprehend the meaning of her words.

"Sharing a cabin?" Winter shrieks, clutching her costume in her hands. "We can't share a cabin."

Crystal thrusts a magnetic key card at her. "You're in cabin twenty-two, near the back of the property. See you in an hour." She rushes back inside, leaving Winter and me standing in shock outside.

Winter spins around to face me, plastering on what I can only imagine is a fake smile. "Well, roomie. Looks like we'll be sharing."

I nod, because boy can I think of all the ways we'll spend in the cabin cozying up. "Sounds like a plan."

Winter narrows her eyes. "Follow me."

We follow the path that winds through the cabins until we arrive at twenty-two. The interior is more spacious than I had hoped. We walk through the living area filled with wood accented leather furniture, back to the master suites, each complete with a fireplace.

Winter heads into one room, so I cross into the other. I drop my suitcase on the sleigh bed and stare at the Santa suit in my hands. When I agreed to help, I guess I forgot how humiliating it would be to wear this suit, but I decide to do it with a lot of class.

I toss off my shirt and unzip my jeans when there's a knock at my door.

"Come in," I say.

"Oh, god." Winter takes one look at me and covers her eyes, turning around. "You shouldn't have invited me in if you were naked."

"I'm not naked." I love her shyness. "Turn around and see."

She slowly spins around, dropping her hands. Her tongue peeks out to wet her lips as she takes in all of me.

It turns me on, and my cock stiffens.

"See something you like?" I drop my pants.

Winter turns back around. "I'll be ready in five minutes. I was just coming in to check on you to see if you were getting ready. I see you are, so I'll leave."

"You can help me get ready," I call after her.

She slams the door, and I chuckle.

This is going to be fun.

AN HOUR LATER, I'm sitting in a red-velvet throne with gold trimming, having kid after kid sit on my lap.

There's a goat off to my side, which was introduced to me as Jack, and dashing about is the lovely Winter, decked out in a Santa's little helper costume, giving her cute book to the children. Fuck. She's got on a curve-hugging green velvet dress that ends mid-thigh, leaving a few inches of skin exposed above her sexy candy cane striped socks. I'd love to throw those curly elf shoes over my shoulders and think of all the ways I need Winter to help me, but I'm trying to be good.

Mainly because kids are sitting on my lap and telling me all their hopes and dreams for this Christmas season.

"I'd like a little brother or sister," a brown-haired little girl says.

"What's your name?" I ask.

"Noel."

"That's a pretty name. How old are you Noel?"

"This many." She holds up four tiny fingers. "That's my mom."

"You look like her," I say.

"Hi, I'm Zoe Steele."

"Nice to meet you. Oh, right. Your husband owns the place."

She nods. "Yes, he does. And you're Crystal's new stepson."

I crack a grin. "That's right."

She beams at me. "It's a pleasure to meet you…" she pauses, "I don't know your name."

"Santa," I say. "Name's Santa Claus." I don't want to destroy the lie for her kid.

"Oh, of course." She gives me a thumbs up and a wink when Noel isn't looking. "Santa has other kids to see, Noel. Let's get going."

At that moment, Winter spots Zoe, and they do a quick hug while another child climbs on my lap.

"Well, hello there," I say.

"I want a pony, and an Xbox. I also want to fly. Do you grant wishes?" the little boy with chocolate-covered cheeks says to me. He holds the rest of his chocolate bar in the other hand, and I lean back so I don't get a mess on my suit.

But it comes with the territory, I guess.

"No, sorry, kid. I can't grant wishes." Although, I wish I could. I'd help Winter see she has a genuine passion for drawing. I could see it in her eyes when she talked about it.

"Then just the pony." He hops off my lap and rushes to his mother.

"Ok, Santa needs a fifteen-minute break," Winter says to the crowd, coming to my rescue.

I stand, stretching my back as I follow Winter to a private room her mother set up for us. It's hidden from the party, behind an enormous Christmas tree, and as soon as Winter shuts the door, I rip the beard from my face.

"I didn't realize there would be so many kids at this thing," I say, grabbing a bottle of water from the mini fridge.

"You're really kind of awesome for agreeing to do this," Winter says, stepping closer.

"I have to say, you look hot in that outfit." I wonder what she'd do if I ripped the fucking thing off.

Her cheeks turn redder than Rudolph's nose. "I feel like a clown out there."

I move closer, reaching my hand out to touch her face. "You absolutely don't look like a clown." My heart slams in my ribcage. She's so fucking pretty.

Her green eyes connect with mine. "Really?"

I breathe her in, loving the magical peppermint smell. "Really," I whisper.

A magnetic pull drags me toward her, and I'm not really sure what's going on. She's all I can see. She's all I want.

I lean in, capturing her mouth with mine, tracing my tongue along the seam of her lips so she'll open up.

She does.

I pull her closer, deepening the kiss and she moans for me. She tastes so good, and I keep kissing her, no longer caring about the ramifications of this kiss. No longer wondering about what this means for our family dynamic. Because having her in my arms feels right. And nothing I've done before has ever felt this way.

Chapter 5

Winter

I can't believe I'm kissing my stepbrother. Is this even allowed? Am I going to hell?

Northy Gumdroppings. Do I care?

He deepens the kiss, his hand tracing dangerously low to the hem of my skirt. I no longer care if this is wrong.

All I care about is having this man's hands all over me. His touch is electric, zapping parts inside me l didn't know existed. I've felt nothing like this before.

Is this all moving too fast?

Actually, it's not fast enough.

Because the kiss-drunk part of me wonders how quickly he can get us back to our cabin and remove our clothes.

This isn't like me.

I don't make out with men dressed as Santa in hidden rooms. I definitely don't make out with men who are also my stepbrother.

This is bad.

"This feels so right," Kane groans out.

"Yes, so bad. I mean, right."

He trails lingering kisses down my neck, over the column of my throat, and finishes by sucking along my collarbone. My fingers plunge into his dark hair, and I tug his head closer, wanting another soul-searing kiss.

There's a knock on the door, and we break apart, panting.

"Kane, Winter, are you in here?" my mother's voice says.

We freeze.

Kane repositions himself in his pants, and I love the fact I gave that massive hard on to him.

I straighten my hair as I walk over to the door. With my hand on the cool knob, I take a deep breath before I open it and peek my head out. "What's up?"

"Your lipstick is smeared," Mother says at first glance.

I wipe my mouth. "I was drinking a soda," I say, knowing full well a soda would never do this to my lipstick.

She brushes past me, into our clandestine Christmas corner.

"Hi," Kane says. "Well, I guess I'll head back out and entertain the children." He's gone in a flash.

Mom fingers the pearls around her neck, giving me side-eye. "Nothing just happened between the two of you, did it?"

It pains me to lie, but… "What? No. Mom, how could you even ask that?" I act shocked, and I'm possibly overacting a bit, but my heart is racing faster than when Kane kissed me.

"Winter, he's our family now. You can't very well be making out with your new stepbrother. Things are fragile between Randall and I."

I perch on the arm of a wingback chair. "Fragile how?"

"Well, everything is so brand new. I don't know how news of our children hooking up would go over with him."

"Mom, we are *not* hooking up."

"I hope not." My mother studies me for what seems like an eternity and finally drops it. "I came to tell you Aspen is here. The ball is tonight so why don't you two go shopping for a new dress in the resort's boutique?" She hands me a credit card. "On me."

I'm horrid about lying and wrap her in a hug. "Thank you, Mom. You don't need to buy me a dress."

"Don't argue, Winter."

I let it go, because I want to get out of here before she can ask more questions about Kane and me.

Because honestly, I don't know how much more lying I can handle.

"WHAT ABOUT THIS DRESS?" Aspen asks, stepping out of the dressing room wearing a sapphire blue gown.

"I love it," I say. "It really makes your eyes pop."

Aspen runs her hands down the shimmery material. "Really? It doesn't make me look like a blueberry?"

"No. You're beautiful, sis. This dress only enhances it."

She laughs away my compliment. "What about you?" she says, changing the subject. "Have you found anything?"

I stare at the ebony satin in my hands, wondering what Kane would think of me in it. "This is pretty, but it's skimpy."

"And that's why you should get it."

Hm. She's right. The simple black dress exposes my back and has a daring slit on the thigh, perfect for Kane to slip a hand inside.

"Ok, done."

After we make our purchases, we stop at the resort's café nestled under the snow-tipped pine trees for coffee. The golden bells on the door jingle when we step inside the merry shop. Holiday music serenades us as we walk past a life-size nutcracker to the counter wrapped in garland. The aroma of peppermint and mocha waft through the air, and I inhale, loving the smell of Christmas.

Once we order our coffees—gingerbread lattes—we find a booth near the back.

"So, tell me about this stepbrother? I saw him walking out of the resort. He's fucking hot."

I shake my head. "You have no idea."

Aspen's known me for so long she can garner an idea just by my tone. She picks up her mug with a tiny reindeer painted on it and blows, then says, "Care to share," before taking a sip.

I sigh. "We may have kissed a little bit."

Aspen sets her coffee down and leans in. "A little bit? Or a lot a bit?"

I suck in a deep breath, releasing it slowly. "A lot. I can't help it. He's just got this pull over me."

"Listen, your mother is going to freak if she finds out."

I cringe. "Well—"

"Oh, no." she cuts in. "Tell me she didn't catch you."

"Not exactly." I stare at the milky Santa hat design atop my latte. "She suspects something, though."

Aspen sets her mug down and gives me her serious face. "Turn it off. Nothing good can come from this. Besides, do you even know anything about him?"

I think about this for a moment. "He works in publishing."

"Anything else?"

I shoot her a half-smile. "He's a fantastic kisser."

"I can't believe you just said that, Winter."

I pinch the bridge of my nose. "I know. I know. What am I thinking?"

"Listen, it's normal. You lost your job, and the holidays are coming. It's stressful. And he's gorgeous. Anyone in your position would act on their crazy impulses."

Is that really it? Am I just acting on an impulse? I feel like it could be more, but every part of my brain reminds me of how wrong it is.

"Tell me about your life," I say, pushing thoughts of Kane out of my mind.

She fills me in on her recent dates and when our mugs are empty, we head to the salon to spend the next few hours getting hair and makeup done for tonight.

It takes longer than expected, so we change into our dresses at the salon.

We rush to the lodge, and as I walk through the doors with Aspen, my eyes seek *him* out.

I spot his dark hair by the makeshift bar in the room's corner. He's stunning in a black suit and tie. The material hugs his broad shoulders and firm ass, showcasing his virile manliness. My core coils into knots, and butterflies flap their wings within my belly. I shouldn't be having this reaction to him, but boy am I.

I can't stop fantasizing about what the two of us will do together alone in our cabin. He spies me from across the room and one corner of his mouth tilts up, nearly stopping my heart.

He's beyond sexy.

He knows it too, because his smile gets cockier the longer our eyes stay connected, like he can read all the dirty thoughts I'm having about him. I try to turn my head, but it's like there's something stuck in my neck keeping me from moving.

He must know what I'm thinking, because he moves away from the bar, crossing the ballroom floor until his shiny leather shoes stop inches from my red tipped toes peeking out of black heels.

"You look, wow." He leans down to whisper in my ear. "Good enough for me to eat."

I grasp Aspen by the elbow. "This is my best friend Aspen." I shove her at him.

He steps away, a polite smile gracing his handsome face. "Nice to meet you."

"Same," she says. "Heard a lot about you. Any brother of Winter's is a brother of mine."

She hugs him, and I wish someone would straight up

murder me because I can't handle the awkwardness of this situation.

"How's the party going?" I ask him, after they've ended their bizarre hug.

"Well, it's going." He rubs at the back of his neck, looking at me from beneath thick lashes. "Much better now that you're here."

"Oh, looky there. I see my father," Aspen says, rushing away from the two of us, leaving me alone with Kane.

Every part of me wants to reenact what happened earlier today, but our parents join us.

"There you are," Randall says. "We're introducing the family soon."

"Great," I mutter as they corral us to the mini stage at the front of the ballroom.

"If I can have your attention, please," my mother says into the microphone.

Oh god, where is that murderer? Do we have an ETA?

Mom launches into a speech, thanking everyone for being here and helping raise money for her charity. At the end of her speech, she announces her marriage to Randall.

The crowd erupts into thunderous applause and my gaze darts up to Kane's. He raises an eyebrow, and I quickly look away before everyone in the audience reads my mind about all the things I want to do to Kane to land on Santa's naughty list this year.

My mother wraps it up by gushing about our happy family. My insides churn, because how many times does she need to say it?

It almost makes me not believe her.

It makes me wonder who she's trying to convince.

Us…

Or herself?

Chapter 6

Kane

Can you sweat during the winter? I feel like I'm sweating a melting glacier as Crystal drones on about family happiness. Mentally, I roll my eyes a few times, especially when she talks about the blessing of her new son getting along with her daughter.

She has no idea.

After this speech, I'm going to find the closest broom closet and stuff Winter in it and have my wicked way with her.

I don't care if it's not allowed. I don't care if it's completely unacceptable. When she walked into this ballroom in that black number hugging all her curves just right, I decided something important.

And that decision is...

I will claim her body as mine tonight. I will explore all those delicious curves.

Hell, I know nothing of substance about her except she comes up with silly elf names and is a naturally talented illustrator and author.

But does that even matter?

Cause I sure know the sounds she makes when she's turned on. I know how her skin tastes. I know how her body feels when I'm holding her close.

Every part of me wants to keep spending more time with Winter.

We finally walk off stage and random strangers introduce themselves to me, welcoming me to the family.

Is it bad I don't want to be a member of their family unless it's from marrying Winter?

Wait.

I didn't just think about that.

"I think my mother has had one too many 'happy' cocktails," Winter whispers, brushing her delectable body against mine.

My heart pounds, thudding in my ears. "Let's get out of here," I whisper back.

Her eyes widen a tad, but hallelujah, she nods. "Ok."

I don't hold her hand, but I sure fucking want to, as we rush out of the ballroom. We hurry past the enormous Christmas tree in the lobby and out the doors into the frigid air. Her legs can't keep up with mine, so I scoop her up into my arms. I know exactly where we're going. Our cabin.

I'm faster than Santa flying across the sky and reach my destination in no time. I set her on her feet and quickly unlock the door.

As soon as we step inside, I kick the door shut with my foot and slam her body against the back of it. "I can't take it anymore."

She grabs my tie, yanking me toward her, and our lips crash together, tongues mating. I moan, thrusting my dick against her stomach. My body ignites into a firestorm, going from zero to sixty in a matter of seconds.

I grab her wrists, raising them above her head. "Tonight, you're mine. Do you understand that?"

She nods. "Yes."

I hover my lips above hers. "Are you sure?"

She blinks. "I think so."

I trail a hand up her quivering thigh, going underneath her skirt and spreading her legs apart. "It means I'll take whatever I want tonight. It means I'm in charge."

She swallows. "Ok."

I spin her around so her front is against the door and run my hands over her ass, bunching her panties into my fist, yanking the material so it falls away from her skin. She groans as I caress her inner thigh, exploring the crevice there, and back over her ass.

"This ass turns me on," I say as I grab a handful. "You should be ashamed of yourself for turning me on this much."

She gasps.

"Should I punish you for turning me on so much I can barely breathe?"

"Yes," she says.

I thrust my hips against her to keep her in place. "You naughty little thing." I palm her ass again, wondering how she'd feel if I spanked her, hoping she'll be into it.

I test it and give her a sharp tap. She moans out the minute my hand contacts her skin.

I massage her right cheek and lean close to her ear. "You like being punished like a naughty girl, don't you?"

"God, yes. Do it again."

I love how needy she is for the slap of my hand. She's perfect for me. I spank her again, harder this time and rub the reddened skin.

"Kane, yes," she cries out.

"You make me so goddamn hard." I kiss her neck and drag my tongue along the shell of her ear. "So fucking hard." My dick throbs for her, and I grind it against her ass so I can feel a semblance of relief.

It doesn't work, and I spin her to face me and hoist her up, telling her exactly how much I want her with the kiss I lay on her.

She wraps her legs around my waist, and I move to the leather sofa, laying her down.

Frantic to taste her, I push her skirt up and dive into the promised land.

"Oh god," she cries out when my tongue makes contact with her pussy.

I feast like a starved man, dragging my tongue through her wetness, ending at her clit. "I'm so fucking turned on by this pussy," I tell her, looking into her green eyes.

She stares at me like she's never wanted anyone as badly as me, and I'm hoping she hasn't. Because I've never in my life been this aroused by another woman.

I continue sucking at her skin, pushing a finger into her wet heat. She bucks beneath me, and I add another finger, moving in sync with my tongue on her clit. My dick is so hard, but I focus on the beauty who has her fingers intertwined in my hair, making the most glorious sounds I've ever heard.

I can't wait to hear her get off.

I speed up my tempo, making sure she's enjoying every second. She squeezes her eyes shut and her back arches off the couch.

"I'm coming," she cries out, but I can already tell by the way her thighs squeeze my head and her walls clamp around my fingers.

I sit up to watch her orgasm wash over her, and she doesn't disappoint as she bites her lower lip and calls out my name.

I remove my belt, unzip my pants, and move over her so I can kiss those luscious ruby lips. Within seconds, I wrap my aching dick with a condom and slide up into her before I can take another breath.

The moment I'm to the hilt, we stop the frenzy and stare

at one another. I'm lost in her green eyes, and my body slowly rocks.

She cups my face, laying a tender kiss on my lips. "I've never felt anything like that before," she whispers.

Emotion overcomes me. Being inside her heat feels so exquisite I kiss her, because I'm afraid I might blurt out the words, 'I love you' to someone I just met.

It's insane, but I feel like I can't breathe unless I'm kissing her. So, I don't stop. I keep kissing her as our bodies find a perfect rhythm. As they play out their own orchestrated melody.

I break the kiss, the words I wanted to say earlier tucked neatly away in my mind, and gaze at her. "You're beautiful," I say instead.

"Kane, this is so wrong."

I shake my head. "Never. This can never be wrong." I spread her legs wider as I thrust inside her. Deeper. Further into her. She moans long and hard.

I run my fingers through her strawberry hair and sniff it so I can remember the fragrance. Everything about this woman is unexpected and refreshing. It makes my mind think I am falling for her.

I push the thoughts away and focus on the sweet feel of her pussy wrapped around me. I pump into her, and she moves with me, her nails scraping down my back.

Fuck, she feels like heaven.

"Kane, don't stop," she says.

I'll never stop. I'd give this woman anything.

My body builds, and I pick up speed. I want this orgasm with her. I want her to come at the same time as me. I want to know the moment she does.

"Come with me," I tell her. "I'm so fucking close."

"Me too," she breathes out.

"Who's fucking you so good?"

"You are," she answers.

I run my lips over hers. "Say my name."

"Kane." Her thunderous cries echo in the cabin.

"Say it again."

"Kane." She grabs onto me, her legs holding me in a vice grip. "I'm coming."

At the sound of her words, I explode in a blizzard of ecstasy. I slam my eyes shut as the powerful pleasure overtakes me.

Her tremors calm, and I pump inside her a few more times, my orgasm lessening with each thrust of my hips.

"You're amazing," I pant out through ragged breaths.

"No, you are," she whispers.

I don't want to break the connection. I want to live in her pussy. I want so many things it scares me, so I kiss her lips before I stand and clean up, discarding the condom.

Her phone pings with a message once I've returned to the living room.

"Is it our parents?" Just saying that sentence sounds so wrong on so many levels.

She shakes her head, sitting up and fixing her hair. "No, it's Aspen. She says they're looking for us."

I pull up my pants and straighten my tie. "Maybe we should head back?"

Winter stares at her phone a little longer. "Yeah, maybe."

Every part of me wants to stay here with her, explore this connection, but I know that's not possible.

Chapter 7

Winter

Things not on my to-do list when I came home to visit my mother: acquire a stepbrother and have the best sex of my life with him.

I can't believe that just happened, and a huge part of me wants to know when it can happen again. Like how soon?

Is now too soon?

I stare at Kane, wondering if we really need to go back to the party.

We dress and he looks like a million dollars while I look like I just got run over by a reindeer. There's a knock at the door, and Kane and I spring into action, taming tangled hair and putting on shoes.

"Winter, are you in there?" my mother's voice calls from the other side of the door.

My eyes widen, and Kane stares at me with what I'm guessing is the same deer-in-the-headlight look I've got going on.

"Winter?" the knock grows impatient.

Kane passes me and opens the door. "Hi, Crystal. Winter wasn't feeling well, so I brought her back here to rest."

Mom pushes through the door, crossing the cabin to stand right in front of me. "Are you sick?"

"Sort of?" I place a hand on my stomach, while my mother places her palm to my forehead. "I think it's something I ate."

"She had the oysters. Maybe they're bad. Warn others," Kane says, stepping closer to usher my mother out the door.

"Well, she can rest, but you should come back, Kane. Your father is looking for you."

Kane gives me a look like he's trying to think of any reason for him to stay. I'm half-expecting him to claim he's had the oysters too. However, he leaves with my mother after telling me he'll return soon.

When the door shuts, I close my eyes and sigh. If she'd come ten minutes earlier, she might have heard me screaming Kane's name. Since I'm not returning to the party, might as well relax my tense muscles. I strip and make my way to the Roman tub in the master bath. As I pass the mirror, I get a glimpse of kiss-swollen lips and love bites on my skin. It's a wondrous sight.

I can't remember the last time I had sex, and I've never had sex *that* phenomenal. Kane definitely knows what he's doing.

Big time.

And I do mean big.

Zoe's special soaps she makes for the resort sit in a wreath on the marble counter, and I select the vanilla goat milk bar and add some bubbles to the water flowing into the tub. The smell emanating from the porcelain is divine as I slide into the mountain of foam, letting the hot water relax my muscles. I lean back and close my eyes, all thoughts turning to Kane.

My core tightens as I remember the way he touched me.

My hands trail over my body up to my breasts, tracing around my hardened nipples. I squeeze the sensitive peaks between my fingers and moan.

"I hope you're not getting off without me," Kane says, standing at the door of the bathroom.

I jerk upright, sloshing water out of the tub. "How long have you been standing there?"

"Long enough." He yanks at his tie. "Hope there's room in there for me."

He removes his clothing and I shamelessly watch, licking my lips when he drops his boxer-briefs.

"Plenty of room." I slide forward so he can get in behind me.

As soon as he's settled, he picks up the loofah sponge and rubs it up and down my back.

"Ahh, that feels so good," I say.

He moves my hair and runs the sponge over my neck. "You're being bad again."

I smile. "How so?"

"I'm fucking hard as a rock. I'm trying to be good here and wash your body, but here you are turning me on again."

"What are you going to do about it?" I look back at him over my shoulder.

"Spanking didn't seem to work with you. Should I be firmer?"

"Or maybe…" Feeling brave, I turn in the tub so I can hover over him, my body coming out of the water. "You can just let this time slide." I nip at his lips, and he gazes up at me.

His stare morphs from hungry to needy as it falls on my breasts. "Fuck, you're gorgeous." His mouth closes on my nipple, and he kneads the other with his hand. I tug him closer, my fingers roaming through his glossy tresses. I love his hair. And the way he makes my body heat.

It's everything about this man. Everything he makes me feel.

Is it too soon to have genuine feelings for him?

Kane positions me where I'm straddling his lap, and I lower onto his thick length, moaning at the slight stretch and fullness.

He isn't slow once he's deep inside me. No, he takes what he needs. He takes what he wants from me, and I give it freely.

Water spills onto the floor, and I no longer care because my body is moving at top speeds. My heartbeat is immeasurable, beating to the sounds of our impact. Of our sex. Of our fucking. Because that's what this is at this point. Pure carnal lust in its simplest form.

His hands cup my face as he plows up into me. "I fucking love the way you feel. So tight."

I slam back down on his lap, matching his intensity. "I love the way you feel."

He groans, and I ride his dick, knowing he completely owns my heart at this moment. There isn't anything I wouldn't give him right now.

Together we come, crying out each other's names, clinging to each other. Our breathing is labored and as I try to catch my breath, Kane's eyes meet mine.

"I think I might be falling in love with you."

My eyes widen at the words he said out loud. Love. Even though I kind of feel the same way, my mind can't process what he said. I ease off him and climb out of the tub, grabbing the robe hanging on a hook.

"Say something," he says, running a hand down his face.

"Jiminy Flusterbuster." This will never work. Our parents are married, for goodness' sake.

I rush out of the bathroom and hear Kane exiting the tub.

"Winter, wait."

I spin around before making it further down the hallway. "We just can't do this," I say to him. "I have to go."

He wraps a towel around his lean hips, staring at me like I've truly broken his heart.

And I head to my room to dress and pack a few things, feeling like I broke mine too.

I OPEN my eyes to the sound of an adamant bird chirping outside my window. "Go to sleep," I yell at the bird, trying my hardest to go back to dreamland.

After I left Kane last night, I headed to my mother's cabin. It surprised me to find her alone.

She said Randall got his own cabin for the evening because they needed some time apart, but swore everything was fine between them. When she asked why I wanted to crash with her, I couldn't tell her the truth, so I told her Kane snores like a train and it was driving me insane.

I don't think she believed me.

"You have half an hour until you have to be at Santa's workshop," my mother says, leaning against the door jamb of the bedroom.

"Don't remind me," I grumble, tossing the covers over my eyes so I can forget about my issues. The thought of hanging out all day with a sexy step-Santa makes my insides burn with acid. Why can't I have a simple life?

Why can't I meet someone normal?

Not saying Kane isn't normal. He's very normal. Probably one of the most *real* men I've ever met.

He doesn't hide behind his job, or his status, or his money. Most of the men I've dated in the past always seemed like they were trying to sell me a gimmick. Like hey, I'm a nice guy, watch. But they were never nice.

They always fell short.

I can see myself building a future with Kane… if the situation were different.

But it's not.

"Get up. I'm sure Kane will wonder what happened if his

little helper is late." She pushes off the doorjamb with a wan smile and shuffles away.

"You can tell him I had to head back to the North Pole," I holler, so she can hear me.

I finally slide my feet from under the covers and onto the warmth of the heated hardwood floors.

After I dress, I head into the dinette area where my mother sits at the small island, holding a cup of coffee, staring out the window. I grab a mug from the cupboard and pour myself some caffeine, adding a copious amount of sugar and cream.

I sit next to her. "Mom, what's really going on?"

Her steely gray eyes gaze into mine. "I'll level with you, if you level with me."

I slump on my bar stool and murmur, "I think I'm in love with Kane Snow."

My mother laughs lightly. "I think I'm *not* in love with Randall Snow."

My eyes widen to saucers. Mom's news is much worse than mine.

"Oh, no." I stand and hug her. "What are you going to do?"

She shrugs. "I don't even know." A tear races down her cheek. "The funny thing is, I don't think he loves me either. How many married couples don't want to spend any time together on their honeymoon?"

I return to my seat and shake my head, thinking about a honeymoon with Kane and how I'd want to spend every second with him by my side. "I don't know."

I listen as she talks about regrets and mistakes. When she's got it all out of her system, and seems to feel better, she asks, "What are you going to do about Kane?"

Ugh. "I don't know. He told me he thinks he loves me."

My mother's face brightens. "That's wonderful, dear. He'd be an idiot not to love you."

"I'm sorry for giving you a hard time about the three-week thing, because that's exactly what I've done."

"Irony at its finest," she says.

I give her another hug. "What a mess we are."

After the hug, I rush off to do my duties as Santa's little helper.

I don't know what I'm going to say to Kane. All I know is I need to tell him something.

Chapter 8

Kane

There are a few things one needs to know to play Santa successfully.

1. Always laugh and make sure your fake belly shakes while doing it.
2. Never promise a kid anything.
3. And never hook up with an elf and then tell them you might love them.

When I told Winter I might be falling for her, I wasn't lying. The only thing I messed up on was saying I might. Because I know now, I'm one hundred percent in love with her. What I'm not in love with is the reaction she gave me when I said the words to her.

I half-expected, ok, fully expected her to leap into my arms and say the words right back to me. I definitely didn't expect her to run from the cabin like it was on fire and I was the arsonist.

Someone places another kid on my lap, who tells me about wanting a new game. I'm barely listening to him because Winter has entered the room and stolen all my attention.

I can barely breathe, and I try not to make an idiot out of myself by standing and rushing over there to kiss her. That would be bad.

That would be a big Santa no-no.

"And I want a Superman action figure, and a basketball, and some skates."

Little man keeps going with his wish list, and I pull my gaze from Winter, who is doing a great job of ignoring me, and focus on the brown-eyed boy on my lap.

"If you're a good boy, Santa might help you with a few things on your list. Just be sure to tell your parents." I don't want the kid to hate Santa forever because he didn't tell his parents what he wanted, and it never showed up.

Winter saunters over, helping him off my lap and handing him a book before he trots over to his mother.

I smile up at Winter, and she smiles back.

Phew. That's the first step.

I knew when I told her last night I loved her, I was most likely making a mistake. First, who falls in love this quickly? And second, why did I say I think I might?

I should have just said I love you. Plain and simple. I love you and we can have a glorious future together.

Have my babies.

But I couldn't go all psycho stalker on her. We've known each other for five minutes, and besides, our parents are married.

I still can't believe this is my reality right now.

Winter assists a little girl with blonde curls onto my lap, and I smile, waiting to hear her requests.

"Hi, Santa," she whispers.

"Hello there," I say back. "What do you want for Christmas?"

"There's nothing I really want." She stares up at me. "What do you want, Santa? I bet no one ever asks you that question."

My eyes meet Winter's. "Well, what I want is a little complicated."

"But you're Santa. You can give yourself anything you want."

I smile at Winter, my eyes still trained on hers. "You're right. I can, but I'm not sure if my elf wants me to have it." I nod toward Winter.

Winter's cheeks turn pink. "Well, maybe Santa needs to remember it's not only about him and what he wants."

Her answer confuses me. "What's it about then?"

The little girl interrupts, petting my fluffy white beard with her hand. "It shouldn't matter. It's Christmas and the only thing that matters on Christmas is getting what you wished for."

I tap her nose. "You're right. And hopefully Santa has been a good enough boy to have my wish come true."

This makes the girl give me a gap-toothed smile, and she hops off my lap.

Winter hands her a book and comes back to stand next to me.

"I think Santa doesn't really know what he wants." She walks away, heading toward the back room.

I rise from my velvet throne and wave to the kids in line. "I'll be back in a few minutes. I need to check on my reindeer."

The children wave back, full of glee, laughing and chatting about Rudolph.

My shiny black boots rush after Winter. "I want you. I know I do. You're what I want," I say as soon as I open the door.

But we are *not* alone.

Winter, Crystal, and my father all stare at me like I've grown antlers.

"Sit down, both of you. We need to talk," my father says, commanding all the attention in the room. Is he going to address what I said to Winter, or ignore it?

I take a seat next to Winter on the small couch. "What is it?" I ask when I can no longer take the suspense.

"We don't know how to tell you both this, but we're getting a divorce," my father says, running a hand through his graying hair. "It's nothing anyone did or said. Crystal and I are very fond of each other, and we have love for each other, but we may have jumped the gun."

Winter rises and hugs her mom, who assures her she's fine.

"I'll be honest," Winter says, "I'm a little shocked."

"I'm not," I say, standing and pacing the room. "This is just like you, Dad. Now you've gone and hurt Crystal and made the Snow name fodder for gossip once again."

Sounds harsh, but my father is notorious for being the child in the family. The black sheep, as you will.

He can never act like an adult.

Ever.

This time, I hoped things had changed, but now I see they haven't.

"This isn't like last time," my father assures me. "This is a very amicable break up."

I stare into my father's eyes. "Then why is she crying?"

Crystal steps forward. "I'm only crying because I know how much we hurt you both."

I scoff. "You haven't hurt us." Winter places a hand on my back. "The only one who hurts people is my father."

Crystal steps closer to me. "No, he's been wonderful. Some relationships come into your life to set you onto a new path." Crystal smiles at Winter as she rubs reassuring circles on my back. "I think I know why Randall and I met."

"Why?"

She gives me a knowing smile before taking my father's hand and walking out of the room.

"Can you believe them?" I jab a thumb over my shoulder in the direction they just left.

Winter says nothing. Instead, she moves to stand in front of me.

"Listen," I start. "About last night…" I'm on the verge of asking her to pretend I never said anything, but she cuts me off instead.

"I love you, too," she blurts out.

My heart leaps in my chest, crashing against my chest, ready to jump into her hands. Anyone who says you can't find true love in three weeks is nothing but a Scrooge.

"Are you sure?" I ask, wondering why I'm even questioning any of this.

She gives me a slow nod. "Yep."

I slide my hands around her waist and pull her into me. "Say it one more time to be certain."

She smiles. "I love you, Kane Snow."

"I love you, Winter Joseph."

Epilogue

Winter

It took my mother longer to get married than it did to get divorced. I want to say they divorced by the next day, but we all know that's not the real story.

And Kane and me, well, we had our own Christmas miracle. He decked my halls so good over the holiday I'm forty-*one* weeks pregnant.

I knead my back with my fist. "This baby is just *not* coming out," I tell Kane as I walk around our two-bedroom condo.

Kane finishes up packing a box. "It'll come. You just have to be patient."

We're moving to a new home, one we just bought together, and life couldn't be better. Kane is killing it in the publishing field, signing on a brilliant author with a large fanbase. And me.

I started fresh adventures for Sparkly Figgybottoms in my spare time, and well, my sales kind of blew up overnight. People love my children's books.

Which is one reason we're moving to a bigger place. Our tiny condo has become the home for my inventory. Lots and lots of inventory.

Besides, I'm sure the baby won't want to sleep in a box of books, so we're packing up the last of our things.

I should say Kane is packing it all up while I rest on the couch larger than a whale. I feel like a whale, full of blubber and water.

"We can always have sex," Kane says with a laugh. "They say it brings on labor."

I stare at him. Yes, I've heard the old wives' tale, but I can safely say Kane and I had so much sex during this pregnancy the baby should have been born by now.

"Kane, I'm serious. Maybe he's stuck. Maybe we should go to the doctor to see if something's wrong."

Kane stops fiddling with the packing tape and sits beside me on the sofa. "I promise you; nothing is wrong. He'll come when he's ready."

"Which is never."

My stomach tightens just as Kane gives me a peck on the cheek. "Ow," I groan out.

I've been experiencing Braxton Hicks contractions for a few weeks, but nothing this intense.

"Everything ok?" Kane asks.

I nod. "Yeah," but before I can say anything more, another cramp comes on even stronger. "Actually, I think I'm in labor."

Kane springs from the couch, grabbing the bag by the door. "We need to get a move on. I've clocked a few different routes to the hospital and at this time of day," he checks his watch, "I think our best bet is down Main Street.

I haven't even gotten off the sectional before Kane is already out the door. "Umm," I say, even though I know he can't hear me.

He rushes back inside. "I almost forgot the most important thing," he says, helping me off the sofa.

I huff through the next contraction, trying to take a step while my uterus contracts.

Kane helps me to his truck, and as he rounds the vehicle and hops into the driver's side, I can see the excitement in his eyes.

Sure, he's excited. I'm terrified.

How badly will this hurt?

What if something happens? I breathe through my next contraction like the Lamaze coach told me, and stare at Kane as he pulls out of our complex.

"I'm scared," I tell him.

He smiles, clutching my hand in his. "Don't be. I'll be there every step of the way. I won't leave you."

If I could smile right now, I'd smile back at him, but an extreme pain shoots across my abdomen. "Get me to the hospital," I say through my clenched jaw.

Kane speeds down the road, disobeying all the rules of the highway. He pulls into the hospital lot and parks the truck.

"Ready?"

I breathe through my nose and out through my mouth. "As I'll ever be."

I'll spare you the gritty and gory details of my child's birth and skip to the good stuff.

The baby.

He's wonderful and healthy.

Kane was a champ throughout the delivery process, and now staring down into the beautiful green eyes of my son, I know life will never be the same.

"Did you call our parents?" I ask Kane.

"I texted them a while ago. I think they're here."

Ten fingers. Ten toes. I keep counting them over and over while the baby stares up at me.

"Hi, handsome," I whisper to him.

My mother knocks on the door as she walks in, carrying a teddy bear with blue balloons. "I want to see my grandson." She stands over my bed, staring at my new son.

It still sounds so weird to say that. I have a son.

A son with no name.

Randall walks in next and smiles at my mother. Even though their marriage didn't last, they're still great friends. In fact, Randall introduced my mother to his accountant, and they've been on three dates.

I still worry about her rushing off to get married, but she's assured me she's learned her lesson. Kevin is a lot more down to earth, and I don't see him even knowing what the word spontaneity means.

I mean, he's an accountant.

"Do you have a name for him yet?" my mother asks us.

I stare at Kane. "Not yet."

Kane smiles. "Nothing seems to fit."

I stare at my son, wondering what name fits him. And then it hits me. "I think we should name him Nick, like Jolly Ol' Saint Nick."

THANK you so much for reading this quick holiday surprise.

Hated By My Roommate

Chapter 1

Sydney

It's true, everything is bigger in Texas. Our great state contains everything from the world's largest pecan to the country's longest Bowie knife. Heck, we've even got Big Tex, the tallest cowboy statue on the planet. Somewhere in all that bigness fits my father's "brilliant" ideas. Bless his heart. He really thinks I can become a spy for his record label.

"Dad, you can't be serious." I offer a carrot to Oreo, our black and white pinto horse, while my father tugs at the corner of his giant mustache, looking me over.

"I am serious."

There is nowhere under the vast blue sky for me to run and hide from his stare, but that doesn't mean I don't crave to hightail it to the barn and burrow down into a bale of hay anyway. You don't say no to Brock Lancaster. The intimidating Stetson perched on his salt-and-pepper hair and the weathered cowboy boots on his feet have sealed many deals over the years. I may be his princess, but I'm also the last of his bloodline and I know the next thing he'll spout is if I wish to one day be queen and rule the kingdom he's carefully crafted, then I need to take one for the team.

"A woman's home is her sanctuary." Oreo nibbles my fingers and prances away from the white fence as if he doesn't want to stick around for this conversation.

My father rolls his gray eyes at me. "Sydney, if you want the piranhas to take you seriously in this business…" I don't even bother listening to the rest of the lecture as it flies past his lips.

This request is beyond the call of duty. I can't believe he thinks I will let a guy I've never met stay with me for a month.

"Doesn't matter to you that he's a stranger?" The sweltering sun beats down on my shoulders as I square them to face off with my father. For good measure, I park a hand on my hip, like my momma would do when she was alive, hoping he abandons his ridiculous plan and sees reason. Granny will lose her bonnet when she finds out what he's got up his sleeve.

"I wouldn't put you in a dangerous situation," he drawls. "You know that, honey."

Ha! That he's asking me to share my home with a potential employee so I can make sure he's not a hack for the competition is beyond the pale. My dad is known for his unorthodox practices, so does it surprise me he's cooked up this scheme? Nope. Even so, they rarely involve *me*.

"But you are, Dad. What if he assaults me in the middle of the night?" It's dramatic but a logical question.

My father balks. "Sydney, he's a respectable, well-known name in LA." He hooks his thumbs beside the gold buckle of his belt. "It'll only be for a few weeks."

I tap my boot on the rain-starved ground, sending a plume of dust onto the red leather. "What if he steals all my things?"

Dad tosses another eye roll in my direction. "Listen, he will not do anything criminal. He's one of the top talent scouts in the country, and I've had my eye on this guy for ages to fill the executive recruiter position. But you never really know someone until you've lived with them. While he's in town, entertaining my job proposal, you'll spy on him and report back to me. You've got my blood in your veins, and you're the only one I trust to see if the assholes over at Halo are setting me up."

To an outsider, he'd sound paranoid. But I've been around my father's business enough to know that his competition wouldn't be above inserting a mole to steal some of the top-earning stars out from under Dad's mustache.

"Whaddya say?" he coaxes. "This will be your company someday soon when I retire, so it's good to get your feet wet. Baby duck needs to learn to swim with the sharks."

A sigh leaves me as I glance out at the horses lazing in the lush green grass of their paddock. Why can't my life be that simple? We both know I'm going to say yes, and I'll just have to journal out my frustration like Momma taught me. Lord knows, she had stacks from dealing with Daddy's larger-than-life personality. The thing is, he raised me with constant talk of taking over Reilly Records, but as much as he planted the seeds of succession and watered them with incessant knowledge, it never took root inside me.

One day, I'll gather the courage to tell him I don't want the business, that I have other dreams. Right now, I don't have the heart to do it. He puts on a grand show for everyone, but as the daughter who loves him, I see the man who fears losing the legacy he built from the ground up.

Halo has slowly been taking money from our pockets with every performer they sign before we can even get to them.

We haven't had a decent artist in years.

"Fine," I relent, wanting to kick myself in the rear for agreeing to such a thing. I have lost my mind. "However, if he touches my cookies"—I narrow my eyes, the same shade as his—"I'll kill him."

My father chuckles. "If he touches anything else, I'll kill

him." He moves closer, wrapping an arm around my shoulder. "We need him on our team. Halo can't win."

"They won't," I assure him. "I'm going to head home and prepare for the intruder." I give him a kiss on the cheek. "I'll call you later."

On the way to my truck, I grab my phone and call my best friend, Callie. "Meet me at my place before we head out tonight."

She agrees, and I point my vehicle in the direction of my condo.

My condo.

⸻

"SO, a stranger will stay here tomorrow night?" Callie asks, apparently not at all appalled by the idea like me.

"Yes. My father thinks it's best he stays with me while he schmoozes him. This way, the press won't know he's in town." I've just filled her in on everything but left out the part about how I'm supposed to spy on Tobias Brentwood. Don't get me wrong, I trust Callie more than anyone, but sometimes she forgets what should remain a secret.

"What if he's good-looking?"

I scoff. "Highly doubtful."

And that's how we end up searching for Tobias on the internet. I'd like to report he's a hunch-backed troll with a unibrow, but there is no doubt Tobias Brentwood is sex in a suit. In fact, he's the most gorgeous man I've seen in my twenty-eight years on this earth. Tall and lean, with clear blue eyes and mussed dark hair.

"Damn." Callie's brown eyes twinkle as she twirls a lock of auburn hair around her finger. "What if he's a sex god who'll sneak into your room late at night, offering his gigantic peen to service your needs?"

I smack Callie's arm and laugh. "You read too many romance novels."

She winks. "Or I watch too much porn. Anyway, let me know if you want to switch places."

"I'm sure this guy will be nothing but annoying, and I already hate my roommate." I hold up an emerald dress that stops mid-thigh, trying to erase the image of his chiseled face from my mind. "What about this one?"

She nods. "I think it's perfect."

"First-world problem solved." Now, if I could solve the sexy new roommate situation, life would be decent.

After we're both ready, we head downtown to one of the hottest spots in our small city, The Golden Spoke Saloon. Callie parks in the crowded lot and I have to admit, I'm excited to blow off some steam. I hardly go out dancing anymore, and I just want one night of freedom before I'm expected to babysit a man who probably has never sweetened his tea or sat in a saddle.

Irritation that I'm still thinking about his handsome face tightens my spine as we head toward the heavy wooden doors of the club. The burly bouncer tips his hat at us as we walk inside the sprawling building. Country music blasts from the speakers, and I sway my hips as Callie mouths the word *drinks*.

I nod and follow her across the worn hardwoods to the horseshoe-shaped bar.

We order two Palomas and I take a sip of my drink, scanning the people on the dance floor.

"Let's go dance," I tell her.

"We have to check out the goods first," she counters.

By "goods" she means the men in attendance tonight. I just want to let loose and shake my body on the floor, so I finish my drink in two gulps and set my glass on the bar.

I hook my arm through Callie's. "Let's check them out on the dance floor."

She slams her drink back and sets her glass down before I pull her away.

We find a spot in the middle, and I sway my hips to the beat as Callie glances around like she's searching for someone specific.

"Who are you looking for?" I yell over the music.

"No one in particular." She points her finger in the bar's direction. "Look at that guy in the black shirt. He's hot."

I glance over my shoulder and see who she's ogling. He has sandy-blond hair that hangs almost to his muscular shoulders, and he's just her type. "You should talk to him."

Callie bumps her hip into mine, nudging us closer to the man in question. "No, I was thinking of him for you."

I shake my head, turning up my nose at the idea of talking to him. "I'm fine. You take him."

She stares at the man once more. "Ok, but I promise I'll be right back. Maybe he has a friend." She shimmies closer to the man at the end of the bar, and I return to dancing.

It's freeing listening to the music and letting your body express itself. I close my eyes and sway my ass to the rhythm. After a few songs, I open my lids and see that Callie has totally hit it off with the surfer-looking dude. They're laughing and having a good time, so I decide to take a break and hit the ladies' room.

I push through the crowd, making my way toward the neon restroom sign at the back of the saloon.

A dim hallway greets me, and I venture down, searching for the bathrooms at the end. I pass by one woman, standing in the hallway on her phone. The light leads the way as I walk further.

A moan stops me in my tracks.

Another moan, more aggressive this time, has me peeking into a lighted alcove.

All I can see is a woman on her knees, bobbing her head in front of what is clearly a man's groin.

Oh, my god. It takes a minute to register that no one is dying or in need of my help. Fairly certain Blondie is a pro at this, considering the way she's hoovering someone's penis down her throat.

I blush, trying to back away from the intimate moment as quickly as possible, but my heel gets stuck in a vent. Like I said, everything is truly bigger in Texas. Including this enormous grate in the floor.

The woman groans, and I wiggle my foot, but it's not helping. If I could only… uh oh.

My shoe slides off at a rapid pace and I lose my balance. I'm going down and there's not a damn thing in the world that can stop me now.

I yelp as my butt hits the concrete floor hard—dress flies up and everything.

For the first time, I get a look at the blowjob recipient and my mouth drops open.

It's him. My new roommate.

A piercing blue gaze meets mine as I push my dress down over my panties and scramble to stand so I can get out of this ridiculously embarrassing situation.

Tobias, with wide eyes, mind you, pulls the woman off his… well, ya know… and shoves himself back into his jeans.

The woman rises to her feet. "What the?"

But he's not paying attention to her pout, instead he's reaching out a large hand to help *me* up.

"Are you ok?" he asks when I'm standing. "You took a nasty spill." He steadies me by placing both hands on my hips.

"I'm fine." I avoid looking at him. "I didn't mean to interrupt."

With a smile that could cure cancer, Tobias bends down to free my black heel. "Here, allow me." He ghosts his fingers along my calf, and instinctively, I lift my foot as he slides my shoe on like I'm some modern-day Cinderella.

The blonde huffs and crosses her arms over her bountiful chest. "Are you kidding me?"

Tobias caresses my ankle before he rises to his full height, which is about a foot taller than me. "Alyssa, we're all good here."

"My name is Melissa." She isn't stomping her foot, but I'm waiting for her to start at any moment, and it makes me feel a million times worse that I've interrupted their private moment.

Tobias ignores her and asks me, "What's your name?"

My mouth figuratively hangs open at this man who could so crudely turn away the woman who was only moments ago sucking on his most private body part. "Look, I'm really sorry. I didn't mean to interrupt… whatever." I hustle to the restroom, leaving them to finish what they were doing or walk away.

Either way, I'm out of there.

Chapter 2

Tobias

Well, this is awkward. Probably shouldn't have had those three bourbons before my plane took off. Or the three on the plane. In my defense, if people were meant to fly, we'd have wings. We don't. And just because someone stuck them on an aerodynamic tube doesn't mean I trust it. So, I needed a little liquid courage to get on board the damn death trap. Throw in some turbulence and more liquid courage and the next thing you know, you've got your dick in someone's mouth when you encounter the girl of your dreams.

I spin on my heel, teetering, rubbing at the back of my neck. "Alyssa, I'm—" Before I can get the word *sorry* out, she slaps me across my cheek.

"It's Melissa." She storms off, and I don't go after her.

I guess I deserved that, but I couldn't help myself when I saw the beautiful brunette with mesmerizing gray eyes staring at me. It's like my mind misfired at the sight of her and nothing else in the world mattered except helping her to her feet. The universe put her in my path and then took her away. She ran into the bathroom before I could even catch her name.

So, that's where I am right now. Waiting outside the women's restroom in this honkey-tonk bar that barely has enough lighting to see properly. But I won't ever forget those gray eyes.

I want to knock on the bathroom door, or better yet, go inside. But bourbon will make you do things like let a stranger lure you into a blowjob in a hallway, so I'm not trusting my judgment at this point.

Another woman walks down the hall, her heels clacking loudly against the floor.

I stop her. "My friend is in there. I was wondering if you could check on her?" I use the best puppy dog eyes I can muster.

"Sure. What's her name?"

"Um..."

The red-haired girl laughs. "Must not be a close friend."

As she walks away, I touch her arm, lightly. "Please. She has brown hair and gray eyes and looks like a goddess."

The redhead sighs. "I'll check."

She probably agreed just to have me leave her alone, but I don't care.

I'll stay out here all night in order to explain to her I don't normally stick my cock in a stranger's mouth. Well, that's stretching it a bit. Don't want to start off lying. I'm no saint, but if not for the alcohol, I would've thought twice about it. My sober dick is selective.

I wait and wait, thinking about what a horrendous meet-cute story this will be for our kids. We'll have to come up with something different to tell them. Hell, it's not like we won't fib about Santa or the Easter Bunny. Neither the redhead nor my mystery woman surface, and a large part of me wants to push through this wooden door and see what's going on behind it.

It's like Grand Central Station outside the ladies' room and another woman approaches. I decide to stop her too.

"I have this friend in the bathroom, and she's been in there for nearly twenty years. I know women take longer than men, but I'm thinking she slipped and cracked her head on the sink. Maybe she's got no toilet paper?"

The lady shakes her head at me, not even a little concerned about my plight of losing a friend. "Maybe they went out the other door?"

"Other door?" I walk around the corner and find another bathroom exit that leads to the dance floor.

Well, what genius thought to do that? My eyes frantically search for the woman from earlier… until I spot Alyssa at the bar, now draped on a guy with a cowboy hat, and I turn in the opposite direction. Earlier, when I arrived, she stopped me dead in my tracks before I could even order my first beer. She had her hands all over me before she could even ask my name. Glad I didn't go out to her car like she suggested, or I'd have never seen the gray-eyed beauty that I currently can't find. I scan every nook and cranny of this joint. Where is she?

I glance around the packed building once more for my mystery woman before heading back to the hotel.

I make a solemn vow to return to this saloon every night while I'm in town, so I might see the brunette once more.

Maybe catch her name.

⸺

"HOW WAS THE FLIGHT?" Brock asks as I stand in his office, admiring the town of Harmony. It's a fascinating small town with interesting vibes that make you feel like you're in the Wild West.

"It was wonderful." I leave out the fact I arrived a day early to get a lay of the land and spin back around to face the man talking to me.

Brock is a merry fellow. He's like Santa Claus without the beard, red outfit, and... reindeer. Ok, I guess he isn't really like him after all.

"Good to hear it. I have a car ready to take you to my daughter's place. And don't worry about Sydney. She's hardly ever home."

When Brock said I'd be staying with his daughter, I nearly choked. But it's a good sign he trusts me.

Brock has been after me for years, trying to offer me a top-level executive position with his company. Most times, I shrugged him off because the idea of relocating to Texas sounded awful, but lately, LA isn't shining with the same sparkle it once had.

In fact, the game of living and surviving in LA is becoming a bit too much.

And yes, I say *game*, because that's exactly what it is. It's all about who you know. What you wear. Who you date.

And for me, I don't *date* anyone.

I don't *know* anyone either.

It's just a bunch of random acquaintances that annoy the ever-loving fuck out of me. It's getting old.

So, the next time Brock called to have me fly out and hear his proposal, I jumped at the chance. I want a change.

I'm not sure if I'll take the job with Reilly Records, but there's no harm in hopping on a plane and seeing what Harmony has to offer.

I decided to get a head start, get a feel for this place before meeting the daughter and officially moving in. One night to clear my head.

I'm the best talent scout in America, and I know it's why Brock's been breathing down my neck. He needs me. And I need him. So, if I have to adhere to his quirky request to stay at his daughter's place, that's what I'll do.

I shake Brock's giant paw. "Thank you so much, sir."

"Please, call me Brock."

"Brock." I leave his office and take the elevator down to the lobby with my bags in tow.

The doors barely slide open before a man in a suit says, "Mr. Brentwood? I'm Brock's driver, Billy. I'll be taking you to Miss Sydney's place."

"Lead the way, Billy."

I follow him outside and slide into his black sedan. He heads down the street, and a few minutes later, pulls up to the side of a smaller building, not even three blocks away. I could have walked. He shuts off the engine, and I step out of the car before he can open my door. I don't need the red-carpet treatment, even though Brock insists.

If I wanted a red carpet, I would have made the man put me up in a five-star hotel. However, I think living with his daughter is a terrific way to get to know the legend behind Reilly Records.

Billy retrieves my luggage from the trunk and sets it on the sidewalk while I stare up at the black, trendy warehouse-style building. I can already picture her apartment with brick walls and exposed ceilings.

I shake Billy's hand and head inside.

A doorman greets me and directs me to a receptionist behind a marble counter. Once I give her my identification and it's confirmed I'm not a random nut, she sends me on my way.

"Sydney has the top floor. Go into the elevator and type in the code 6-1-6-3. I'll call her and tell her you're on your way up."

I thank her and head into the elevator. As soon as I reach the top floor, the doors open into a hallway with a front door leading to a penthouse suite wide open, and I guessed completely… wrong. Nothing is exposed except the gorgeous view of sapphire sky and Texas terrain outside the glass wall in front of me. A stone wall with a humongous fireplace is to my left and warm earth tones paint the surrounding walls.

"Hello," I call out, wheeling my luggage across the wide wood planks toward the center of the large room filled with southwestern furnishings.

There's no answer.

I gaze up at the antler chandelier that drops from the lofty ceilings above the charcoal-colored sectional and wait for a response. Nothing.

The kitchen is off to my right, and I smell the makings of something delicious coming from that direction.

"Hello. It's me, Tobias Brentwood." Before I can call out again, a brown-haired goddess is standing before me, gazing at me with familiar gray eyes.

My heart stops beating.

This is the same woman I searched for last night.

Sydney.

Chapter 3

Sydney

I'm not very hospitable right now. After I pleasured myself to the memory of Tobias' face last night—something I'm not proud of but thoroughly enjoyed—I decided the best way to get through this forced-roommate situation is to hate the man standing in my living room.

To say witnessing his hallway hummer confused me is an understatement. So I wrangled Callie, and we left without looking back. Journaling my annoyance suggested that I was most annoyed over the possibility I might've been a little envious it was her and not me.

It's downright preposterous to feel that way, so despising him will fix the problem. If he wants to do scandalous things the minute he arrives in town, so be it. Why shouldn't he enjoy the perks of his good looks? I'm sure women throw themselves at him daily.

He blinks at me, most likely trying to find the words to

explain his man-whoring. As I ogle his broad shoulders imprisoned beneath a black dress shirt, it occurs to me I don't really think that's my fundamental problem with him.

My problem is that he's gorgeous. Plain and simple. All that tuggable dark hair and those plush lips make me want to rip my clothes off and let him feast upon my body. I'm not sure I'm ready to throw myself at his big feet, begging him to take me to my bedroom.

"Rule number one," I start, wanting to lay down some ground rules. Who cares if this guy is hotter than the Texas sun in July? I can keep a level head around him.

"I'm sorry?" His gaze drifts across my face, stopping on my mouth. "Rules?"

"Yes. If you're going to live here, we need clear rules." Remembering my manners, I tilt my lips up and head back toward the oven to check on the cookies I'm baking. "You can do whatever you want, just don't bring your skanks around." The last part slips out before I can stop it, but I never claimed my manners were impeccable.

He follows me into the kitchen. "After meeting you, I would never. There'll be no skanks ever again."

I spin around to face him. "Oh, I'm sure."

"I *am* sure," he whispers, handing me an oven mitt.

There's not an ounce of mockery on his face. He's standing there like he's serious, but I know it's just a game guys like him play.

"Let me grab my cookies, and then I'll give you the grand tour," I say, ignoring his comment. He probably wants to charm me into finishing what blondie at the club started.

I'll never give him that chance.

Gorgeous, but an asshole. I've no proof of that critique, but I'm going with it anyway to fight this attraction.

I slide the baking sheet of cookies from the oven and set them on the stovetop.

"Mm," he says behind me. "Sugar, my favorite."

I glance over my shoulder at Tobias, nearly coming into contact with his chiseled jaw as he leans in for a sniff. My blood pumps at an alarming rate. "Well, you're not getting any. These are for Bob downstairs."

He grabs for one anyway, and I lightly smack his hand away. "Ouch. I see you like to play rough." He takes a deep inhale, but I swear he's really sniffing my hair. "Smells delicious."

My nether regions heat at his casual mention of playing rough, and I hate that I'm having this reaction to him. I think it's because it's been so long since I've had any sort of action. Jason, my last boyfriend, was a joke, and terrible in the sex department. I faked more orgasms than I care to admit. Now that I reflect on it, I've never had anything that would count as world's best sexual experience.

I bet Tobias could give that to me. Just look at his strong hands.

Oh, his hand.

While I'm fantasizing, he's reaching for another cookie, and this time, I grab it. I should let go, but I study it, memorizing the strength of it.

"I can do a lot with this hand if you'd let me," he murmurs, standing entirely too close.

I drop his hand immediately and step back. "Fine," I say, defeated. "Have a cookie."

He smiles as he stuffs the treat into his mouth, and when he's done, the tip of his tongue finishes off the lucky crumbs. "Delicious." He sucks on his fingertips and it's too much.

I shuffle around him and cross the kitchen tile with rapid steps. "Follow me." I head down the hallway. "Your room is just through this door."

"Right across from your room, I see." He peeks his head into my bedroom.

I cruise across the floor to block the doorway. "You'll never need to go in there." I'm standing too close to his body, but I can't move because the smell of sugar cookies and a woodsy scent fills my nostrils, and the combination makes me dizzy.

Or maybe it's his intense stare that's making me so light-headed I wobble on my feet when I reach for the door to close it.

He rests a hand on my hip, and a lazy grin spreads across his face. "You're having the same effect on me too, baby girl."

My eyes widen at his endearment and at how much I like it. "Don't call me that." I snap out of my Tobias trance and head into the guest room. "Here's your key"—I set it on the dresser— "and there are towels in the closet. You'll find extra blankets in there as well if you get cold at night."

He moves through the room, over to the tall windows. "You won't keep me warm at night?"

I jab a thumb over my shoulder. "I'll be sleeping in *my* room. With the door locked."

He locks his hands behind his neck, causing his shirt to lift enough for me to see the thin trail of dark hair leading into the front of his pants. I also see a well-defined v on his hips, pointing to the bulge in his jeans. "Well, if you ever get lonely, I've always got room in my bed."

I snap my eyes up to his. He's messing with me, because who says these things? And why do I find it thrilling? "No, thank you." I turn to leave. "I'll let you get settled in and unpack."

"Have dinner with me," he says before I walk out of the room.

"I already have dinner plans tonight with a friend."

Tobias stalks toward me. "A guy friend?"

"Does it matter?" My plans are with Callie, but it's not his business.

"I just want to see my competition."

I laugh, but it comes out shrill. "Competition? I would

never date you." I don't mean it to sound rude, but it's the truth. When I met him, he was getting action from another woman. "It wouldn't be prudent. You're here for an interview for my father's company, for one thing."

He stops in front of me, toe-to-toe, and I breathe in his delicious scent once more. "You will date me. You just don't know it yet."

I suck in a sharp breath at the audacity of this man, and also because I think I stopped breathing. "Don't count on it." I leave his room, bound across the hall, and shut my door.

What the heck? Once my pulse is no longer racing like a thoroughbred, I spend the next hour getting ready to meet Callie. Dad would toss Tobias out on his muscular butt if he knew about this, but I don't think I'll include his overtures in my spy report.

When I leave my room, Tobias is nowhere to be found. Good. I hide the cookies to remind myself I hate him.

It's really hard to hate Tobias. The three days he's been in my home, he's made breakfast every morning. Even put fresh flowers on the table. He's a phenomenal cook and my attraction to him has grown tenfold, because not only does he wake me with the smell of bacon and fresh coffee brewing, but he also cleans the mess.

As part of my asinine spy assignment, I'm forced to have conversations with him. I know too many things now that have nothing to do with the task at hand but fulfilled my curiosity about him.

Favorite color—gray.

Favorite animal—turtle.

Favorite book—anything Sherlock Holmes related.

I also now know what he looks like fresh out of the shower, wrapped in a towel. That was a doozy I didn't see coming. Every day I've reported to my dad that there have been no signs he's a mole, but maybe Tobias is just that good. Regardless, journaling is not easing my frustrations, and I need him out of my house ASAP before I masturbate myself to death. Or before he discovers my secret and lets it slip to my father.

"SORRY I'M LATE," Callie says, sliding onto a stool at the white marble bar of The Black Oyster Bar. "Are you writing a love note to Tobias?"

I shove my journal in my purse. "Hilarious. I'm just letting out a few frustrations."

She signals the bartender and orders a mojito. Once she's settled in with her beverage, she turns to me with a gleam in her eye. "I still can't believe Mr. Blowjob and Mr. New Roomie are the same person." She laughs. "What are the chances of that happening?"

I peer at Callie over the rim of my butterfly pea flower martini. "A zillion to one?"

"Are you going to have sleepovers in your room? Make obscene shadow puppets on the wall?" Callie asks with a straight face, her dark eyes shimmering against the stark-white light of the club.

Before I can say anything, I'm stunned into silence when I glimpse Tobias in the mirror that lines the back of the bar, walking straight toward us with a smile on his handsome face.

"Hi, Roomie," he says.

Callie's jaw drops open. She's staring at him like he's an enigma, and I nudge her with the tip of my cowboy boot.

"Hi. What are you doing here?" I ask.

It's like sexy is a second language to him because he gives a half-grin that could melt hearts and says, "I heard there was an open mic night tonight, so I made the journey."

Callie interrupts his gaze-fest on me and sticks out her hand. "I'm Callie."

He shakes her hand. "Nice to meet you. I'm Tobias."

"Better to meet you," she coos, dreamily gazing into his striking azure eyes.

"So, I guess the better question is, what are *you* doing here?" Tobias stares right at me.

"Well, if you must know, I too work for a record label, and I'm scouting talent." I don't want to tell Tobias the real reason I'm here.

He nods and gestures toward the bartender. "Two more of these drinks for my ladies, and I'll have any hazy IPA you have on draft."

"You don't have to buy us a drink," I say, wondering why he's wasting his night on us when he clearly could have any woman in this place.

"What kind of man would I be if I didn't buy you two a drink?"

"Fine," I relent. One drink, and then he'll move on.

Callie makes idle chit-chat with Tobias until the bartender sets our fresh drinks on the bar. Then we both fall into a lust-drunk stupor when Tobias reaches between us to grab his beer and slowly brings the mug to his lips. His mouth plows into the frothy head and I watch as he swallows down the first drink of amber-colored alcohol. It must taste as good as he looks, because he savors it, closing his eyes and licking the residue from his lips before taking another gulp.

I can't stop watching him, and then I notice Callie is hypnotized as well.

I snap out of it because we must look like a couple of loons, salivating over this gorgeous man standing between us.

"So, you never answered why you're here," Tobias says.

"Well, actually, Sydney is going to—" Callie says but I shush her before she can finish.

"What is Sydney going to do?" Tobias asks Callie.

"It's nothing." I shoo away the conversation like it's a pesky fly. "It's dumb, really."

Callie gives me a stern stare. "It's not dumb. You should be proud."

My face flames red, and I wish Callie would stop talking. Seriously. What if this makes its way back to my father?

Tobias leans in, clearly interested in something I don't want him to know. "Tell me, Callie."

She can't escape his charm. His charisma. "She's singing tonight."

I cover my face when his stunned eyes shoot to me.

"This I have to see."

Chapter 4

Tobias

Baby girl has secrets. Twenty dollars says her father doesn't know she's loving up on a microphone when she's not on the clock. If she's got pipes, I fully intend to support her musical endeavor. That's what a partner does in a healthy relationship. Things might get awkward if she sounds like a shrill cat, but I'll cross that bridge when the time comes. We can get a vocal coach if we have to… work some wizardry in the studio. Hell, I'll wear earmuffs if needed.

Hopefully, it won't come to that.

I'm no stranger to an open mic night. In fact, I can safely say I live at them. It's the best place to spot talent, and as the best talent scout in the country—it's what *US Weekly* dubbed me—I hang out at them all the time.

It's sort of my office.

"I won't be singing tonight." Sydney glares at her friend Callie.

I interrupt before Callie can respond and lightly touch

Sydney's arm. "Please don't let me be the reason you're not going to sing tonight."

She looks nervous, worrying her plump bottom lip with white teeth. I have all kinds of questions about Sydney's singing, but don't want to ask right now. Because I want this brunette enchantress to answer them while she's naked. Riding my face.

I've never been this crazy about a girl.

My motto has always been "Do 'em and move on." I've never pursued a woman. But there's something about Sydney. She may be my potential boss' daughter, but this magnetic pull is too strong to ignore.

Sydney walks away from us after telling us she's going to sign in. She walks over to a small booth with a pink-haired girl taking names, and right after, she's ushered backstage.

The lights go down, and Callie wiggles in her seat next to me.

"Just you wait," she says, leaning over, beaming with pride.

I find it endearing that Sydney has someone she can call her best friend.

With me, I never had that person I could trust. I felt like the connections I made in LA were all fake. Everything about them.

Fake. Fake. Fake.

I guess it's not entirely true. I have one friend, but other than that no one I can truly count on.

A blond-haired kid, not even eighteen, walks on stage with a guitar slung over his shoulder. He wraps his hand around the microphone and adjusts it to his tall height. "I guess I'm starting things off today."

He sits on the bar stool behind him and strums his guitar. I listen as he performs an off-pitch melody, and already I go into work mode, wondering if this boy has what it takes to be a star. Would he appeal to the masses? Does he have the total package?

Nope. The song is decent, but he possesses nothing special.

Several more singers take the stage, and sad to say, none of them are headed for superstardom.

After a bearded guy wails a pop song, Sydney walks onto the stage, looking like an angel in her white sundress and matching boots. All that's missing is the halo above her glossy hair.

My breath hitches in my throat.

Why the fuck am I so nervous for her?

The spotlight loves her, but my gut feels like someone punched it. She sits with a straight spine on the stool, bringing the microphone to her lips as the music plays.

The entire bar is silent as she sings the first line, sweeping the air from my lungs.

Her voice is mesmerizing and not a note off pitch. The song is one I've never heard, and I lean over to Callie, asking if it's an original.

Callie nods, and my eyes snap back to the girl on stage, who has the enraptured crowd in the palm of her hand. My mind reels with pleasure from the falsetto she hits. Why has she never pursued a career in singing?

She works for Reilly Records and could easily get signed.

Sydney belts out the chorus about a love gone wrong, and it makes me wonder if she's ever been in love. Has she had her heart broken?

I should pummel the asshole who could hurt her in such a way.

When the song ends, sadness permeates my system that I can't keep listening to her voice. Every part of me wants to rush the stage and hold her, caress her soft skin, and kiss her tender lips.

A vision of her singing lullabies to our sweet cherubs forms in my mind. I don't know how to handle the overwhelming emotions coursing through me right now, and if Sydney comes over to sit with me, I might just snatch her up and toss her over my shoulder and carry her caveman-style out of here to stake my claim.

"I gotta go," I tell Callie. And then I rush out of the place like there's a fire in the center. When, in all actuality, the fire is burning deep in my chest.

As soon as I'm outside, I breathe like I'm suffocating. I lean over, placing my palms on my knees, trying desperately to fill my lungs with air.

What's happening to me? I'm supposed to be here for a job, not planning my life with Brock's daughter. I legit have floor plans for our two-story house in my brain. We'll need a spacious backyard for our kids to play. Fuck. What if she's on the road?

I straighten and force one foot in front of the other until I'm heading around the block. Yes, earlier today I teased Sydney about needing me to warm her up at night, but I would keep her warm for eternity.

And that thought frightens the fuck out of me, because I just met her less than a week ago.

I walk the streets, not sure where I'm headed, just trying to make sense of my irrational feelings. I hated how the other men in the club stared at her like they'd seen nothing more alluring in their pathetic lives. I mean, I can relate, but I despised seeing the lust in their eyes.

I'm sure I mirrored them, and I should know about pathetic lives. I lead the most pathetic of all.

My childhood was the opposite of Sydney's. I didn't grow up with wealth or with parents who loved and supported me. Most days, I was sure my father couldn't wait to be rid of me. My existence was nothing more than a meal ticket for my parents with the government. A check every month. Food stamps. Health care. Every assisted program they could apply for, but I never saw a single benefit.

Few people realize this about me, because I keep it well

hidden, buried deep inside. No sense in complaining about something you can't change.

Besides, it's what made me into who I am today. And who is that? I guess I'm still trying to figure that out. People have asked many times why I don't open a talent agency. I don't know the answer to that question. There's always been something holding me back.

Some fear of committing.

My thoughts drift back to Sydney. I've only just met her and have all but put a ring on her finger in my head. Maybe it's because she's different. In LA, I mention my job and the women flock to me, wanting their fifteen minutes of fame and hoping I'm the man who can deliver.

And yes, I'm the asshole who took advantage of their desire, using it to fuel my own desire. Not an admirable way to live, I know.

It's what drew me to Texas.

Now, I'm wondering if that same thing is driving me toward Sydney.

Loneliness.

"HOW ARE YOU LIKING TEXAS, SON?" Brock asks, while loading his Colt's magazine with .45 ACP ammo.

I can appreciate a man who interviews at a gun range. Not sure how I feel about this cowboy hat he insisted I wear. Last night, I ended up finding a hotel room to finish getting my head together. If I'd sensed Brock would request an impromptu meeting this morning, I probably would've postponed my pre-mid-life crisis. As it is, I rolled out of bed, showered, and dressed in the same clothes so I could Uber over to the Alamo Gun Range. Because one thing I figured out last night is that I want this job.

"It's definitely different," I say, glancing at the surrounding set up that looks like the OK Corral.

"Is it somewhere you could put down roots?" He slams the magazine into the Colt 1911, racking the slide. "As talented as you are, I'm not looking for someone who won't stick around."

Oh, I'm sticking around. Sydney's gray eyes and angelic voice drift into my mind. "Yep. I'm pretty connected to this place. So what does Sydney do at your company?"

His gaze slides to me. "She dabbles in everything. Marketing, contracts. You name it, I've taught it to her."

"And she enjoys it?" Cause with that voice, I can't help but think she's meant for things besides the mundane.

"Why wouldn't she? It's her birthright." He aims his gun at the red bullseye a good distance away from us. "Someday, she'll marry and pass it down to my grandchildren."

Well, I get his wanting to keep it in the family, but really that will be up to Charlotte and Lucas. I won't force them to do anything they don't want to do with their lives. And there I go again. For fuck's sake, I've named our kids. I'm sure Sydney would want a say in that.

"Anybody special in her life?"

"No, why?"

I laugh it off, especially since he has a weapon in his hand. "Just getting to know everything about the people I'll be working for."

He accepts my answer, and we spend the next hour blowing holes in the wooden targets. My performance isn't marksman, but it's good enough to get a hearty handshake and slap on the back when we're done. We make plans to meet up again for dinner sometime soon at his ranch and then he calls a car to take me back to Sydney's place.

I get to the condo in record time and use my key. A pang of disappointment fills my chest, making my shoulders sag, that she's probably not here.

Everything is quiet when I enter, but then I hear a groan

coming from the back of the apartment. I move in that direction, ready to defend this home with my bare hands if needed.

When I reach the hallway, I hear a moan, and pause. It's definitely coming from Sydney's bedroom. Holy fuck. Did she bring home a guy from the bar?

I move in stealth mode down the hallway, keeping my breathing even so as not to disturb Sydney and her possible guest.

Not gonna lie… My head is ready to explode at the thought of some other man enjoying all the pleasure I'm sure Sydney could dole out. The closer I get to her room, the louder the moans.

My cock hardens at the sounds she makes, and I imagine her naked and spread out. Is she thinking about me?

Is this guy doing everything he can for her? Is he doing it right? I can do a much better job.

I'd have her screaming and waking the neighbors with her cries of ecstasy.

I'm not even sure why I'm still moving closer to her bedroom. I should leave the apartment. Or should I barge in and stop this asshole from taking what's mine?

I creep closer, like the sick fuck I am, and notice her door is ajar. Fuck.

To peek or not to peek, that is the motherfucking question. And all I've got are bad answers.

Answers that cross some major lines of this whole roommate agreement.

I push away the gentleman part of my mind telling me not to look and side with the devil on my shoulder.

My cock throbs as I listen to her moans.

Fuck. She sounds so intoxicating.

I peek my head around the door, and oh, my god.

I'm not ready for what I see.

There is no other man—repeat, she's alone—and I don't understand what to do with all of this new information.

She's lying on her back, eyes closed beneath a thin blanket… with her hand between her legs. I'm stunned, frozen in place.

My cock turns to granite. Harder than the fucker has ever been before.

I'm at a loss of what to do.

A small piece of me says I should turn away, but I laugh at that notion. I couldn't turn away even if I tried.

I watch with rapt fascination as she works her body, her legs spread wide. I'd give a million dollars I don't have if the blanket would fall to the floor right now. I'd live in debt the rest of my life for one peek at her pussy.

She opens her mouth, and I'm expecting another moan to fall from her lips, but what she says stops my heart.

"Tobias," she whispers.

Her eyes remain closed, so she isn't seeing me.

Every fucking part of me wonders what would happen if I made my presence known right now. Would she let me make her come?

She's losing control before I can make up my mind, and with that glorious image burned in my brain, I slip down the hall, into the bathroom, before she notices me. I shut the door and turn on the shower. I've got a massive fucking hard on and the only thing that will calm me down is fisting my cock to the image of her until I come.

Chapter 5

Sydney

Please don't let that sound be what I think it is. I sit up and yep, I hear the shower running in the bathroom down the hall. Shit. That means Tobias returned. My gaze fixates on my cracked door. Did he see me? *Hear* me?

My hormones have been out of control since he arrived in town. After being onstage last night, combined with all the nervous energy I felt after the show, I finally had to take care of things.

I've been so worked up since I saw Tobias sitting in the front row, listening to me sing. The way his eyes never left me. The way his mouth hung slightly open as I sang my heart out.

It turned me on.

So much so, I was a little heartbroken when he rushed out of the club after my number. Did he hate it?

Am I a terrible singer?

Why did he leave?

Stop being obtuse, Sydney. He didn't come home, so obviously, he found a woman to occupy him all night. I tried not to think about the way he ghosted us, while I had another drink with Callie at the bar.

Finally, I called it a night and lied to her, saying I needed to be up early for work. What I really did was rush home to see if Tobias was here and find out what he thought of my performance.

But now, I don't care.

I slip out of my room and pad to the kitchen to make lunch. This seems like a carbohydrate kind of day, so I grab the bread, deciding to make myself a grilled cheese. Not to brag, but I really do make the best. The secret is loads of butter. I pull out the skillet from the lower cabinet, and when I straighten, I see Tobias in nothing but a green towel wrapped around his hips. For a quick second, I peek at his yummy abs before I turn toward the stove.

"I wasn't aware you were here," he says, moving in my direction.

I breathe a sigh of relief that he didn't see me getting off to x-rated fantasies of him in my mind. "I didn't know you were back."

"Yeah. Sorry I left right after your performance." My belly churns at his mention of me singing, hoping he doesn't tell me I sucked.

He steps closer, taking all the oxygen in the kitchen with him. The bright light in the kitchen spotlights every nook and cranny on his torso like a magnifying glass. "I wanted to tell you," he breathes in, and then lets it out slowly, inching even closer. "You were amazing. Your voice…" His words fall away and my cheeks heat.

"Oh, please," I say, waving off his praise.

He lifts my chin, so I have no choice but to meet his gaze. "I mean it. You have a voice like no other. I'd sign you right now if I thought it's what you wanted." It's like he's looking into the deepest recesses of my soul. "Is it?"

I'm too lost in his eyes to understand the question. "Is what?"

"Is that what you want?"

I'm in a daze, and my mind can't comprehend what he's saying to me. He's casting some sort of voodoo magic over me, so I move away and focus back on the task at hand.

Grilled cheese.

"I don't know," I whisper.

He hops on the counter, and it would take a stronger person than me not to look when his towel gapes open a little, exposing muscular thighs.

He winks and adjusts his towel. "Ah, no peeking," he says. "I mean, unless you want me to remove it?"

Yeah, I do. But I laugh at his words. "Like I'd ever."

He braces his hands on the counter, studying my tank top and cotton shorts. "Mhm."

He's so cocky, and overwhelming. And totally didn't mention where he stayed last night. Well, it's not my business and I refuse to ask.

"I'm going to change clothes," I say, spinning on my heel and leaving my grilled cheese mess on the counter.

"What about your sandwich?" he calls after me.

"I no longer have an appetite." Without a look back, lest I turn into a pillar of salt, I escape to my bedroom and slam the door. I jerk my journal off the nightstand and let my frustration out on the page.

Even his balls are sexy. Yes, I got a glimpse. They are manscaped and perfect. Not too big and not too small. Just right. And that just annoys me more because I sound like a porn version of Goldilocks. And now he's in my kitchen, cooking my grilled cheese. How much longer am I supposed to live with this man? I need to talk to my dad tomorrow, tell him he should send Tobias back to LA. We don't need him.

I'm lost in thought as a knock at my door halts my pen.

"What do you want?" I call through the wood.

"I made you my famous grilled cheese."

I toss the notebook on my bed and cross the floor to open the door. Tobias is now dressed in black sweats and a t-shirt that reads, "I have neither the time nor the crayons to explain this to you." He's holding a white plate with a golden-brown grilled cheese, cut diagonal—exactly how I like it.

"You didn't need to cook me anything."

He grins. "I wanted to, because you looked... hungry." The way he says the words leaves little to the imagination. He's implying I was hungry for him.

"Well, I'm not."

He nudges the plate toward me. "You're not going to eat this deliciousness?"

My mouth waters because it's cooked to perfection, with crisp edges and the right amount of cheese. It's like he's my sandwich soulmate. "Ok, maybe I am hungry."

"I'm hungry too, but not for food." His eyes rake over my body as I take the plate, and I recognize exactly what he means.

A shiver runs through me, starting at the top of my head and ending at the tips of my toes. I pick up the sandwich. "Thank you," I say, ignoring his hunger remark, but then think better of it because I understand what type of man he is. When he's hungry, any dish will do. I just happen to be the closest female within proximity to him. "And about your hunger problem, I'm sure there were many women last night who'd be happy to feed you. Maybe one did on your overnight stay."

He gives me a sheepish grin, and it's adorable. Almost bashful. "I stayed in a hotel, alone, because I had some things to think about. There's only one woman who can satisfy this craving I've got."

I take a bite of the grilled cheese, loving every second of its cheesy goodness and his answer. "And who would that be?"

"You, Sydney. Only you."

I stare at him, speechless. When I finally find my voice, I change the subject. "This is delicious."

"Thanks. Had lots of practice cooking for myself growing up. We didn't have much, but we had lots of cheese and bread. When your parents don't give a shit, you learn to take care of yourself."

The sandwich gets stuck in my throat. His eyes widen, like he didn't mean to reveal so much to me. But… I'm glad he did. "I'm sorry you had shitty parents. I think it's admirable you took matters into your own hands. Fuck them for making you fend for yourself."

At my words, his awkwardness disappears and then we have a ten-minute conversation about his childhood, and I tell him about my mom passing away when I was ten. It's unexpected. It's *special*. And absolutely not how I thought things would go when he knocked on my door.

"WHAT DO YOU THINK, Sydney? Do you think Tobias would like it here in Texas?" my dad asks, entering my office, his smile full of life.

"I think you'd have to ask Tobias that question," I say with a smile mirroring his.

Tobias laughs but covers it up with a cough. "Everything's been amazing. I even made it to an open mic night."

"Ah," Dad says as I stiffen in my chair. "Anyone we should take a look at?"

Tobias glances at me and I drop my head, hoping he doesn't mention anything about me. "There was this one act I couldn't stop thinking about."

They chatter about finding talent, and I hold my breath. Two days have passed since I sang in that club. Since I thought about Tobias while I touched myself. In those two days, I've discovered nothing that shows he's up to anything except what he says.

Dad, ever the paranoid one, thinks we need a little more time to be certain. Easy for him to say, since he's not the one having to live with Tobias. Just look at him in those perfectly fitted slacks and dress shirt, oozing sensual masculinity out of his pores. He's even had the nerve to roll his sleeves up to reveal some arm porn.

As if reading my illicit thoughts, my father says, "Texas looks good on you, son. Don't you agree, Sydney? Don't you think Texas loves Tobias?"

"Sure," I mumble, not wanting to give my true opinion.

The Texan ladies certainly love him. I saw the way Tracy in accounting stared at him when he arrived for his tour of the building. Holly from HR nearly knocked me over with her big hair, whipping her head around to get a second look at him. Even Millie, the sixty-year-old receptionist, raised her painted-on brows. And she *never* raises them because of all the Botox in her forehead.

"Tobias is coming out to the ranch tomorrow for dinner. Sydney, you'll drive him."

It's not a question, so I nod my confirmation, wanting to end this charade so I can evict Tobias from my home. And my head.

Tobias gives me a sparkling Hollywood smile. "I'm looking forward to it."

When they leave, I finish up my work so I can hightail it out of my father's building. I should probably stay because there are things to discuss with my father. Like, why is Tobias still my roommate? But I don't want to talk about any of that right now. Instead I'd like to go home, relax, and not think about Tobias without his shirt on. I press my fingertips into my temples because I can't do *any* of that since Tobias *lives* there.

There's a knock at the door, and the bane of my existence barges in.

"What do you want, Tobias?" I ask, leaning back in the leather chair behind my desk.

He shuts the door and rests a shoulder against the frame. "You seemed stressed when we were here earlier. I don't like you being stressed. Just wondering if there's anything I can do to ease some of that unwanted pressure." I swear he makes everything sound sexual.

"I'm good."

He takes a step forward. "I think you want it."

I narrow my eyes on him. "Want what?"

"Me."

I don't even know how to react at this moment. I'm more stunned than anything else, but I'm also turned on, because I do want him. And I wonder if I should just act on these impulses.

"And what makes you so sure I want you?"

He stuffs his hands in his pockets, rocking back on his heels. "I heard you the other day."

Chapter 6

Tobias

If looks could murder a person, my little songbird's death stare would slay me in a second. But I can see something else hidden in those smoky depths. Desire.

And that's not me being narcissistic or not reading the room correctly. It's a fact she's thought about me. I heard her. And if my ears deceived me, my eyes sure didn't. They saw how fucking stunning she looked, stroking her pussy with her neck arched and those long lashes dusting her flushed face.

I need to make her come again. There's no denying I want this woman beneath me in every sexual way possible.

I'm so tempted to tell her to get on her knees right now. To suck my cock into submission.

Hell, I'm hard right now.

I stare at her plump lips, wondering what they'd feel like wrapped around me. Heaven. That's what they'd feel like.

"Get out," she finally says.

Hm. I may have gone too far. I can't let her throw me out

and never talk to me again.

I step forward, placing both palms flat on her desk, leaning over. "No need to fight this attraction you have for me."

She zips up from her chair and moves around the desk until she's standing right in front of me. I rise to my full size, challenging her.

"Let's get one thing straight." She pokes me in the chest with a dainty finger. "I am not like all the other women out there who fall at your feet. That was a moment of weakness you overheard."

I glance down at her finger and then back to her fiery gray eyes. "Moment of weakness, huh?" And then I do something I know I shouldn't. I palm the back of her neck, pulling her closer. "I guess this is my moment of weakness, then."

I crash my lips to hers.

I expect her to push me away for being so brazen in kissing her, but she melts into me. Her hands glide up my chest, and she opens up for me, like a flower blossoming beneath the sun. I groan and take my time exploring every inch of her sweet mouth. Take my time gliding my tongue over hers. My heart pounds in my ears and the louder it beats, the deeper this kiss goes, until I'm ready to throw everything off the desk and ravage her sinful body on the sleek mahogany wood. She's wanton, tugging at my hair and pressing her tits against my chest. The sensual moans she's making right now are literally killing me. I splay my fingers in her silky hair, driving my knee between her legs, because I can't take much more.

Before I can grind my thigh against her pussy, she pushes me away. "See, that proves it."

"Proves what?" I ask, panting, my head still in a daze.

"Proves that I don't want you."

This wakes me up a little. I lean back, staring into her bewitching eyes. "Ah, how so?" There's a hint of laughter in my voice because our kiss proves she is totally into me.

"If I could kiss you like that and push you away, that means I don't want you." She straightens her hair, returning to the chair behind the desk.

"Well, it doesn't change the fact that I fucking want you." I grip my hard cock through my pants. "See how badly I want you?"

She licks her lips.

Doesn't want me, my ass. She's practically panting.

"Get out," she says again.

I let go of myself and smile. "One of these days you're going to stop fighting this attraction you have for me and you're going to beg for it."

She slow-blinks. "You wish."

"Ask me if I ever think about you while jerking off."

"No way." Again, if looks could kill. But there's no denying that kiss.

"Ask me. I know you're dying to know." I move over to where she's sitting and lean in, gripping the arms of her chair.

She holds my gaze. "Well, since you're right here, do you?"

"Every night." I dip my head to whisper in her ear, "And every fucking morning too." I nip her earlobe before I turn on my heel and leave her office.

———

MY LITTLE SONGBIRD is always surprising me. You'd think someone as delicate as her would have a snazzy sports car. A Mercedes or a Porsche. Cue the buzzer sound. Sydney has a white Ford truck with red leather seats. And damn, it only makes her sexier.

She's driving me to dinner with the family. I'm kind of excited, because it's almost like she's taking me home to meet her parents, even though that's not the case at all.

After the kiss yesterday, I came home to an empty house. I woke up to an empty house too.

"What did you do last night?" I ask when I can no longer suffer through the silence.

"I stayed with Callie."

Automatically, I'm gutted for coming on so strong. "I'm sorry about yesterday," I tell her.

She stares at the road ahead of us. "No, it wasn't because of that. Callie just broke up with a guy she went out with a few times and was upset."

"You sure about that, pretty girl?"

"Yes." She glances at me one quick second. "And in case you're wondering, I still *don't* want you."

I relax in my seat, unbothered by her lie. "Good."

She laughs, and it's soothing to my ears. I can honestly say that I want her. Bad.

I've never met someone so happy all the time. Well, unless she's around me. Yet, I sense it's all an act. Maybe she's afraid I'll hurt her. Given my track record, it would seem it isn't a question of *if* I'll hurt her, but *when*. She's wrong, though. I'll never hurt her.

She flips on the radio, and we ride in comfortable silence for miles and miles. I gaze out the window at the golden wheat fields as far as the eye can see and wonder how anyone can live this far away from a big city. The further we drive, the more I can understand it. It's peaceful and I might be so relaxed I sing along to a few country songs on the radio with Sydney.

Best decision I ever made. The smile doesn't leave her face as I screw up the words.

Too soon, we come to a wooden arch that reads Reilly Ranch. Once we pass through it, the scenery changes. It's lush green grass with horses spread out in the pastures. A sprawling white house—more like a rancher's wet dream—comes into view. It's a two-story home with lots of windows and a wrap-around porch. Brock, wearing his Stetson, stands near the steps as Sydney pulls around the circular drive. A petite older woman with a silver bob waves at us. Why are my palms sweating?

Sydney throws the truck in park, and I take a deep breath before stepping out. I have to remind myself that this guy is trying to woo me, not the other way around. This doesn't even identify like a job interview though. Instead, this feels like me wanting to impress an overprotective father because I'm dating his daughter.

That thought hits me square in the chest, and I think about it for a second. What would it be like dating her?

I stare at her as she bounces up the porch steps and wraps her arms around the woman in a yellow dress with an apron over it. "Hi, Granny."

"Hi, love." She squeezes Sydney tight. "Introduce me to this fellow."

Sydney makes the introductions and Opal sizes me up as Sydney greets her father.

"Hi, Daddy," she says, happier than life.

As soon as their hug is over, I reach out to shake his hand. "This is quite the spread you have here."

"Close to one hundred acres. I'd have more, but I don't have time to work the land."

"It's stunning. I've never been on a ranch before."

"There's only one thing you really need to understand," Opal says. "If anyone tells you they need to go see a man about a horse, that means they want out of the conversation. Don't follow them."

I grin. "Good information."

Brock leads us into the foyer.

"This is cool," I say, admiring the open layout with high ceilings accented by wooden beams. To my right is an enormous living room, featuring a stone fireplace and lots of plump furniture filled with colorful pillows.

"If you'd like, Sydney can give you a tour while I cook dinner," Opal says.

"I'd love that," I say.

"Thought you would," Opal says with a cheeky lift of her brow. "I need you to finish peeling the potatoes, Brock."

"You got it," he says.

They head to our left and when they disappear, Sydney's eyes meet mine. "We'll start over here," she says, jabbing a thumb over her shoulder toward a long hallway. "Dad's office is down at the end, and I think you'll really like it."

I connect my hands behind me, following her down the oak floors. "Lead the way."

Her hips sway as she moves down the hallway, and I can't stop my eyes from checking out her ass. She's gorgeous in a red sundress with strappy brown sandals. As I'm imagining lifting her dress to see what color panties she's wearing, she opens a door and steps inside a large room.

I follow her in and let out a low whistle when I see all the platinum and gold record plaques hanging on the wall. "This is amazing." I check the names, in awe of such royalty. "I didn't know they signed Gene Gray with Reilly Records."

Sydney perches on the arm of a leather club chair. "He's a great friend of Daddy's."

I stare at her ruby lips as she smiles at me. "What about you?"

"What about me?"

"Do you want your name on one of these plaques?"

She shrugs and the thin strap of her dress slips from her shoulder. "I enjoy writing songs more. I don't think I want the headache fame brings."

I step closer and ease the strap back into place. "You have that star quality."

"Do I?" She rises, but not before I see the goosebumps my touch gave her. "Do you say this to all the women?"

"Never. I never lie about talent." Which is the truth.

"Is it true you signed Trinity?"

I rub my jaw. Trinity is the biggest diva in the music industry right now. The hell she put her ex through has never been lost on me. "Yes, I did."

"Do you believe the story between her and her ex-boyfriend?"

I shake my head. "I'm not sure. He moved to Alaska, I heard."

"I like his shark movies."

I laugh. "I've never seen them."

"They're god-awful, but funny."

"Maybe we'll watch them together one night."

"Maybe."

"We can cuddle close," I say, inching closer.

She places her hand between us, resting it on my chest. "Did you want to see the rest of the place?"

"Yeah, I'd like to see your bedroom. And not for clandestine purposes." Technically, that's not a lie, because my curiosity about her is outweighing my need to rip that dress off her tempting curves.

She laughs, moving away from me. "Ok, but no judging."

"Promise."

I follow her back through the house and up the grand staircase that leads to the second floor. When we step inside her old bedroom, it's like I'm catapulted to a different time.

"Nothing that special," she says, guiding me into her room.

Pfft. Everything is special. The platform bed with a pink quilt she cuddled under, the bay window full of white pillows where she probably sat and stared out at the landscape a time or two. On the yellow wall by the door are notches marking her growth. This room is full of history, and I want to learn it all. I study everything, trying to get clues about the woman in front of me.

I cross to the dresser and glance at a framed picture.

Sydney's probably eleven or twelve, standing next to a black and white pony.

"That's when we first got Oreo," she says, coming to stand next to me.

I gaze at the picture where she's beaming at whoever held the camera. "You look so happy here."

"I was happy. I love that horse."

"Where is the horse now?" I don't want to bring up a sensitive subject if the horse is no longer with us, but I felt I had to ask.

"He's in the barn. We'll go there after the house."

I smile. "Lead the way."

We continue moving throughout their home, and I'm in awe of how she grew up. All the pictures of her with her family show a stable upbringing filled with happy times. Much different from the way I grew up, that's for sure. I can tell she's Brock's pride and joy. It's evidenced by the shrine of photos he has of his daughter in every stage of her life.

When we step outside to check out the property before dinner, I keep close as we amble across the sun-scorched grass toward a red barn. "What was it like growing up here?"

She slows down a bit. "It was great."

"Really?" I give her a half-grin. "Why don't I believe you?"

She stops walking, her mouth parted just a bit to take my breath away. What I wouldn't give right now to touch those lips of hers with mine. "No, really, it was great. But… being here makes me miss my mother."

"I'm sorry." I'm an idiot for not making the connection of this ranch to sad feelings because she told me her mother died here and she misses her more than anything.

I reach out, wanting to touch her in some small way. "Want a hug?" I graze my fingers down her forearm.

She watches the movement. "You don't seem like a hugger."

"Are you kidding? I'm an award-winning hugger. I've given some of the best hugs around."

She raises a skeptical brow, but her eyes twinkle with laughter. "Really? Who would ever give an award for that?"

I smile, happy that I've cheered her up. "You will, after I've given you the hug." I open my arms, hoping more than anything she accepts my offer.

She flies into my chest, like she needs this hug more than anything. I wrap my arms around her, holding her a second longer than I probably should, breathing her in. I'd like to soothe her in any way possible, but she steps away and I shove my hands deep in my pockets, so touching her more won't tempt me.

We continue the tour, entering the barn, and it's not what I imagined. It's pristine with a wide center aisle and four large stalls on each side. In the back is a variety of saddles and things I'm sure are used to groom the horses. I spot Oreo right away in the mix of horses peeking their heads over the wooden doors.

Sydney gives each of the four majestic animals a pat and tells me they used to have more horses but her dad is too busy running Reilly Records.

"Why is it called Reilly Records and not Lancaster Records?"

She nuzzles Oreo. "It's my mother's maiden name. My father started the business right before she died, and they came up with that."

I smile. "I love it." I move closer to Oreo and watch as she runs her hand along his long nose. His large black eyes inspect me. "What about you? Do you want to run Reilly Records?" I know I have no right to ask these questions, but I can't stop wanting to learn everything about this woman. I want it all.

And that's vastly different from how I normally am.

"We should head back," she clips out, and right then, I realize I screwed up and the tour is over.

Chapter 7

Sydney

Do I really have the desire to run Reilly Records? I wish I knew the answer to that question. A huge part of me wants to be in the saddle, writing songs for the rest of my life, living a good life here in Texas. Another piece of me wonders if the main stage is a place I'd like to visit from time to time. But I see the way singers and pop stars get exploited in the worst of ways and it's a bit like selling your soul to the devil.

To be honest, what I want right now is for Tobias to kiss me again. While giving him a tour of the ranch, all I can think about is having his hands all over me.

I avoid his question, because I can barely think of a way to express it that would make sense. Instead, I say, "My father decided my future a long time ago."

Before we get back to the main house, Tobias stops me. "I think you can have any future you want. Your father just wants you to be happy. I'm sure he'd be ok with you bowing out of running Reilly Records."

I glance up at him as the tangerine sun dips low in the sky, casting a halo around his head. Although, I'm aware he's no angel. "How can you be so sure?"

"I think it's pretty obvious."

"Maybe you're right." I lead him back into the house and the aroma of dinner catches our noses and we both breathe in deep.

"That smells delicious," he says.

"Gran is an amazing cook."

"I can't wait to eat."

I lead Tobias into the dining room and my father's already sitting at the head of the table with Granny to his right. Tobias takes the chair to his left. It's a smaller table, so I sit at the other head and it's all very cozy as I look at the food waiting for us. My father reaches out his hands to say grace before we eat, and I stare at Tobias when he mirrors his action, reaching out a hand to me.

I place my tiny hand in his much bigger one and avert my attention from him by bowing my head.

My father says a simple prayer and finishes with thanks that Tobias could be here as well.

Am I thankful he's here?

Yeah, I am, and not just for physical reasons. There's no hiding the fact that I want his lips and hands all over me, but I also find myself enjoying his company when I'm digging for information about whether he's up to something nefarious.

"Opal, I haven't had a home cooked meal like this in… well, never," Tobias says, placing the linen napkin in his lap. "Thank you for your hospitality."

His gracious statement makes my chest clench. I've been a horrible hostess in my attempts to keep him at a distance. Now, I want to whip him up something delicious every night. But damn, he's a better cook than me.

Grandma preens under his praise and stands to scoop him

an extra-large helping of pot pie. "You need a wife," she says. "You're a handsome fella. Why aren't you married?"

Tobias nearly chokes on his sip of water. He sets the glass on the table. "Good question."

My father intervenes. "I'm sure Tobias just hasn't found the right woman yet, Mom."

"I'm betting she's here in Texas," Gran says.

Tobias lifts a brow, glancing in my direction. "You may be right about that, Opal."

I blush and go through the motions during dinner, listening to their chatter about everything from horses to Tobias complimenting my grandmother about her flaky crust, trying my best to keep my attention on chicken pot pie and off my dirty thoughts about Tobias.

"What about you, Sydney?" Granny asks.

"I'm sorry, what?" Everyone at the table is staring at me.

"Are you dating anyone?"

I chew for longer than necessary. What is it with my grandmother today? She's never inquired if I have a boyfriend. So what gives?

I finally swallow. "I like to keep my options open."

Granny side-eyes me. "I think you and this young gentleman should come back another day to have lemonade with me. There's a soiree after church coming up, you two would have fun."

"Granny, he doesn't have time for things like that. He's—"

Before I can get the rest of my words out, Tobias is already saying, "I think that's a great idea."

"Thought you might," Granny says. "I'm going to put some coffee on." She rises and heads to the kitchen with a pleased grin on her face. My father, however, does not look so pleased. I try to right the wrongs when Granny disappears from earshot.

"Tobias, you're not here to socialize with me. You don't have to agree."

Tobias leans back in his chair. "I don't mind, really. I love soirees."

If he's genuinely interested in the job, which I believe he is, now it all sounds so forced. Like, *Hey, want the job? Entertain my daughter and that should get you on board.*

"We're all getting a little ahead of ourselves here," Daddy says, trying to regain control, but I'm already out of my chair.

"I think I need to go talk to a man about a horse."

Tobias stands. "Sydney, wait."

I don't hear what else he says because I'm already rushing out the front door. I'm overreacting, and I don't even get why I'm so mad right now. I think because I want Tobias, and I can't have him.

Not under these pretenses.

Tobias rushes after me as I hustle away from the house. "Sydney, can you please wait?"

I stop near my truck. "Tobias, I don't want you to think there's any foul play going on here. Or that I'm a clause in the contract."

Tobias pushes a hand through his dark hair. "I would never have thought any of that. From what I see, your father is a very respectable man. Can I also point out that your use of the horse phrase was perfection?"

I can't help but smile.

"Come back inside?" he coaxes.

"You can stay. I'm gonna head back to my place. Dad can find someone to give you a ride home. Please stay," I say to him, hoping he won't leave because of me.

Tobias steps closer. "I want to do the right thing here. And I realize that means I should stay and chat with your father about the business, but every cell in my body is screaming to take you home and show you what you do to me."

I can barely breathe. "What do I do to you?"

He grabs my hand, placing it between his legs and pressing it against his zipper. On the hardness bulging beneath my palm. "You make me so fucking hard." His lips are so close, and I want nothing more than to taste them against mine again.

"Get in the car," I say. I can't believe I'm doing this.

I've never seen a man get in a car so quickly in all my life. But then he hops out. "We can't just leave Opal hanging. We need to say goodbye."

Wow. If there was ever a sign that he's a good man, it's that he would turn down sex to say goodbye to my granny. It just turns me on more that he thought of her feelings.

Our few minutes to say goodbye turns into thirty when Granny talks us into having a slice of lemon pie. When we finally leave, I don't know how to act because I'm not sure if he's changed his mind now that he's had time to think about it. He clears that up about five miles down the road.

"Pull over," Tobias says.

I glance at the wheat fields. "Here?"

"Yeah, I have to tell you something."

I turn down a dirt path, moving away from the road. "What do you need to tell me?"

He leans close, pulling at the nape of my neck. "This," he says before laying his lips across mine.

And this kiss is so much more than the first one. It's slow and tantalizing, but makes my pulse race, like galloping on a horse at top speed. His tongue traces over mine and he cups my butt, lifting me onto his lap. I straddle him as he deepens the kiss, moaning into his mouth, pressing closer, searching for relief from the ache in my core.

What is happening here?

His hardness presses against my center, and I grind against him.

"Feel how badly I want you." He squeezes my ass. "Now let's see how much you want me." His hooded eyes hold mine as his warm hand glides under my dress and up my thigh. He reaches my panties and slips his fingers under the silky fabric.

"You're so fucking wet for me." He smirks against my lips. "I knew you wanted me."

I rock into his hand. "You're so cocky." However, his cockiness right now is an aphrodisiac.

"That day you were touching yourself," he whispers against my lips, "I heard you say my name. Do you understand how fucking hot that made me? How hard I jerked my cock in the shower? I've wanted you since the first moment I saw you." Before I can process his confession, he devours my mouth.

Now we're pawing and groaning as we try to get at each other as quickly as possible. I kiss his jaw, his neck, and earlobe, memorizing the sexy sounds he makes. His hand explores inside my panties until he's got two fingers sliding in and out of me, making me so close to coming undone right here in my truck.

He unzips his jeans, pulling out his massive dick, and I moan at the sight of it. Heat fans out from low in my belly, warming every nerve ending.

"Please, don't stop," I beg, rocking my body on his skillful fingers.

"Oh, I won't. I need you to come on my fingers. I want to taste you." He pushes another finger deep inside me, reaching a sensitive spot that triggers a crescendo of tingles in every cell of my body. "Look at how you look at my dick. You want this?" He fists his long length with his other hand.

I nod, licking my lips. "Yes."

He shakes his head at my answer. "Not until you give me at least one orgasm right now. All over my fucking hand. I won't give you anything more until you do that. Understood?"

I nod again, loving his bossiness. Loving the way it ignites something deep within. "Understood."

He brings his lips close to mine and murmurs, "You're so fucking pretty." And then our tongues tangle together in a kiss so deep, he reaches recesses of my heart I didn't realize existed.

My eager body grinds against his hand, wanting him inside of me. "Tobias, please."

"I'll give you everything you want, baby girl. As soon as you come for me."

"I'm right there," I whisper against his lips.

He presses his thumb against my clit, and I grip the seat behind him as the pressure builds, expanding until it's ready to combust. "Give it to me," he demands.

"It's yours." My eyes lose focus and I explode all around him.

"That's it, my greedy little songbird." He stills his hand as my powerful release shakes everything I thought I knew about orgasms off its foundation.

"Fuck, yeah," he husks out. "Keep coming all over me."

I shamelessly ride out my release until the storm in my body passes and calm returns. He swipes his thumb along the pre-cum leaking from his cock and removes his fingers from inside me. My body ignites again when he glosses my bottom lip with his pre-cum at the same time he sucks his fingers into his mouth "You taste so fucking sweet."

I lick my bottom lip, savoring his essence. "Mm."

His eyes blaze and he palms the nape of my neck, bringing our lips together in a mind-blowing kiss.

He breaks away to fish a condom from his back pocket. In a flash, he rips the foil with his teeth and slides the rubber over his dick. "You felt so good coming all over my fingers. I can't wait to feel that all over my cock."

"Ah, god. Give it to me now."

He presses the fat tip at my entrance and eases me down on him. My hand slaps against the foggy window. He's so big. So thick. So perfect.

My body takes a minute to get all of him inside me, but once he's all the way, he stills, gazing at me with those pretty blue eyes. "Fuck, you're tight. Look how well you've taken my thick cock. Such a needy girl."

His words turn me on in the worst of ways. I lean my head back, closing my eyes as I rock against him. And then the tempo increases until I'm riding him like the star of a rodeo. Giddy up for this cowgirl.

Tobias closes his eyes as he groans out a string of unintelligible words. He clutches my ass with both hands, lifting me up and slamming me back down over his hard length. I grip his shoulders, loving every second of him owning me.

The way he moans out my name.

The way he slams inside me.

The way he looks at me like I'm a rarity.

I could get used to a thing like this.

I never want it to stop.

"You want another orgasm, you greedy little thing?"

"Yes," I moan as he rocks up into me again, over and over. "Yes, Tobias, yes."

"Good. Give it to me. I want your orgasms." His eyes meet mine and he cups my cheeks so I can't turn away. "You got that? From here on out, I want every single one of your orgasms. Days when you want a quick hard fuck. Or nights when you want it slow and lingering. However you want it, I want to give it to you. Understood?"

Wow. I want that too.

"I need to hear the words, Sydney. Do you understand?"

I stare him in the eyes and answer with a simple, "Yes."

"Good girl." He continues pumping inside me, his hands returning to my rear, and his dick is even harder than before. "Now come on me."

My body hums a sweet melody as I focus on getting off again. I'm so lost in everything he's saying to me it doesn't take much to see my next orgasm on the horizon.

"Come with me," I pant out.

He growls and slams into me with ferocious thrusts as he

rubs my clit until I'm chanting his name. It's like he has the directions to my body seared into his brain.

"I'm close," he rasps. "You feel so fucking good."

My orgasm tears into me, ripping me apart, and I spasm around him.

"Jesus Christ, Sydney. Fuck," he says, his orgasm mingling with mine. He holds onto me tightly as his body shudders, and after, we end up driving home and doing it all over again. I just hope my father never finds out.

Chapter 8

Tobias

It's been two days since I first had sex with Sydney in the front of her pickup truck. Since then, we've fucked on pretty much every surface of her condo.

Today, however, we're back at her father's ranch. We're here to have lemonade with Granny. Yes, she's also Granny to me now, and I just hope she's around to meet our little ones someday. I've never been much of a lemonade drinker, but as I sit out here on the front porch with Sydney on one side and Granny on the other, I can see the appeal of country living. There's a soft breeze coming in off the fields and it's relaxing as fuck out here.

"You should take Tobias riding. Show him the ropes," Granny says to Sydney.

Before Sydney can agree, I cut in, "No, it's ok. I'm not much of a country boy." The closest I've come to a cowboy is watching old spaghetti westerns on TV. I don't know anything about wrangling cattle or hog tyin' a calf.

"Well, we'll have to change that." Sydney sets her lemonade on a nearby table and stands from her rocking chair.

I stare up at her. "Really? You can't be serious."

"Oh, I'm dead serious," she says with an enchanting smile on her face.

After I reluctantly get up, we say our goodbyes to Granny and walk down the back porch steps.

"What exactly does this entail?" I ask, leery I'm getting myself into something that might kill me before I have a chance to share my life with her.

"You'll see."

She sneaks a saucy wink to me and leads me toward the large wooden barn like she didn't just get my blood pumping faster. Damn. Now, the urge to kiss her is overwhelming, and I glance over my shoulder to check whether Granny went inside the house. We haven't told anyone about us dating, so I want to make sure we're not caught red-handed. Once I see the coast is clear, I sweep Sydney into my arms.

"Come here," I say right before I fuse my lips to hers.

She wraps her arms around my neck, and for a moment, we get lost in each other's touch. For a moment, the world fades away.

I back her against the side of the barn. "I want to take you right here and now," I tell her, gazing into her eyes.

She giggles. "Tobias, we can't have sex here. Someone might see us."

"Let the whole damn world see," I say, grinding my hips into her to keep her in place.

She pushes me away with another laugh. "Come on. After I show you the ropes on the ranch, if you still want to have sex, we will. Anywhere you choose."

"Oh, don't tease me with that. I'll definitely want to have sex." I move away from her, and we enter the barn.

A horse neighs as soon as we close the doors, and it almost scares the ever-loving shit out of me.

"Hi, Oreo," Sydney says, stepping closer to the black and white horse. She grabs a carrot from a nearby bin and feeds it to him.

"Great looking horse," I say, because his large eyes are pinned on me.

"You want to pet him?"

I stuff my hands in the pockets of my jeans. "I wouldn't even know how."

Sydney crooks her finger at me, her gray eyes shining. "Come here, silly."

"Absolutely." I move closer to the horse and reach out my hand to slide it along his face.

"This is called the horse's muzzle."

"Muzzle," I repeat, like I'm learning a new language.

"Ok, I think you're ready to ride," Sydney says, opening Oreo's stall gate.

I step back. "Wait? What?"

"It's easy."

"I've got a better idea. How about we find a bale of hay to get busy on?"

This makes her laugh. "Don't be nervous. You wanted to learn the ropes."

Seems to me she didn't take that as tying her up, so I think back to earlier today when I said I wanted to learn about ranching. I'd rather wear chaps—bare-assed—than get on this horse but looking at the smile that splits Sydney's face makes me a happy man. I want to be the one to always put a smile on her face. And because of this, I am about to mount a wild animal.

Ok, maybe not wild, but still an animal.

Sydney goes through the motions of saddling the horse and bringing him out to the paddock. "You'll just ride him around here and I'll have the reins in my hand the whole time."

"Why don't you ride it with me?"

"Him," is her response.

"What?" I ask.

"Him. Oreo is a *him*, not an it."

"You know what I mean. Why don't you ride *him* with me?"

Sydney purses her lips, and after a few moments of contemplation, says, "Ok, cowboy. You have a deal."

We mount the horse—which was a process, let me tell you—and once we're both settled in the saddle with her in front of me, away we go.

As we trot across the grass, the way Sydney's body moves against mine has my cock stirring to life. All of that turned-on-ness goes away as soon as Sydney has the horse run a bit. Now, I'm just trying to hang on for dear life.

"You ready for a real ride, cowboy?" Sydney says over her shoulder.

I grip her hips tighter, not sure what she has planned. "Whatever you want." Because it's here and now, I realize I will do anything for this woman.

She leads the horse out of the paddock area and into a field blooming with wildflowers. The horse takes off in a quick gallop, and my curse words get carried away by the wind.

It's a lovely countryside, but I didn't take note of any details before I squeezed my eyes shut from fear of falling off. After a good distance away from the house, she slows the horse.

"We can get off here and let the horse rest." She dismounts, and I climb down more gracefully than I got up on this ride. "What did you think?"

Now that I'm on the ground, I guess it wasn't horrible. "I can see the appeal." My phone rings, and I pull it from my pocket. "Let me take this," I tell her when I see who is calling.

She nods, and I walk toward a row of bushes as she strokes Oreo's long neck.

"I'm busy," I answer.

"Tobias," Mark McManus, owner of Halo Records, says into the phone.

"What do you want?"

"I hope you took some time to go over what we discussed the other day."

I roll my eyes, moving further away from Sydney until I'm behind a crooked oak tree. "Not gonna happen," I grit out.

He chuckles. "Oh, it'll happen. You'll see. I'll call you tomorrow with the details."

I disconnect before he can say anything more and head back toward Sydney.

While Oreo wanders around poking his nose in the patches of bluebonnets, we sit in the sea of grass.

"Who was that on the phone?" Sydney asks, shielding her eyes from the afternoon sun.

I shove the phone into my pocket. "Nobody."

She studies me for a second before she drops her hand and leans back on her palms. "It's so peaceful out here."

"Yeah." I pluck a blade of grass and twiddle it between my fingers. "I couldn't imagine growing up like this."

"How did you grow up? I mean, you told me a little bit." Her gray eyes focus on me, and I want to tell her everything about my life. Every single aspect. Every minute that led me to this spot here with her.

"Alone, mostly. My parents were always out getting high, and I was an afterthought. We lived in a dangerous neighborhood, so I guess I was always on high alert. Took me years to lose the constant worry that something bad was about to happen." The reason I tell no one about my past is because I don't want to face the pity in their eyes.

However, Sydney has none shining there. And I want to thank her for it. She scoots closer. "And look at everything you've achieved. I bet if you had everything handed to you, you probably wouldn't have worked so hard to get away. You're living the dream."

"Are you living *your* dream?"

She shrugs. "Yes, I love my life."

I raise a brow. "Really? That's your dream? To run your father's company?"

She sighs. "I don't know." She leans close to me, and I wrap an arm around her shoulders. "I just want to be happy. And I'm happiest when I'm writing songs."

"Then, write."

"You make it sound so easy."

I smile. "It *is* that easy."

"I like the way you're so certain about things."

She has no idea. I've already thought about my whole life with her, and in our future, she's not running her father's company. Instead, I'm helping her father while she pursues what interests her. Because I would do that for her. I'd do anything for her.

"So, um, want to guess something else I like?" she asks.

"Me?"

"Mhm." Her fingers tiptoe up my thigh until she palms my dick. "And this."

I glance over at Oreo who is standing still, not watching us, but hm. "As much as that turns me on, there's a horse here."

"He's napping," she says.

"He's standing."

"Look closer. His eyes are closed. See how his neck is relaxed and his head is drooped?"

"Yeah."

"That means he's dozing. Horses sleep a lot standing." She waggles her brows. "He'll never know."

She's the expert, not me, so I'm all in. The way she's looking at me right now makes my heart pitter patter in my chest, and this will be perfect practice for sexy times when Charlotte and Lucas nap. I lean in and lock my lips to hers. She moans against my mouth, and it brings my dick to life. My heart thunders like a stampede of wild horses as I deepen the kiss.

"I'll never be able to get enough of you," I tell her, wanting to have her right here and now. "Take off your jeans. If I don't get inside your pussy, I might go insane."

"Well we don't want that," she says.

"Lose the panties too." As much as I'd like to play with her right now, this isn't really the place. "On your hands and knees for me."

She does exactly as I requested, pushing her naked ass in the air. "Like this, cowboy?"

"You're such a naughty girl." I unzip my jeans and pull out my cock. She licks her lips as I fist it in my hands, rubbing my thumb over the drop of pre-cum shining at the tip. I drop to my knees behind her and find the condom in my back pocket.

"Hurry," Sydney whines.

I smack her ass before I rip the condom open. "Is somebody hungry for my cock?"

"Yes, hurry, Tobias. I'm so ready."

I slip my fingers through her seam, discovering how wet she is for me. I lean over her body and line my dick up with her pussy. She pushes back against me, but I tease her, rubbing the tip of my cock through her wetness, letting it press her hard at her clit. "That feels good, baby? You ready for my dick?"

"Yes," she says, spreading her legs apart.

I spank her ass once more before I enter her in one forceful strike, pausing as soon as I'm buried to the hilt. "Fuck, your pussy is so good." I run my hand up her back and wrap my fingers around the base of her throat. "You're such a good girl taking all of my cock deep in your hot cunt."

"God, I love when you talk dirty."

I pull out and push back inside her with a punishing stroke. "You like this dick, don't you?" I repeat the action a few more times before I fully fuck her. "You look so fucking good handling my cock so well." I slam into her slick warmth, over and over, my body edging closer to explosion.

But not until I make her come first.

I let go of her neck and play with her clit, toying with the bundle of nerves until she's crying out my name. Her pussy grips my dick tighter as her body vibrates from her pleasure. Sydney's orgasms are quickly becoming one of my favorite things.

"I want you to come again," I husk out.

She pushes her ass against me as I keep slamming into her, determined to get her off once more before I seek my release.

"Tobias," she moans out, and it drifts through the air, into my ears, and settles into my heart. I love the sound of my name on her lips.

My balls tighten and I hold back another minute so I can please this blessing beneath me. "I need you to come, Sydney. I'm so fucking close. Can you come for me? Please," I say, my voice strained with the need to shoot my load deep inside her.

I press on her clit, working the perfect rhythm that has her legs shaking. "That's right, Sydney. Come all over this dick. Show me how much you like my cock."

"I'm coming," she sings out, like a chorus of angels. "Tobias," she says once more before I squeeze my eyes shut.

The exquisite pulse of her pussy coming on my cock gets me every time. I couldn't hold on any longer even if I tried. The waves of my orgasm drown me, damn near killing me with its intensity.

"Fuck," I groan out. I fill the condom with my seed and pepper kisses along her back as I finish. "Sydney, I'm falling for you," I whisper against her skin. "I'm fucking falling for you."

Chapter 9

Sydney

I couldn't be happier than I am right now. I'm nearly floating down the halls at work.

"Sydney, come in here," my father's voice booms from his office.

I get my head out of the clouds and make my way into his office. "Yes, Daddy?"

"Something's different about you. What's going on?"

His question causes a chain reaction of nervous movements—tucking my hair behind my ear, scratching my eyebrow, fidgeting with the buttons on my shirt. My father can't discover I'm sleeping with his potential employee. Actually, Tobias is more than that. Daddy plans on making him head of his own division, and here I am sleeping with a future executive. Possibly fucking it all up. "Nothing's different."

My father studies me, and I do my best to keep my face passive even though my heart is racing. He finally relents, deeming me the same, and says, "Let's discuss Tobias. Tell me everything you know about him."

Instead of telling him he enjoys kissing me and snuggling close, I simply shrug. "I've told you everything I know." Well, relevant things. Not personal things Tobias told me in private.

"No strange calls? No mystery guests? Nothing?"

I shake my head. "No." My mind quickly returns to the other day when he took a phone call, and when I asked who it was, he told me no one. But how can I even think it's something Halo related?

"Have you talked to him about staying here?"

I don't want to get ahead of myself, but I hope Tobias is feeling even a smidge of what I am. Would he stay for me? Do I want that? Yeah, I do.

"I haven't talked to him much," I say, hoping my father finds a shred of honesty within that statement.

"Interesting." It's like my father senses something and I wish he'd just say it instead of beating around the bush.

"What's up, Daddy?" I ask, parking a hand on my hip.

"Nothing. I'm just wondering about Tobias' character."

"What about his character?"

"Well, is he a good guy? Does he generally care about the people he signs?"

How could he even ask this? I think back to Tobias encouraging me to go for my own singing career. To chase my dreams. So yes, he cares about the artists. And I need to tell Dad about my dreams.

I suck in a deep breath, knowing I need to have this conversation one of these days. "Daddy." I step closer. "Can I talk to you?"

My father's already sifting through papers on his desk and doesn't even look up when he says, "Sure, what's up?"

I want to tell him about my songwriting dreams and how I'd love to work in that field, but I can't find the right words. "Um…" My words fail me as my father's phone rings. He stares at me, and then holds up one finger to take the call. "It's nothing." I spin on my heel and head out of his office as he answers the phone.

One of these days, I'll tell him. Yet, one day flows into another and then another goes by. Time will keep ticking, and it'll be another ten years before I tell my father what I really want.

"Hey," Tobias says, walking up beside me as I turn a corner. He reaches out to me, but I sidestep him.

"You can't touch me here." I shuffle him into my office. "We can't be seen together like that."

Tobias' brows draw together. "I know."

I blow out an exasperated breath. "I'm sorry, but I can't tell my father I've been sleeping with his star recruit."

Tobias looks different. Despondent. His tight-lipped smile is forced as he stands with his hands at his sides. "I get it."

I plop into my office chair. "My father will never understand." I study him. The worn out look in his eyes. Like he's been fighting a battle. "Is everything ok?"

Tobias steps closer but remains on the other side of the desk. "Sydney, I need to talk to you."

I gaze up into his eyes, but he's not meeting mine. Must be serious. "Sure, what is it?"

He rubs the back of his neck. "I… um, I…" His words never come because the door bursts open and my father barrels into the room.

"You asshole," he says, pointing a finger at Tobias. "Did you think I wouldn't find out?"

I bound from my chair. "Daddy, what's going on?"

Tobias doesn't say a word, just stands there, letting my father continue his assault.

"You gonna tell her or should I?" My father's mustache twitches with anger at Tobias. I don't think I've ever seen him this mad.

Oh, god. Did he find out about us?

"I can explain," I say in a rush to get the words out before my father assumes the worst.

My father turns to me. "You knew?"

I give him a pointed look. "Of course, I knew." Are we talking about the same thing here?

"Why didn't you tell me?" He's so angry.

I inch closer to my father. "We didn't know how. We wanted to wait. I really like him, Daddy."

My father tilts his head. "Like him? What do you mean?"

"I've been involved with Tobias for a few weeks."

Dad's head whips between us and I swear if a head could explode, his would. But he's staring at me like this is all new information, and now, I'm confused.

"I care deeply for your daughter, Brock," Tobias says from the other side of the room. "I never meant to hurt you." He stares at me. "Either of you." And then he walks out the door.

My father and I blink at each other.

Confusion builds.

"What's going on?" I ask.

"He took a job with Halo Records."

It's been three weeks since Tobias left. Three excruciating weeks of trying to make sense of everything. Was he really just a playboy who used me for his own gains?

My mind can't come up with any other possibility.

I thought he cared for me, but I was stupid to think that.

How could I have been so silly?

I didn't even realize Halo offered him a job, but of course, they did. They probably swooped in with a bigger and better job as soon as they caught wind Daddy was offering him one. And Tobias accepted theirs. And then he left. Like, cleared out his stuff and flew away before I got home. That stung the most. No goodbye. No explanation.

I'm a horrible spy. What a joke I tried to hate him. Instead of uncovering if he was a mole, or a bad guy, all I figured out is that he's a fabulous kisser and a fantastic lover. I fell for him and he flew away with my heart, without looking back.

THE DOOR BUZZER sounds as a tear trickles down my check. I toss my journal aside and pull myself from the comfort of my couch. I open the door to find my father with a frown on his face.

"Can we talk?" he asks.

"I think we should." I've been avoiding my father the past few weeks. I've been avoiding everyone, if I'm being honest.

We move into the living room, and I plop down on the couch, hugging a yellow throw pillow close to my chest. "What's up?"

"I get you're upset about Tobias, and I'm not here to make you feel better about him. Those city boys are a different breed. They don't value family and honor. They don't understand loyalty."

I pick at the stitching on the pillow. "I guess." I thought Tobias did care about those things, but I was so wrong.

Silly me.

"I wanted to talk to you about the company."

It's now or never. I can't hide from this any longer. "I wanted to talk to you too, Daddy. I don't want to run your company. I understand it's your dream, but I just don't want it." That was easier to say than I thought it would be.

His laughter is not the response I expected. "I kind of figured you didn't. Besides, you're not very good at it."

With pretend shock, I gasp at his statement. But truer words were never spoken. I suck at it.

And I can't believe he's not angry. Or yelling. Or throwing things.

We should have had this discussion ages ago.

"Seriously, you're not. I think it's why I sought out Tobias. I thought if he took my offer, I could one day turn the company over to him." My father removes his cowboy hat from his head.

"I'm sorry it didn't work out," I tell him, meaning it in so many ways.

He sits beside me, and I tell him about the open mic nights. I explain to my father about how I've been writing songs for over two years now. How every Friday night I've been singing those songs for a small crowd.

He listens. He absorbs what I'm saying to him.

"So, you want to be a singer?"

I shake my head. "No. I'd rather stay behind the scenes and write songs."

My father pats my knee. "There's nothing wrong with that. I wish you would have told me sooner."

"I'm singing some of my songs tonight. Would you like to come?" I'm nervous as I wait for his answer.

My father smiles, holding his Stetson in his hands. "Yeah. I would like that."

We should talk about Tobias. I should tell him how I really felt about him. How angry I am, but I keep it bottled inside instead. I'm sure my father knows how upset I am about him leaving. It's so clearly written all over my face.

There's another knock at my door, and I get up from the couch to answer it. It's Callie. She's all dressed up in a light-blue sundress and tan cowboy boots. Her hair is pulled to one side, and I'm happy to see her.

"Are you ready to sing your heart out tonight?" she says, with a bright smile on her face.

Dad stands. "Hi, Callie," he says in a deep voice.

"Mr. Lancaster, hello."

My father puts his hat on his head. "Text me the details and I'll be there. See you girls later."

Once he's gone, Callie spins to face me. "Let's get you all dolled up."

I roll my eyes. "Can't I just go like this?"

She stares at my baggy white t-shirt and gray sweatpants. "Um, no."

"I miss him," I confess, as I let her lead me back to the bedroom.

"Don't beat yourself up too hard," Callie says. She crosses to the bed and lies across the comforter while I rummage through my closet, looking for the best outfit to wear for open mic night. This will be the first time Daddy will hear me sing in public since a chorus concert in second grade.

"I still can't believe I trusted him so freely."

Callie frowns. "You're a good person, and he took advantage of that."

I want to cry, but I refuse to give Tobias anymore of my head space. I rummage through my closet, pulling out a hot little number.

Callie gives her approval to the red dress I hold up. "Yes. Go with that one." She rolls on her back, staring up at the ceiling. "Good-looking guys like Tobias should come with a warning label."

I laugh. "Yeah, *Don't trust the sexy*."

Callie laughs with me, and for five seconds, I feel better about everything. My father listened to me about what I want for my future. I never thought I'd see the day when Brock Lancaster would bow down to his own daughter and give her what she actually wants, even though it differs from his own dream.

Sure, I'd love to keep the business in the family, but I can't ignore my dreams any longer. I won't ignore what I want any longer.

Although, what I want most in the world, I can't have.
Tobias.

How could I have been so wrong about a person?

I try to push the negative thoughts away as I slip on the dress and turn toward the mirror. "How do I look?"

Callie sits up. "Wow, you're going to knock 'em dead tonight."

"Do you think everything he said to me was a lie?" I ask Callie for the millionth time.

We've dissected my time spent with Tobias and learned two things:

1. He's good at the lies. He really made me believe he was really into me. Every touch. Every kiss.
2. I fell in love with him.

It's ridiculous to think someone can fall in love so quickly, but I know what's in my heart. This burning in my soul is unmistakable love.

"I think he cared, Syd. You can't fake that. No one is that good. I saw the way his eyes lit up the first night you sang for him. There's no pretending that."

I want to believe her words, but it's so hard when the man I love didn't tell me he accepted a job with the competition. It came out a few days after he left that he leveraged my father's offer against his offer from Halo. Who does that?

Not someone who cares about you. And it sure seemed like he did.

Tobias needs to discover himself because he's a darn good actor.

He played the part of the doting boyfriend perfectly.

And I fell right into his trap.

Chapter 10

Tobias

Everything is smoggier in LA. A thick haze blankets the tall buildings outside my skyrise office at Halo, like a cruel reminder of the fresh air in Texas I left behind. Of my little songbird I left behind. All I can think about is the look on Sydney's face when I walked out of the office that day. The way the tears brimmed, so ready to fall. Did she cry after I left?

Did I?

I have to admit I may have shed a tear or thirty. Not really. But maybe. Ok, yes, I did.

It's been a few weeks since the day I left Texas, and my heart still hurts like it was yesterday.

"What do you think?" Mark McManus, head of Halo, slams a hand down on my shoulder with pride. "It's phenomenal, huh?"

He's talking about the office, and yes, while it is a gorgeous space with a view people would probably rob their children's college funds to access, I find no happiness here. But I go through the motions, pretending it's everything I've ever wanted. "Yep."

Mark chuckles and the sound grates on my nerves. "I'm really glad you finally joined our firm."

As if I had a choice.

I turn to face him, shrugging his hand off my shoulder. "I bet."

Just because Mark MacManus forced me to work here doesn't mean I need to play nice.

"I guess I'll let you get back to it," he says, losing his smile as he stares at me.

I nod, no longer having the energy to get out any words for him.

As soon as Mark leaves my office, I slump into my office chair. How could I let this happen? The woman at the club my first night in Harmony. The actions that transpired. All of it. I should have sensed Mark would play dirty.

Yet, I never expected him to have me followed. Or have his spies snap pictures of me getting head in the back of a club and snap even more photos when I was out with Sydney. There was even a video. And then to use all of that to blackmail me into a position here. All to get back at Brock Lancaster. I swear, Mark and Brock's competition has got to stop. It's literally ruining lives.

It's ruined my life.

However, I couldn't let my actions ruin the lives of Brock or, worse, Sydney.

I love her.

Plain and simple.

I absolutely love her.

And I love her too much to ruin her life. I can't think of any way out of this situation. I can't allow Mark to go to the press with sordid information about me and the Lancasters. It would hurt Sydney too much.

It would hurt Reilly Records.

I try to imagine the story coming out. It's not just photos of me with Sydney. There's a video of Sydney and me having sex in her truck late one night. How they even got that video, I have no idea. But they did. And a sex tape would be bad news for their company. And her new career.

She's better off without me. Without all of this drama.

Right? Right.

If I tried to go to her now, all of Mark's threats would come to fruition. I can't allow that to happen.

It's better this way.

My cell rings, and I accept the call when I see it's my friend Ethan Hale. Big bad movie star, Ethan Hale. I wish I was the one who discovered him, but sadly, I wasn't. We met a while back on the set of one of his movies.

"Hey, man. What's up?" I say.

"I thought you were staying in Texas. It surprised me to hear you're back," Ethan says.

"I wanted to stay in Texas. Believe me. I could have been happy in Harmony."

Ethan sighs. "Sounds like you met somebody there."

"She was the best person I've ever met."

"So, what happened? Why aren't you there making babies with her?"

I laugh. "It didn't work out."

"That's bullshit. If it's meant to be, it'll always work itself out." Ethan should understand about impossible love situations. He's a big-shot movie star, who fell for his stepsister before their parents' wedding. He never thought it would work out either, but Ethan and Nova are happy and expecting their first child.

"There's no plausible scenario where this story can have a happy ending," I say.

"Nonsense. It can have a happy ending if *you* make it have one."

I've always valued the way Ethan looks at life. So simplistic. So carefree. It's a way I wish I could live my life.

I cross to the glass wall and stare out at the place I've called home my entire life. However, it's never been much of a home. It never loved me back in all the years I've been here. No family to call my own. No roots, so to speak.

I stare at the line of cars on the freeway and wonder if this is my future. My life. A life of solitude, because I know I'll never find another Sydney for as long as we both shall live.

I want to marry her.

I want to fill her with all of my babies.

I want to create a forever home with her.

"You still there?" Ethan asks, breaking me from my epiphany.

"I have no idea how to make things work." Because in all honesty, I just don't know.

"Let me worry about Mark McManus. I've got my own dirt on him and the actions he did at a certain award's party a few years back."

"Oh, this I got to hear."

Ethan laughs. "No, it's probably best if you didn't. Now go get your girl."

"Seriously?" I ask him, unable to think of a possibility where I can walk away from this job.

"Yes, go. And you better bring the big guns when you try to win her back."

I stop in my tracks, thinking about how I could ever deserve Sydney. The groveling I am happy to endure to let her know how sorry I am.

"I'll talk to you later," I tell Ethan as I grab my things and rush out the door.

"Mr. Brentwood," my new secretary calls out after me. "Where are you going, sir?"

I hit the button on the elevator bank and yank at my tie. "I quit." I'm enraged as I say the words, because I let Mark manipulate me into walking away from Sydney.

But I'm going to make it right.

On my way out of the building, I stop in the lobby and book a one-way ticket to Dallas. I need to get there as soon as possible.

There's nowhere else I'd rather be.

I'm all in on this shit. And if Sydney doesn't forgive me… well, I'll cross that bridge when I get there. But I'm not leaving Texas until I've proven my worth to the woman.

"Where do you think you're going?" Mark stops me before I can leave the building.

"I've thought about it. I can't work for you," I say as I slide my phone into my back pocket.

He laughs—short and curt—before saying, "What do you mean? We had a deal. I would hate to publish the pictures and video I have of you."

"Oh, I know you won't." And I don't bother explaining further because I know Ethan's got me.

And with those words, I walk out the glass doors, not bothering to look back.

Chapter 11

Sydney

"It's a full house out there," Callie says with a big smile on her face.

I run my sweaty palms down my dress. Everyone in Harmony is here tonight, waiting to see me, because my father tweeted an invitation to the town, telling them I'd be performing at an open mic night. This is another reason I'd never want to be famous. There's no way I could perform for millions of people. Especially when my heart is in a gazillion tiny pieces.

"I can't do this," I tell Callie, turning to escape out the back door.

She grabs my arm. "Are you kidding? Your songs are brilliant. Sing them for your father." She smiles wider. "For everyone."

I'm sick to my stomach. "I can't. I just miss him a ton."

She wraps her arms around me. "I know you do, sweetie. But he wasn't a good guy."

Tears fill my eyes. "You're right, but I sure wanted him to be."

"I wanted him to be too."

"It's silly," I say, moving out of her embrace. "But I could see a life with him. I really think we would have been good together."

Callie gives me a look of pity. "Listen, forget about him. Just go out there and sing your heart out. You have an amazing voice and soul-touching lyrics. Everyone's going to love you."

I give Callie another hug, grateful to have her in my life. "Thank you. You'd better go if you want a seat."

"Your dad and grandma are saving me one. Break a leg," she says as she gives me yet another hug.

"Stop hugging me already and go." I squeeze her tight and then release her.

She hurries away and when I hear my name called by the announcer, I make my way on stage. The bright lights make it hard to see the crowd before me, which is best. I know my father is out there somewhere, and that thought brightens the darkness that's lingered inside of me since the day Tobias walked away.

I adjust the microphone and smile. "Thank you all for coming out tonight. Now, this is a song I just wrote a few days ago." The lights go down, and a lone spotlight in the back of the club lights up, allowing me to see the crowd. My father, Gran, and Callie sit in the front row, all beaming from ear to ear.

I'm grateful they're here, but melancholy seeps into my bones when I sing the first lyric about meeting someone in the most unusual way. I gaze at the spotlight, trying to hide myself in the brightness of it. Even though I'm in front of a large crowd, I still feel lost somehow. I will not cry on stage. I will not cry while I sing. No matter how much everything hurts.

I belt out the chorus about loving someone you just met.

About how a grand love when lost can hurt so painfully you relive the pain over and over.

After the song, and I've poured my heart out, I head into the crowd to sit with my family. My father hugs me, telling me how proud he is of me. It actually makes me feel a bit better.

I will not cry.

"We have a late addition to the roster," the emcee says.

The lights dim, and I debate on whether I should just head home or stay here and enjoy the night out. Before I can make up my mind, a soft blue spotlight hits the man on stage, and I gasp.

Tobias stands there with a microphone in his hand.

Is he going to sing?

"Hi, everyone," he says to the crowd, and then his blue eyes land on me. "I'm not a great singer, and I'm an even worse song writer, but I've put something together. I hope you don't hate it too much." He winks at me. "This one's for you, Sydney."

A tune plays through the stage speakers, and Tobias sings the first few words, "I was an idiot to leave."

I listen in rapt fascination as he belts out lyrics he wrote himself.

"I should have never went and saw a man about a horse. I should have found you instead."

His voice isn't half-bad, but it's not his voice I'm listening to. I'm hearing the words he's saying just to me. He sings about how he screwed things up, and how he'll forever love me. By the end of the song I'm in tears, and my father nudges me as the crowd cheers.

"Go up there and tell him you love him back," my father says.

I gaze at Tobias on the stage and wipe away more fat tears from my cheeks. I know I want him to wrap me into his arms, but it's like I'm frozen about what to do.

He betrayed me.

Callie elbows me. "Go. Go," she urges.

I stand on shaky legs and walk toward the stage. Before I can walk up the steps, Tobias jumps off the stage and lands right in front of me.

"I'm so sorry," he says.

"What are you doing here, Tobias?" I still can't believe he's really here. In the flesh. Standing right in front of me.

"I was a fool for leaving."

"Doesn't change the fact that you *did* leave." Tears threaten to spill over. "Why?"

The crowd is listening, trying to hear everything we're saying. Tobias stares out at the people, and then pulls me toward backstage. There are a few grumbles as we walk away and the emcee thanks everyone for coming out tonight.

Music plays through the bar as Tobias leads me further backstage where we can have some privacy.

"Sydney, these past few weeks have killed me being away from you."

"Why did you leave?" I ask again, knowing that I've been dying a little inside each day since he's been gone too.

He shakes his head. "I couldn't hurt you."

I gaze into his eyes. "But you *did* hurt me. You hurt me so much."

He steps closer, like he wants to touch me but thinks better of it. "I'm so sorry. I was a fool. I was scared."

"Scared of me?"

He shakes his head. "No." He steps closer. "Sydney, Mark blackmailed me with videos and photos that would hurt you and your father's reputation. He said he'd release them to the public if I didn't come and work for him. I had to take that job, or risk hurting you." He fills me in on the details about our sex tape and how he needed to protect me. "I love you," he says, staring into my eyes.

I can't believe the words he's saying, but it sounds like something Mark would do. "Why didn't you tell me?"

Tobias steps even closer, erasing all the distance between us. "I couldn't risk the chance of him releasing the tapes."

"Why are you here now?"

He smiles. "Because I have a friend taking care of it all. Because I can't stay away from you for one minute more. Even if it means risking everything."

I think about everything he's saying to me. About a possible sex tape of us. "Do you think Mark could have been lying about a tape? Did you see it?"

Tobias stares at me. "No, I haven't seen it, but I think he has one. He's that big of a snake that I think he would have me followed."

"I think you're right." I grab both his hands. "Tobias, whatever happens we deal with it together."

He gives me a smile. "Agreed." He wraps his arms around me. "I love you, Sydney."

I fling my arms around his neck. "I love you too."

He visibly relaxes. "You don't know how happy I am to hear you say that."

"I feel the same way."

He leans in, capturing my lips with his and I know nothing will ever be the same. We'll always be together.

No matter what life throws at us, we've got this.

Epilogue

Sydney
Six Months Later

Do you know what's funny? Threats. Threats make the person doing the threatening appear like they hold all the cards. And the threatened one feels like they have nowhere to go. A lot of times, they're empty, as is the case here. Mark McManus never made good on his threats.

I bet he never had the video to begin with. Who knows? Perhaps, he's saving them so he can use them at the inopportune time. But it'll never matter.

Daddy's already accepted Tobias into the company with open arms. As for me, I'm writing songs for some of the top performing artists in the world. It's crazy to think about the exciting whirlwind of the past few months.

Once Daddy found out about Mark's blackmailing scheme, he exposed him and let's just say we'll never have to worry about Halo anymore.

"Where are you taking me?" I ask Tobias as he guides me

to his new Chevy truck. It's amazing how quickly a city boy can turn country when given the right motivation. Tobias says each day he spends in Harmony he's more and more at home. And I love that about him.

"You'll see." He starts the engine and pulls away.

A few miles down the road, he turns on the radio and a song I wrote blares through the speakers.

"It's surreal the masses can hear something I created," I tell him.

"I love your words," he says, reaching over to hold my hand. He lazily runs his fingers over mine and brings my hand to his lips. "I love everything about you, Sydney."

I gaze over at him. "I'm sure not about *everything*. Yet, I do make a better grilled cheese than you."

His laughter fills the cab of the truck. "No way"

"Yes, I do. Admit it."

He laughs harder. "Never." He turns down an isolated county road. "But maybe you can be the one who makes them for little Charlotte and Lucas."

"Who?" I ask him.

He drops my hand. "I…uh, nevermind."

I twist in my seat. "No, who are Charlotte and Lucas?"

A smile splits his face as he continues driving, peeking over at me quickly. "The names of our future children."

My chest warms. "You named our children?"

He doesn't answer right away, but then finally says, "Is that bad? We don't have to name them that. I mean, if you hate the names. If you have an ex named Lucas, I get it."

I love this man.

I laugh softly. "Never had an ex named Lucas." I pause before continuing, "I actually love the names." I can picture our life together, little Charlotte and Lucas running around, raising trouble.

"I'm glad." He focuses on the road.

"Where are we going?"

"You'll see," he says, shooting me a wicked grin.

After a few more minutes on the road, he pulls into a long driveway that leads to a magnificent two-story white farmhouse with about five acres of front yard alone. It has a wrap-around porch with a swing swaying in the wind. Off to the side of the house is a stable and paddock. "Are we here to see a man about a horse?"

Tobias cuts the engine. "Not exactly."

"Whose house is this?" I ask, as Tobias gets out of the truck.

He bounds around to my side of the truck and opens the door. "It's *our* house."

I stare into his blue eyes and then my eyes snap back to the house. "What?" I can't believe what I'm hearing.

I hop out and Tobias leads me up the front walkway, up the steps of the porch, and to the front door. He reaches into his pocket and produces a silver key. "I said, it's our house. That is, if you want to live here with me."

My eyes well with tears. We've been living together since the moment Tobias said he was sorry, but never in a place that we could call our own. It always felt like he was living at *my* place, not *our* place. "I love it."

He opens the door and drops to a knee. "Before we go inside, there's something I'll be needing to ask you."

Now, the tears are streaming down my cheeks. "Oh, god," I whisper.

He fishes a black box out of his pocket and opens it, showing off a round diamond ring. "I've loved you since the moment I first met you. Even if that wasn't the best moment in my life."

I laugh through my tears.

He continues, "I knew you were the one for me the moment I first saw you and every moment after that. I couldn't stop picturing a life with you, but nothing can compare to the real thing. I love my life. I love having you by my side every step of the way. Sydney Lancaster, will you marry me?"

"Yes," I say, frantically nodding.

He slides the large rock on my finger and stands. After a dizzying kiss, I'm lifted into his arms and carried across the threshold of our new home. He sets me down in the living area.

The house is empty, but I can already see the possibilities. The feature I love most is an enormous bay window, and I walk over to it, sitting on the red cushion.

"This is where I can write songs," I tell him.

"I plan on building a shelf right here for all the Grammy's you're going to win," he says, pointing to the wall next to the window. He points outside to the paddock area. "And Oreo will love it here."

I jump up, wrapping my arms around his neck. "It's perfect."

"You're perfect." Then he melds his body into mine, kissing me deeply. Before long, the slow-burning embers are a blazing wildfire. He sits on the window ledge and has me straddle his lap. "Let's christen this new home. Ride me like you own me."

I smile against his plush lips and grind against the hardness growing inside his jeans. "Happily."

He lowers his zipper, freeing his already hard length. The sun pouring in the window highlights his masculinity as he hikes up my dress and pushes my panties to the side. "I need in this wet pussy."

"It's yours, Tobias. Whenever you want it." I slide down his dick.

"Fuck," he says on a groan once he's completely inside me.

I rock against him. "You feel so good. So big." The way he fills me up so perfectly is heaven.

"That's right. Ride my cock, baby. This is all for you.

Every hard inch is yours." He slams inside me, gripping each ass cheek in his hands.

Our lips are mere centimeters apart as I breathe in his words. I keep riding him, loving his hardness deep inside me, knowing this is the man I want to one day call my husband.

"You feel so fucking good," he says. "Turn around." He stands me up, turning me around to sit reverse cowgirl style on his lap. I lean forward a bit as he grips my hair in his fist. "I'll never get enough of your hot pussy," he groans out. "You were made for me."

He keeps working my body like he owns it, and he does. He owns every part of me. Forever and ever. I could never leave this man. Not after finding out what even one day away from him feels like.

I ride his cock as he jerks up into me. "I'm close."

His fingers fly under my dress, finding the bundle of nerves and rubbing just right. I grip his thighs, leaning my head back as my body nears its release. "Yes, Tobias. I'm coming," I shout as he keeps working my clit, faster and faster.

"Don't stop coming all over me, baby." He growls as his body picks up speed. "Fuck, this pussy is mine."

"All yours," I whimper, squeezing my eyes shut, as my body builds toward another release. Stars line my vision, and a white-hot heat presses at the corners of my chest as my body explodes into something new. I've never had an orgasm like this in all my life.

It just keeps going.

"Fuck, I feel you. I feel your pussy tightening all around me. Can't hold on," he says in a pained voice. "Gonna come," he grunts out.

His hands reach around to fondle my breasts as he breathes into my hair. "I love you," he says against the shell of my ear as his body erupts and quakes. "I love you," he says on repeat as his body pulses through his orgasm.

"I love you, Tobias," I say, tilting my head so our lips can join in a kiss.

"I won't ever stop loving you," he tells me as he breaks the kiss.

And I never will either. This is ours. Our life we're building together. A life I've dreamed of one day having. Tobias is my everything.

My roommate who is now my soon-to-be husband.

Thank you for reading Hated By My Roommate.

Holiday Hideout

Chapter 1

Fender

"So, lay it on me. How many death threats today?"

"Around fifty-thousand," my assistant, Noreen, says on our will-this-nightmare-before-Christmas-ever-end conference call.

"Not horrible," I tell her. "Things are calming down."

"Well, that's only on Twitter." She pauses. "Combined across all social media platforms, you have more today than yesterday. They despise you most on TikTok."

I groan, throwing a pillow over my head.

"This will blow over soon." Noreen's reassuring voice continues to lilt from the phone, finding the bright side of my tarnished career, but I barely hear her. I barely hear anything anymore.

Except *her* songs. The woman who demonized our breakup to her millions of fanatics.

"This isn't my fault. People want to kill me because I want a happier life?"

Noreen sighs. "Fender, things will get better."

I shake my head. "I should just let the public do it. Let them have their way with me and…" I breathe out, "whatever."

"Save the dramatics for the big screen," my manager, Les, chimes in. "Pull yourself up by those massive biceps. On a positive note, the studio sent the script for the next *SharkQuake.*"

I groan again. "This will be the eighth movie for the franchise. It's time to say enough is enough. I mean, how they can't catch the killer shark by the eighth movie eludes me."

"Well, it's the baby of the original killer shark attacking everyone in this one," he says.

I sit up and toss the pillow across the room. "That's even worse."

"The script isn't half bad."

"So, it's only half good?"

"Ok, ok," Noreen cuts in. "Do you have everything you need in your cabin? I had someone stock beverages and food for your stint as a hermit. I can have whatever you want delivered. Christmas tree, perhaps?"

"No, I'm fine. I'm not celebrating the holidays this year." I glance out the floor-to-ceiling glass wall with nothing but the Alaskan woods to see. "Until this thing with Trinity blows over, I don't want any contact with the outside world."

"Well, you won't have to fret about that in Polar Bear, Alaska," Les says. "No one will find you there."

True. I'm in the foothills of the Mistletoe Mountains, and it's secluded.

"Not even Santa," Noreen adds, in a disappointed tone. "Are you sure you don't need anything else? It's a shame you have to hide away during the holidays until this nightmare ends."

"My cabin is nestled right outside of town," I tell her. "If I need anything, I can… ski to the store."

"You should have let me rent you a vehicle," Noreen mutters. "What if the holiday spirit strikes and you want to shop for gifts? Polar Bear looks like a Christmas Village, such a shame to—"

"I'll be fine," I cut her off. "I'm sure Santa wants to murder me too."

I semi-listen as Noreen and Les assure me things are not as dire as they seem. Easy for them to say. They aren't hiding out in Alaska for God knows how long. It's fine. I can grow a beard and become a recluse who whittles animals out of tree limbs.

"I'll send the script over," Les says.

I groan on the inside. "Fine." I end the call and toss the phone.

I'm thinking someone cursed this film series. If not for the *SharkQuake* movies, I would've never met Trinity on set and this death debacle would've never happened. When I dated her, she was a struggling actress and singer, working on an album, and wanted a deal more than anything. Well, she's got one now, worth millions of dollars.

I flip on the television, hoping to distract my mind from the Trinity trouble, and there she is staring back at me from the stage of Dancing With The Stars, singing the newest hit song she wrote about our breakup, while couples pirouette around her like figurines in a music box.

Her dark hair shines under the studio lights as she wails into the microphone.

I should've run away when you asked me out on a date.
Thought it was fate.

SHE ASKED *ME* OUT. The killer shark had just devoured her character, and when the scene wrapped, she strolled over covered in fake blood and suggested we get drinks at a nearby bar. I don't date co-workers, but figured why not.

*Life was perfect.
I put on my prettiest red dress.
But your success meant more than me, I guess.*

AS SHE CROONS, her slim frame shrinks between my narrowed lids. Um, it was absolutely not perfect. We were both struggling to make a name for ourselves in the brutal city of Hollywood. My success? Yeah, I thought I was heading somewhere big with the *SharkQuake* franchise, but it's a typical B-flick budget, and not enough to launch me into superstardom. She's the one who teased non-stop about doing something scandalous for her 'big break.'

Morbid curiosity keeps me listening as she belts out the chorus to cheers from the audience.

*Your pretty eyes hid all the lies.
Everything was alright until your shark bite…*

FINALLY, something true. I do have pretty eyes. Blue with a hint of green.

She warbles about me ripping out her heart in the middle of a restaurant, humiliating her for all to witness. The audience cheers while she nods her head to the beat of the song.

My god. None of this is true. Trinity and I were ok, but then small things turned me off. She became a diva. She fixated on fame and wanted to eat at celebrity spots. Pay paparazzi to take our photo. Shit I had no interest in doing with her. I wanted more. I wanted normal. So, I sat her down one evening—at her place, *not* a restaurant—and told her we were headed in the wrong direction.

We had a great talk. Or so I thought.

Little did I know, six months later, she'd release an album about our failed love story with me as the asshole who trampled on her heart and her, the tragic victim. Her album, "Ex, Y, Z… Now I See," was the number one download on iTunes within a week, and it thrust her into superstardom.

She's adored by the world.

And I'm the evil man who broke her heart.

She even has a Trinity Tribe now. I think they named her fan club 'Kill Fender Fallon.'

Needless to say, I tried to contact Trinity, tell her to call off her fans, but their hate for me is its own entity now.

She ends the lies coming out of her red lips with a coy smile and receives a standing ovation.

"Fucking great."

I turn off the TV and head into the kitchen. My frown reflects in the stainless-steel fridge when I open the door and grab a Heineken. I guzzle the cool beer while I ponder my predicament, propped against the granite topped island.

Am I in the wrong? I've asked myself this question a million times.

The internet says I'm a jerk, so it must be true.

"Fuck 'em," I grumble to myself, because I guess I should get used to talking to myself in solitude.

I want a woman to laugh at my jokes, not that I'm hilarious. I want a woman who makes me feel needed. I want a woman who gets me.

And Trinity wasn't that person for me.

I could have been selfish, kept dating her even though she deserves a man who's crazy about her. That wasn't me.

My phone pings with a message from my sister, Felicity, who always seems to have a psychic ability.

"You ok?"

"Oh, I'm great." I snap a picture of the snow-covered mountainous backdrop surrounding my rental property and send it over to her. "There's an actual chill room in my cabin."

It's a thing.

Similar to a foyer, but not. Alaskans call it an arctic entry. It's a modest room which serves as a place for the snow to melt before entering your home. Noreen said it keeps the interior of your house warmer.

Insanity.

"Brrr. I got frostbite from looking at all the snow. You hate cold weather."

"I hate murderous fans more."

"You can't hide forever."

I snicker at her naivete. "Watch me. I'll become one of those mysterious creatures that only leaves my tracks in the snow."

"Stop," she types back. "You're not living out the rest of your days as a yeti. It's more like you're taking a minute to breathe. To reset."

True. I need to figure out a plan for my life. When I first started acting, I thought I'd be this mega-action movie star, and everyone would love me. Ha.

At twenty-nine, I realize this might not even be what I want anymore. The Trinity backlash has helped me see how brutal it is in the public eye. People come at you with pitchforks just because they can, and I don't want to be murdered while I'm snug in my bed.

Felicity laments about my lack of Christmas spirit, and the

hairs on the nape of my neck rise when a crash sounds from somewhere in the house. My sister is back in California with her husband and three kids, so I know she's not standing in my cabin.

My survival instincts kick in, and I grab a knife from the drawer and slip out of the kitchen with it gripped in my hand. The cabin has an open floor plan, and I see the living room is clear, so I strain my ears to find the thumping noise I hear. In stealth mode, I cross through the living area to peek into the arctic room. The firewood previously stacked neatly in the corner now litters the wood floor like matchsticks.

A hunched over woman, bundled in a puffy pink coat with a matching hat covering her dark hair, shrieks when I leap in front of her.

"Penguin piss," she shouts, jumping about twenty feet off the floor.

"What the hell are you doing in here?" I ask.

"Um, hi," she says, giving me a blank stare. "What are you doing here?"

My gaze flits across the crimson staining her cheeks and drops to her pouty lips when she pulls the bottom one in with pearly whites and flickers blue eyes to the weapon in my hand.

"Answer the question," I say.

"You and your steak knife need to move aside. I have a job to do."

She's a ballsy little thing, but it's possible she's packing heat inside that marshmallow of a coat.

"Do you have a gun on you?"

"No."

As I've learned from Trinity, a pretty face doesn't make you a truth-teller.

"Take it off." I point the knife at her jacket. "Slowly."

She slides the metal zipper down with pink nails and shrugs it off with a wiggle of her shoulders.

"Fuck," I mutter. And not because of the spectacular breasts straining beneath her purple t-shirt. It's the words scrawled across those beauties that have my mind reeling—Kill Fender Fallon.

She's one of them.

Chapter 2

Rachel

Fender Fallon looks sexier in person, if that's possible. No wonder Trinity is heartbroken.

Even though he's scowling at me like an angry maniac, I can still admire his beauty. The scowl on his handsome face only emphasizes the rugged angles carved above a strong jaw covered in dark scruff. He's always clean-shaven on screen, but this new facial hair works fabulously on his tall frame. It reeks of a sexy mountain man.

I'd like to see him whip out his big axe.

I stare into his mesmerizing eyes and remind myself to breathe.

No. Stop fangirling. Who cares if he's the star of my absolute favorite movie franchise of all time. Not me. I certainly don't care that he stands there looking every bit as scrumptious as he does on screen. And I *really* don't care his eyes are twinkling sapphires. Because that would mean I don't care he's holding a knife, and that would mean I'm a loon.

"Sorry about the wood," I say. "I bumped into it and knocked it over."

"Are you sorry about the wood or sorry I caught you?"

"I didn't know you were here—"

"I'm sorry," he interrupts. "Did I screw up your attempt to murder me?"

"Excuse me?" I laugh. "I'm not here to murder you, Mr. Fallon. I'm sure there're many people out there who'd love to do that, but I'm not one of them."

His brow lifts. "Ah, so you know me. What do you want? An autograph?"

"An autograph? Unless it's on the check you're paying me with, then I don't have any use for that."

"Pay you?"

"Yes, we agreed on twenty dollars an hour."

He crosses his arms over his chest. "Who are you?"

"I'm your maid. Rachel Shepherd." I reach into the pocket of my jeans to show him the key I used to enter, but he lunges at me, twirling me around, enveloping me in a bear hug.

"Not so fast," he growls against my ear.

"What are you doing?" I squeal.

"There are a ton of unstable people looking to find me and get revenge."

"You might be the unstable one," I say and then apologize because it's probably not good to criticize in this situation. "Sorry for saying that. Can we start over at the part before you wrapped around me tighter than garland?"

"You're wearing a shirt that says Kill Fender Fallon, so I want to make sure you're not carrying a weapon on you."

It might make things worse if I say I wore this shirt as solidarity with Trinity against heartbreakers everywhere. We've established it was a poor decision.

"Look, I'm here to clean your cabin. I should've been here this morning, but life got in the way, so I'm late. My boss said you would arrive tomorrow, so I didn't expect you'd be here. And not to be rude, but I don't have time for this. If I wanted to hurt you, there's an axe in the corner and I know how to use it. But I am not, nor have I ever been, a *murderer*." I struggle against his firm hold, contacting his groin, and he drops his arms, stepping away.

He runs a hand through his dark hair, leaving it in disarray. "I don't need a maid."

My shoulders slump because I need this money for Christmas. "It's in your rental agreement I clean twice a week, so you might as well let me do the work."

He opens his mouth to speak, but I can't let him say no so I ramble on about cleanliness being next to godliness and he won't even know I'm here.

"I'll be as quiet as a mouse."

He drops his arms from his chest and shows an even row of white teeth.

Whoa.

I've never felt dazzled by a smile until now.

"I'm going to take your silence as a yes. I'll start in the kitchen." I jab a thumb over my shoulder. "If you need anything, let me know."

He nods, not giving me a verbal response.

That's fine. Dad says it's good manners to say nice things. If you have nothing nice to say, keep your mouth shut. Perhaps that's why Fender remains silent as his eyes clock me going into the kitchen. It's unnerving having him watch me as if I'm prey.

I set my bucket of cleaning supplies on the curved island, assessing the large area with my eyes. The granite countertops are clear of messy debris, and the stainless sink holds two dishes. Well, at least he isn't a complete slob. The place is immaculate, and I wonder if he's cooked here at all. Doesn't matter what he's doing in his private time. I need this job more than water, so I'll play nice with the statue of a man standing in front of the fireplace and clean things that are already clean.

I take out my sponge and the expensive cleaner my boss, April, likes us to use and get to work, wiping the stove. When I glance over my shoulder, Fender is *still* staring.

"Am I doing it the wrong way?" Who knows, people in California may clean with rose petals, or something else just as fancy.

Fender shakes his gorgeous head and his eyes dart away. "No, you're fine. I'll be outside."

He stalks across the living room, past me, and out the patio doors. A brief laugh escapes my lips. Of the few things I know about California, one of them is endless sunny and warm weather.

Well, here in Alaska, it is not either of those things. I'm sure Fender will discover that after being outside for two minutes.

Once the stainless appliances sparkle, I move onto sweeping the tile floor. It's too quiet, so I grab my iPhone and put on my favorite playlist.

As I sweep behind the breakfast table, I glance out the patio doors. Fender went outside five minutes ago, with no coat, mind you, and he's still out there. As I move to the sink to wash the plates, I worry he froze to death.

Nah. I'm sure he gained survival skills from those action scenes in his movies.

Confession: I know those scenes by heart.

I'm a shark movie junkie. Cheesy shark movies are even better. Corny shark horror movies are the best. If I had to rank them, *SharkQuake* is my favorite shark movie of all time. Actually the whole series is top of the list.

Second, *SharkZilla*. Fabulous ending.

Third, *When Sharks Dream*. This is kind of a *Nightmare on Elm Street* meets *Shark Week*. Fun times.

Fourth, *Sharks On A Plane*. Yes, you guessed it. It's so ridiculous that it's hilarious.

Last, is a little low budget number. *Shark Master*. I think I'm one of the few people in the world who has seen it.

My younger sister, Joanie, and I discovered our mutual love for cheesy shark movies when *Sharknado* came out. She's a senior in high school, so she doesn't enjoy hanging out with me too much these days, but we've drooled over Fender Fallon many times. Since he split with Trinity, not so much anymore.

I'm not the type to dwell on the lives of famous Hollywood actors or singers, but sad to say, I was rooting for them. Probably because Fender was perfect to me in every way.

What's not perfect is my luck.

When Fender slams the patio door shut, my favorite Trinity song pipes into the kitchen.

"It's fucking freezing outside."

If I ignore the tune, hopefully, he won't notice. "It's Alaska."

He gives his perfectly sculpted arms a brisk rub. "Yeah, but I never imagined it would be so…" He stops talking and stares at me.

I stop scrubbing the dishes. "What?"

He folds his arms. "You're going to make me say it?"

The lyrics to Trinity's song, 'You no-good son-of-a-bitch,' waft through the air, and I reach for my phone, hands all sorts of sudsy, to turn the music off. "Sorry. It was on my playlist," I say.

His sapphire eyes look defeated. Without a word, he crosses the kitchen floor, heading into the living room and disappearing down a hallway. A door slams shut.

Why wasn't I more careful about what music I picked? In my defense, it's my cleaning playlist, and I wasn't intentionally trying to be insensitive. Nor is it my fault he broke her heart. Sometimes you have to live with the consequences of your actions.

Once I finish in the kitchen, I head into the living area, searching for messes. The cabin is spotless, but I dust the bookshelves and polish the oak coffee table, taking my time, dragging it out to get in my hours.

It's a beautiful place, full of character. Exposed logs topped by cathedral ceilings and plush rugs beneath plump leather furniture make me wish I could just sit and stare at the stone fireplace, sipping hot chocolate. But I can't, so I head down the hallway. On the left must be the bathroom because the hum of a shower cuts off as I pass.

I hustle toward the master bedroom.

Same thing in here, spotless. The rustic king-size bed is unmade, but there are no clothes strewn around the room. I guess it's surprising to me he's tidy, because one of Trinity's lyrics says she picked up her dignity instead of the mess he always left everywhere. Hm. Maybe he's turned over a new leaf.

An acoustic guitar rests in the corner, and I walk over to it, trailing a finger along the neck, wondering if he plays. With a name like Fender, he must.

Whether he's musically inclined isn't my business, so I pull back the red and black buffalo check comforter to strip the sheets and throw them in the laundry. As I bundle them up, I catch a whiff of cologne. It smells like sunshine and pine... so good. Before I can stop myself, I bring them to my nose and inhale the intoxicating scent like a weirdo stalker.

Bad idea.

Because a deep voice says, "Are you sniffing my sheets?"

Chapter 3

Fender

"I, uhm…" She frantically tugs at the pillowcase, not answering my question. "I'm just going to throw these into the laundry. They could use freshening."

I smirk. She's not fooling me.

And I know she knows I know she's caught.

I'm still miffed over the Trinity song, so when her sparkling blue eyes flit to my chest, I decide to give a little payback.

Hands on hips, I flex my pectorals. "Ok, I'm going to get dressed."

She doesn't move, eyes homed in on my chest.

"Ok, that's a good idea." Her gaze drops to the white towel low on my hips.

She licks her pink lips, and damn, if I don't mirror her action. Unexpected lust courses through me, and I try to ignore it by clearing my throat.

"I'm going to get dressed… alone," I say.

Her eyes reach mine after taking a slow exploration up the length of my stomach and chest. Finally, she nods. "Yes, I'm outta here." She rushes past me, out of the room.

I'd say I won that round. Right? It's not uncommon for women to swoon over my body. I typically spend more hours in the gym than I do on set filming. I'm not sure the pain and gain were worth it, because she did something to my heart. It flipped, or stopped, or something catastrophic when she stared at me with those big baby blues.

A woman has never affected me like her. I wish I could say I had this pulse racing phenomenon with Trinity, but I didn't. Maybe if I did, we'd still be together, and I wouldn't be trending on Twitter. Probably not, because, well, she's a liar.

For all I know, Rachel is too. It's not like it matters, though. She may be beautiful, but my stay here is temporary. I do not need to break another heart while I'm here in Alaska, so it's best I don't have these unwanted heart flips when she's around. Because one thing I've realized about being in Hollywood, it's that the paparazzi love when you mess up, but when you mess up twice… they go ballistic.

I won't be messing up.

Ever.

"DO you think you can go to the store for me?" I ask Rachel before she leaves.

She cleaned the house in record time after our *moment* in the bedroom. Pretty sure she just freshened the sheets in the dryer.

"If you make me a list, I can bring the stuff by next time I come to clean."

I cross my arms over my favorite *Jaws* t-shirt. "When will that be?" I'd go myself, but who knows what type of publicity I could run into while I'm shopping. Let's just say if the paparazzi catches wind I'm hiding out here in Alaska, my life will be over. This small town will turn into a breeding ground for men with cameras. I'm sure the locals would despise me more with the paparazzi lurking around their winter village, popping out of the tinsel and Christmas trees to snap photos of yours truly.

"The contract is for me to clean twice a week." She slides on her gloves. "April said the owner of your cabin specified an extra day in the housekeeping contract. April's my boss. Gracious lady. Very good to her employees."

I think it's cute how Rachel rambles. I wonder secretly if I make her nervous. Her defiant little nose scrunches up the longer I stare at her. I like staring at her.

"That won't do," I tell her. And it won't. I need things right now. Like a toothbrush. When I left LA, I was in no mood to pack, and I realize that was stupid of me to leave without grabbing the essentials.

She shrugs. "Well, I guess I could go after…" She stops talking when I step closer.

"Can we just go together now?"

"Together? As in you and me?"

I nod. "That's what together means."

"Don't you Hollywood types usually have people to shop for you?"

"I do my own shopping. I'm a B-list, wait, a D-list celebrity."

She scoffs. "That's not true."

"No one knew who I was before Trinity made me famous. Or should I say infamous?"

She looks very put out by my statement, as if I've offended her, snapping up her coat and shoving her arms in it. "I knew who you were before you ever started dating Trinity."

She did? "Really?"

"I'm a huge fan of *SharkQuake*."

I raise a brow. "You are?" I didn't know *SharkQuake* had

any *huge* fans. I didn't realize we had any fans at all, if I'm being honest."

"Yes, my little sister, Joanie, and I watch all the movies. I have to say out of all the ridiculous shark movies, yours is the best."

"Ridiculous?"

She blinks. "Well, um, yes. I don't mean any disrespect to you. You're a great actor. But you must know the plot is—"

"Ridiculous?"

"Yeah, but that's what makes them amazing. I mean, sharks coming up from a crack in the earth during an earthquake? Shark movies have a cult following."

I'm flabbergasted by her enthusiasm. I knew *SharkQuake* was a pile of shit, but I didn't think a *huge* fan would say this. Let's be real here. Rachel and Joanie are probably our *only* fans.

She laughs, and it's the sweetest sound, soft yet sensual. "There's a group on Facebook."

"A group? For what?"

"It's a cult film appreciation group for people who love low-budget shark movies. We all agree, *SharkQuake* is the best."

"In that case, I'm sure they'd tell you to take me to the store."

Her lips twist with hesitation and she's silent for a few seconds before she finally speaks. "What would Trinity say?"

"Doesn't matter. We're no longer together."

Trinity shouldn't factor into anything I do with another woman. I can be around another woman all I want, right?

"I mean, would she be ok with me helping the no-good son-of-a-bitch?"

"I think she would be ok with it." I give Rachel my best Hollywood smile. The one I'd like to think landed me the role of Robbie in *SharkQuake*.

"We can go to the store outside of town. That way no one should spot you."

"Thank you." I snag my jacket and gloves before she can change her mind. "Let's go."

I lock the door behind us, and we make our way to her Jeep parked in the driveway. It's colder than the North Pole, and I secretly wonder if we'll run into Santa Claus out here.

She starts the engine once we're huddled inside and turns the heat on high.

"How can anyone live here?" I ask.

She shrugs. "It's not as bad as you think. Besides, the summers are gorgeous."

"How long is summer here? A month?"

She laughs as she backs out of the driveway. "About three weeks."

"I thought so. What do people here do for fun?"

"You don't want to know." She cuts her eyes to me, then back to the road.

Now I'm intrigued. "Of course, I do."

"Many people, not me, but a considerable amount of people spend the winters, well…" Her cheeks turn pink, and I wonder what on earth she's going to say.

"They do what?"

"You know…" She trails off, gripping the steering wheel, and won't look at me.

"No, I don't." But I have an idea and now I want to hear her say it. "Tell me."

What she says is the last thing I expect, "Shove the clown in the cannon."

Chapter 4

Rachel

I can't believe I just said that out loud. Yes, it's a euphemism for sex. I'm twenty-six, not a child, but I can't bring myself to say it in front of him. Fender doesn't say a word, and he's back to laser-focusing his gaze on me.

The silence is deafening as I try to drive in a straight line down the narrow lane toward town. I flip on the music to drown out the silence, but a Trinity song blares into the cab of my Jeep.

Our hands brush as we both reach for the radio.

Even though my hand is tingling from the brief contact, I win the race to the dial and click it off quickly. "Sorry about that."

He twists a bit in his seat to face me. "So, um, you go to the circus a lot?"

"No," I answer. "How do I say this delicately? Slay the Vadragon… Release the Kraken."

"People have sex all winter long? Is that what you're trying to say?"

I'm mortified. "Yes." I sneak a peek at him. "Some people do."

It's a long-standing joke about people screwing all winter long to stay warm, and with the amount of babies born the next year, I believe there's validity to the notion people do the horizontal hula continuously.

Not me, though.

I can't remember the last time I had sex. I remember it wasn't good, though. It's fine. Polar Bear is a small town, and there's a two-to-one ratio of men to women, so it's not like I couldn't have my stocking stuffed if I wanted to ride someone's pole. It's more the lack of time left in my life between working and taking care of my dad and sister, which is most likely why April and Joanie are my only friends.

"What about you?" Fender asks.

My cheeks flame like lava, and I turn down the heat in the Jeep before I incinerate. "No, like I said, not me."

"That's a *damn* shame."

I like the way he drew out the word damn, like he could think of all the ways to bend me over and give me the sex I so desperately lack.

"We also plunge," I blurt out to change the subject.

"What's that? Some sexual position I don't know about?" He chuckles, like it's ludicrous there could be a sex position he hasn't tried.

I blush *again*. "No, everyone jumps into the icy waters of a popular lake around here."

His brow crinkles. "Why would people do that?"

I sneak another glance at Fender as I drive. If I weren't driving, I could stare at this man all day. "Because."

He laughs, and this time, it's a hearty laugh. Not the one from his movies that's a gruff rumble. Like a genuine laugh. The sound makes my insides turn molten.

"That's not an explanation," he says. "There has to be a reason people jump into a freezing lake."

I shrug. "It's for charity."

"Do you plunge?"

I smile and tell him a secret. "This will be my first year."

I may dip one toe in and chicken out, but I'm going to at least try it.

"Why are you doing it? You don't look like an adrenaline junkie to me."

"I'm not an adrenaline junkie."

"Then why do it?"

I make a right into the parking lot of the General Store, located just outside the city limits of Polar Bear, and park the car, not shutting it off just yet.

"My sister says I'm not daring enough."

He studies me for a moment. "And you think taking an ice bath will make you more daring?"

I twist in my seat to face him. "I'm hoping. Joanie has been saying for years I stick to myself, work too hard, and never make friends. So, this year, I plan on taking the plunge and diving headfirst into the frigid water with hundreds of other people."

He breathes in and out, tilting his head a bit, before saying, "I can think of a few ways to make you more daring."

I blink back the vision of me riding Fender like a cowgirl. "How?"

"I have time on my hands." He smiles his million-dollar smile. "I can dare you to do outrageous things. It'll be fun."

Oh, man, I see why Trinity fell so hard for this man.

"No thanks. I'll just plunge instead." I exit my vehicle and rush inside the General Store without waiting on him.

Fender follows me inside, placing a gentle hand on my bicep. "What have you got to lose?"

His touch causes a shiver to race through my body, and I

spin around to face his intense eyes. "Well, I should be able to dare you to do things too."

He steps back, dropping his hand. "What kind of things?"

I shrug. "Oh, I don't know. Daring things."

He laughs. "I don't need to be more daring, remember? We're working on you."

I throw his line back in his face. "What have you got to lose?"

He gazes at me. "Nothing. I just need all this paparazzi madness to go away so I can get back home."

"Then it's settled." I remove my glove and stick out my hand.

"What are you doing?"

"You're supposed to shake it, duh."

"Did you just duh me?" He chuckles.

"It's customary to shake after making a deal."

He removes the glove from his right hand and wraps his fingers around mine. His warmth envelops me in a way I shouldn't enjoy, but I do. "We have a deal."

I don't want to break the contact, but I know it's for the best, so I drop his hand and face the aisles stocked with groceries and necessities.

"Ready to shop?" I ask.

Fender does a quick sweep through the store, grabbing the essentials one may need if they packed nothing before leaving their house. Toothpaste, toothbrush, deodorant, hairbrush. It makes me wonder if he left California in a rush.

I watch as he takes his things to the register. He laughs about something with Earl behind the counter, and I smile.

"Earl, charge him extra," I joke, stepping up to the counter.

"I should get a discount for hanging out with this one." Fender jabs a thumb in my direction.

I've known Earl since I was a little girl, and there's no way he'd ever take Fender's side in anything.

"She's a heartbreaker, that one." Earl chuckles. "You should watch out."

My mouth drops. "Earl, how could you say such a thing? I've never broken a heart in my life."

Fender winks, and warmth floods my veins. "Good to know, Earl."

"If anyone breaks hearts around here, it's him." I point a finger at Fender.

Fender drops his head, grabbing the bags from the counter. "Thanks, Earl."

He walks away from me, and I wish I could have stopped myself from sticking my foot in my mouth, figuratively.

THE CAR RIDE is silent as I drive Fender back to the cabin he's renting from Mr. Richter.

"I'm sorry for what I said back there," I say when I can no longer suffer in silence a second longer. "I didn't mean to be insensitive."

He shrugs. "It's cool. One day Trinity will see the truth."

I would love to know the full story, but I won't ask him.

"Well, if you'd like to dare me to keep my mouth shut…" I don't finish my sentence because I wonder if I could ever keep my mouth shut for any period of time. I don't talk a great deal, but when I do, my mouth runs away with random thoughts.

He laughs. "Now why would I do that?"

"I like to ramble, I guess."

"I don't mind your rambles."

I blush because that means he noticed them. "Thank you."

"What are you doing for dinner? It's getting late, so you must be starving."

"I don't know. Nothing planned." On cue, my stomach growls at the mention of food.

Fender grins. "Let me repay you for the trip to the store by cooking for you."

"You can cook?"

"Yes, does that surprise you?"

I guess it does since Trinity sang about being his personal chef, but I won't tell him that and fib. "No, not at all."

"I worked in a kitchen before I became a movie star."

"That's so fascinating." I blink. "Your kitchen didn't even look like you had eaten in it."

"I can clean up after myself too."

I smile. "I guess you're right. Sorry, I just assumed since you're a famous movie star and all…" I don't finish my thought because Daddy says not to judge people. And I judged Fender before I even got to know him.

Not that I know him now.

"Your brain must be busy at work."

I snap back to reality. "Why do you say that?"

He points out the windshield. "You've slowed down to fifteen miles an hour, and you're veering off the road."

"Sorry. Dad says it's not nice to judge people, and I guess I judged you a little."

"I don't mind." He leans back in his seat as I step on the gas pedal. "Most people judge me. That's why I get all the death threats."

Death threats?

Chapter 5

Fender

It's cute the way Rachel stares at me while she drives. She peeks over at me beneath her lashes, every so often, the sparkle of her blue eyes competing with the light of the stars.

Whoa. Where did that come from? Alaska has frozen my brain. Have I mentioned how weird Alaska is? I haven't seen the sun since I got here.

"So, you get death threats?" she asks as soon as she's pulled into my driveway and turned off the engine.

"Yes, lots." I step out of her Jeep into the frigid air.

"Wait," she says, chasing after me. "Real people want to kill you?"

"Does that seem so hard to believe?"

She tilts her head at me. "But why would anyone hate you enough to end your life?"

Her innocence is a major turn on. "Trinity. I broke her heart, remember?"

"That's no reason to kill you."

"Look at your shirt." I shrug, trying my best to get the key into the lock with these gigantic gloves making it impossible to accomplish. "It's not going in."

"That's what she said," Rachel murmurs, making me laugh and I drop the key.

I stoop to pick it up at the same time as Rachel, and our heads collide into each other.

"Ow," she calls out, wobbling.

"I'm sorry. Let me look at your head." We move inside the cabin. "I've got ice in the freezer." I stride toward the kitchen, and she follows. "Or we've got pounds and pounds of snow outside."

Rachel smiles up at me, holding her hand on her forehead. "I'm sure it's fine."

"Come here."

She stops a few feet in front of me, dropping her hand, her big blue eyes gazing at me like I'm the Big Bad Wolf who might eat her. Yum. It takes all my willpower to not look at her pussy now that I'm thinking of my head between her thighs, feasting on her.

"Come here," I repeat, but my voice has dropped an octave or two.

She removes her coat and gloves and places them on a stool at the island. It's a real pain having to remove layers every time you come inside, but I shuck mine off too.

"This isn't necessary," she says, but steps closer to me.

Gently, I brush back her silky hair and inspect her forehead, looking for a bump. There isn't one, but I take my time, breathing in her scent.

She smells fresh and sweet, like a Christmas tree decorated with sugar cookies.

"I don't see a bump," I rasp out, feeling intoxicated by her.

It's got to be the Mistletoe Mountains making me want to taste her lips. I knew I should've nixed the cabin and hid out in a van. She glances up at me, and I remind myself why I can't bend down and plant my lips on hers.

I can't start anything with her because I'm leaving to film a movie after the holidays. Bad timing. Either way, I step away from her like she's lava, threatening to melt all the well-constructed walls around my heart.

"Dinner?" I hustle toward the fridge.

"Right, what are you going to cook?" She sits on a barstool, her elbows resting on the counter in front of her.

"Halibut."

"Are you cooking it just for the halibut?" She laughs at her corny joke. "Get it? Just for the hell of it. Halibut, err nevermind."

I crack a smile. "Yeah, I get it." This woman is adorable.

Snow falls outside the window behind her, and I stare at the serene scene for a moment.

Rachel's eyes follow mine to see what's caught my attention. "Never seen snow before?" she asks in a soft voice.

"Once, when I was little."

She stands, moving from the kitchen to the bay window in the living room, peering out at the puffy snowflakes. "It's so peaceful when it falls."

"You'll be safe driving home in this, right?"

She turns to face me, a wry smile on her face. "I've lived in this town all my life. I'm safe to drive in anything."

I turn my attention to preparing dinner, because a big part of me wants to hear every detail of her life, and that's crossing major boundaries I've set for myself. Cooking for her doesn't count. This dinner is just a repayment for her taking me to the store. That's all. It's not a wrap-the-beautiful-woman-in-your-arms-and-kiss-her-madly-because-the-Mistletoe-Mountains-have-possessed-you kind of thing.

I snag the fish from the fridge, plopping the paper wrapped halibut on the counter, thankful my assistant had the house stocked with food. While I gather the ingredients,

Rachel makes herself at home, picking up my guitar and strumming the strings.

"Do you play the guitar?" she asks.

I chop an onion, adding it to the mango salsa I'm preparing. "I do. I was actually the one who taught Trinity how to play." And she backstabbed me, so that's a regret.

"Ah," Rachel says and turns back to the bookshelf to browse the collection of reading material stocked by the owner of the cabin. "Do you like to read?" she asks, turning around to face the kitchen.

As she flows through the house, I watch her. Even though I shouldn't. I can't help it if I'm being honest. She has a glow about her.

"A little. Mainly scripts."

"Do you read a lot of scripts?"

I chuckle low. "Actually, I don't." I sigh. "For a celebrity fighting to make it big, the parts are few and far between in Hollywood. With the contract for the shark movies, and how badly they bombed, no one's knocking down my agent's door to book me."

"Well, they should be. You're an amazing actor."

I crack a smile. "Thanks. What about you?"

"What about me?"

"Is cleaning houses your dream?"

She blinks up at me as I bring a pot of water to boil for the broccoli. She crosses the living room and takes the small step that leads into the kitchen. "No, it's not."

"What are you passionate about? Besides cheesy shark movies." I still can't believe there's a group on Facebook about shark movies.

"One day, I might tell you." She stares into the bowl of salsa and sniffs. "Smells good."

"How am I supposed to dare you to do things if I don't know what you're passionate about?"

She wags a finger at me. "Oh no, mister. You can't lay that on me."

I laugh. "Ok, fine." Can I dare her to kiss me? Why is it the only dare I can think of?

"It all looks so good."

"I've got a dare for you," I say, gaining her attention.

She swallows. "Ok, what is it?"

"I dare you to tell me what you're passionate about."

She laughs. "That's not fair."

I move closer, wondering if I can smell the fresh scent of her again that I'm secretly becoming addicted to. "Tell me," I say in a husky voice.

"Why?" Her blue eyes beam up at me.

"There's a chance I can fuel your passion. Bring it to life in a new way."

We're so fucking close.

"Maybe you can."

I lean in, ready to capture her lips when the timer dings for the broccoli. Fucking broccoli.

I get to work on the rest of dinner while Rachel asks if she can help. I put her to work making a salad, so I don't do something stupid like dare her to kiss me, even though it's all I can think about while I cook.

Once dinner is on the table, we sit down to eat.

"Taking pictures," she says.

"Excuse me?"

"I'm passionate about photography."

I lean back in my seat, seeing her with fresh eyes. "What do you like taking pictures of most?"

"Alaska is so beautiful. I just want everyone to appreciate it."

"So, scenery and landscapes?"

"And sometimes people."

Over dinner we talk non-stop. She laughs at a few of my jokes, and tells me she lives at home, helping raise her younger sister. She tells me stories about her childhood. About what it was like growing up here in Alaska. How she worries her father will never find a woman to replace the mother she lost so long ago. I tell her insider details about filming *SharkQuake*, and she stares at me like she can't get enough. It's never been this easy to talk about nothing and everything with someone, and I wonder if she can feel this thing between us. This growing entity I won't be able to ignore for very much longer.

I need to make sure Rachel never stays for dinner again.

Chapter 6

Rachel

"So, is he as gorgeous in person as he is in my dreams?" Joanie asks while I prepare dinner the following week.

"He's better."

I remove the roast beef from the oven and think back to Fender in nothing but a white towel hanging low on his hips. I'm so proud I didn't do something rash like yank it off and run with it. Believe me, I wanted to tear that towel off and see what he had hidden beneath the plush material.

Part of me felt these intense moments when we were alone together at his house having dinner. Am I wrong?

I must be.

He's leaving soon.

"I have to meet him." Joanie stands right in front of me, so I can't ignore her. "Take me to work with you."

I stop piddling around the kitchen. "Absolutely not."

"I'll just go in your place. He won't even notice," she says.

Joanie and I look practically identical, except she has hazel eyes and I have blue. Her hair is a smidge lighter than mine, but other than that, we're nearly the same. Except she's boisterous, and I'm… I wouldn't say I'm boring, but I'm not as social as my sister.

I also have tact, something my sister lacks. It's the main reason I won't let her anywhere near Fender.

"No," I snap back.

"Why can't I meet him? Are you afraid I'll tell him how you used to write the name Rachel Fallon on all your notebooks in college?"

"You wouldn't dare."

"Let me meet him."

I park a hand on my hip. "I can't take you to work with me. How would that look? Hello, Mr. Fallon, I brought my kid sister along to ogle you all day."

"I will *not* ogle."

I give her a stern stare.

"Ok, only a bit of ogling, and light stalking."

"No way." I swipe the bowl of green beans we're having for dinner from the counter and walk out of the kitchen to set them on the table.

It's been one week since I had dinner with Fender. A part of me wishes he would cook for me again. Ok, all parts of me wish I were back at his place. Ogling.

"Meet who?" my father asks.

"No one," I say as quickly as possible.

"Fender Fallon," Joanie says louder and quicker.

"The guy you girls like from that awful shark movie?"

I drop my mouth, same as my sister, and together we say, "It is *not* awful."

My father laughs, the crow's feet at the corner of his eyes deepening. "Is that who's shacked away up in Richter's cabin?"

I nod.

"Yes," Joanie whines. "And Rachel won't let me meet

him."

"It's not my place. April told me to be very hush-hush about who was staying there. I shouldn't have even told you."

My father carves the sirloin roast and slides several pieces on Joanie's plate. "Rachel's right. You can't just invade someone's privacy."

Joanie huffs, piling roasted potatoes on her plate. "Need any help at work?" she asks, trying another approach.

I laugh. "I promise if Fender is up for meeting people, you'll be the first to know."

Joanie pouts, slumping in her chair. "What's he like? Is he a no-good son-of-a-bitch like Trinity says he is?"

"Language." Dad motions with his knife for my plate, and I hold it up for a few pieces of roast while I defend Fender to Joanie. "Actually, he's nothing like that at all. He's very down-to-earth." He's also sexy, amazing, and gorgeous. But I won't tell her any of that. Sometimes with sisters, you don't need to say anything.

"You're crushing on him, aren't you?"

"I'm not." My cheeks turn fire-engine red. "I'm really not." I don't know who I'm trying to convince, her or me. "Dad, tell her I'm not."

Our father chimes in, taking his seat at the head of the table. "It's ok to be a little star-struck when you meet someone you've watched in movies. Just know he's a different breed than us."

"What do you mean, Dad?" Joanie asks with a mouth full of food.

"People from Hollywood, who live that extravagant lifestyle, rarely know how to treat others very well."

I think about my father's words. I also think of Fender saying he did his own shopping in Hollywood, and how people didn't know who he was until Trinity made him famous. Or I should say infamous.

"It must suck for him," I mumble between bites.

"Why do you say that?" our father asks.

"Well, nobody knew him, and now he's famous for being a heartbreaker. Famous for crushing the very essence of Trinity."

"I think Trinity's a bitch," Joanie says.

"Joanie, that language isn't necessary," our father chides.

"Well, it's true. She cries about how he broke her heart. Maybe he just didn't love her. Should he have stayed because if not, she'd air all their personal laundry to the world? It's pathetic blackmail. Her songs aren't even that good."

"I like her songs," I whisper.

I do, they're catchy. But they're wrong in a way.

Joanie's right. She shouldn't have aired their personal lives to the mainstream. And so far, Fender seems nothing like the guy in her songs.

"She couldn't think of anything better to write? I bet that will be her only hit album. No one's gonna care about her singing about other things. Will she have to sing about exes forever? It will scare guys to date her."

Dad and I laugh at Joanie's words.

"I think you may be right," my father says. "Tonight, after dinner I have to go out for a while."

"Where are you going?" Joanie asks.

He shifts in his seat. "Uh, I just have to help Roger with something in his garage. He's working on another woodworking project and needs help to mount the thing." His eyes bounce between Joanie and me.

"Ok, I'll clean up dinner."

He smiles. "Thank you, Rachel."

I shrug. "No problem." Honestly, I need to keep myself busy, so I won't think about the man in Richter's cabin.

I can't stop obsessing about the way he looked in that towel. For once in my life, I'm looking forward to going to work.

ON THURSDAY, I'm out of the house before Joanie can beg for the umpteenth time to tag along. I want to decorate Fender's house before he has the chance to change his mind. He has no clue I've brought a few holiday decorations to jolly up the place.

Before I leave, I grab my camera, gingerly placing it in its case. After work, I plan to head up to Reindeer Glacier and take cool pics of the landscape. The sun will be kissing the horizon today, and I want to capture the rays reflecting off the ice.

If I can get it just right, it should look like a magical wonderland.

I head off to Fender's and when I spot him on the porch, I almost want to snap a photo of him. He looks so peaceful, staring at the landscape, drinking from a mug with a blanket around his body.

I smile at him when I step out of my Jeep. "I have a surprise."

He stands and walks toward me, wrapping the blanket tighter around him. "I didn't think you were stopping by today."

I pop open the back of my Jeep and grab the first box of twinkling lights. "Surprise."

"What's this?" Fender asks, peeking over my shoulder.

"I figured I'd deck your halls."

Fender cracks a grin. "You know where I come from that has a different meaning than what you probably mean."

I nearly drop the box of decorations, but Fender grabs it from my hands, balancing the cup of coffee with the blanket very nicely. "I meant I could give you a little Christmas cheer."

Fender only smiles wider. "Again with the innuendoes."

I grab another box, rolling my eyes. "You know what I mean. I'm going to decorate your cabin for Christmas."

"Absolutely not."

"You sound like Ebenezer Scrooge."

He heads to the cabin to bring in my box of lights. "Bah humbug," he says with a laugh.

Once we get all the contents of my vehicle unloaded, which Fender said looked like enough stuff to decorate the North Pole, I stare up at him. "I'll make sure it's very festive."

He rubs the back of his neck. "That's what I'm afraid of." He sets his coffee down, and tosses the blanket onto the couch. "Look, it's just me here. I don't need all this stuff." He grabs a strand of silver garland from one of the boxes and inspects it.

"That's more of a reason you need some holiday cheer. I am not going to pretend to know what you're going through, but I think this can help make you happy for the holidays."

He steps closer. "What if I don't want to be happy?"

"Everyone wants to be happy," I tell him, breathlessly.

"Are you happy?"

I wink. "I will be if I get to decorate your place."

He waves his arms. "Well, by all means, deck my halls."

I giggle. "Do you want to help?"

"Sure."

We spend the next hour or so transforming his cabin into holiday heaven. The only thing missing is a tree. As I'm placing the last gnome in the snow on the mantle, Fender steps outside to chop firewood.

After I light the pumpkin pie scented candles on the coffee table, I hustle to my car to grab my cleaning supplies. Since I'm already here, might as well make the place sparkle.

"Fuck you, wood. And fuck you too, axe. And fuck these gloves most of all," Fender curses from the side of the house.

I make my way to where he stands chopping wood… unsuccessfully.

Sometimes in the movies you see a man with strapping

muscles chopping wood, and you suck in a lusty breath at the sweat trickling down his six-pack abs.

While I know Fender has the body to fulfill that fantasy, it's not what I'm seeing right now.

First, he's wearing his gloves and a thick winter coat. A gray beanie masks his dark hair, and as he tries to chop the log, he's having the hardest time.

"Need some help?" I ask, stepping closer.

He stops and looks over at me, and it nearly knocks me off my feet. I mean, he's good-looking, but I forgot *how* good-looking.

"My damn hands froze solid, and I can't aim this axe with this heavy coat." He tries again and misses the block of wood completely.

I laugh a little.

"Great, and now you're laughing at me."

"Here, let me show you a little trick."

"Oh, that's right. You know how to chop wood too." He drops the axe in the snow and the look in his eyes says he doesn't believe me.

"It's all about placement. Doesn't matter how many muscles you have."

"This I gotta see." He steps back, folding his arms across his chest.

I grab the axe handle. "So, you want to hit the block of wood dead center and bring the force behind it."

"You've got the force?"

I raise a brow. "Maybe not in my guns, but I do in my legs."

He laughs, and it's cute and playful. "Guns?"

"I've got guns." I hold up my free arm and flex my bicep. Even though he can't see it behind my coat. Actually, my gun is more of a small kitchen knife.

"Mhm. Sure. Ok, Miss Rachel, show me how it's done."

"It's all body movement."

"If you chop this wood, I'll do anything you ask."

I laugh. "Well, get ready then."

Dad taught Joanie and me how to chop wood at a young age. It really is all about placement and bringing the right force behind it. Which I can do.

"Watch closely."

"Oh, I'm watching."

At his words, butterflies swarm into a frenzy as his eyes stay on me.

I lift on tiptoes, bringing the axe behind me. I lower my body to build up momentum and swing the axe over my head as I drop into a squat, hitting the wood squarely in the middle so it splits in two.

"Wow."

"You have to build up momentum and put your whole body behind it."

"I see that." he steps closer. "I'm impressed."

My whole body warms. "Do you want to try?"

He takes the axe from me. "Sure. I can't let you show me up." He laughs.

"Now get your whole body behind it and drop at the same time as the axe."

He does as I instructed and splits the next piece of wood in two. "Wow, cool."

"You're becoming a real mountain man," I say with a laugh.

"I could definitely get used to this."

Chapter 7

Fender

I've been looking forward to Rachel coming by again since the moment she left my place a few days ago. It's sad to say, but not only do I miss the human interaction, I missed her.

Now that she's here, I kind of don't want her to leave.

However, I had a stern talk with myself about all the reasons I can't feel an attraction to her, no matter how irresistible she is right now. The need to hold her in my arms causes me to cross them to fend off the urge to scoop her up and whisk her away to my bedroom as she chops more wood, showing me the proper technique.

You would never catch girls in LA chopping wood, at least the women I've dated. They'd rather hire out for things like manual labor.

Rachel's definitely different.

And I like it.

I chop another piece of wood with ease and Rachel laughs.

"Now you'll have enough firewood to keep you warm." The way she gazes up at me makes my chest fill with warmth.

I swing the axe again, splintering the wood in half. "I could think of other ways to stay warm."

Her cheeks tinge pink and I set the axe down. "Should we get this wood back inside?"

I nod, helping her collect a pile of wood to bring into the arctic room. I can't believe I'm here in Alaska chopping wood.

When we head back into the house, Rachel says she's going to clean.

I feel bad about her cleaning my place, so I say, "I already did everything."

"You're not supposed to do the cleaning," she scolds me with a playful glint in her eye.

I shrug. "I don't mind tidying up after myself. I've never had a maid before."

"Not even in California?"

"Remember, I'm not rich and famous. I'm just an average guy who is in a few movies."

"You're anything but average."

The air sizzles with heat, and I instantly forget the reasons I can't kiss her right now.

She stares at me, standing in the middle of my living room, and I need to cool off. "I guess I'll bring the rest of the wood inside the house."

She smiles. "Perfect. I'll just do a few things and head out, because the sun is fading fast."

"You got big plans or something tonight?" The thought of her having plans, or worse, a date, makes me ragey.

She tips her shoulder up in a cute way. "I'm going to Reindeer Glacier to take pictures."

I've never been to a glacier before, and it sounds like the coldest place in the world, but right now, every part of me wants to go with her. "That sounds like fun."

She takes out a cloth and a spray bottle. "You could come

with me. There'll be no people out there, so no one will see you."

"Ok, I'd like that." I smile at her before I head back outside to grab the wood we chopped. Well, that she mainly chopped.

When I get back inside, Rachel is on the phone. "No, I said no. Ok?" She shoves her phone into her back pocket.

"Everything ok?"

"It's just my sister bugging me about something."

"Sorry. Anything I can do to help?"

She stares at me for a moment with her mesmerizing blue eyes, then she shakes her head. "No, it's fine."

"What does she want?" I know I have no right to pry, but curiosity and all. Is it weird I want to know everything about this woman?

"She wants to meet you. Like I said, we're both huge fans of *SharkQuake*."

I take off my coat and hang it on the coat rack. "I don't mind."

She shakes her head. "Absolutely not. No way."

I laugh. "I don't mind. I don't have many fans." Sure, I have tons of women *claiming* to be fans so they can get into my pants, but I bet many of those women have never seen *SharkQuake*.

I wouldn't know because I've never been that guy. I started in the movie business in my teens after a talent scout saw me at a high school soccer game and contacted my parents.

My mother had a long talk with me, telling me to make sure this is what I wanted to do with my life. She said something about once you start, it'll be hard to leave the industry. Especially if you become famous.

If only my mother could see me now. I'm famous all right. But for all the wrong things.

"Well, maybe a brief meeting one of these days."

I nod. "Sure thing. I'll leave you alone so you can clean. I don't want you to miss the sun." I walk into the back bedroom, grabbing my phone from my pocket and pulling up Felicity's contact info.

"Hey, little brother, how's Alaska?"

"It's definitely different. I tried chopping wood, and that didn't go over too well."

She laughs as I recount the story to her, and when I mention Rachel's name, I swear I can picture my sister's brown eyes lit with glee.

"Tell me more about the girl."

I shake my head. "She's intriguing, but I can't get involved with someone right after the whole Trinity thing."

My sister has never liked Trinity, even while we were dating. She said she never trusted her. "It doesn't hurt to clear your mind and relax. I'm not saying you need to get involved with this woman, but it might be good to have someone to talk to about everything that's happened to you this last year."

I sigh. "Yeah, it would be nice to get a few things off my chest."

"I know you're hurting, Fender. Just try to have fun while you're out there."

"Yeah, how's the family?"

Now it's her turn to sigh. "The kids wear me out every day."

"I wish I could be there to help."

"It's ok. I have Scott and we're doing good. The paparazzi stopped coming around when they realized you weren't here."

"Yeah, sorry about that. It's so funny how many times I wished I could make it into the big leagues, and now that I have the paparazzi chasing me, I can't remember why I ever wanted to be famous."

"Funny how those things work, isn't it?"

"Yeah."

We talk a few more minutes and then I have to end it. "Let me let you go, because Rachel and I are going to a glacier."

"Oooh, have fun."

"It isn't like that, at all." Even though every bone in my body wants it to be just like that.

After I hang up with my sister, I put on another pair of socks to wear out to the glacier. I can't believe how many people live here in the cold.

When I came to Alaska to hide from the press, I didn't think through what it would be like to live here. I figured I'd watch movies, chop firewood, and live my best recluse life. I never realized how much there is to learn about living in extreme weather.

"Are you ready to go?" Rachel asks when I step out of my bedroom. She takes one look at me and laughs. "You look like the abominable snowman."

"I fluffed up." Sure, I may have thrown on a few extra layers to stay warm while we're on the glacier. "It's manly, right?"

She laughs harder, and it's adorable. "It's supposed to be warm today."

I laugh, loud and short. "I highly doubt that."

"Ok, well, when we get up there, you'll start shedding those layers." She snaps her mouth shut and her cheeks tinge pink.

Hopefully, she's thinking about me undressing around her. Something I'd be happy to do for her, if she ever requests it.

I try to pull up all the reasons I can't get involved with Rachel, but they fade with each smile she casts my way.

"I doubt that, too."

She laughs and grabs her things, and we head outside to her Jeep.

"Ready?" she asks as she starts the engine.

"As I'll ever be."

I don't know what to expect about being on a glacier, but I'm excited to be out of my element and trying new things. Trinity never wanted to do new things. I once offered to take her rock climbing, but she complained about messing up her nails, and we never spoke of rock climbing ever again.

"Polar Bear is a lot different from LA, huh?" Rachel asks as she drives through the town.

"Yeah," I say, peering out my window.

It's the first time I've seen it, and it's definitely small. But it has a quintessential charm. When I flew into town, I didn't even bother looking out the cab windows, trying my hardest to remain as hidden as possible. I should have looked because this town is fascinating. Each building is topped with lights twinkling below the frosted snow caps on their roof. Green garland with enormous red bows drape across the street creating a tunnel to drive underneath. Pine trees decked out with Christmas ornaments decorate the storefronts, and the whole place feels like a Thomas Kincade winter painting. I'm just waiting for a horse-drawn sleigh to slide by.

"Does Santa live here?"

Rachel laughs. "What? No, he lives in the North Pole, silly."

"I swear this is secretly the North Pole. Look," I point my finger out the window. "That's a candy cane."

Rachel smiles. "That's not a candy cane."

"Yes, it is. There's a candy cane on that building."

"It's a barber pole."

"A what?"

"A barber pole. Many barber shops have them."

"I've never seen one."

"Yes, it used to symbolize blood and bandages, or something crazy like that."

I laugh. "I don't believe you." I pull out my phone to Google a barber pole. "Red to represent the blood and white to represent the bandages used to stem the bleeding from bloodletting." I shut my phone off. "Interesting."

"See, no Santa."

I point out the window again. "Well, explain that." I point

to a snow-covered wooden cabin with puffs of smoke floating from the chimney.

"That's just a shop."

I laugh when I read the sign. "It even says 'Santa's Workshop' on the sign."

"Well, it's not the *real* Santa's workshop."

"How can you be so sure?"

She doesn't say anything right away as she drives through the town, until finally she says, "Well, I guess I can't."

A few miles further down the road, I turn in my seat. "So, what kind of wild animals can I expect to find on this glacier."

"We shouldn't run into any."

"No polar bears?"

She shakes her head. "We shouldn't."

"You don't sound very confident."

"Like I said, we should be ok."

My nerves twist. "Should I be afraid?"

"I'll keep you safe," she says.

"I should be the one saying that to you."

She smiles, and I stare a beat too long at the way her mouth curves. Her lips are kissably sweet, and I wonder for a moment what they taste like.

And who will keep me safe from her.

Chapter 8

Rachel

The temperature inside my Jeep is at an all-time high. It has everything to do with the man sitting next to me, and nothing to do with the temperature gauge.

I wish I could undo the way he makes me feel.

Then, I wouldn't be sitting here sweating.

Sad part is, I don't think he'd ever see me as someone glamorous, like the women in Hollywood. I'm more of a plain Jane compared to those women.

I try to push the negative thoughts out of my head as I drive down the highway to take me out to Reindeer Glacier. It hasn't snowed in a few days, so the weather should be perfect.

It made me laugh when I saw Fender exit his bedroom, all bundled with clothes. Poor guy.

The warm temperature on the glacier will surprise him. I know most would think a glacier would be freezing, but I swear the ice reflects the sliver of sun there is and makes the air warmer.

"I should warn you about all the safety precautions about visiting a glacier. We won't be going out onto the main glacier at this park, but we will be at the base of Reindeer Glacier."

"I should look out for animals, right?"

"No, keep your eyes peeled for moss-covered ice. It can be very slippery. Stay close to me."

"Absolutely," he breathes out.

My insides tingle, and once again the temperature in my Jeep rises. I enter the parking lot of the Reindeer Glacier National Park and pull into a spot. There're few cars, and I'm happy with the fact too many people shouldn't disturb us. Few people visit the glacier in winter.

I must be crazy.

But today's forecast said it will be one of the warmer days, so it should be perfect for taking pictures.

"What do you do with the photos once you've taken them?" Fender asks as I grab my camera bag from the trunk area.

"Edit them. What do you mean?"

He smiles, grabbing my bag off my shoulder and swinging it over his own shoulder. "I mean, do you sell them?"

"No, I don't." I thank him for taking my bags and we head onto the trail that leads to the base of the glacier.

"Why not?"

"I don't think anyone would buy them."

He laughs. "You'd be surprised."

"I guess I just lack the confidence."

He steps closer, swiping a stray strand of brown hair that flies around my head. "You have no reason to doubt yourself in anything."

"Thank you," I breathe out.

One guide for the longer hikes steps up behind us, ruining our moment. "How far out are you folks going today?"

I turn around to see an old friend. "Hey, Sam. Not very far today."

"Rachel, I didn't know that was you." He wraps me in a hug with his burly arms. "Taking pictures today?"

"Yep."

Sam's brown eyes land on Fender. "Who's this?"

"This is my friend, Fender." They shake hands. "Sam and I grew up together. Our fathers have been friends since we were little," I feel the need to explain.

"Nice to meet you," Fender says.

"You too. Stay safe, Rachel. And tell your dad I said hi. I haven't seen him in forever."

I raise a brow. "What are you talking about? He went over to help your dad with some woodworking the other night. He's actually been going there often to help him."

Sam tilts his head. "Really? I don't think so."

"He said your dad has been working on some new projects."

"Dad hasn't worked on anything new since last April when he hurt his shoulder."

"Oh, ok. I'll let my dad know." Where has my father been?

I push away the thought of asking my father later of his whereabouts and head down the trail.

"It feels good to be out in the fresh air. LA has such dirty air," Fender says once we've traveled a ways down the trail.

"Do you get out a lot?"

"I used to. This past year has been a little rough."

"I'm so sorry."

"It's ok. There's nothing anyone could have done. Life comes at you hard sometimes."

I want him to tell me more, but I can tell this is one of those stories I don't want to pressure him into telling. Hopefully, when he's ready, he'll share with me, and until then, I'll stay silent.

"We can stop here, and I can take a few pictures of the glacier before we get there."

"Is that the one we're going on?" Fender stares up at the enormous chunk of ice.

"That's the one."

He sucks in a deep breath. "Ok, looks fun."

I take the bag from his shoulder. "It will be, promise."

"I'm trusting you." He touches my arm. "And I don't trust many people."

My core temperature rises. I swallow as I blink up at him, the chemistry between us turning me into a mute.

We find a sizeable rock to sit on, and I take out my camera, connecting the lens to the base. "Look over there." I point to a white bear in the distance.

Fender stiffens. "That thing won't bother us, will it?"

I shake my head, snapping pictures of the bear moving through the area. "No, he won't."

"Look at you being all confident."

I laugh at his words. "I guess there're some things I'm confident about." I peek up at him.

He's staring at me with wide eyes, like he's never seen anything so amazing. It makes my palms sweat and my belly feel like it's sliding across the ice.

"Why are you looking at me like that?" I find the courage to ask.

"You're so pretty," he whispers.

I dip my chin, trying to hide myself from his intense stare. "Am not."

He places his fingers under my chin, bringing my eyes up to meet his. "Yes, you are." His gaze darts toward the bear. "He's moving."

The moment is broken, and I silently curse the bear that would have to cross a giant gorge to get to us.

We sit in silence as I snap a few more pictures.

"Can I ask you something?"

"Sure," he says, leaning back on his hands. "Ask away."

"You said last year was rough. Was it because of breaking up with Trinity?"

He leans forward, and I stop snapping pictures. "No, it has nothing to do with Trinity at all."

I stay silent as he breathes in deep and lets it out slowly.

"My mother was diagnosed with pancreatic cancer at the beginning of last year, and within five months, she died. The cancer ate away at her so quickly we didn't even have time to say goodbye. I was away filming the last *SharkQuake* movie, so I didn't get to spend as much time with her as I would have liked."

"I'm so sorry," I say to him, placing my hand over his. "Death sucks. It isn't fair. But I'm sure your mother would be really proud of you."

He blinks at me. "Thanks."

"I know what you're going through."

I suck in a deep breath and let it out slowly. "Yeah? What was it like when your mother died?"

"I was young. I barely remember her, and every time I think about it, it pisses me off more. It's not fair that I can't remember her. I can remember something stupid that happened in first grade, or I can remember the square root of pi, but I can't remember her smile."

He brushes a piece of my hair out of my face. "I'm so sorry, Rachel. I bet she had a smile like you. One that takes your breath away. One that lights up any room."

"I don't smile like that." I turn away from him so he can't see me blush.

"Yes, you do. You have a stunning smile."

I stare into his eyes, unsure of what to say, not wanting to break this spell he's cast on me. "You do too," I lamely say. I snap out of the trance he's put on me, and stare around us. "It's beautiful here. I think our mothers would have loved it."

Fender breathes in the fresh mountain air. "I know they would have."

We sit in comfortable silence for a while, and then he turns to me. "Can I ask you a personal question?"

I shrug. "Sure."

"Anything going on with you and Sam?"

I nearly fall over. "No, why would you even think that?"

Now it's his turn to shrug. "Just making sure you're completely single."

I suck in a deep breath. "Can I ask you something now?"

"Sure."

"Is that why you broke up with Trinity? Because you had just lost your mother?"

His finger trails across my cheek, and his eyes drop to my mouth. "I broke up with Trinity because I didn't love her. And when my mother died, I realized life is way too short."

"Life *is* short," I hear myself say. "You should go after what you want." I feel like I'm trapped in a dark tunnel, and the light shining at the end is Fender's blue eyes. Our eyes are locked in an intense battle, neither of us turning away.

"You're right. I should go after it," he breathes, and then he leans in, capturing my lips in a searing kiss.

He moans, and my world explodes into a million tiny pieces. His lips are perfect, soft yet firm, and I cling to him, lest he try to pull away. His hand moves into my hair, gripping my scalp, and he deepens the kiss, tangling his tongue with mine. I let him because I can't find a good enough reason to stop him. I've craved this since the first moment I saw him on screen in *SharkQuake One: The Beginning*.

I need his hungry kiss to last forever and a day.

Heat flares inside my body, and if he keeps making that sexy noise deep in his throat, I may accelerate global warming. It's making me *that* hot.

But dammit, he breaks the kiss, wrenching his lips away, panting.

"I'm sorry—"

I cut in, not wanting to be a regret for him. "Please don't apologize for kissing me. That would break me."

"Rachel—"

I stand. "Let's just move on from it." He obviously got caught up in the moment from our conversation. "We should get to the glacier before night falls."

It's almost like a giant elephant is walking with us as we trek across the snow toward the glacier. My mind works overtime, trying to understand the life-altering kiss Fender Fallon just laid on me. Joanie would turn as green as the Grinch if she knew. Not that I'm going to tell her, or anyone. No, this kiss will make it to the grave with me. It'll be something I can look back on when I'm older. And living with my cats. Ugh.

"Please, stay close to me," I warn Fender.

"You don't have to tell me that twice."

A fire burns through me as Fender wraps an arm around my waist, bringing his front to my back. "How's this?"

"It's delightful, but not the safest way to travel."

His grin is contagious, and I'm smiling ear-to-ear when he releases me.

"Now, remember, it'll be very slippery. Stay close."

"Yes, ma'am."

"Ready?" I ask at the base of the icecap. The sun reflects off the water not too far away. It's peaceful here, a serenity flows through the water and I take a second to appreciate nature in its purest form.

"As I'll ever be."

We step onto the crystal-like glacier.

"It's like walking on ice, so go slowly. This isn't a race," I tell him.

He's a good listener because he moves slower than a turtle. "Baby steps," he whispers.

"You can walk a little faster."

He smiles. "Nope, I'm doing good."

We head out a few more yards, and I stop so I can capture

a few pictures of the sun glinting off the ice. It's beautiful at this time of day, and I inhale a deep breath, mesmerized.

Fender must think the same thing because his eyes wander around, taking in all the beauty of our surroundings. "It's breathtaking," he says.

I want to tell him the only thing breathtaking around here was his kiss. The very kiss I'd like to repeat over and over.

I wasn't expecting Fender to confide in me about his mother. My heart broke for him when he leaned on me at that moment about losing her.

Trinity really got it wrong in all her songs about the break up. She never mentioned what *he* was going through.

Probably because she never truly cared for him.

I snap a few more pictures and then glance over at Fender once more. His cheeks are as red as Rudolph's nose, and he bounces a little in place, as if his whole body is shivering.

"We can go now," I say, putting him out of his misery.

If you're not from around here, you have to get used to the frigid temperatures. I'm like Elsa from *Frozen*. I've got ice flowing in my veins.

Growing up in Alaska gives you a thick skin, but even I'm not impervious to the cold, and it's best to leave before we both turn into blocks of ice.

We make our way back down the trail and out to my Jeep in the lot. I don't want this day to end. Because once we get back to Fender's place, the majestic beauty from this glacier will have worn off. And whatever reason Fender kissed me will have most likely worn off too.

I'll just have to make sure I never forget it.

I'm pretty sure that'll never happen.

Chapter 9

Fender

I know I said I would never put a move on Rachel, but the way she looked with the sun glowing behind her as she spoke to me, I couldn't help it. I really couldn't.

However, I know better than to let that happen again.

"When is that thing in the lake you mentioned the other day?"

Rachel turns off the highway and onto the road that leads into town. "The plunge?"

"Yeah, that."

"It's actually on Saturday." Her whole face glows. "Want to come?"

I get my mind out of the gutter at her words and smile. "Yes, I would. I won't be going in the lake though."

"It'll be fun. You should try it. I dare you."

I lean my head back against the soft leather. "You can't dare me to do something like that."

"Why not?"

"Because you can't dare me to do something that might get me killed."

"You won't die from it."

"Let me ask you something."

"Ok," she says as she drives back through Santa's little village. I swear this is where the man really lives, if I were to believe in something so ridiculous.

"Have you been practicing?"

"Well, yes. I need to get my body prepared."

"I haven't been. So, I'll definitely die if I jump."

She scrunches her cute little button nose at me. "Hm. I still think you'll be ok."

We leave town and she heads into the mountains toward my cabin.

"You can dare me to do anything else."

How bad is it I hope she dares me to do something naughty? Downright dirty. Because the naughtiness running through my head whenever she smiles at me is in overdrive. I never imagined it'd be possible to have so many filthy thoughts running through my head all at once.

She pulls up to my cabin and shuts off the Jeep.

"Want to come inside for a minute?" I have absolutely no reason to ask her inside that comes to mind. I have a million reasons I *want* her to come inside but can't voice any of them.

"No, I should head home."

"Right." I can't leave this vehicle just yet. My body won't move.

"I had a lot of fun today," she says, glancing up at me.

"Me too." Her eyes call to me like a siren, making me lean closer. "Dare me to do something."

Fuck, this woman makes me want to do things. Crazy things. Like kiss her again.

As if she wants the same things too, she leans in. "I dare you *not* to kiss me."

I blink at her, not sure if I heard her correctly. Her dare was unexpected. How can I not kiss her? Especially right now with the sounds of winter playing in the background. I tug her closer, slanting my lips over hers, and kiss her hard. This is one dare I don't mind losing.

She opens her mouth for me, and a moan escapes her lips. I pull her onto my lap, and she straddles me. I kiss her harder, wanting to keep her in my arms forever.

"You lose," she says, breaking the kiss.

My body hardens and I smile. "Yeah, this whole daring each other to do things is stupid." I laugh a little.

Rachel grinds her body against me. Slowly, ever so slowly. Agonizingly slow. "I agree."

Our eyes connect, and I curse under my breath. "Rachel, I…" I can't get the words out in the right way. I want to tell her…

I shouldn't be doing this.

I should leave.

I want you so fucking badly.

But all I can do is grip onto her hips and grind her body into mine. Her heat rubs along my hardness.

"Rachel, this is how badly I want you." I grab her hand, pressing it along the ridge of my dick. "You make me so hard."

She leans her head back, and I trail kisses along the sweet skin of her neck. "Fender," she moans.

"Yeah, look how hard you have me. Look at how turned on you've got me, baby."

Her eyes widen as she continues to ride me. Even though we're both fully dressed, it's still the most erotic thing I've ever done in my life.

"Is this what you want?" I take her hand and guide it to my raging cock that wants to be touched by her bare skin.

She nods, rubbing her hand up and down my thick length.

I go to unzip my pants to pull him out, but Rachel stops moving.

"I should probably go," she says, her eyes meeting mine.

My breathing's heavy, and I try to calm my body down as quickly as possible. "I'm so sorry I got carried away."

"No, it's ok." She climbs off my lap, and I want to hit myself for what an idiot I am.

Women like Rachel don't want a quick fuck in the front seat of a Jeep. No, they deserve to be wined and dined, and I basically made Rachel feel cheap after spending one of the most beautiful days with her.

I'm such an idiot.

"I'm sorry. I didn't mean to go so far." And I didn't. I only meant to give her another kiss goodnight, but one touch from her wasn't enough.

"It's ok. Have you ever seen *Shark Master*?"

I breathe in deep through my nose, letting it out smoothly. "Excuse me?"

"There's this movie called *Shark Master*, and it's really good." She's nervous. I can tell, because she's rambling on about a movie.

Listen, there's zero part of me that wants Rachel to go home right now. I've never heard of this movie she's talking about, but every piece of me wants to watch it with her.

Right the fuck now.

"Let's watch it." I don't give her a chance to answer and hop out of the Jeep, hoping more than anything she follows me inside.

I smile to myself when I hear her slam the door to her vehicle.

We get inside and she cuddles into the couch cushions while I bring up the streaming service she says *Shark Master* plays on.

"Do you want snacks?" I ask, flipping through the remote to find the movie.

Rachel stares up at me, and I swear it does something to my chest. Her eyes sparkle as she smiles. "Sure, what have you got?"

"Popcorn?" It's almost a bit awkward because both of us are pretending what just happened in her Jeep moments ago never happened.

Or maybe we're just trying to prolong the night so we can stay around each other longer. And I'm quite all right with doing just that.

I don't want her to leave.

I want to keep kissing her.

I don't think I'll be able to even focus on this movie. But I will, for her.

"Maybe just a water?" Rachel asks, and I click the movie to play and rush into the kitchen to grab two water bottles.

Once I return to the living room, I find Rachel in the dark and under the red and white moose blanket I had draped over the couch.

I sit down inches from her. "Can I get under here with you?"

She moves the covers over both of us.

I raise an arm to the back of the couch, and she snuggles in closer. I could really get used to this.

The movie starts, and I immediately understand what she means by cheesy low-budget shark movies. This shit is awful, but Rachel remains enraptured in the movie.

She turns to face me. "Isn't this great?"

I smile, dropping my arm to drape over her shoulders. "This is perfect."

She doesn't return her attention back to the movie, instead she watches me. Our eyes are locked and I lean in, capturing her lips once more, unable to stop.

"Fender," she moans out.

I cup her cheeks, bringing her closer to me so I can keep

kissing her. I don't want to stop, but alarm bells sound in the back of my mind.

I ignore the fuck out of them.

Rachel, however, does not. She breaks the kiss, pushing back just a bit. "I should go."

"The movie isn't even halfway through."

"I have laundry." She bounds from the couch. "Right, I have lots of laundry."

"Oh, ok."

I guess I can't argue with laundry even though I know it's an excuse. I rise from the couch and follow Rachel to the front door. She rambles on about dryer sheets as I help her into her coat.

I barely get a goodbye in before she's out the door.

This woman turns me on.

My body's still fired up, and after shutting off the movie, I head back to my room. I change into my night pants and climb into bed.

I think back to the way Rachel stared up at me during the movie.

Damn, she smelled like heaven, and the scent lingers in the air, turning me on even more.

I lower my pants and pull my cock out, rubbing my hand up and down the steel length.

"Fuck," I groan out, wishing I was with Rachel instead.

Kissing her was insane. My heart beats frantically around my ribcage as I stroke my dick.

"Fuck, Rachel," I moan out, wishing more than anything she were here with me right now. On her knees, sucking my cock. Her big blue eyes staring up at me as her sweet lips wrap around my hard on.

I imagine it all in my head, jerking my dick as hard and fast as I can. I keep seeing those lips. That mouth that kissed me with all the fervor she had. Fuck, her kiss is something I won't forget anytime soon.

I tug on my dick, moaning and groaning as loudly as I can as my body lights up. I come, hurtling into my orgasm with such speed it's hard to contain it all. Fuck, Rachel.

I picture me in her, on her, all around her as she takes me in deep.

My orgasm barrels through me like a freight train as I lie in bed.

The need inside grows as I keep coming and coming, groaning out Rachel's name as I do.

Fuck. I don't think I'll be able to stay away from her.

"I'M DOING MUCH BETTER," I say to my manager, Les. "When does filming start?"

If you asked me a few months ago if I wanted to do the next *SharkQuake* movie in the franchise, I would have said no. But now that I know Rachel and her sister are huge fans, it makes me proud to be Robbie in the films.

I stare out the window at the night sky, wondering how I came to be in Alaska. Sure, when my assistant Noreen mentioned an uncle who owned a secluded cabin, I jumped at the chance to get away. But now, I can't believe I'm here.

I'm not the type of man to rush into a relationship without a connection. I thought I had one with Trinity, but now I see it was more of her wanting to connect with me to build off what little star power I had to launch her own career. And she did just that.

Yet, Rachel is so different.

I've only known her a few short weeks and yet, I feel something strong pulling me toward her.

"Filming starts right after Christmas."

"I'll be there."

SharkQuake always films on a Hollywood set. The movie doesn't have enough of a budget to film anywhere exotic. So, in less than a month, I'll be back in California. Without Rachel.

Why am I so melancholy?

I don't even care about running into the press in LA. I just want to hide out here for a little while longer, spend more time with Rachel. I know that can never happen, but a part of me wonders, what if?

I hang up with my manager and pull up Rachel's number.

I text her, "Should I take a cold shower?"

She answers back within a few seconds. "I'm so sorry to leave you in such a state. Yes, a cold shower should help."

I laugh to myself. "I meant to prepare for the plunge," I text back.

She sends an emoji with pink cheeks and I smile, thinking about all the times I've made her blush. "I knew that. You can take a cold shower for that too."

"While we're on the subject… I'm sorry for getting carried away." My fingers fly over the screen of my phone.

I move away from the window and stretch out on the couch.

"No, it's fine. I'm the one who got swept away by everything. I never should have kissed you," she texts back.

I stare at the phone. How can this gorgeous woman think she did something wrong? "No, it was all me. You do something to me, Rachel. You make all my inhibitions disappear."

"Really?"

"Yes, really. You have to know the effect you have on me," I text.

"I figured you'd have many women to choose from back in Hollywood."

I laugh at how wrong she is. "Negative. Do you know how turned on I was in your Jeep?" My body heats, and all I hear is the pounding of my heartbeat in my ears.

"Are you turned on now?"

I read her text over and over, knowing exactly where I want this conversation to go. I tear my shirt over my head, tossing it on the floor.

"Very turned on," I answer back.

And then I do something rash. I dial her number.

Chapter 10

Rachel

Am I really doing this? I'm so turned on right now I can barely see straight. My father and sister both left for the evening, and I sit here, wondering how on earth this is happening.

When I rushed from his place the other day spouting out about laundry, I thought for sure Fender hated me for leaving. I got scared, and even now my nerves flutter throughout my system like a shockwave, making me tingle.

This is all my dreams come true, times ten.

"Hello," I whisper.

"Rachel, just the sound of your voice has me harder than a rock." He sucks in a deep breath. "Tell me you're just as turned on."

"I am." An avalanche of passion barrels through me.

"What are you doing right now?"

"I'm lying on my bed. My free hand is tickling my stomach." I move my free hand up and down my torso.

"What are you wearing?"

I've never had phone sex in my life, and just the thought of Fender turned on has my insides turning to molten lava.

"I'm just wearing a long t-shirt and panties."

"Do you know what I would do to you right now if you were here?"

I close my eyes. What am I doing? Is this really happening?

His words ring in my ears, *"Do you know what I would do to you right now if you were here?"*

"What would you do?" I ask him.

He breathes in deep. His voice is low, controlled, with a hint of huskiness that turns me on even more. It's the same voice he used in the Jeep. "First, I'd remove that shirt and lick a path down your body."

I imagine him doing just those things. "All the way down?"

"Fuck, yeah. Then I'd kiss you, Rachel, the same way I kissed you tonight in your Jeep. I'd kiss the ever-loving fuck out of you. I'd show you who you belong to."

"To you?"

"Yes, to me. Are you touching yourself?"

I run my hand down my stomach, dipping underneath the waistband of my panties. I rub my finger through my wetness, putting pressure on my clit. "Yes."

"I'm stroking my hard cock just for you. Do you know how hard you make me?"

"No."

"Harder than I've ever been."

"Really?"

"I haven't been able to stop thinking about you since you dropped me off."

"Same," I say, breathing into the phone.

Images slam into my mind as I visualize Fender lying on the bed, stroking himself.

"Imagine I'm the one slipping my fingers inside you. I want to feel how wet you are."

"I'm soaked."

"When I get you alone, I'm going to take my time with you. I'll fuck you nice and slow, making sure I show you how deep I can go."

I can barely think straight, and I rub faster, imagining Fender's fingers are the one bringing me so close to an orgasm. "Fender," I moan.

"Tell me you'd let me pound your pussy as deep as I can go."

"Yes, yes." And a million more. I wouldn't be able to get enough of him. I'd never want him to leave. My mind spirals out of control as image after image of what Fender could do to me plays like a movie.

"You're going to make me come so fucking hard."

"Yes, Fender." I bite my lip. "I'm so close."

"Do it. Come for me. Let me hear you."

My body arches, my orgasm coming out of nowhere, blindsiding me. "I'm coming." I feel so carefree at this moment. I feel like I'm floating on a cloud. Breathless, I keep rubbing myself as the last few waves of my orgasm subside.

Fender's husky voice groans through the phone. "I'm going to come for you, Rachel. Just for you." He groans louder as his orgasm barrels through him.

It's the sexiest thing I've ever heard, and I memorize the sound.

As soon as we're nothing more than ragged breaths on the phone, I hang up.

I do.

Without even saying goodbye.

Without even acknowledging what just happened.

I let the fears of what we just did eat away at me as I stare at my phone, wondering if he'll call back. I can say it was a faulty connection. My service provider dropped the call. That happens. Right?

I continue to stare at the phone when a text appears from Fender.

"Sleep tight. The next time I see you it is on."

TODAY, it's on. It's Saturday morning, and as I get ready for the plunge, my stomach twists into a pretzel.

"So, he'll be there?" Joanie asks me for the millionth time.

"He said he would."

"So, that's a yes?" Her big eyes question me.

I shrug, exasperated. "I don't know, Joanie. I don't know if he means what he says. I don't know him that well." I hope he means what he says, because if so, then today when I see him, it is *on*.

"No need to get your panties all in a bunch," Joanie says with an eye roll.

Sometimes I wonder if we're even related.

"Is Dad coming today?"

"He said he had a few things to do, but he'd meet us there."

I look at my sister as she tosses a sweater over her t-shirt. "Has he been acting weird?"

"What do you mean?"

"It's just I ran into Sam, and he said Roger hasn't worked on any new projects since he hurt his shoulder last April."

Joanie's eyes widen. "No, that's impossible. He said he had to go over there today to help Roger out before the plunge."

"I don't know, something weird is going on with him." I purse my lips, wondering why on earth my father would lie to me.

"Maybe he's sneaking off to have a torrid love affair."

I laugh at the ridiculousness of her statement. "There's no one he could be dating."

Joanie stares at me. "You're right. I don't know then. Maybe he picked up more hours at work and doesn't want to let us know?"

Hmm. "Maybe."

"Are you ready to go?"

I look at myself once more in the mirror. I'm glad the plunge takes place in freezing temps. No need to wear a bikini in front of Fender.

My thought drags me into a world of self-doubt, and I shove the insecurity away. No, I won't let the idea of me in a bikini ruin my mood today.

"Think warm thoughts," Joanie says as we leave the house.

Warm thoughts, exactly what I feel when I think of Fender and our phone sexcapade the other night and what's coming.

People pack the lake when Joanie and I pull up in my Jeep. The sun hangs low in the sky and there's a slight chill in the air. A small crowd stands near a white tent, with steaming mugs of hot cocoa in their hands.

"Wow, can you believe Levi is here?" she asks, talking about the boy from school she's been obsessing over since the seventh grade.

"Is he?" I scan the crowd, but I'm not looking for Levi. I'm only looking for Fender, and I spot him near the entrance to the tent in a hoodie and sunglasses.

From this far away, you wouldn't even be able to tell who he is. I make my way toward him, letting Joanie wander toward Levi on her own.

"Hey, you came."

"Quite a few times since talking to you," he says with a smirk.

I blush. "I meant you showed up."

He leans in closer to whisper in my ear. "I knew that."

"Are you going in the lake with us?"

He raises a brow, staring out at all the people standing by the lake. "I want myself in perfect functioning order when we leave here."

I blink up at him. "Why?" I know exactly why, but a part of me needs to be reminded. Because as many times as I pinch myself, I still can't believe this is really happening. To me. Of all people.

I wrap my fingers around his bulging bicep. "I have faith you'll be just fine."

He steps back. "No way. I'm not gonna let you convince me to jump into that lake."

"Oh, come on. It'll be fun."

He shakes his head. "Yeah, right. Probably as much fun as having your teeth pulled."

"You'll feel alive once you jump in."

"I feel very much alive just standing here where it's warmer."

Head-to-head people huddle together to get that last bit of heat before jumping into the lake.

"You'll feel even more alive."

He wraps an arm around my waist. "Rachel, you make me feel more alive than I could ever feel. If you want me to follow you into some frozen lake, I will. Because I'm realizing I'd follow you anywhere. It's why I planned ahead and brought a change of clothes."

I gaze into his piercing blue eyes, unable to even breathe. Before I can say anything, Joanie interrupts us.

"Fender Fallon, oh my god, all my dreams have come true."

I step away from Fender, breaking the connection between us.

"Fender, this is my sister, Joanie."

Joanie steps forward with a wide grin plastered all over her face. "I can't believe I'm meeting you." She sticks out her hand, and Fender laughs.

"The sister. Ah, so you have lots of stories about Rachel, huh?"

"Loads," Joanie answers with a mischievous glint in her eye.

My mind races through memories she could bring up to embarrass me. Please don't let her tell him about the time I fell flat on Mrs. Rutger's apple pie I brought to school in the tenth grade. I'll never live that one down.

"Can't wait to hear them." He glances over at the lake. "Are you doing this craziness too?"

Joanie scrunches her face. "Hell no."

I smack her arm. "Watch your language."

Fender chuckles, and it's all sexy how he does it. I don't think this man knows how to *not* be sexy.

"I'm not killing off my brain cells by freezing them to death." She steps closer so only we can hear her. "You know that's what the cold water does, right? Kills functioning brain cells."

I give her my best snarky smile. "Good thing for you, you don't have any."

Her mouth opens. "How dare you?" She grabs Fender's arm, locking elbows with him. "I have so many more stories to tell you now."

He laughs and they walk off together.

"You're really doing this?" my father's voice sounds from behind me.

I spin around to face him. "Sure am."

He smiles, his frown lines disappearing. "You have nothing to prove to anyone, you know?"

"Dad, do you not want me to do this?"

He shakes his head. "No, it's nothing like that. I want you to do it for you, and not for anyone else."

I give my father a side-hug. "I am." I step back, giving him a stern stare. "I ran into Sammy."

"Oh, yeah?" His eyes no longer meet mine as he scans the crowd for no one in particular. "How's he doing?"

"Well, he told me to tell you he hasn't seen you in a while. To say hi to you."

"That's nice, dear." My father appears distracted, and I know it's because I'm questioning into dangerous territory. Every time my father has tried to avoid us girls, or not tell us something, it's always been the same thing.

No eye contact.

An aloof voice.

"Dad," I get his attention, "what's really going on?"

He nods. "Nothing. Nothing at all." He scurries away before I can ask him anything else.

I size up the lake, taking a deep breath and blowing it out super slowly. I spot Mrs. Green, my high school English teacher, and step up closer to her. "Have you done this before?"

"Last year, it was a blast," she says. "You'll be just fine, sweetheart."

I wish I could believe her. I jump in place to warm up as I look for where Joanie and Fender have rushed off to.

As I glance around, I spot Fender returning with Joanie and a few of her high school friends dragging behind.

"I see you found a fan club," I say to him.

He smiles. "Yes, I did, and my fans want me to jump."

Joanie and her friends plead with Fender as he smiles down at me.

"Well, you can't disappoint the fans."

He laughs harder. "I can't believe I'm about to do this."

"It's for a good cause."

Chapter 11

Fender

She could tell me the money was being used to fund Trinity's next album and I would still jump with Rachel.

Because I am just that smitten by her.

Unlike I ever have been in the past.

I stare out at the lake, and then at the crowds of people gathered out here today. Everyone bounces on their toes, trying to stay warm.

I'm a complete block of ice, so I can only imagine what this water will do to me.

"What if I catch hypothermia?" I ask Joanie and her friends.

"We'll warm you up." They all giggle in unison.

Rachel studies me with a smile on her face. I'd love to know what she's thinking about. Is she thinking about the other night?

Is she thinking about all the things I said to her?

I wasn't lying when I told her I would take my time with her, and I plan on doing just that.

After I jump into this freezing cold water.

We head off to a public restroom to change into the clothes we'll wear to jump in the lake. Once I emerge, Rachel smiles at me.

"Ready?"

I shrug. "As I'll ever be."

They roped a small part of the lake off with paramedics standing by, just in case anything wrong were to happen. Women with oversized, fluffy towels stand just outside the roped off water, ready to wrap the participants in warmth.

We move to the starting line and a man with a whistle announces the plunge will begin. The whole town is here, and there's other games and activities.

Everyone gathers around the lake. Other people are dressed as elves, Santa Claus, and there's even a man dressed as Superman, waiting to jump into the freezing water.

There're reporters everywhere, most likely filming for the local news stations, but either way I do my best to avoid them.

I don't need the paparazzi getting wind I'm hiding out here.

"Once I blow the whistle, you'll jump in and make your way to the other side. The paramedics will help you out of the water if you need help. Ready?" the announcer says into a microphone.

The crowd cheers us on, and already I'm regretting doing this. I give a quick wave over to where my fans have accumulated.

"Don't let it get to your head," Rachel says.

"What?"

"The fandom."

I laugh. "I've never had legit fans before. It's nice."

She smiles and the whistle blows. I just do it. I take the plunge and jump into the water.

Holy fucking shit, that's some cold ass water. My head, full of tiny pins, bobs above water. I move as fast as I can to make sure Rachel's not a popsicle.

She laughs beside me, her eyes widening when she glances over at me. "Fuck," she curses, "this is cold."

"Language," I deadpan.

She laughs even harder and I join in.

The paramedics help us out of the water and an older woman wraps me in a large white towel. A heated towel.

My teeth chatter as we move toward an area with a heated large tent. I can't wait to go in there. I grab Rachel's hand, leading the way.

"I can't believe I did that," she says, her lips a delightful shade of blue.

"Come here." I envelop her in my arms, wrapping my towel around her too. "Let me warm you up."

"I'm warmer already," she breathes against me.

I need this woman like the air I breathe, and I'm ready to tell her that when Joanie and her friends join us.

"That was so cool. How cold was it?"

I let go of Rachel.

"Colder than your dead, black heart," Rachel teases.

She beams as she recounts it, like jumping in the freezing lake makes her proud.

I couldn't care less that I jumped in, but suddenly a warmth floods through me at how much this all means to her.

I hold my hand to the small of her back as Joanie and her friends congratulate us. I feel as though I'm in a daze, wanting more than anything to get Rachel back to my place and alone. All to myself, so I can show her all the naughty things I've been thinking of since we talked on the phone.

We head to the restrooms, getting changed out of our wet clothes. I knew I'd jump, it's why I brought a change of clothes. After another twenty minutes of walking around, meeting a few people, and having a quick snack the organizers arranged, I walk Rachel to her Jeep.

"Can I catch a ride? I took an Uber here."

She grabs her phone. "Let me just…" her words fall away as she taps away at her phone.

"Are you ordering me an Uber?" I ask.

She laughs, shoving her phone back into her pocket. "No, I was texting Joanie to hitch a ride with my dad."

"He's here? I'd like to meet him."

Rachel stares up at me with her big blue eyes. "Maybe another time."

A tremor of lust travels throughout my body at the urgency she wants to get back to my place. "Absolutely."

We hop into her Jeep, and she heads toward Mistletoe Mountain.

The ride home is silent, and more than anything, I want her to tell me all the things. Everything about her life growing up here. But I can't bring myself to ask the questions.

She has nothing to say either and tangible lust fills our ride home, wafting through the air.

It lingers, swirling and swelling until it's suffocating me when we step inside the arctic room.

I tug her closer, needing to quench this hunger driving me toward a collision with destiny.

Her cool blue eyes roam over my hardening body and there's a fire hidden there.

I step closer, and before we move into the house, I wrap my arms around her, folding her into my chest and kissing her, letting my tongue explore hers.

I open the door, leading her inside.

"I need you, Rachel."

"I need you too, Fender," she says, her breath a little shaky.

The air crackles and I lean in claiming her sweet lips

again. The kiss deepens and I hold her closer, swallowing deeply, roughly, breathing her all in.

My gaze drifts down to her pebbled nipples beneath the soft fabric of her shirt. Her body's like a road map, showing me exactly where she needs my touch.

I lift her shirt, and take it off in one quick sweep. Her light-blue bra does little to hide her arousal, and I strip that away just as fast.

She moans as my fingers trace over her breasts. Her skin's so soft, and my pulse pounds in my eardrums.

The sounds she makes are criminal, downright dirty, and all for me. My cock grows, straining against the zipper of my old worn-out jeans.

I kiss across the delicate skin of her collarbone, making my way down the column of her throat. I work my way back down to her tits, and stare at them before closing my mouth around a nipple, and then the other.

Her moans are killing me.

The feel of her hands weaving through my thick hair does my head in. I'm dizzy with lust, and I press my hard on against her, seeking relief.

She steps back, her eyes widening a bit. "Is this a good idea?"

"It's the best idea," I tell her, sweeping my mouth across hers in a desperate kiss.

We somehow manage to make it back to the master suite, and I get her onto the king-sized bed. Our bodies move in tandem as we rip the rest of our clothing off.

Once she's fully naked, I gaze at her, memorizing her soft curves and delicate frame. She lies back, giving me full access and I take my shot. I'm definitely right where I want to be. Here with her.

Rachel smiles up at me. "Having second thoughts?"

She took my moment of appreciation for a moment of hesitation. "Not at all. Stop thinking I might have some sort of regret about this. I regret a lot about my life, but you will never be one of them. I've wanted you since the moment I first saw you."

Her breath hitches. "Even with my Kill Fender Fallon shirt on?"

I kiss the tip of her nose. "You've been on my mind since that day. So many naughty things I've thought about you since then."

Her eyes grow heavy with need. "Show me."

Oh, I plan on doing just that.

I lean in, capturing her lips with mine, loving the sweet taste of her lips. I'm not lying when I said I've thought about this woman since the first moment I saw her. Because I have. She's been on a constant loop inside my head, and all the dirty things I've thought about doing with her.

I feel like I'm on a rollercoaster, my heart pounding rapidly inside my chest. The adrenaline spikes higher and higher with each touch. Her nails trail down my back and again the desire I've had for her shines through my eyes.

"The things I want to do to you," I murmur in her ear.

"What things?"

"I want to spread you wide open, slide my tongue through your dripping wet pussy."

Her cheeks tinge pink when I start the dirty talk, and it eggs me on.

"Do you like it when I talk to you like that?"

She nods, her nails digging into the skin of my back. "Yes, Fender."

"Spread those beautiful legs wide open for me."

She does as I command, and I groan. White hot heat flames my vision, and I move down her sweet body.

Wetness gathers between her legs, and I swipe my tongue, ending right on her clit as she moans out my name. I continue sucking, pushing and lapping at her skin with my tongue, until her fingers dig into my hair and she's bucking underneath me, calling out my name.

"Fender, please, don't stop." She's so close, I can tell by the way her legs open wider and her grip on my hair tightens.

I don't stop, letting her know I'll always do anything to fulfill her needs. "I've dreamt about this," I tell her right before I roam my tongue over her slit.

"You don't know how many times I've dreamed about you."

Those words flood my chest with warmth and a sense of pride washes through me. I press a finger inside her and then another. Before I know it, I'm finger fucking her with all the need and want I feel for her.

She cries out. I watch as she unfolds before me, her hands gripping onto me tighter than before. I work her, taking her orgasm for myself.

She relaxes her body, and before she can calm down from her release I grip my cock in my hand.

"You're so ready for me," I tell her, lining my dick up with her entrance. I slide into her, my body rocketing to new heights. I'm soaring as I push deeper inside her, feeling her pussy clamp down around my hardened flesh.

I sink further into her heat and still once I'm all the way in. "Fuck," I breathe out, loving the way her body fits perfectly with mine.

She stares up at me with her big baby blues, and as I gaze into her eyes, I slowly rock inside her. We find a perfect tempo, both of us panting and moaning out in pleasure.

My body builds and builds. Red heat flashes behind my eyelids as I pump deeper inside her. Harder. Faster. My body picks up speed and I can barely hold on any longer.

My hands fly into her hair as her nails scrape down my back.

"I'm so close," she tells me.

I want to say a million things to this woman right now.

Things with words like love, commitment, and happily ever after.

But I keep my mouth shut, not saying all the things I hope she'd like to hear from me.

Instead, I kiss her lips, tasting the forever promises I wish she'd whisper to me.

We both crash, tumbling into an endless blissful abyss as we come in unison, our bodies holding each other closely.

As soon as my body's calmed, I gaze into her eyes...and I know.

Chapter 12

Rachel

Fender's light snore in my ear and his arm across my chest wakes me the next morning. Is this heaven? I'm sure this is what heaven feels like. Endless orgasms given to me by Fender Fallon.

I slip out of bed, sneaking off to the bathroom to freshen up.

I need coffee. In the kitchen, I look high and low but can't find any. Who doesn't like coffee?

I open the fridge and remove eggs and bacon to make breakfast for Fender. I'm still not able to come to terms with what happened between us last night. My body gets all tingly when I think about how his strong arms held me all night long.

My god. He's somebody I could fall in love with at the drop of a hat. Hell, I'm already seventy-five percent of the way there.

I start on the bacon, and once it's sizzling, I fry the eggs in a separate pan.

"I thought I smelled something good," Fender says, walking into the kitchen with only a pair of black boxers slung low on his hips.

"Morning, sleepy-head. How did you sleep?"

"Better with you in my bed."

My chest warms at his words. "I slept better too." He crosses over to the stove and I rise on my toes to plant a kiss square on his lips.

"I like waking up to that," he says.

"Me too." I finish up the eggs and slide them onto a couple of plates already loaded with bacon. "Did you want some toast?"

"Nope, just the protein for me, please. I've got another movie filming soon."

"Oh, right." I hand him the plate and make my way over to the table in the dining room.

I never thought about the ramifications of what sleeping with Fender would mean for the long term.

Of course, he's going back to Hollywood. Of course, my heart will break when he leaves.

We sit down, both of us silent as we eat breakfast.

"Listen," Fender finally says. "I don't know what's going to happen when I get back to LA, but I really like you."

I smile. "I really like you too."

He reaches out his hand for me to take, and I do. "Let's not think about the future and just enjoy our time together."

I nod. "I'd like that."

Yes, I would like that a lot. Because any time with Fender Fallon is golden. A once in a lifetime agreement. Don't think about the future.

That should be easy.

"What are your plans for today?"

He arches his eyebrow at me with a soft laugh. "You're such a smartass." He grabs me, pulling me into a hug.

I laugh. "Maybe."

"WHEN I ASKED what your plans were for the day, this is not what I had in mind."

"Oh, come on, it'll be fun."

"The things I do for you, Rachel. I want you to know I've never done these sorts of things anywhere else."

I glide around the frozen pond on ice skates as Fender watches in amazement. We've been skating at this pond for as long as I can remember, and it always gathers a crowd at this time of the year. They've commercialized this pond as much as possible by adding food trucks and making other refreshments available. It's quintessential, and exactly what you'd imagine a small-town skating pond would look like.

I zip back and stop right in front of Fender. "Don't worry, I won't let go of you." I take his arm, and together we glide, ungracefully I might add, around the pond. "You're doing great," I tell him.

He teeters on the ice but stays upright. "This is definitely not for me."

"No, I'm serious. You're doing better than I expected."

He wraps both arms around my waist, making us lose our balance and tumble down to the ice. I land on top of him, and he kisses my nose. "So, you had no faith in me?"

I pinch my forefinger and thumb together. "Just a little."

I help him to his feet, just as Mandy O'Brady swoops in next to us. Mandy, and her little gang of wannabe models have always been the town's typical mean girls. I've never gotten along with them, and I don't plan on starting now. "Who's this, Rachel?" She studies Fender. "Haven't I seen you somewhere?"

"No, you haven't." I try to move Fender away without crashing to the ground but her get-along gang joins us before we can escape.

"Yeah, you look familiar," Shannon Greene says, flipping her long strawberry-blonde hair over her shoulder. "Aren't you the guy who dumped Trinity?"

"It is you." Mandy's finger almost touches Fender's nose.

"In the flesh," Fender says with an easy-going smile.

I must applaud him. I'd want to crawl away in a hole and never resurface, but he's handling it like a champ.

Shannon, Mandy, and Gretchen launch into a million questions regarding the breakup. Taking Trinity's side, of course.

After a few minutes, Fender holds up both hands in a surrender stance. "Listen ladies, the heart wants what the heart wants, and mine wanted something else." He drapes an arm over my shoulder.

Shannon clocks the action. "Your heart wants Rachel?"

Fender's smile is delicious. "Damn right, it does. Now if you'll excuse us, ladies."

We leave the pond, heading toward a stretch of land for my next surprise of the day.

We hop out of the Jeep after I park along the side of the road.

"What's this?" Fender asks, staring at the snowy field filled with nothing but Douglas Firs.

"You're going to chop down a Christmas tree."

Fender stuffs his hands into the pockets of his winter coat and turns around, heading back to the Jeep. "Oh, I don't think so."

I laugh. "Come on. You're a real mountain man now. And here in Alaska, we chop down our own trees."

He spins around, his blue eyes blazing into mine. "Who says I even need a tree?"

I park a hand on my hip. "Quit being a baby."

"Fine." Fender steps up closer to me. "How about that one?" He points to a fat Douglas Fir sitting in the middle of the field.

I smile wide. "It's the exact same one I would have picked."

I head back to the Jeep, grabbing the saw and rope so we can tie it up once he chops it down.

We get to work, both of us working the saw back and forth until finally, I let Fender finish chopping the tree with the axe. He swings a few times, and then yells 'Timber' as the tree falls to the ground.

"You're a pro," I tell him.

"I could get used to a life like this," he says as we tie the tree to the roof of my Jeep.

As soon as all the tools are put away, Fender grabs me, pulling me close to his chest.

"I had fun today," I say, staring up into his eyes.

"Me too." He kisses the top of my head. "And I really meant it about getting used to this."

I close my eyes as I hug him harder, trying my best not to read too much into what he's saying, because then that would mean I'd be planning a future with him, which is what I want to do.

I can't tell you how quickly we exit the field, or how fast I drive to Mistletoe Mountain to let Fender have his wicked way with me, but I will say this—it was faster than Santa's reindeer flying across the sky.

Once we're in the cabin, Fender kicks the door shut. "I've been thinking about slamming my cock inside you all damn day."

"Fender, for tonight, let's not think about tomorrow. But tomorrow, I think it's best we never do this again."

I just can't afford my heart the pain it'll have when he walks away. I'm already in too deep.

Chapter 13

Fender

I don't want only tonight. Tomorrow we pretend like this didn't happen? No. It happened. It *is* happening.

It's happening to her. It's fucking happening to me. I can't make sense of what is happening, but it's monumental. As I scoop her up in my arms and carry her to the bedroom, the thought of her wanting to pretend like it's not life-changing crushes me.

But I won't let her know it does. Tonight, I'll give her everything she wants.

I lay her on the bed and start with a kiss, moving our tongues in tandem, tracing along one another, opening my heart to her, laying it right there before her, sliced open, bleeding and wounded. And I pray she knows how to make it whole again.

I slip a finger past the material of her panties and bury it deep inside her. She moans into my mouth, and her legs spread, eager for my touch. She's soaked when I remove my finger and pull her to straddle my lap, grinding her down onto me.

"Feel that? This is how much I want you."

The moonlight streams into the window, highlighting her beauty. Her tits are so close to my face I reach out and smooth my hand over one.

"Fender," she moans as her body continues to grind against my hardness.

With hunger, I move Rachel under me and gaze into her eyes. "I want to own your body."

She palms my face. "It's yours."

I kiss her with all the trust, fear, lust, and every other emotion rippling through me.

I'm rock hard, and there's no stopping now. The only thing my mind can think about is being deep inside her. Being fused as one.

My hands rip the lace of her panties to shreds and toss them across the room.

Her eyes widen at my carnal ferociousness. It only fuels me on.

She removes her shirt, and I growl at the sight of her. We shed the rest of our clothes, and she lies back, licking her lips when she sees my cock.

I run my dick through her wetness, and she bucks up to grind against me. "Such a needy girl." I smile down on her.

"Please," she begs.

As fast as I can, I sheath my cock with a condom and position myself at her tight entrance.

The moment I'm completely inside her, I stall. Fuck, nothing should feel this damn good.

I start slowly, pumping my full cock inside her as she takes every inch.

She moans my name, and it's like music to my ears.

There's meaning behind her touches, and I want to understand everything she's telling me every time she places her hands on my body. I keep pumping inside her, claiming every inch as mine. And tonight, I won't let her forget it.

My gaze drops to her full breasts and I lean down to take a nipple into my mouth. I gently bite down, applying more pressure the longer I suck on her.

Our bodies climb together now, her moans growing to high-pitched screams as I ravage her body harder and faster.

She begs me not to stop. She begs me to never let her go. And more than anything, I want to keep these promises to her.

For tonight only, I treat her as if she's the only star in my sky. And tomorrow, when the sun rises, and all the stars fade, I'll be man enough to walk away.

Her nails rake down my back and it turns me into something wilder, something crazier with lust, and I pound harder. Our bodies are both so close, and I want to give her the ultimate pleasure. To treat her like the princess she is. To give her everything I am.

My one and only Rachel. For tonight, anyway.

Outside, the wind howls through the pine trees, screeching like laughter through the night, knowing full well I won't be able to keep my promises to her.

But I ignore the wind, I ignore the stars and moon shining down on us, knowing I can never be the one for her. Even if we're made for each other. I give and she takes. I push and she pulls. A symphony of bodies mingling in perfect harmony.

If one can ever believe in repeating moments, or warping time, let them warp this night to replay for the rest of my life.

I run my finger over her clit, and she moans a long, low moan. "Fender, I'm so close."

"I know, baby. Give it to me. Give me yourself."

Her eyes slam into mine, and our hearts beat in tune as we rock into each other.

Sweat slicks our bodies, and tangled together, we reach that precipice. She's the first to jump, tumbling down around me.

"Never forget me," I whisper against her cries of passion, speaking only for her heart to hear.

My body plunges full speed ahead, and I lose control, thrusting, pounding, fucking her with everything I have. Everything I am.

And tomorrow, this will be a ghost of a memory.

⸻

THE NEXT DAY, Rachel leaves without so much as a word in my direction. I slam a hand against my pillow, dragging my ass out of bed. I can't believe she just left me.

Should I go back to LA and return to my life?

Is that really what Rachel wants?

I sit in the chair by the fireplace in my living room. I grab a few logs Rachel chopped and toss them into the pit. I can't leave here without telling her how I feel.

But honestly, how do I feel?

I want to be around her, always. And that's enough for now.

Actually, I could see it all with her. A house in LA and another in Alaska for the summers.

Am I naive to believe something with Rachel could work out? Should I even bother trying? She was adamant about wanting me to stay away.

My phone dings from the counter in my kitchen. I answer the call.

"Fender, just who I wanted to talk to," Emmett Garfield says into the phone. He's one of the top agents in the field, but even he can't get me out of my contract with *SharkQuake*. And because of this, I'm not able to book any other gigs. "How's Finland?"

"Alaska," I say.

"Same thing." He laughs. "Listen, big news. I've spoken

with Les, your agent, and I'm willing to take you on as a client."

"Oh, wow." My mind spins.

"*SharkQuake* is pushing up the schedule, and once you're done filming this movie, I've got some pretty big things lined up just for you."

"Doesn't everyone in Hollywood hate me?" I ask, confused.

"Are you kidding? Trinity put you on the map. You're famous now, buddy. *SharkQuake* has doubled in profits overnight. And it's all thanks to their big star."

"So, they moved up production because of me?"

"That's what it's like to be a big star."

I rub at the back of my neck, not believing what I'm hearing. "I'll get back to LA straight away."

"Good thing." He hangs up, and I set my phone down, staring at it like it holds all the answers of what to do with Rachel.

I pick it up, dialing her number.

I launch into a full monologue. "I have to be on set earlier than planned, so I'm leaving tomorrow. I want to see you before I go."

"Come for dinner. Tonight, six o'clock."

"I'll be there." I suck in a deep breath before telling her, "I just can't leave Alaska without seeing you one last time."

She hangs up without another word, and I'm hoping it's because she feels the same way I do. Maybe there is something real here.

I show up at her house precisely five minutes before six.

"You're early," Joanie says to me as she swings the door open. She pulls me into the arctic room before we enter the house. "Rachel's upset."

My eyes widen. "Why? Is it something I did?" Or didn't do?

Joanie shakes her head. "No, my father got caught lying again."

I smile. "Lying about what?"

Joanie smiles. "You'll see." She opens the door to the house, and as I step inside, I spot Rachel in a soft red dress. She looks ravishing, and I try to keep myself in check while I'm in her father's home.

Rachel stares at her father. "We'll talk about this later, Dad." She crosses her arms, clearly upset.

"Good to meet you, sir," I say, shaking her father's hand when he steps closer to me.

His blue eyes, same as his daughter's, study me. "Heard a lot about you." He's smiling, so I don't know whether to take that as a good thing or a bad thing.

"Don't believe any of it," I say back.

He slaps me on my shoulder blade, bringing me into the kitchen and further away from Rachel.

Joanie follows us into the kitchen, sticking by my side.

More than anything, I want to be alone with Rachel. I'm leaving tomorrow, and that thought alone slays me. I don't want to go away.

I want to take her with me.

Always.

Chapter 14

Rachel

After dinner, I lead Fender up to my room so we can talk.

He walks around my room, inspecting every tiny detail. I'm a little mortified he's seeing all my personal items, but he's seen me naked, so there's that.

He holds up Mr. Wrinkles, my stuffed boxer puppy I've had since a child, and smiles. "Cute."

"Mr. Wrinkles always kept the bad dreams at bay. I couldn't get rid of him."

"Wish I was Mr. Wrinkles," he mutters, placing him on the bed. "Rachel, I don't want to leave."

"But you have a movie career." I sigh. "It's fine. We had an expiration date from the beginning."

He moves closer to me, wrapping his arms around my waist and kissing the top of my head. "Come with me."

I step out of his embrace. "I can't go anywhere with you."

"Yes, you can. You can stay with me. Come with me."

I shake my head, half of me contemplating moving to LA with him. "I can't."

My father needs me. My sister needs me.

I can't leave them.

"Please. I've never felt this way before in my entire life."

I nod, silently agreeing with him. "Me either."

He wraps his arms around me again, holding me tight. "I can't leave Alaska without you."

"My family needs me."

He appears dejected. "I can come up in between filming. I can come back once we wrap. We can move in together, up here."

"You hate Alaska."

He leans his forehead against mine. "I'd live anywhere if it meant I could be with you."

My heart swells. "Fender, I just don't know."

"Be with me," he breathes across my lips. "Rachel, please be with me."

I close my eyes, trying to picture a life with him. It comes so easily. Us spending time in Alaska, and then jetting to California every time he has to work. I think about my father all alone, needing me, and my sister getting into trouble.

"Fender, I can't leave." I step back from him before I kiss him and forget every reason I have to stay.

"I'll come up. We can make this work."

I think about his words for a second, but I can't live this life where he visits me on weekends, trying to cling to a new relationship. As much as I think it could work, doubt creeps in. Long-distance relationships are hard, and we're just beginning.

"No, we can't," I say, tears welling in my eyes.

"We can."

"I don't want to hold you back."

"You're not holding me back."

I turn away from him, because if I keep looking into his

eyes, I'll lose all my resolve. I won't be the reason he ruins his career. I won't do that to him. "I think you should go."

"Rachel," he pleads.

"Please go."

He stands behind me for a minute or two before heading out of my room. Tears fall as soon as he shuts my bedroom door.

Chapter 15

Rachel

It's been a whole week since Fender left to return to Hollywood. An entire week filled with tissues and me second guessing myself.

Fender told me he'd call me when he went back to LA, but I begged him not to. One word from him and I'd leave Alaska so fast and never look back. Just one whisper of begging me to move away with him and I'd be a goner.

"Where's Dad?" Joanie asks when she walks into the house after school.

I hang the last ornament on the full tree and raise a brow. "I thought he was picking you up from school?"

"I waited, and he never showed up."

I yank out my phone, furious with my father. He doesn't answer, and then the front door opens again.

"Hey, what's going on?" he asks, walking into the house like he didn't just forget to pick up his seventeen-year-old daughter from school.

I slide my phone into my pocket. "Dad, we never finished our fight."

His gaze volleys between Joanie and me. "Um, ok."

We all take a seat on the couch, and I stare at my father. "What is up with you lately? You forgot to pick up Joanie after school."

His eyes widen. "I completely forgot. It won't happen again," he says.

"But it *has* happened. Many times. You haven't been going to Roger's."

He scrubs a hand down his face. "I've been…"

"Are you sick?" Joanie asks, interrupting my father.

He shakes his head. "No, no. It's nothing like that. I've…"

Joanie and I both cross our arms. "Tell us, Dad."

He blows out a breath. "Fine. I've been seeing someone."

"What? Who?" we ask in unison.

"Jenny Fisher from the library."

"Mrs. Fisher? Are you joking?" Joanie screeches. "You've been hooking up?"

My father gives her a harsh stare. "It's more than that. I've been meaning to tell you girls, but we wanted to make sure it was solid before making it official."

I snap my eyes to his, still in shock. "How long have you been dating her?"

"A few months."

"Months?" Joanie nearly screams. "Months?" she asks again, like she can't believe her own ears.

She's clearly not handling this as well as I am.

To be honest, I'm happy for my father. He put his whole life on hold to raise us girls.

"Good for you, Dad," I say, and Joanie widens her eyes at me.

"I am shook," Joanie says, sitting back and crossing her arms.

"I didn't do this to hurt you girls. Everyone deserves love, and I was lucky enough to meet the woman of my dreams, and have two beautiful daughters with her, but my heart is ready for love again."

My heart goes out to my father, and Joanie's scowl softens.

"I can't wait to have her over for dinner," I say.

"When are we having the shark boy over?" my father asks.

I shake my head. "He went back to Hollywood. So, that's over."

My father frowns. "I'm sorry."

"You should have gone with him," Joanie says.

"Well, he asked me to."

Joanie launches forward on the couch, her eyes nearly bugging out of her head. "And you said no? Why?" she whines.

"I can't leave you and Dad."

"Why not?" my father asks.

"Because you both need me."

Dad and Joanie share a look.

"Let me ask you a question, Rachel," my father says. "Do you love him?"

"Of course, she does," Joanie answers for me.

Do I love him? Joanie's right. Of course, I do. I think I have since the first minute I laid eyes on him. I've never known anyone so laid back, like Fender.

"It doesn't matter now."

"Why not?" Joanie asks, her voice softening.

"He's off to Hollywood to be a huge star."

"I saw the way he stared at you at the plunge. He loves you."

I laugh. "He does *not* love me."

Does he?

It's too soon for love. I've only known him for a short while. It can't be love. It can't be something that could last a lifetime.

"Yes, he does," my father adds. "I could see it at dinner the other night."

"Well, it doesn't matter now."

"You should go to California. Go be with him," Joanie says. "You'll always regret it if you don't."

THE NEXT DAY, as I clean Mr. Henderson's place, dusting and vacuuming, all I can think about is going to LA.

What if Fender's already forgotten me?

What if he doesn't want me anymore?

What if I get there, and he turns me away?

I think about what my father and Joanie said, about how I'll always regret it if I don't go.

Which is true. I will always regret it. What if our love is the kind of love that can handle any challenges thrown its way.

I think it can be.

Because the love I feel for him is the forever kind.

The kind that can stand the test of time. He's my shark mate, and I don't ever want to let him go.

I smile wide as I think about heading to LA, showing up at his place, and kissing him madly.

"You do such a good job here," Mr. Henderson says, breaking me from my daydream.

"Thanks," I say. "But I think I'm quitting."

Mr. Henderson's smile drops. "What? No."

With my mind made up, I give him a quick nod. "Yep, I quit." I grab the duster I was using on his TV. "Don't worry though. April will send someone new over."

I leave his house and hop into my Jeep, ready to tell Fender exactly how I feel.

Chapter 16

Fender

Thoughts of kidnapping Rachel flit through my mind for about five minutes before I realize it will never work. Obviously.

Every day I think about some new way I can convince my girl to move to LA with me.

Since I've been home, it's been a whirlwind of activity. Rehearsals. Fittings. New gym hours to get into shape for the movie. So many things have kept me busier than a bee. Yet, I can't seem to stop thinking about Rachel.

About making a life with her.

The other thing that has happened since I've been home is the paparazzi still follow me everywhere.

And anywhere.

It gets old, quickly.

I return home to my one-bedroom apartment and hang my keys on the ring just inside my front door. The loneliness I feel swallows me whole.

I think I've been lonely my whole life, always searching for my other half and never finding her. Until Rachel.

I've picked up my phone many times to call her, but I always chicken out. Even though every part of me wants her here, there's a bigger part of me that wants to be back in Alaska with her.

Sure, I've dreamed of becoming a big star in Hollywood and living the glamorous life, but honestly, it's not all it's cracked up to be. Having the paparazzi up my ass all day, every day, makes me realize this isn't what I want.

What I want is Rachel.

What I need is her.

And if she must stay in Alaska to take care of her father and sister, then I'll be in Alaska too.

"What do you mean you want to quit?" Emmett asks. "You can't quit. You have so many movie producers lined up, wanting you for their films."

I scrub a hand down my jaw. "I get that, but my heart's not in it. I think it never left Alaska."

Emmett stares at me for a minute before realizing I'm not changing my mind. "She must be pretty special."

I smile. "She is. Obviously, I'll finish the movie I'm contracted for, but after that I quit."

Emmett stands and shakes my hand. "If you ever change your mind."

"I won't."

I leave his office and run smack into the woman who started this whole thing. Trinity herself.

She appears different. Like being with her was over a century ago. It's funny how those things work.

"Trinity," I say to her as her entourage glares at me through fake lashes.

"Fender, what are you doing here?" She raises a quizzical brow.

"Quitting."

"Can we talk?" She glances over her shoulder at her friends and then stares at me.

Every bone in my body wants to deny her request. I've got more important things to do, like winning back Rachel.

Trinity doesn't really give me a chance to answer as she pulls me away from her little gang of 'yes' girls.

"I've missed you, Fender. Don't you miss me?" She bats her long lashes at me.

I chuckle. "Well, actually…" I spot the exit, and inch closer to it.

"My record went multi-platinum. Any man in the world would be lucky to have me." She parks a hand on her hip.

"That's great." I inch even closer to the door leading to the outside.

"Fender, I'm trying to talk to you," she screeches, gaining the attention of some passerbys in the office. "Don't you want me?"

I stare at her, wondering how on earth I had ever really wanted her. Rachel's blue eyes pop into my head and I smile, thinking I need to get to Alaska before she's moved on and forgotten all about me. "No. Trinity, I don't want you." I walk away from her, heading toward the exit, then glance back at her from over my shoulder. "Oh, and Trinity, call off your fans, or I'll tell my side of the story." I wink. "You wouldn't want me to do that, right?"

She looks like she could start a fire with her eyes right now. I almost laugh as I head outside, and breathe in deeply. I've got a plane to catch.

Chapter 17

Rachel

"Deep breaths," Joanie says. "You'll be ok."

"I've never been on a plane before. What if it crashes?" I start to panic.

Joanie shakes her head. "No, it's more likely Fender says no to being with you than the plane crashing." Leave it to Joanie to give it to me straight.

Now, I worry, but push the thoughts away. "Thanks for that."

I sling my carry-on bag over my shoulder and head toward security with slow steps. There's a slight commotion coming from the line, and I stare back at Joanie.

"What is that?" Joanie asks, looking at the small gathering of people with cameras. "Oh my god, it's Fender." She points to the center of the crowd.

I strain my neck, trying my best to see him. "What is he doing here?" I ask Joanie.

"Maybe he forgot something."

And then I see him. He looks sexier than he did before he left. His tousled dark hair hangs low over his sunglasses. His jeans and white tee are probably the hottest thing I've seen this man wear. He spots me and stops walking, a slow smile spreading across his face.

He's so gorgeous.

The crowd parts, and he crosses the airport to stand right in front of me.

A tingle radiates throughout my body. "Did you forget something?" I ask him.

He removes his sunglasses, his eyes blazing into mine. "Yeah, you." He wraps his strong arms around my waist and plants his lips right on mine.

Our tongues crash together like old friends that never want to be parted again. He tugs me closer, and I fling my arms around his neck, running my fingers through his hair.

I don't care if people gawk at us.

I don't even care if someone snaps a photo of the two of us making out like teenagers in the middle of an airport.

All I do care about is this man, holding me like his whole life depends on it.

"What are you doing here?" Fender asks after he's broken the kiss.

"I was heading to LA to be with you." I show him my ticket in my hand.

"I love you, Rachel. After this last shark movie, I'm quitting, and I want to live here with you."

My eyes fill with tears. "I love you too. But you don't need to quit for me."

"But your father, your sister."

I shake my head. "They're both fine."

Fender's arms are still around me, and he smiles. "We can figure it all out. Just know that I don't plan on ever letting you go."

I rise on tiptoes, and right before I kiss him, I say, "And I won't ever let you."

Epilogue

Rachel

And the stockings were hung by the chimney with care. Well, as much care as Fender could muster.

In his defense, we've been very busy since we left the airport, and the fact that he was able to even hang the stockings at all was a major feat.

"The house looks great," Fender says, staring at all the holiday decorations we've put together in his cabin. "I can't believe you think I needed more."

I prop up on an arm, while lying next to Fender on a red buffalo check blanket in front of a roaring fire. "Yes, Christmas only comes once a year and it's a time to be festive."

Fender smiles that brilliant smile that makes me love him ten times harder every time he lays it on me. "It is peaceful here." He holds me close as he tickles my bare back with his fingers. "I'm not happy I have to leave in the morning."

"It won't be too bad. I'll be going with you this time."

"I can't wait to show you LA." He kisses the top of my head. "And I really can't wait for you to meet everyone on the set of *SharkQuake*."

My stomach flips. "I can't believe this." Basically, all my dreams are coming true. If you would have asked me last Christmas how I thought I'd be celebrating the next year's Christmas, I'd never have pictured this scenario. Even though I've imagined this scenario every time I watched one of the *SharkQuake* movies.

"Believe it, Rachel. And if you forget it, I'll remind you everyday how much you mean to me." He slants his lips over mine, tugging my body closer.

I break the kiss. "There's only one thing I haven't seen yet."

Fender smiles. "What's that?"

"Will you play something on the guitar for me?"

His cheeks are actually turning pink as he moves to the other side of the room to grab his guitar. "I guess I can play a little something." He strums the strings, playing a chord that floats through the room.

It's perfect.

He starts a slower tune, and sings the first line about meeting the right one.

I hold my breath as he continues.

"Sometimes in life, it's too short.
Sometimes in life, you meet someone.
Sometimes in life, you get surprised.
You meet the one you're meant to."

My heart burns in my chest as he sings about meeting me. And then the chorus starts and I laugh a little.

"A meet cute gone wrong.
I thought you wanted me dead.

*But you just wanted me out of the way to clean.
And I just wanted to get you into bed."*

"I love it," I tell him as he strums the last note. "You have such a good voice. You should do an album."

Fender shakes his head. "No, never. I'm happy right where I am." He sets the guitar down and moves back over to where I'm lying under the blanket.

The fire roars as Fender makes love to me for the third time tonight. And in the morning when we wake, we'll be heading to California, for Fender to start filming the last *Shark-Quake* movie, and then who knows what will happen.

The world will be ours for the taking.

And I plan on taking it all with him.

Thank you so much for reading Holiday Hideout.

Hard Ride

Chapter 1

Betty

We may need a cleanup in the produce aisle. He's back, and if he doesn't stop looking so delicious in that leather vest and tattoos, I may combust right here between the eggplant and avocados. Jenna will have to mop me up from the floor...

"Betty, where are the sweet potatoes you have on sale?" Mrs. Fuller, a faithful shopper of The Hungry Grocer, asks. "Gonna make Richard a pie and the canned ones won't do."

I point her in the direction of the baskets of potatoes, casting a sneaky glance toward the muscled man browsing the fruit like he's picking out a car.

"How's your father?" she asks as she digs her frail hand through the potatoes, inspecting them, and inadvertently reminding me I should not be sneaking glances at the man currently fondling melons like they are a lover.

"He's well." I hustle across the tile floor to the berries in the far corner to avoid further questioning about my dad that I know is coming. As chief of police, my father knows everyone in this small town, which means everyone knows me too.

Sometimes, it can overwhelm me.

Normally, I love my job managing the local grocery store—somebody has to do it, and I do it exceptionally well—but many people thought I'd follow in Daddy's footsteps, joining the police force right out of high school.

As if I'd ever want to be Daddy's deputy.

Don't get me wrong, I love my father, but I'm not interested in leading the type of life where I'm critiqued through society's magnifying glass.

Although, I am anyway. I can't step a smidge out of line or else my father hears about it. Most of the time, I don't mind following the rules, but now and then, I dream of a wilder life. A night full of naughty fantasies that would blow the wig off Mrs. Fuller's head.

It's just a dream though. The men of this town are a joke in the romance department. Trust me, I've dated a few in my twenty-three years, and they wouldn't know the difference between my bellybutton and the spot between my legs. I want to be ravaged by a *man*, not the dweebs running around this small town.

"Excuse me, Miss," a deep, growly voice says from behind me. "Are the strawberries sweet and ripe?"

The masculine voice rumbles through me like a freight train, setting off flashing red lights in all my erogenous zones.

I spin around and my eyes land on the leader of the Legendary Villains Motorcycle Club.

The hottest produce shopper in King's City, Nevada.

Once a week, he comes in and peruses the fruits and vegetables, and once a week, after my shift, I go home and do scandalous things to myself, imagining he's touching *me* with those tattooed fingers. It's wrong, wrong, *wrong*. It's forbidden. My father says if there's anyone I should stay away from, it's these guys. They're bad news.

"Of course they are." I step out of the way of the tall man and all his muscles. "These are from Marvin Zimmerman's farm."

"I like them juicy," he says, reaching past me to pick up a container of plump strawberries and eyeball it.

He wears a tight, white t-shirt beneath his club vest, and the way his biceps poke out from his sleeves makes my mouth water. I scoot further away from his woodsy scent, trying not to stare at the big bulge behind the zipper of his worn jeans.

Or—Lord, help me—the sexy smattering of gray in his tousled dark hair, right by his temples.

Or—Jesus, take the wheel—those succulent lips surrounded by a close-trimmed beard.

Better yet, I move myself out of his tempting vicinity to the display of apples.

"Excuse me," he says again, huskier this time. "How are these for pie?"

He selects a Red Delicious apple and holds it in his palm, tempting me.

"You bake pies?" seems the logical question here, so I ask it.

"Is that a problem if I do?" His brown eyes skim over my pink Hungry Grocer polo and khaki pants.

"Perhaps," I snap at him, knowing I should be nice to all customers, but Silas Irons is not a man I want shopping in my store and making me the subject of gossip at church bingo because he's talking to me. He's not supposed to have a conversation with me. He's supposed to quietly drift through the aisles and let me watch him. "Why are you shopping here?" I ask, my voice reflecting the turmoil churning inside me.

"Pickin' up a few things." His voice is rough and low—layered—like he's lived a life full of experience. I bet he knows how to touch a woman the right way.

I stare at his big hands for a second and then snap my eyes back up to his brown ones.

My father would most likely kill me for talking to this man. He'd be even more upset knowing Silas Irons has even stepped foot on this side of town. My father and the Legendary Villains have a truce, a treaty of sorts. They stay on their side of town and my father looks the other way when they party a bit too loud.

"If you're looking for a balance between sweet and tart, Braeburn is the one you want."

His gaze fuses with mine, sending my body temperature soaring. "That's exactly what I'm looking for."

I give him a curt nod. "Happy to help."

He drops the apple back into the pile and reaches in to snag a banana from the display by my shoulder. His potassium levels must be excellent because it's the one thing he buys each week. With a chin dip, he tips the banana in my direction and then stalks off, and I hate that I stare at his ass filling out his jeans just right.

It's been too long.

Jenna sidles up beside me. "Now, that's a man I'd let touch me in all the wrong ways." She sighs.

My head whips to her. "I can't believe you just said that."

Jenna's an employee of mine, and nearly twice my age. Actually, she's probably more Silas's age than I am.

"You must agree with me? You wouldn't let him give you a hard spank or two?"

"I wouldn't let him touch me at all."

"That's your problem." Jenna smacks her cinnamon gum like she's just solved the riddle of my existence. "You're too wound up. You need to let loose. Live a little."

I glance at Silas and wonder what it would be like to let loose with him. "You know he came in just for a banana," I tell her. "Again. Isn't that strange that he doesn't get a bunch?"

Jenna laughs. "I bet he's coming in here to get a good look at you."

I slap at her arm playfully. "No, he is not."

We watch as Silas pays for his banana, and before he leaves the store, he tosses me one last glance over his broad shoulder.

"See, I think I'm right," Jenna muses. "He's wanting to share that banana with you."

"He's old enough to be my—" My words halt when Jenna puts her hand up to stop me from speaking.

"Do not say *father*," she butts in. "He's not *that* old. Probably forty, forty-one."

"I'm only twenty-three."

"Who cares?"

"Everyone in town," I remind her with a raised brow.

"I think you need to go out." She shakes her hips. "Find some handsome stranger and get freaky with him."

I roll my eyes. "My father would murder him, and then murder me."

"Well, maybe you should go to the bar across town. The Cool Cactus."

My eyes widen. "I can't go there. My father would have a heart attack."

But the more I think about going to a secluded bar on the edge of town, I realize maybe Jenna is brilliant. Go to a place where nobody knows me and find a hookup. I'm so over dating. I just need to… unwind.

"Only if he finds out," Jenna says, adjusting her blonde ponytail. "Which he won't."

Maybe Jenna's right. Maybe I should have a night of fun. I have a few days off coming up, and I could easily slip into something a little more revealing and have a night or two on the town.

I work hard six days a week and never get any time to play. It's been years since a man touched me, so yes, tonight I'm going to find someone to take away all the stress I'm under from running this store.

Jenna beams when I tell her I'm going to do it. "Just looking at you right now, you definitely need a little fun. Maybe you should head over to the Legendary Villains' complex and ask Silas to show you a good time. A little appetizer before the main course."

I gasp. "I would never. I don't want those rough hands all over this," I lie, moving my hand over my body, showcasing the goods.

"Oh, I think you'd change your mind if you saw him with his shirt off."

"Have you seen him with his shirt off?"

"Only in my dreams, sweetie." Jenna makes a sharp turn and straightens cucumbers. "Don't look now," she whispers. "Mr. Redford is here."

I knock Silas out of my mind and turn my attention to the store owner striding in my direction.

"Hello, ladies," he says, as cheerful as ever. The crow's feet nestled beside his faded gray eyes crinkle deeper when he smiles at us.

"Hi, Mr. Redford. How're things?" I ask.

"Great. Betty, can I see you in my office?"

I give Jenna a nervous glance before following Mr. Redford to his back office.

Once we're both inside and he has taken a seat behind his desk, he drops a bomb on me. "Betty, I got an offer on the store."

"You're selling?" I hold my breath. I love my job, I really do. I've worked hard to make The Hungry Grocer everyone's favorite store in the area, and who knows what might happen if he sells to a huge corporation that will want to bring their own managers and key players in to run things.

My job will be obsolete, and I'll have nothing.

"Yeah. It's an excellent offer. I hope you understand."

My worst nightmare has come true. "I understand."

He shuffles through a stack of papers on his desk. "I'm not sure if they'll get rid of the entire staff, but I asked them to keep you and as many of the employees here as they can."

"When will we know our fate?"

"They are still deciding, but soon. You're not out of a job yet."

Lucky for me. He follows up that doozy with a quick run over the store's earnings and profits. When he dismisses me, my shoulders are knotted tighter than a pretzel, and if there was any doubt in my mind about hitting the bar tonight, it's gone.

Bye bye boring life.

Chapter 2

Silas

"Another banana? I don't want this shit, Silas." My younger brother, Dragon, tosses the banana I bought at The Hungry Grocer at me.

"You know I hate bananas," I say back to him, setting the banana down on the bar. "And you know I don't like to waste things."

"Then why do you keep buying them?" Henley, the Sergeant at Arms, asks.

I stare at the ripe fruit, unable to answer the question. More like won't answer the question.

The meeting for the Legendary Villains just ended a few minutes ago, and I'd like them to clear the fuck out, but now this has turned into a banana situation.

"I think he enjoys looking at that pretty little store manager," Duke says, smirking.

"Shut the fuck up before I punch the ever loving fuck out of you," I snap back.

"Whoa," he says, holding his hands up in surrender, "someone's testy."

"I think you guessed right," Jagger, another member of my club, says.

Their remarks don't get deep under my skin. I've been president of this club for years, and these men are as real of a brother as my blood, Dragon. So, I'll let their teasing slide. Although, they're right about Betty down at the Hungry Grocer. Women in King's City are a dime a dozen. Too many of them come to our club, trying their best to get my attention, or any member of the Legendary Villains' attention. Most times, I turn the other way. Most times.

Lately, I turn away all the time. No one gets me excited.

Not like the raven-haired daughter of King's City police chief. Inky-dark hair, eyes the color of the deep blue sea, and a smile that could knock you out within seconds of witnessing it. She's a bombshell, in the-girl-next-door kind of way. I must be out of my mind. There's something about her I can't quite put my finger on. Although I'd like to put my fingers all over her.

I'd never do it though.

She'd probably call her father to have me arrested.

He'd love the chance to lock away the leader of the LVMC. Hell, sometimes I think he'll lock me up for way less than just looking at his daughter.

So, I stick to shopping at a store I don't need to shop at, just to steal glances of the pretty Betty Hutton.

"Are you going to be the one to meet up with Lewis at the Cool Cactus tonight?" Dragon asks.

I nod. "Yeah."

A government shipment full of AK-47s and other military grade weapons got boosted off a semi in the middle of the night out on Route 42. Chief John Hutton's been sniffing around, trying to place the blame on this club, and I couldn't be more pissed off by this preposterous accusation. My club is clean, mostly. We may dabble here and there in illegal activities, but nothing as big as stealing guns from the government.

My gut says someone's trying to frame the Legendary Villains for something we didn't do. Worst part is we can't even come up with a good alibi because we stick to our compound and drink at our own bar. So, tonight, I'm heading across town to sniff out the name of who's framing us, and more importantly, why.

"You sure you don't want me to go with?"

I shake my head. "Nah, it'll be easy… just get the name from Lewis and leave. A baby could do it."

Dragon's brown eyes, the same color as our father's, studies me, like he doesn't believe me. "Just don't stop by that store and buy more bananas." He laughs.

"Or at least buy something else," Henley says, picking up the banana and peeling back the skin so he can take a bite.

"You look so sexy doing that." I joke, and everyone laughs.

After I say my goodbyes, I walk outside and hop on my Harley Softtail Deluxe, ready to get this shit over with once and for all. As I drive through town, I think about who hates us enough to frame us for their crimes. A few names come to mind. Another rival club does too, but nobody who is smart enough to pull off this type of heist.

It's a little after ten p.m. when I pull up to the Cool Cactus and park my Harley near the front. I've been to this bar before, and never had too much trouble here. It's run by a friend of the club so in essence, it's *our* club.

I take a seat at the oak-covered bar and order a beer. "Busy here tonight," I say to the bartender, Curly.

"Rowdy bunch of college kids playing darts at the far end," he says back.

I look over in that direction and spot the kids he's talking about right away. Like a fraternity that took a wrong turn and ended up here. They certainly don't belong in a club like this, but it's none of my business.

"They giving you trouble?"

Curly shakes his head. "Nah, I'm watering down the shit outta their drinks."

I laugh as I sip my beer. "Smart move."

I scan the crowd for Lewis, making sure I haven't missed him. If he can help in any way to figure out who's framing us, I'll be forever grateful. "Lewis here?" I ask Curly, and he nods toward the rear of the club.

I glance in that direction, but something catches my attention as I do. Betty Hutton dancing near the college punks in a tiny black number that shows off entirely too much of her perfectly porcelain skin.

Damn.

I take a long pull of my beer as I watch her dance for some twenty-something college asshole who wouldn't even know how to fuck her properly if he tried. She backs her ass up against him while he runs his hands over her hips.

I set my beer bottle down, wondering what on earth she's doing. I've never seen her at this bar before. Hell, I've never even seen her out. She's not the type of woman who does this sort of thing.

So, why in the fuck is she here tonight? In a skimpy tight dress for that matter. Is she looking to get wild?

Is living under her father's thumb finally taking a toll on her?

The way she twists her body and moves those graceful hips, I can tell she's wound up tight and needs a good fuck to relieve all of that tension. I watch as she plays along with the dirtbag who's getting too close to her. He kisses her cheek, obviously getting a bit too flirty. My blood boils.

"Hey, Curly," I say. "Do me a solid and turn the music off? Got a killer headache."

He doesn't push back, just drops his towel on the glossy bar and does what I asked. Betty and her jackass dance partner look puzzled for a moment but move along to the dart area in the back.

"Long time," someone next to me says, breaking my attention from Betty.

I glance over and meet the hard blue eyes of my friend and owner of this club, Lewis Stockton. "Hey," I mutter, my mind itching to turn its attention back on Betty and the college guys.

"Heard you were here looking for answers."

I nod, spinning in my chair to where my back rests against the bar, and I can see Betty in my line of sight. I won't be taking my eyes off of her again. She doesn't belong in a club like this, hanging around boys like that. "Got anything?"

Lewis shakes his dirty-blond head. "I wish I did, man. Everyone's been tight-lipped about this heist job. I don't think it was anyone local."

I rub at the stubble covering my chin. "We were thinking that too. There's no way the Golden Snakes could master a plan as detailed as this one."

Whoever did this knew exactly where to find the trucks and killed the guards with semi-automatics. They were in and out within a matter of minutes. The Golden Snakes are a rival MC, just outside of Vegas, and know better than to come anywhere near King's City or it'll cause a war between the clubs. Honestly, when we first heard about this heist, we thought maybe it was them, but there's no way those inbreds could have pulled off something this clever.

"I have to get back, but I'll ask around."

I shake Lewis' hand and say, "Somebody has to know something, because it wasn't us."

Lewis nods. "Yeah, it's not your style. Besides, you guys wouldn't have the distribution to offload a shipment that large."

"That's another thing that's got me wondering. Whoever

took it has to be running them somehow. I'm sure they can't move a shipment that big on the back of their bikes."

"This is definitely a well thought out job."

"Yeah, that's what worries me most. I don't want to be goin' down for someone else's crime."

"I'll ask my man down in Vegas, see if he's heard anything."

Betty laughs, gaining the attention of the skater punk college boy with blond hair and a team jacket for the state college. She runs her hand along his shoulder, and I watch the guy lick his lips.

She has no idea what she's playing with there. That guy isn't good enough for her. Hell, neither am I, but at least I know what she needs right now and could definitely deliver those goods for her.

I shake his hand again, harder this time. "Thanks, man. You've been a great friend. Even if you let some young punk asses into your club."

Lewis laughs, staring at the boys in question. He lets out a sigh when he spots Betty. "Is that the police chief's daughter?"

I nod. "Don't worry. I'll take care of her. Make sure she makes it home safe."

"Be sure that you do. I don't need that kind of trouble in here." He gets up from his stool and nods to Curly before slipping away into a door near the back.

I return my attention to Betty. I know exactly how I'm going to take care of her.

Chapter 3

Betty

"Bullseye," I say with a sway of my hips. "And that, gentlemen, is how you play darts."

"*Throw* darts," one of the college guys corrects me. "You don't play them, you *throw* them."

I roll my eyes. "Whatever, Dart Police."

Preston, the guy I've marked as a potential candidate for a night of letting loose, defends me. Sort of. "Leave her alone, Brent. Who cares if she calls it the wrong thing?"

I should call this night a bust.

When I was getting ready tonight, I had big dreams of having a little fun, but these guys are anything but that. Every time they speak to me, it's like they bring me down a notch. I haven't even had a sip of alcohol, because I didn't want to be drunk and make bad choices. However, I'm still hanging out with these guys, making bad ones.

I study Preston's blond hair coiffed perfectly to one side and picture having sex with him tonight.

Ugh. I can't.

Just the thought of sex with him makes me more stressed out than I already am. I want someone who will think for me, so I can just relax and enjoy what he's giving to me.

Someone like Silas.

This is all his fault. If not for him and his banana, I probably wouldn't be here seeking sex in the first place. If Jenna hadn't mentioned his abs in the store today, I'd most likely be at home, fantasizing about him in the safety of my bedroom, not trying to hook up with a guy whose gelled hair looks like it could survive the winds of a Category 5 hurricane.

"I'll be right back." I rush away from the guys and head toward the women's restroom to compose myself and possibly climb out a window.

Once inside, I cross to the marble counter and splash cool water on my face. What was I thinking? I should just head home.

Before I can turn around to leave, someone steps into the bathroom with me. The click of the lock ricochets against the lime green walls, and my pulse races when I stare at the man reflected in the mirror.

"What are you doing here, Betty?" Silas asks. His voice is raspy, like he's in pain just talking to me.

"I…" I have no answers for him.

"This isn't a place for someone like you."

"What's someone like me?"

"Someone sweet. Classy. Someone who takes the time to help Ms. Wegman get her groceries 'cause she can't see to read the labels, even though she's an ornery old bird. Someone smart enough to run the town grocery store, but too young to know she can't expect a boy to do a man's job."

Whoa, I sound amazing. Well, except for that last part about my age.

I spin around, leaning against the sink to move away from the man who's taking up all the small space with his big muscles. "I…" I decide to tell him part of the truth. "I needed something."

His eyes catch fire at my words. "I know what you need."

I suck in a breath. "You do?"

He steps closer, landing his hands on my hips, lifting me onto the counter. "You need to be fucked the right way." He crushes his lips against mine, and my body comes alive like it's my first day of living.

My heart beats at a frantic pace as his tongue tangles with mine. I can't believe Silas Irons is kissing me.

He breaks the kiss, his chest rising and falling just as fast as mine. "You taste just as sweet as I imagined you would."

I want to pull out my cell phone and record this event, because it's too unbelievable. "You've thought about this?"

He touches my hair, tugging lightly at the strands. "I've thought about a lot of things, sweetheart. Things you probably have no business knowing." He steps between my legs, and I squeeze my thighs around his lean hips, holding him in place.

"Like what?" I ask, feeling braver than I ever have in my life.

A worry line forms between his brows, like he's deciding if he should act on his impulses. Please Lord, let him keep going.

The silence drags on too long, and I wrap my arms around his neck. "Please, tell me," I whimper, unable to handle the suspense about what he's thought about doing to me.

Everything about this situation is naughty and forbidden, and my panties are already wet.

"I know you've probably never been fucked hard," he says, melting my bones. "Fucked right. Like a woman should be fucked. And hell, I've been jerking off nightly, thinking about doing that to you."

I'm soaked by his words, and I tilt my hips, seeking some sort of relief from the ache in my core.

He rocks his dick into me. "You turned on? Your little pussy craving my touch?"

"It's so craving your touch."

His big hand lands on my leg, inching up my skirt as his fingers glide further up until he's nearly at the hem of my panties. I knew this man was good-looking, but never realized just how spectacular he was until he's right up on me, breathing in my same air, pecking kisses along my neckline. His hand hovers over my thigh, barely touching me, and I want to push him to the finish line. What is he waiting for?

He stares at me with hooded eyes. "When's the last time you've been fucked good?"

I shake my head. "I don't think I ever have." Sure, I've had sex, but none I'd consider good by any means.

His nimble finger slips my panties to the side so he can touch me there.

There. Mm.

Oh, right there.

Yes.

He runs his finger through my wetness, and I moan out long and low. "You're so goddamn wet for me. How perfect."

I twist my hips, thrusting against his hand, seeking any type of relief. "Please," I whimper.

"You're so fucking needy. Look how bad you want it."

"I do. Give it to me," I beg.

"I'm gonna give it to you, sweetheart."

Finally, he slides a finger inside me, and I nearly buck off the sink. "Damn, you feel too good. Hot and tight. It should be a sin," he growls out before his lips capture mine once more as his finger pushes in and out of me. His thumb circles my clit, and I nearly have an orgasm right here and now.

I've never come so quickly, not even with my vibrator. I want to feel him everywhere. All over me. Inside me. Deeper.

I ride his hand, grinding, unashamed to let him gift me

what I need. Frustration flows off me in waves, and I tug at his shirt.

I need to see what he looks like without a shirt.

He shucks off his leather vest and helps me remove the soft cotton, and damn, I hope my body looks this good at his age. Ink flows over his skin like exquisite paintings framed by the ridges and grooves of abs and muscles.

"Wow," I whisper, trying to take in all of his tattoos at once.

He smirks, obviously liking the way I'm studying him. "You keep looking at me like that and we'll be in here all night."

"I'm actually ok with that," I tell him as I bring my lips to his chest, kissing a path over a heart tattoo above his left nipple.

He keeps working me, sliding his fingers inside, stroking my clit, making my nerve endings hum in a chorus of pleasure with each jerk of his hand.

"Oh god," I moan out.

"You're a tight little thing," he says, squeezing my ass with his other hand, bringing me closer to him. "I can't wait to be fit snug inside you."

I fumble with his belt buckle, trying my best to release the beast hidden behind his pants. "Please."

"I love how needy you are for my cock." His lips crash to mine once more as my body nears its crest. And then it breaks, flooding my body.

"I'm coming," I moan, my body picking up speed as he groans his approval. Pinpricks of lights flash behind my eyelids, and I swear I leave my body and float straight to the heavens. Silas has finger banged me so good, I died. As soon as my body calms, I open my eyes to find Silas staring at me, as if he's amazed by what he's seeing.

He removes his hand and licks his fingers as I climb off the sink and stand on shaky legs.

My dress falls over my body and the only sound is our heavy breathing. What now? I don't know what to do, and for a moment, I feel awkward.

I can't believe what I've just done with Silas Irons.

"I… uh…" I can't even think of what to say, so I revert to what I tell my customers at the Hungry Grocer. "Thank you for your business. Come again." I mean, it kind of fits. I'd certainly like to come again. Oh god, what do I do?

"I can definitely make that happen." As if Silas can read my mind, he spins me around, to where my back is against his front, and I can feel the ridge of him through his jeans, pressing up against my ass. All of him. Every hard inch.

He catches my gaze in the mirror. "Don't leave. I think I need a hard ride more than you."

Feeling brazen, I push my ass against his erection. "You promised to give me exactly what I needed tonight."

"That's right. I did." He licks his lips and leans in to rub his handsome face along my ear, nipping at my lobe. "I always keep my promises."

"Well, then," I catch his attention. "Give it to me."

Like lightning, he lifts my dress past my hips and leans me forward to where my forehead rests against the mirror. "Look at this ass." He smacks it, spinning me around so fast I almost get whiplash. "I'll always give you anything you ask for." He unzips his jeans and pulls out a gorgeous but monstrous dick.

Survival instincts kick in, and I recoil at the size of it, backing away slightly, unsure if it will fit. "Uh," I say, squeezing my thighs together. "Will that even fit?"

His eyes roam over all of me. "Barely," he breathes out. "But I'm gonna make sure you're nice and wet for me."

I believe him, and now I'm second guessing everything. "Uh," I say again.

Silas looks vulnerable right now, staring at me with sad eyes. "Please, don't back out," he says, strained.

It's like he wants me to be ok with his size, and not shy

away from him. It makes me yearn for him, want to please him, and not be afraid of his size. But to welcome it.

"Give it to me," I whisper, spreading my legs further apart as he moves me onto the counter.

One side of his lips tip up and the sight of it turns me on more than anything. "I knew you wanted to be my little naughty plaything."

I nod. "I do."

He reaches into his back pocket, pulling out a condom and opens it, ripping the package with his teeth.

"Gotta protect that banana," I say.

His heated gaze meets mine, and he chuckles. "Yeah, but I am clean. I want you to know that."

I gaze into his eyes. "Me too. I'm on the pill," I tell him.

His muscular chest rises and falls as he stares at me, mouth open slightly, as he debates whether he wants to do this without a condom.

It might seem foolish of me, but something in my gut, a connection to him, makes me want to feel him bare inside me.

"I've never fucked a woman without a condom before," he whispers.

I take the condom from his hand. "I've never fucked a man in a bar bathroom. There's a first time for everything."

He leans closer, capturing my mouth with his luscious lips. He kisses me rough, possessive, encompassing as he holds me tight against his hard body. I'm wet and ready when he breaks the kiss. He presses his thick cock at my entrance, nudging in the head, and I suck in a breath.

This is really happening.

"Fuck," he rasps, his eyes falling shut, "you feel so good." He moves slowly at first, easing in, letting me acclimate to his size.

His very *big* size.

I moan, holding onto him for dear life as he gives me

exactly what he promised. He moves inside of me, in and out, over and over. God, he feels so good.

I can't believe this is really happening.

I squeeze my eyes shut, letting him pump in and out of me.

"Open your eyes. Be here with me," he says, his husky voice so close. "Betty, look at me. Look at my thick cock pushing inside you."

I open my eyes, staring into the dark eyes of Silas Irons, and then glancing down to the connection we're forming.

He slows his pace. "Just me and you right here. Right now."

I nod, my eyes snapping back up to his, letting him fill me completely. "I know." This is the wildest thing I've ever done in my life, and I can't imagine doing it with anyone else.

With one hand on the small of my back and the other gripping my hip, he continues moving inside me, melting my insides with every touch he delivers. I moan louder the closer my body builds toward an orgasm. The first of many I'm hoping for with him.

The whole city would shun me if they knew I was here right now, head thrown back, my nails digging into the flesh of Silas's biceps as he pummels me.

It just feels so good.

A kind of good I've never experienced before, a kind of good I want again, because I'm pretty sure I'll never experience this with anyone else.

It's like Silas has the map to my body memorized, and he's driving to all the best places, taking his time admiring each and every attraction. I love it.

I meet his thrusts, and Silas groans.

"Fuck, sweetheart. You were made for me."

My toes tingle, my legs wrapped tightly around his back. Warmth spreads through my veins as my orgasm blossoms low in my belly. Silas's dick tends to it, nurturing it, feeding it with his ragged breaths and deep pumps, until it blooms and blinds me with its dazzling beauty. Silas Irons, this man making me feel so alive, has fucked me so good, I'm blind.

I moan through my release, and Silas holds me tight, close to his body, grunting through his own release, stringing together a mix of curses as he does.

As soon as our bodies have calmed, reality sets in and I worry about what I should say next. Do I just leave? Should I rush out of this bathroom and never look back? I mean, he's not a commitment type of guy, I'm sure.

Once I straighten my dress and run shaky fingers through my hair, I exhale. "Thank you, I needed that," I say as I hightail it out of the bathroom and rush out of the Cool Cactus.

"DAD, the doctor said you need to lay off the junk food and eat more fruits and veggies."

My father, in his usual grumpy style, rolls his eyes at my words and brings a jelly donut closer to his lips. "They make jelly from grapes. That's a fruit."

I park a hand on my hip. "Don't try to win this argument on semantics." I dig through his refrigerator, looking for anything I can put together to make him a proper breakfast. Every Sunday morning I head to my father's house to cook breakfast on his one and only day off. Today I was a little late, and he fended for himself.

I can't press him too hard on his unhealthy breakfast, because I don't want to delve into the reason I was late. I can't very well tell him I was getting busy with the city's MC president last night at a bar across town and overslept.

So I have no choice but to let his jelly donut slide and smile. "I'll bring you some groceries this afternoon. I have to run into the store today to grab a few things anyway." Because no one can ever get everything they need in one shopping trip.

I feel like I live at the Hungry Grocer and still never have all the ingredients I need to make a meal.

"I heard Silas Irons was in the store yesterday." My father licks a bit of jelly from his fingers. "Did he cause any problems?"

Dammit, Mrs. Fuller. My insides coil tight as I try to act nonchalant. "Uh, no. I mean, he got a banana. That's not a problem."

My father sets his half-eaten donut on his plate. "Banana?"

"Yes, even criminals eat their fruits and veggies." My father studies me for a quick beat before taking a sip of coffee. "I want you to stay away from him."

He eyes me over the rim of his mug, and I suck in a deep breath, unsure of when I'll ever be releasing it. I finally do one quick exhale and try to keep my voice calm. "Never planned on hanging out with him."

"He's into some bad things, Betty. I wish he wouldn't shop at your store."

I should change the subject, but nosiness wins out. "What kind of bad things?"

My father shrugs his broad shoulders. "Someone stole a government shipment of guns out on Route 47. We think they were involved somehow."

I don't need to ask my father who *they* are in that sentence. It's obvious he believes the Legendary Villains stole the guns. And who am I to say anything different?

I try to think about Silas stealing guns from a semi off the side of the road. It frightens me I let him touch me when he's obviously a criminal.

I'm going to hell.

Right along with him.

At least we'll be able to keep each other company.

Hell can't be hotter than Silas's orgasm face.

Ugh, I can't believe I just thought that.

My father finishes his donut and grabs the last one from the box.

I snatch it before he can reach his mouth with the pastry. "Oh no you don't." I take a big bite of the donut and grab my purse and keys from the counter. "I'll be back in an hour. Just gonna get you some groceries."

My father chuckles as I leave the kitchen. "I've got more donuts hidden away."

I shake my head as I shut the front door, hopping into my SUV to head off to the store. That man will always have donuts hidden away and I wish he would eat better. He's got a demanding job, and with all the stress the donuts are most likely wreaking havoc on his system. I push the thoughts away as I start the engine and back out of the driveway.

As I drive, I think about Silas and the gun shipment. He's a dangerous man, and I need to stay away from him.

So why am I secretly hoping he'll be shopping for a banana at my store when I show up there?

Chapter 4

Silas

I haven't been able to stop thinking about Betty since the moment she left me standing in the bathroom after having the best sex of my life. I haven't *wanted* to stop thinking about her, if I'm being honest. Fucking her was highly unexpected, but now that I've had her, there's no stopping me from trying to have her again.

She felt like a dream, and my head's already ten miles high in the clouds as Dragon tries to get the meeting together for the LVMC.

"What did Lewis say?" someone asks, but I can't get my brain to work right. All I can think about is *her*.

"Are you even listening, Silas?" Dragon says to me in a gruff, no-nonsense voice.

I run a hand through the thickness of my hair. "Yeah, man. I'm trying."

"Late night?" Duke asks with a grin.

Every motherfucker around this table knows I went to the Cool Cactus last night looking for answers.

"What happened last night?" Henley asks, before taking a sip from his cup of joe.

I blow out an exasperated breath. "Nothing." There's no way I'd tell these assholes I hooked up with Betty. They'd think I was making it up because a girl like Betty doesn't hang out in low-life clubs like the Cactus.

Hell, she's too good for a place like that.

She's way too good for a guy like me.

"What did you find out last night?" Dragon asks me, his eyes holding a hint of worry.

I shrug. "Lewis is checking a few leads. Nothing concrete."

"Fuck." Dragon slams a fist on the table and the guys all stare at him. "I won't go down for a job like this. Stealing a government shipment is hard time. We don't mess with guns."

"I don't think the police would believe you," Jagger says.

"Look, we'll figure this shit out," I say, trying to bolster my club's confidence. "We won't go down without a fight."

They all nod, and we turn the topic onto stupid club shit. I shouldn't say stupid, because I love this club. The men are like my brothers, but for some reason I just can't focus on any of it. We end the meeting, and I stand, pushing my chair in.

As I'm walking out, Dragon pulls me aside, and his dark eyes study me. "What happened last night?"

"Nothing," I answer.

"That's a lie," he says, like some kind of psychic. "You did that thing."

"What thing?"

"Tugging your eyebrow. Like Dad did about Mom."

This is the thing about working with your blood. They notice little shit, 'cause they know you inside and out.

I shake my head. "You wouldn't believe me."

"Try me. You're hiding something."

I stare into my brother's eyes. "Betty was at the bar last night."

Dragon steps back with shock on his face. "No shit?"

I run a hand across my jaw, resisting the urge to tug at my eyebrow. "Yeah, she was…" I don't even know where to begin, but I trust my brother. He knows me like the back of his hand and won't stop digging until he unearths the truth. "A little out of control. I ended up helping her regain that control in the bathroom."

Dragon punches my shoulder. "No way. I don't believe you."

"Believe it."

"Fuck, what are you thinking?"

"I don't know. When it comes to her, I don't think much."

Dragon chuckles. "What did she say afterward? Her father won't find out, will he?"

"She didn't say anything. She said thanks and ran out the door."

This makes Dragon laugh harder. "Listen, once was good." His face drops the humor, and he clasps my shoulder. "You got your fix and can get rid of whatever the infatuation is with her, but you can't keep doing it. Her father would kill us all, and they're already giving us trouble with the shipment."

"Yeah, I know." I do know. I've been thinking about that all morning. About how Chief Hutton is looking for any excuse to lock us all up.

Fucking his daughter would be a good reason.

"I mean it, Silas. No more."

"Yeah, I got it."

But I don't, because as soon as I leave the clubhouse, I hop on my Harley and head to the Hungry Grocer.

I just need to see her one more time.

AS I BROWSE the produce section of the Hungry Grocer, my thoughts are a complete mess. I'm trying my best to look like an ordinary customer, checking the quality of various items, but I'm sure I'm failing miserably by the frantic look in my eyes as I scan the store, searching for the raven-haired beauty I can't stop thinking about. The only woman who will satisfy my appetite.

Last night was a dream, one I keep checking to make sure I didn't imagine the whole thing.

I move through the Sunday shoppers, glancing over the grapes and apples, when I spot Betty standing next to an older man near the back.

I think he's the store owner, but I can't be too sure.

Betty's a damn gourmet feast, wearing jean shorts and a little top with cherries all over the material. Cherries. Right on her nipples. Yum. Her dark hair is twisted in a messy bun atop her head, begging me to free it. The sight of her instantly takes me back to last night when I was with her, feeling her. Kissing her. She's a fantastic kisser.

Normally, I don't spend a second time with a woman I've fucked. I'm more of a one-and-done kind of guy, but Betty isn't just any woman. I'm already planning what I'd like to do to her next. I'd love to have those ruby-red lips wrapped around my hard dick. Watch her take me deep down her throat.

Betty pushes a shopping cart away from the older man, coming in my direction, and I don't like the expression on her beautiful face. Her lips are turned down, and she looks upset.

"Hey," I whisper when she's a few feet from the baskets of corn.

She glances over, her mouth dropping open, shock written clearly on her face. But there's something else there too. It's brief, but I saw it before she shuttered it. Desire. "Silas, I… uh… didn't see you there. Shopping for a banana?"

I chuckle. "Nah, I think I'll upgrade to plantains. Ever had them?"

Betty glances over her shoulder, and then back at me. "I'm sorry, what?"

I step closer, my boots stopping inches from her sandals. "Plantains."

She laughs, but the pitch is all wrong. She's nervous. "Sure."

I don't know if I'm the one making her nervous, but I'm definitely going to find out what's troubling her. The more I stare at Betty, the more I realize I'd do anything for this woman. Anything.

"Are you ok?" I ask, reaching out my hand to touch some part of her. I land on her elbow, and I stroke it gently. "You looked upset earlier."

She pulls her arm away from me. "I'm not upset. I just have a lot going on." She looks up at me and then blows out a deep breath. "About last night—"

I don't let her finish before I cut in. "Please, don't."

"Silas, we…" Before I can stop her from saying how we should have never happened, which I'm sure is about to slip past her lips, she snaps her mouth shut.

"Don't say it was a mistake." The only mistake here is that I didn't make my move on her long ago.

"But it was," she says, all wide-eyed and short of breath.

I watch her chest rise and fall, trying not to point out the way her nipples have pebbled underneath the fabric of her shirt. "It wasn't."

Her gaze caresses my beard and lips before she snaps out of it, squaring her shoulders. "It was," she says, more determined. "And it will never happen again."

She marches away, pushing her cart like she's in a shopping competition and I laugh slightly under my breath.

"Oh, fuck yes it will," I say to myself.

Chapter 5

Betty

Walking away from Silas Irons has to be the hardest thing I've ever done in my life, but seriously, I can't let anyone see us together. I swear just one look from some nosy customer, and they'll all know what I'm trying to hide.

They'll know I spent last night enraptured by his attention, reveling in a world of lust and passion. They'll know I'm quickly falling for a man I can't have.

I wouldn't say I'm falling for him in the love department—an outlandish thought—but there's just something about him I find tempting. Alluring. So incredibly hot, and I can't stop thinking about him.

His hands exploring me.

The way his lips curled into a smile when I came all over him.

That leather vest full of patches over his t-shirt and worn jeans.

Those sexy faint lines of wisdom beside his dark eyes.

My face feels redder than the cherries on my shirt remembering our passionate time together as I push my cart through the store, looking for healthier foods for my father to toss into the cart. What I really want to throw in here is Silas. Everything I pass reminds me of our tryst in some crazy way.

The big salami sticks in the deli, most of all.

As I round the corner of the bakery section, Silas appears right in front of my cart. I nearly run right into his groin.

"What are you doing?" I ask him.

"Shopping." He holds up his basket with plantains.

I maneuver my cart around his hotness. "Well, I can see that. Why are you following me?"

This makes him chuckle. "I wasn't following you."

"Were too." Before I can argue with Silas anymore, I spot Mr. Redford by the loaves of fresh baked Italian bread. He waves for me to come and speak with him. "I'll be right back," I tell Silas, avoiding his penetrating stare. Because let's face it, I won't be back.

I can't be back to chat with him. Even though I'd love to get to know the personal side of him. What movies does he like? Is he a country music fan like me? What side of the bed does he sleep on? Favorite superhero. Important things. The things that make him tick. Things I'll never know. Sadness fills me as I move across the glossy floor.

"Betty," Mr. Redford says as I approach him, leaving Silas standing in the middle of the bakery. "I wanted you to meet Dan West. The new owner." He gestures to the tall man standing next to him.

I have to lean back just to get a glimpse of his face. "Hello, Mr. West," I say, sticking out my hand for him to shake.

I stare into his blue eyes, trying my best to produce a genuine smile, but my lips don't want to cooperate. It could be because he's very intimidating in his black suit and matching tie.

"How do you do?" he says, shaking my hand with a firm

grip. He glances over my shoulder at Silas, and then returns his attention back to me. "You shopping with your boyfriend today?"

I let go of his hand, smoothing my palms on my shorts. "No, he's just a… a…" I can't think of what he *just* is.

"A friend?" Mr. West asks.

"A customer," I reply quickly, letting this man know I'm all business when I'm in this store. "I'm very friendly with all my customers."

He studies me for a moment, like he's trying to decide if my words are true or not. "I see."

"I'm excited to work for you," I say, changing the subject. "Mr. Redford says you have a lot of ideas on how to make the Hungry Grocer even better than it already is."

This makes him smile. "Yes, yes, I do." He steps back. "We can discuss that during your work hours. We won't keep you on your day off. Nice to meet you."

"You too." I shake his hand again and say my goodbyes.

When I turn around, Silas is still standing there, waiting for me to return. I walk right past him, not wanting my new boss to see me chatting it up with the president of the local motorcycle gang.

"Betty," he says, gruff and growly. It's almost like he demands my attention. Like there's no other choice but to talk to him.

"I'll meet you outside." I don't need to draw any more attention to this attraction by talking to him right in the middle of the bakery. I don't need the gossip mill rushing off to tell my father what I'm doing. Not only for my well-being. I don't want Silas facing the blow-back from my father. God, I'm already protecting him. Next, I'll be sneaking things into the jail for him to shank people with.

I'm sure it's pointless to pretend here, because my father will probably find out anyway. I swear that man has a spy on me or something.

I wheel my cart to the checkout lane and pay for my items. When I step outside with my bags, Silas is waiting by my car.

"Don't act like last night meant nothing to you," he says as I open the back hatch of my SUV to put the groceries inside.

"It's not that." I don't even know what it is, so I focus on getting my groceries into the back of my vehicle.

Silas takes over, removing the brown paper bags full of dad's food from my hands, and I shamelessly watch his body as he leans into my Ford, neatly arranging them. "What is it then?"

"You're a criminal," I whisper-yell, glancing over my shoulder, making sure no one can hear me.

The store is fairly slow with most people out to lunch after Sunday morning services, and we're pretty secluded by my car in the back corner of the lot, but one can never be too careful. Wouldn't surprise me if Mrs. Fuller and her friends disguised themselves as the birds trilling in the tree shading my SUV.

"Where'd you hear that? Daddy?" he asks, and I don't like his tone. His rumbly chuckle pisses me off.

"As a matter of fact, yes." There, that'll teach him.

"Yeah? What else did he say about me?"

I lean closer. "He says you stole some shipment of guns. *Guns*," I repeat, still whisper-yelling, nearly losing my cool.

He grabs my upper bicep, yanking me closer to him. To where our mouths are just a breath apart. "I never stole any guns."

"You didn't?"

"Hell no. That's not how the Legendary Villains work."

I can feel the anger rolling off him from my thinking he's guilty. "Who stole them, then?"

He shakes his head, visibly relaxing the longer he stares at me. "Don't know. That's why I went to the Cool Cactus last night. To ask around. It's too big of a job for me and my guys."

"My father says they're building a case."

He blows out a deep breath and closes the back gate of the SUV. "That's what worries me. Whoever stole this shipment is framing us good."

I lay a hand on his bicep. "I'm sorry. I wish there were some way I could help."

"You can."

"How?"

He leans closer, nipping my earlobe. "Don't believe things until you talk to me first." He runs the pad of his thumb along my collarbone, skating it up my neck, and the gentle action causes a cascade of shivers to race all over my skin. "Who was that man you were talking to?"

"Mr. Redford?" I ask, my mind in a fog now that he's touching me.

"No, the other one." Silas presses kisses along my neck, and my body heats hotter than the bright sun beating down on us.

"Uh, the new owner."

"He got a name?" He licks the base of my throat.

"Dan West."

"I don't like the way he was staring at you."

I laugh, breaking the moment. "He wasn't staring at me in any special way."

"I didn't like it," he growls, his body hardening against mine. "I know every dirty thought he was having about you."

"No you don't."

"I do, because I'm having the same thoughts."

We're completely alone, shielded by my SUV but I'd feel better inside the vehicle.

I swear if I didn't know any better, I'd say he planned it.

"Want to go for a ride?" I ask. "Talk in private?"

He doesn't even answer, just strides to the passenger door and hops inside.

Five minutes later, we're parked on a deserted road, hidden by cactus and brush.

And we are *not* talking.

I swore to myself last night before I crashed in my bed that I wouldn't do this again with Silas Irons, but the way he's touching me right now makes me forget about all that nonsense.

It's just noise.

Worrying about what the town thinks. What my father would think. It's all just a flurry of indecipherable sounds.

He races his finger up my arm and I shiver. "Are you still needy? Did I not ease this ache you've got for me last night?"

I shake my head. "No, I need more." I'm like a heathen, trying to get any scrap of Silas I can.

He fists his hardness in his hands through his jeans. "Look what you've done to me," he groans out, his hand rubbing over the denim material. "Look how hard you've made this fucking cock. It's all your fault."

I bite my lip. "I can't believe I'm doing this."

He stalls. "Betty, I don't want you to have any regrets."

I stare into his chestnut eyes, and see a glimpse of vulnerability again, one I want to ease with just my touch alone. All my insecurities about being with him disappear. Now, I want nothing more than to please him. Pleasure him in every way possible.

I raise my hand to his face, letting my fingers glide through the stubble along his chin. "I don't regret any of this," I tell him, before I scoot back to my seat and unzip his jeans. "It's my turn to make you feel good."

"Oh fuck," Silas says, closing his eyes and leaning his head back on the seat when I free his dick. His hands fly into my hair, and he clenches the strands in his fists. "That's right. Take care of this problem you've created like a good girl."

I run my hand up his velvet length and his eyes open to watch me.

He's in awe. I can see it so clearly on his face.

"I want to suck you," I tell him, licking my lips.

Last night in the club, I didn't get a good enough look at his size and girth, but today it's all I see. So much of him.

I swipe my tongue along the engorged head, and he hisses low and long. Closing my eyes, I take another lick, like a lollipop, and then I slide his length into my mouth.

His hands dig deeper into my scalp, pushing my head just a bit further, as his hardness grows inside my mouth. "Fuck, this is a beautiful sight. Take my hard dick deep down your throat. Make me come." His breathing is ragged. "Oh fuck, make me come."

I glance up at him, and our eyes meet.

"Is this turning you on? Having your man's dick in your mouth?" he asks, his hips jerking forward ever so slightly.

I breathe through my nose as I take him further and further, letting him fuck my mouth.

He pistons his hips, dragging his cock in and out, and I want more and more of him. I don't even care that we're outside, hiding away on some deserted road.

I don't care that at any moment someone could catch us. I just don't care, because the want and need I have for this man is just too powerful to resist.

As if he knows exactly what I'm thinking, he pulls me from his mouth. "Take off your shorts and panties," he commands. "I'm gonna fuck you right here. Give my sweetheart exactly what she needs."

Within moments, I'm straddling him. It's like his body is in tune with mine. He presses the head of his dick along my entrance, and my body welcomes it, easing down on his thickness in one smooth movement. He hisses, looking down at where we're joined.

I moan out his name when he guides my hips up and down his length.

"Betty, fuck," he growls out. "I'll never be able to get enough of you."

I'm kind of feeling the same way, but I don't voice that

sentiment. Instead, I repeat his name over and over like my personal mantra. Like saying his name somehow brings me closer to him.

I kind of feel like it does.

He pumps in and out of me, gripping my ass so hard I'll have his marks. It turns me on more, and I meet him thrust for thrust.

My nerve endings tingle and I can't tell which way is up or down as he continues to fuck me, making me his woman.

"You're mine, Betty," he says. "Mine." He rams up inside me. "Mine." A shudder passes through his frame. "*Mine.*"

He reaches between our bodies, pressing the pad of his thumb to my clit and my body reacts almost violently, splintering in two, my orgasm hitting me so fast and hard I can barely keep up. My heart feels like a battering ram smashing against my ribcage with such force I can barely contain it all.

"So fucking needy," he tells me, his body moving faster now. He leans his forehead against mine, gripping me tighter. "You're mine," he grits out as his orgasm takes over, turning him into a beast of a man while he gets off.

So feral.

So primitive.

So completely mine.

I don't know what all of this means exactly, but I know I'm not ashamed to be seen with him.

I'll need to tell my father.

Chapter 6

Silas

I've been sneaking around town with Betty for about a week now. The first few days after claiming her as mine when we left The Hungry Grocer, I didn't mind. I knew she needed time to get used to the idea of what being my woman would entail.

As I sit here at the table, waiting for my Legendary Villains brothers to come together for our weekly meeting, I can't help wondering how Betty's getting along at work.

Even though she brushed it off, I still don't like the way her new boss looked at her the other day. It pissed me off so badly that I had to claim Betty that day, so there was no doubting how I felt about her.

And I'm sure she knows how serious I am about her. Because I've never felt this way about anyone.

Betty is it for me.

Now I just need to keep convincing her of that fact until I marry her and make her my girl forever.

"You've got hearts in your eyes," Dragon, always the first to show up at club meetings, says to me.

"I can't stop thinking about her. Like I physically miss her when she's not around."

Dragon stares at me, mouth hanging open like I've been possessed. "Dude, don't let anyone else hear you say that shit."

I have no shame in my feelings for Betty. She's my woman. "I'm in love."

Dragon fingers his thick beard. "You're not in love. You're just pussy whipped."

I shake my head. "No, it's love. Pure love."

He smacks me on the top of the head. "Did you fall down? Or something? What the fuck is wrong with you?"

"Love," I say as I slap him back. "One day, you'll fall in love too."

Dragon shakes his head, his brown eyes appalled. "No, I never will."

I laugh, staring at my younger brother. "You will. And you'll act just like I am."

"Doubt it." He sits in the chair across from me. "Did you hear from Lewis?"

I shake my head. "Hasn't called."

"Maybe we should call him. I'm thinking about going down to the Golden Snakes and asking around."

"Like hell you will." I won't let my only brother take on a job like that. "I'll do it."

He shakes his head. "It's too dangerous."

I lean back in my chair. "Fuck you. I'm the president and older brother. You think I'm gonna let you do this?"

Dragon raises a brow. "Yeah, but I'm more of a badass than you are."

I laugh, knowing he's joking. "Yeah fucking right. When the rest of the guys get here, we'll figure it all out."

As if by magic, the rest of the guys show up, entering the room one at a time.

Henley, Duke, Blaze, and Jagger take a seat, each of them ready to figure out how we get our name out of the mud.

"Silas is thinking he'll head to the Golden Snakes compound and ask around," Dragon informs them.

"You should take someone along with you," Henley says.

I nod, knowing Henley's right. "You want to come with?" I ask him.

He nods back. "Yeah, I'm guessing I can."

Henley's a good man to have with you in a fight. He's a quick shot, and an accurate one too. He's served real hard time, and also served time in the military as well. Rough as they come, and I'm honored to do any mission with him.

"I'll head back to the Cool Cactus, get with Lewis," Duke says. "Find out if he's heard anything."

"Let him know we need answers now," I say.

"Speaking of the Cool Cactus," Blaze says. "I heard you and the police chief's daughter have been spending some time together."

"Obviously," I grunt out. They know I'm spending time with her. "She's mine. And as my woman, that means we *all* protect her at any costs."

Blaze's smile drops. "Absolutely. Does her father know yet?"

I shake my head. "No, and I don't want him finding out until Betty decides to tell him."

"I'd hate to be at that exchange," Jagger says. "Should we prepare for backlash from that convo?"

"Probably not a bad idea," Dragon says.

"Why?" I ask.

Dragon hits me with a pointed stare. "Do you really think he's going to welcome you into their family with open arms?"

"I hadn't thought about it." I mean, yes, I've thought about it a little. Basically, I figured he'd be pissed for like five minutes until I explain to him I love his daughter more than I've ever loved anyone.

And I think she's feeling the same way.

The table erupts into a fit of laughter at my answer.

"You'd better think about it. There's no way he's going to be happy that you stole his little girl," Blaze says.

"I didn't steal her."

"Don't tell me that. Tell him," Blaze replies.

"I have to be heading home. Betty's meeting me there," I tell the guys, then I turn my attention to Henley. "We'll head there tomorrow."

He nods, agreeing. "Sure thing. If the chief hasn't killed you first."

The whole table erupts into a fit of giggles, like a bunch of schoolgirls. I leave them, slamming the door shut as I do.

I hop on my Harley, heading home, wanting more than anything to see the woman waiting for me there.

"I CAN'T BELIEVE you can cook," Betty says, and I raise a brow at her. She sits on top of my granite counter, swinging her legs back and forth.

I step between her thighs, leaning my hands on the counter beside her. "And why don't you think I can cook?"

"Well,"—she twines her hands around my neck—"you never shop for anything other than a banana or gummy bears."

I lean back with a smile. "I'll have you know, gummy bears are a delicacy."

This makes her giggle. "Really? I'm not a fan."

I step away from her, feigning shock. "I don't know if we can be friends."

She hops off the counter so she can trail after me. "I don't want to be your friend."

This stops me in my tracks. "What do you mean?" I gaze into her fiery blue eyes.

She wraps her arms around my waist. "I want to be more than friends."

I lay a kiss on her, lifting her back on the counter, my heart hammering in my chest. "You already are more to me than just a friend." I cup her warm cheek with my palm. "Betty, you're it for me."

Her smile spreads like rapid water rushing into a canyon. "You're it for me too."

My chest does this thing it's been doing all week and squeezes with warmth. I capture her plump lips, sliding my tongue in her mouth, letting her know she's the only woman in this world who I want to be kissing.

Once I've kissed her breathless, I lean her back to where she's propped up on her elbows and I remove her shorts, taking her panties along for the ride down her long legs.

And then I toss those golden beauties over my shoulder so I can get to her sweet spot. She moans, and the sound is perfect here in my home.

Like she belongs here.

"I want you to move in," I tell her.

She sits up. "You do?"

"Yes." I won't take no for an answer. I hope she's prepared for that.

Her eyes sparkle, and it takes my breath away. "Ok, I'll move in."

"Good." I spread her legs apart, nestling my head between her thighs. "Now your man is gonna show you what else he can do besides cook."

I swipe my tongue through her wetness, loving the taste of her. When she's bucking her hips against my face, I move to her clit, working the bundle of nerves until she cries out for more. My cock is so hard as I keep giving it to her, moving my fingers to her entrance. I push a digit inside, crooking it at the knuckle to reach that special spot that makes her fall apart.

I want to be in her slick heat, but I want to show her that I am all about her right now, giving her what she needs.

Betty rides my face and it's such a turn on. "I want to feel this sweet pussy come all over my tongue," I tell her.

I keep sucking her clit between my lips, pressing just enough for her to get a good rhythm. My cock is harder than concrete as she bucks and tugs my hair, all quick pants and breathy moans.

All mine.

I groan while she rides my face, my tongue working magic as she puts me further under her spell. When I add another finger, pumping and sucking her pussy, she shatters. Her legs tighten around my head as she calls out my name through her orgasm.

As soon as her body calms, she pulls me up. "I can definitely get used to that," she says with a lazy grin.

I kiss her pink lips. "And I'll definitely be willing to give you that every day."

She gets dressed as I cook chicken for a salad. She glances around the counter. "No bananas?"

I shuffle a hand through my thick hair. "Nah, don't like them."

This makes her laugh out loud. "Why do you buy them?"

I don't want to confess my truth to her. But the way she stares at me right now, doe-eyed and gorgeous after a fresh orgasm, I can't deny her. "I would sometimes get flustered in the store and just grab the first thing I saw."

This makes a soft look pass over her face. "I can't picture you being nervous." She grips my bicep.

"Well, you used to make me nervous."

She parks a hand on her hip. "I don't anymore?"

I peck a kiss on the tip of her nose. "No, you don't."

The only thing that makes me nervous right now is that we'll never find out who's framing us, and I'll live a life behind bars and not right here where I belong... with Betty.

Chapter 7

Betty

Life can't get any better than this. Well, at least I don't think it can.

"You're way too pretty to be with him," Dragon says.

I laugh. "That's very nice. But it's not true."

I came to their compound to meet Silas's motorcycle members, and they've all been so friendly. At first, I was a bit nervous, not sure what I was getting myself into, or if they'd expect me to know their lingo, but now that I've met everyone, I'm happy Silas has these men in his life.

It's obvious they are a brotherhood and protect each other at all costs. They've told me a little about the issue with the gun shipment, and I'm hoping this afternoon I can talk to my father before work.

Dad still doesn't know I'm dating Silas, and now we're moving in together. Things have happened at warp speed, but I know it's right. I can feel it deep in my bones. Every time Silas looks at me, I know it.

This man would do anything for me.

Anything.

And I would for him too.

"She's too good for you," Henley calls out as Silas grabs my hand and leads me toward his bike in the lot.

Blaze, Jagger, Dragon, Henley, and Duke came out to see us off, and as I wave goodbye, I smile.

"They were all so nice," I tell Silas before sliding onto his Harley.

"Of course. You're my woman. They know I'd kill them if they were anything but nice."

"Gee, thanks."

Silas cups my face in his big hands. "You're a good person. Anyone who meets you will see that light and fall in love with you immediately."

I blush. "Thank you."

He slides onto the bike and I slip my arms around his body, snuggling against him. He revs the engine, and the machine vibrates between my legs as Silas takes off.

Life is good.

We're heading to my house so I can grab a few things I'll need until we can officially move all of my stuff into his place. I feel free with the wind in my face and nothing confining me as Silas navigates the roads. Just the blue sky, fresh air, and my man. I've had nothing but swarms of butterflies flapping their excited wings since I agreed to this new life I'm starting with Silas.

Who would have ever thought?

All those good vibes fade when sirens blare behind us. Silas pulls off to the side of the road and puts down the kickstand to his bike.

We both get off his bike as the officer exits his vehicle.

Motherfucker.

My father.

He's not a patrol officer, so I never expected to see him walking toward us.

"What are you doing, Dad?" I ask him before he can speak.

"I should ask you the same thing." His face is hard, each line accentuated by anger. "What are you doing riding on *his* bike?" The way he says *his*, all twisted with disgust and judgment, makes me furrow my brow.

"He's my boyfriend."

Silas steps forward. "Before you say anything, you need to know how much I care about your daughter."

My father laughs, but there's zero joy in it. "Do not tell me how much you care for her. You don't even know her." He returns his attention back to me. "How long has this been going on?"

I don't want to give him the truth, but there's no lying to Daddy. "A few days, maybe a week."

"A week?" His voice is loud, nearly to the point he's screaming.

Silas tries to step forward, calming my father down, but he's not having any of it.

"Don't get any closer or I swear I'll shoot you."

"Daddy, you wouldn't dare." I scowl.

"Like hell I wouldn't."

Silas backs away, holding his hands up. "I care about your daughter, sir," he says, and my heart splits in two.

"Dad, please let me explain."

"Get in the car," he says to me but looking at Silas, his hand idling slightly above his pistol. "Now."

"No, I won't." I cross my arms, tears threatening to spill out, but I won't back down. I won't give in.

"Betty, I'm not asking you."

"What? Are you arresting me?"

"Maybe you should just go and talk to him," Silas says, stepping closer to me.

I stare at my father, his red face and rigid posture, knowing he will never be ok with Silas and me. We're from two completely different worlds.

Is he right?

Is this all a mistake?

What if Dad refuses to give Silas and those nice men in his group any peace because of me?

I blink back the tears. "Silas, maybe we're rushing into things." He looks like I've just kicked his puppy. "I just need some time to think."

My father smiles, like he's won this war, but I stare at him next.

"Doesn't mean I won't be moving in with him, Dad. I care about him too."

"You can't know that after just a week, Betty."

Tears stream down my cheeks. "You're wrong."

"Get in the car, now. I'll take you home."

I gaze at Silas, and I'm not sure what to do. Time to think is what I need. "I'll call you," I tell him.

"Betty, I'm not giving up on you. Ever. I'll give you your space to figure things out, but what's going on between us is real." He nods to my father and heads back to his bike.

I cry as I rush into the front seat of my father's car.

"What were you thinking?" my father asks as he pulls away, leaving Silas standing by his bike on the side of the road.

I have no answers for him, because right now I'm not even sure what I was thinking. It is real, right?

It has to be.

"Silas isn't the man you think he is," I tell my father as he drives down the main street of King's City.

"I know exactly what type of man he is. Jesus, he's twice your age."

"Age doesn't matter. He knows what I need. He protects me, Daddy."

"No, I won't allow you to be with a man like that."

"You can't keep me from him. I'm an adult."

"Like hell I can't."

"You can't stop my heart from loving a man I choose."

"Yes, I can. He's a criminal for Christ's sake."

"He didn't do it."

"Do what?"

"The gun shipment. He didn't do it."

My father laughs, gripping the steering wheel. "Oh, is that what he told you?" He can't stop laughing as he pulls into my neighborhood.

"I believe him. Why would they lie about it?"

This makes my father laugh harder. "You don't know why a criminal would lie? He stole those guns, and I'll be throwing him in jail for a long time. You'll be throwing your life away by being with him."

I shake my head as he parks in my driveway. "You're wrong. They're trying to figure out who did it. You'll see."

My father twists in his seat to stare at me. "No, you will. He's not right for you."

I get out of the car and lean in. "Yes, he is. He is right for me, Daddy. And I'm moving in with him."

I've decided. I want a life with Silas. I want it all with him.

WORK DRAGS BY... and by. I want to leave this place and rush over to Silas's house and tell him I want him.

My father never came around about Silas, but I'm hoping once he realizes the Legendary Villains didn't steal the gun shipment that he'll see he's a good man.

That he's a good man for me.

He cares about me. I know this.

So, I've decided after work I'm going to let Silas know I'm not going to back out of this thing with us. I flit around the store, thrilled with my decision. I'm also happy that my father knows about us. Now I don't need to worry about what he's going to do.

Most likely disown me.

No, he won't do that.

He'll see everything is going to work out for the best.

It just has to. Now if work will do the same, life will be one happy circle jerk.

Dan West has been in the store all morning, and well into the afternoon, making sure things are running up to speed.

He's been a complete gentleman, and I'm excited to work for him. He has expansion plans and wants to open more stores across Nevada.

This could turn into a promotion in a few years. He mentioned I could be a divisional manager in the future.

On my way to the stockroom, I wave at Dan as I pass him in his new office.

"The shipment just came in," Hank, an older employee, tells me.

"Thanks." I make my way to the back of the store to sign for the shipment. The driver isn't waiting for me, so I slip through the employee door that leads to the loading dock and stop cold in my tracks.

"Put the boxes near the front of the truck. We can hide most of the AKs with the canned goods. Once it gets to where it's going, they'll know what to do with it," a man with a deep voice says.

"We just need to make sure the guns make it across the border without a hitch," another deep voice says.

"They will. Dan assured us this plan is foolproof." The man laughs. "No one's even onto us."

Both men laugh and I try to peek around the corner.

AKs? As in guns?

Chills race down my spine. Dan West is using this grocery

store as his front to ship guns across the border. I need to tell my father. I need to tell Silas.

I need evidence. Right now, all I have is my word, which should be enough, but it's not enough to build a case in the legal system.

"We just have to get it to the Golden Snakes, and they'll help get the guns over the border," the deeper voice says.

"Through Arizona?"

"Yeah."

Golden Snakes? I've heard of them from my dad. They're a Mexican motorcycle club based in Las Vegas. I remember my father speaking about them a long time ago. They are true criminals. Men so bad, even the jails spit them out, hoping they'll leave. Usually, they stick to Vegas, never venturing into our small town.

I pull out my phone, pressing the record button so I can get this all on video.

"Can I help you with something, Miss Hutton?"

Blood pumps in my ears as I whirl around and my eyes crash into Dan West's. "I, uh, just needed to check my messages." I tap at my phone, getting into the messenger app.

"I don't think so." He snatches the phone from my hands. "I know what you were doing. If my men had kept their mouths shut like they were supposed to, you'd be fine." His voice is like venom, and I wonder what he means about me being fine.

Is he going to kill me?

He grabs my wrist, flinging me around the corner where his two men stand next to a semi filled with large wooden crates.

"Help me get her into the truck," Dan says to his men. "If you two would have kept your fucking mouths shut, we wouldn't be having this problem."

"No, please," I stop walking but he drags me with him.

"No one has to know anything." I try to free my hand, but his grip tightens.

"You're not going anywhere."

The two men step closer, one grabbing me by the ankles and the other grabbing my shoulders as they lift and toss me into the back of the semi.

As soon as I land on my ass, they shut the doors, locking me inside.

I slam my hand against the metal door, screaming out, telling them they can't do this. I scream and scream as the semi's engine roars to life.

Fuck this.

I search the crates, trying to find one of the guns. The semi pulls away, and I stumble but catch myself from falling.

Finally, I spot one of the guns, but of course, they're not loaded.

That doesn't mean I can't use the butt of the gun as a weapon.

I sit near the door, waiting, biding my time until we get to wherever we're going. There's no way I'll give up without a fight.

Chapter 8

Silas

Betty leaving was the worst thing to happen to me. I hated her father wouldn't listen, but I respect that she's his daughter.

And now she needs space.

"What is with you man?" Henley asks, pushing his glasses further up his nose as he drives his F-150 down the interstate.

"Just thinking about Betty." I told him the story earlier, about how her father pulled us over as soon as we left the club.

My guess is he was most likely spying on the clubhouse, waiting for one of us to fuck up.

We know better than that.

"Listen, I saw the way she looked at you. She'll come around."

"Yeah." She better, 'cause this ache in my chest just keeps getting stronger.

Heat rolls off the blacktop as we ride in silence. I turn the air higher, hoping it'll help this burn in my heart. I hope we get the answers we're looking for and Betty's dad accepts the truth.

We pull up to their complex just before dark, knowing that we'll need to stay out of sight. A semi sits near their clubhouse, and Henley glances at me.

"What do you think is in the semi?"

I raise a brow. "Guns?"

"That's what I'm thinking too. If we can sneak inside, I can plant a few bugs."

The action at the club appears to be happening in a bar they've got on the property, so we should be able to slip inside their main clubhouse, which is its own separate building. Hopefully.

Either way, we're ready to fight for the answers we so desperately need.

Right before we walk down the hill toward the clubhouse, a man opens the doors of the semi, and we crouch behind a van in the abandoned lot across from their complex. We're not close enough to hear what anyone's saying, but we can see what's going on.

"Is that Betty?" Henley asks as the door swings open and a woman, yielding a gun, whacks the guy across his face.

Fuck. "Yeah, that's her."

I pull out my phone, texting Dragon. "Come now. Send the police too."

He answers back, "Heard."

Another man yanks the gun away from her and wrestles her to the ground. I'm going to pulverize him. No one touches my woman. And that's when I see that motherfucker from her store.

I nod at Henley, letting him know we've got backup on the way. And we make our move. I replace my phone with the gun in my waistband, make sure it's racked, and head closer to the clubhouse in a full on sprint, knowing I need to get to Betty before they do.

Henley's hot on my heels as we race across the abandoned lot and rush along the semi from their blind side. No one sees us and we both aim our guns, knowing once we reach the back there'll be plenty of Golden Snakes club members to fight.

"Let her go," I say, aiming my gun at the man who's holding her.

"Silas," she whispers, and I nod at her, letting her know that we've got this.

"How did you get in here?" one Snake hisses. I think his name is Patch, or Snatch, or something else just as ridiculous.

"I told you we needed a fence around our property," another member says, one I don't recognize.

"I won't say it again." I keep my gun trained on the man who holds Betty in his grip.

The man glances at Dan West, and I focus my eyes on him. "So, you're running this shit show?"

He nods. "I am, and you're not invited." He aims a weapon at me, and before he can even get a round off, I'm squeezing my trigger.

He goes down in a flash and before I can aim my gun at anyone else, Henley's already in action, bringing the other men to their knees.

The man holding Betty lets go, and she stands there, tears streaming from her eyes.

I rush over to her, making sure no one hurt her. "Are you ok?" After disarming my gun and placing it back in its holster, I pull her into my arms. "You're safe."

A few minutes later, police sirens fill the air.

"I can't believe that just happened," Betty says, crying into my chest. "I saw them at work and tried to get a video of it."

"Never try to play detective again. You got me? You call me first. You ever have that happen to you, you call me first." I pull her from my body, staring into her eyes. "You call me. Got it?"

She nods repeatedly. "Yes, I've got it."

I pull her close to my body again, happy she's safe here with me.

"Betty," I hear her father call out, and I release my hold on her.

She rushes into the chief's arms, and I step closer, letting him know what happened here.

The police officers with him get busy making arrests, and before long, the place is roped off and an ambulance has arrived, along with the coroner.

"Silas, I'm sorry we got the situation all wrong," John says to me.

I stare into his eyes, never looking away, letting him know right here and now what type of man I am. "Yes, you did get it wrong."

He steps closer. "I got a lot of things wrong." He holds out his hand. "Thank you for saving my daughter."

I nod, shaking his hand, my eyes meeting Betty's blue ones. "I'd do anything for her."

"You better."

"Always."

Another officer approaches me, needing my weapon. He takes me into custody as a formality and will drive me to the station for my account.

Before I go, Betty rushes over to me. "I'll be waiting for you at our place."

I smile. "Good girl."

She rises on tiptoes and kisses me on the lips.

"Make sure she has keys to my place," I tell Dragon as he comes onto the scene. "And watch her until I get home."

Dragon nods. "Sure thing."

I give my girl another kiss before I'm hauled away.

Epilogue

Betty

It's been three months since the ordeal with Dan West and the shipment of guns. Three whole months of loving Silas Irons.

A few weeks ago, Silas came to me and said he wanted to hand over the Legendary Villains to his brother. He said he wanted to retire, that he wanted to focus his time on me.

Of course I agreed.

He now works part time with me at *my* store.

Yes, I bought The Hungry Grocer after the whole thing happened. I should have bought it in the first place, but never thought I'd be approved for a loan. However, I got approved, and now I'm the proud owner of the store.

With help from my boyfriend, Silas.

Daddy finally came around.

He was happy Silas saved my life, even happier when Silas left the Legendary Villains, but still hated the fact his baby girl was in love and didn't need him anymore. Although, a girl will always need her father.

"Honey, I'm home," I say as I enter our house after a long day at the store.

"We're out back," Silas yells through the open patio door.

I can hear the laughter and commotion coming from the backyard and wander in that direction.

The entire lineup of the Legendary Villains sits on my back porch, drinking beer with their past leader, Silas.

I say my hellos, sliding onto Silas's lap as Henley explains some new app on his phone to the other guys.

"It's an app that tells you how to spend your money," he says, pushing his glasses up his nose.

"I know how to spend my money," Duke says with a laugh. "I don't need some app to tell me how."

"It's for budgeting," Henley explains, and all the men laugh at his words. Henley tries to explain more, but nobody is listening to him.

"How was your day?" Silas asks me with a kiss.

I wrap my arms around his neck, kissing him fully. "It was great. I hired a new girl to work the register and promoted Jenna."

His hand slides over my ass. "That's good." He trails kisses down my neck, groaning against my skin. "Everybody get the fuck out. Party's over," Silas says, removing me from his lap.

I stand. "Silas, they don't have to leave."

Silas stares at me with a certain hunger in his eyes. "Like hell they don't. Get the fuck out."

The men groan their disapproval as they set their empty beer bottles on the patio table.

"You're an asshole," Jagger says, stepping toward the back gate.

"One day you'll be in love, and you will all do the same thing," Silas says, scooping me up in his arms.

They all laugh, each of them saying they'll never fall in love.

As soon as they've all left, Silas holds me in his arms. "I do love you."

I kiss his lips before answering back, "I love you too."

WANT MORE of Silas and Betty? Silas has a big surprise for his new girlfriend, Betty.

CLICK HERE to read now.

The Favor

Chapter 1

Abby

Have you ever had a secret? A secret you can't tell anyone? A secret so dirty and dark it makes you blush?

I have one. It makes my skin heat every time I think about it.

Everyone has something, right?

A kink?

A secret desire?

A fantasy?

I've been holding onto my fantasy for way too long, and it's consuming my every thought.

Sometimes, when you have these wants that are never met, they grow. They build. They climb higher and higher, until you can't control it anymore.

And that's what's happened to me.

Right now, I have the utmost need to have a stranger's hands all over me. Someone who doesn't know who *I* am.

For me, that's a difficult feat. I'm not being narcissistic when I say—*everyone* knows who I am.

People see me and immediately want a picture, autograph, or just to touch me. That's the trade-off when you're one of the biggest movie stars Hollywood has ever seen. My agent's words, not mine.

The last movie I starred in topped one billion in the box office. One billion. That's a lotta dough.

Unfortunately, the lack of anonymity wreaks havoc on my dating life. My sex life. If I wanted, I could get a line of men wrapped around the block, hoping to make *all* my dreams come true. That doesn't turn me on, though. I want someone who has no clue as to who I am.

Is that so hard to find?

I'm wishing on a star. Pardon the pun. Is there no one here in LA who hasn't seen my latest film? Is there anyone anywhere who hasn't seen it?

It doesn't help that the movie highlights me as a superhero goddess in a black leather suit. Which, don't get me wrong, I loved everything about the role of Seraphina. But, trying to get a man to see me as anything other than that character is damn near impossible.

It's entirely impossible.

Not one person knows me as Abby Carmichael anymore. No one knows me as Abby, the woman who has a need for someone to take care of *her*, and not all the characters I've played over the years.

What I want sounds so simple, but it's not.

I've tried to date. I've tried to do the single gig, but it just doesn't work. Trust me.

And maybe, I just don't want any ol' stranger to touch me.

There's only one thing this girl wants for Christmas this year.

"Abby, thanks for meeting me today," my agent, Emmett Garfield, holds out his hand for me to shake, pushing his black-rimmed glasses further up his regal nose with the other.

I slip my hand in his. It's large. It's strong. And it turns me on a little.

But, honestly…the glasses do so much more for me than any ol' handshake ever could.

I transform into my character of Hollywood bombshell, and offer my signature million-dollar grin. "Always happy to please."

His eyes darken from their normal chocolate-brown to black ink. "Step into my office." And I'm kind of hoping there's mistletoe hanging overhead. But, sadly there isn't.

He moves his tall frame aside for me to enter the spacious area where he makes some of Hollywood's most lucrative deals. His clean scent surrounds me as I take a seat in one of the leather club chairs in front of his desk.

A perk of being famous is I don't have to ask for much. Case in point, Emmett's assistant, Warren, sets a Diet Coke with a fresh glass of ice onto the side table by my seat.

"Thank you," I say, even though I'm not thirsty.

Emmett nods him out of the office, and then turns his attention on me. "I have three projects you'd be perfect for. And also, Karl Devon is producing a movie and," he pauses for full effect, "he might want you."

Emmett's eyes scan my face, and I wish more than anything he'd said the words, "I want you," instead.

I know it's absurd I've got this obsession with my agent. Hollywood is like being in high school. It really is. Actors bounce from relationship to relationship like popcorn popping. From what I've seen, it's true what they say—couples in the limelight just don't make it.

I'm at the height of my career, and I don't want anything to slow down my momentum. So, I don't want a relationship with my agent. Like definitely not. I just want his hands all over my body. Preferably, in the suit he's wearing today.

That won't happen with the dynamic we have going on right now. He definitely doesn't see me as Abby Carmichael. I think he sees me as profits in his tailored slack's pocket. I think he sees me as another Seraphina sequel. As a paycheck.

Too bad, because I'm pretty sure Emmett could deliver in the bedroom. He'd check all my boxes, and fulfill all my fantasies. I can tell by the dominating way he stands in this skyrise office that overlooks all of LA. It's in his dark eyes that study everything with such precision, such a careful approach, that I know this man would take his time going downtown. If you know what I mean.

Chills flare across my skin, and I try to shake off the arousal. "Wow, a Karl Devon movie," I finally say. "Did you have something to do with this?" I cross my legs, deliberately showcasing my Prada heel with a wag of my foot.

He watches the movement for a moment before a slow smile spreads across his face. "I may have had my assistant mention your name when he was having lunch with his assistant."

"Ah, using the assistants to do your dirty work?"

He smirks a bit as he brings his water bottle to his lips. "Dirty is the only way I play."

That statement feels like a promise of things to come. But, I know playing this game with my agent is like playing with fire.

There's no way I can do it. Unless.

No.

Although.

Not happening.

Maybe?

Nope.

I squash the thought immediately, rising from my chair. I thank Emmett and give an excuse of having another meeting before I leave in an ungraceful rush. On the elevator ride down, I repeat in my head that I can't have thoughts about my agent in any way, shape, or form. He's my lifeline. He makes the movies happen for me.

Starring in a Karl Devon film is huge, and I can't screw this up just because I have a thing for Emmett Garfield.

Karl Devon is to Hollywood as diamonds are to women. Everyone loves Karl's movies because they're more serious, more challenging, more rewarding. Doing a Karl movie means I can possibly be on my way to an Oscar.

I stop walking, the idea of accepting an Oscar floating through my head. Wow. Can you imagine?

I've heard the rumors Karl Devon's next new role is a Christmas in July movie, and it's all about a woman, struggling to make ends meet so she can have a better life. I'm not sure of the outcome, but it's definitely something I've never done before. A more serious role. Something that showcases my acting, and not just me in a leather suit.

I hop in my car and head into town to my favorite little cafe. When I exit my car, I do a few poses for the paparazzi, and then head inside to meet my friend, Raven.

It's cool, the owner of the place doesn't let paparazzi inside, so it's a natural hotspot for celebs and the like.

I spot Raven's short black hair and horn-rimmed glasses in the corner, reading a book. She's seriously the only one who can pull off her signature sexy librarian look. Me, I'm a chameleon, changing my look with which role I'm offered. Usually, I like to have my hair darker, more brown. Like before I was famous. Right now it's lighter than usual and tumbling in waves almost to my ass with highlights and strings of gold flowing through my tresses. I call this the 'Seraphina' look. My most popular character. A badass superhero from the planet, Gyphor, in search of her long-lost race, bringing peace to the intergalactic order. Listen, it's a huge hit with men of all ages. And I do mean, *all* ages. I get tons of fan mail from boys still in high school.

Ugh, sorry to put that mental image in your head, but

imagine how I feel when I open those letters. I'm still in my prime too, only twenty-four, and have already amassed a lot more than any other actress my age.

"Hey," Raven greets me. "How'd your meeting go?"

You'd think most movie stars just hang out and party in their downtime. But not me. Not usually. You can normally find me at my house, reading, writing, and watching Netflix. Raven and I even started a book club with other Hollywood stars who love to read. Our favorite is romance...of course.

"Ok, get this," I take a seat across the table from her, "ready?"

Raven leans forward. "Are you going to tell me that Santa isn't real?"

I laugh a little, and then smile, leaning in to whisper, "Karl Devon…"

Before I can even get the whole sentence out of my mouth Raven recites, "Oh my God," over and over.

"It's like all my dreams are coming true," I tell her. "This is the role I really want."

"That's incredible." She beams at me. "You need to sprinkle some of that magic on me."

"You're doing great on your own," I tell her. Raven isn't lacking in magic. Emmett has kept her busy with jobs. She has a gig on a popular TV show, and is one of the few actresses who can do both TV and movies seamlessly. She has a new movie coming out soon, and then for her, it's right back to TV.

"Did Emmett say it was definite?" she asks.

"No, just that Karl Devon might want me."

Raven points her black straw at me from her cocktail. "Kind of wish Emmett wanted you instead, huh?"

I press my lips together so I don't say yes. It's a complicated wish, though. It's one of those types of wishes you could make and have come true but have a ton of conditions tacked onto it.

Like I wish I could eat all the cake in the world. I love cake. But, I don't want the calories. See, it's called a conditional wish. I just made that up, just now, but let's make it a thing. Maybe I'll tweet it.

Anyway, I'm losing track. Emmett is the type of man I wish would want me, with conditions. A whole lot of conditions.

Like for example, I would want our working relationship to go unaffected. And trust me, I've heard all the stories about people saying they can sleep with someone and still act the exact same way around them.

And who knows, maybe I wasn't born with that certain sector of my brain. Because when I sleep with someone it changes everything. Most times it ends up with my naked nudes in some silly gossip rag, and my PR works double time to nip it in the butt...quite literally. It only happened once, and I wasn't completely nude. Thank god.

But still.

Do you see why dating is next to impossible?

And oh sure, I could date an actor.....puhleease. No thank you. The only thing more conceited than a male movie star is their ego. Trust me, they're the worst.

So, for me, it's been months and months of solitude.

The closest I've come to having an intimate evening was with BOB, my battery-operated-boyfriend.

But, it's ok. Most days I'm so busy working, studying my craft, or trying my hardest to land new movie deals that I hardly even notice being alone. Other days, especially around the holidays, I just yearn for a warm body to hold me close.

Instead of answering, I laugh as the waitress stops by to get my order, and I tell her I'll have a peppermint mocha. Let's face it, Emmett's out of my league. And he's the type of guy who knows it. And I've heard he's dated half of Hollywood, well, he's slept with half of Hollywood.

Raven smiles. "Do you have a date for my premier?"

And I answer, the same answer I've had for every other premier we've gone to together. "Yes, you."

She laughs. "Not this time, hun. I have an actual date."

My eyes widen, and my heart beats faster. "You let me sit here for however long before you decided to lay this on me?" I laugh.

She shrugs. "It's nothing so great. Just a new producer wanting to get into rap music."

"Oh. Do you even like rap music?"

She laughs, shaking her head. "No, guess not." She takes the last bite of her sandwich and shuffles from her seat. "I have to get going. I can't be late for Timmy Tallon tonight."

"Have fun," I call off to her, and then let my mind wander back to Emmett. The one man I can't quite figure out.

I want him, but how would it work.

And then, an idea hits me.

Chapter 2

Emmett

Have you ever had one of those days? Where nothing too spectacular happens, but for some reason you know something bigger is on the horizon. Having the Karl Devon movie land in my lap is not the only huge thing I have going on in my lap right now. Yes, I'm talking about that. Most men will say they've got a nice long package, but I've got the references to back it up. And guess what, it's not as many as you may think.

Sure, I've been labeled Hollywood's bad boy agent, complete with a track record of dating every super model who passes my path. But, hey, guess what? It's so not true. You can't believe everything you read in the gossip column.

Trust me, sometimes I think I need to hire a PR person just for me.

I'm the top agent in all of Hollywood. I know I know. Some people may say, hey Emmett how can you be so cocky. But, it's not an opinion, it's not cockiness....I really *am* the top agent in all of Hollywood. In all the world if we're speaking honestly here.

And my roster of actors and actresses is long and thick.

Like other things. My agency is the biggest in all of La La Land.

I guess I like big things.

And a Karl Devon movie is just that, a big fucking thing. Karl Devon is one of those producers who comes around every ten years, makes a movie, and bam, it's the next hottest thing. Remember, Doomsday? Yeah, that was him. One of the top grossing movies of all time. The only movie to ever come close to those numbers is Seraphina, two years ago. And yeah, I have the hot little actress that played Seraphina on *my* roster.

She just happens to be one of my top clients.

But, let me let you in on a little secret. Man, oh fuck, if she wasn't a client I'd have her bent over my desk in a heartbeat screaming out my name.

I've never wanted anyone so badly in all my life.

Is that wrong to think that?

Yeah it is, promise I won't have that slip up ever again.

I'm all professional, baby.

Ok, where was I? Oh, right. Karl Devon. The moment I got the info he was sniffing around for a lead for his next top secret project I just knew I had to get my girl on the front lines. I knew I had to get Karl Devon to want her...as badly as I do.

Ok, ok, I know, I slipped again. Sue me.

"Warren, get in here," I bark, frustrated that I can't have the one woman I want.

Warren's a good kid, and wastes no time rushing into my office. "Sir?"

"How long do we have to wait for Karl Devon to make up his mind? What can we do to nudge him in the right direction?"

Warren squirms, biting his lower lip in nervousness. I've known the kid for years and he has a ton of nervous tells, but he's getting more and more confident the longer he works for me. "Uhh, I…"

I stand from my desk. "We need to get an impromptu meet and greet between Abby and Karl."

Warren scrambles to my calendar. "You're free tomorrow night, and I can find out where Mr. Devon will be."

"Get on it," I shout out. Yes, this will be perfect. I just need to get Abby and him in the same room, so he can see for himself how perfect she'd be for his project.

And yeah, I only know his movie is a more serious role, which I think Abby can do in a heartbeat. She can do anything, and then some. She's one of those actresses that can mold into whatever character you need her to play.

It's fucking sexy as hell, but like I said, I don't think about her that way. Or at least, I don't think about her that way starting now.

I'll just jerk off to her later when I'm home and alone, and I'll be cured of thinking about her.

Although, it hasn't worked in the past to exorcise her out of my system.

Fuck.

I grab my phone, punching in the familiar numbers. "Abby, don't make plans tomorrow night."

"Ooh, what did you have in mind?" See, it's when she talks all seductively and in a low voice that I get turned on. Lord, help me.

"I want to get you and Karl Devon in the same room, so it'll speed up his thought process."

I can tell she's smiling. "I love the idea. Just text me all the deets."

"Will do." And I hang up on her as quickly as I can before I say something stupid like what are you wearing right now?

Even though I just saw her less than two hours ago.

I'm going to Hell, well ha, that's a given, but I'm going to a different type of Hell reserved for idiots with unrequited sexual desires about someone they shouldn't even be thinking of.

I need to get laid.

"He'll be at the Lancaster Room tomorrow night," Warren calls from his desk right outside my office door.

"Get all the details, and text me." I rush out of my office, with one thing on my mind. I need to hit the gym before I combust from all this sexual energy floating around in my head.

I swear, it happens every time Abby comes to my office.

Chapter 3

Abby

My idea is risky. It's downright silly, but it can possibly work. Although it has many moving parts I'll need to make sure all come off without a hitch. But, Emmett would give me the type of night I want from him, no strings, and he'd have no idea who I am.

I know Emmett is as blind as a bat. I just need to orchestrate a rendezvous between him and... that's the thing, who?

I don't know anything about Emmett's love life. All I know are the rumors I've heard. But, what I've heard is enough to go on. Setting up a little blind date for sex should be a cinch. Like I said, many moving parts.

And I'll make sure the room is dark, and my hair is different, and I'll disguise my voice. It's good to be a wonderful actress.

I just need Emmett to take the bait. I need him to want to hook up with a stranger, and to want to rock her world more than he ever has before.

Like I said, based on his track record this should be easy.

All the possibilities.

All the wants.

The needs.

The desires.

Everything I yearn for, and somehow I can't stop thinking about this man, and I need him to scratch the most unitchable itch I've ever had in my life. But, when the body wants sex with someone who doesn't know who you are, well, the body will nonstop obsess over it for months.

And I'm at my breaking point here. I can't go through another day without Emmett inside me, with me riding the Emmett express all the way to orgasmville.

I need reinforcements. I need Warren. Yes, Warren's the only man that can get close enough to Emmett. He's the only one who can put that whisper of a thought into Emmett's ear. Slip the essential possibility of it all.

I text Warren, and my best actor bud Chris. Yes, there's tons of Chris's out here in Hollywood, and he is, in my opinion, the funniest one. And Chris and Warren are great friends.

It might be starstruck on Warren's end, but on Chris's end it's purely entertainment for him. He loves going out, and he loves seeing his most favorite person in the world…me.

I text the boys and make plans for an emergency session for tonight.

I need them to go over my plan, fill the holes, and make sure it's foolproof.

THE CLUB IS PACKED on a Friday night, and my security detail hangs back as I scan the place. It's dark, with gold chandeliers draping from the ceiling. It's all glitz and glamour and the people inside are dressed just as elegant. I fit right in with a gold, shimmery skirt and black top. My favorite pair of gold heels finish off the outfit.

I head toward the bar, watching as men turn their heads to catch a peek of me.

The night holds an air of possibility to it all. Like anything can happen if you just believe in fairytales and sparkly dust. And maybe a bit of the Christmas spirit. I want to believe. I really do.

Warren's first to arrive, kissing my cheek and ordering me a cosmo to match his own.

Chris, as always, is fashionably late with an entourage following closely behind him. He lights up the club when he walks in. He's got charisma coming out of every pore.

He kisses my cheek, and orders a cosmo to match.

"What's the emergency?" he asks, his eyes roaming the club like he's on an African Safari. Like he's looking for a lion to make him roar.

"I need both your help." I give them my best I'm-so-fucking-serious look.

And then I go into all the details, leaving no stone unturned, telling these two men my innermost fantasies that have plagued me for months about my agent.

They're both shocked. "Oh damn," Chris breathes out. "And you don't want him to know who you are?"

"I can't have him know. I just can't."

Warren nods, like he understands. "I get it, girl. It would ruin the whole work relationship." He sips his cosmo. "Can't say I'm really surprised."

"What do you mean?"

He sets his glass down very carefully so as to not spill any. "Come on, the chemistry between you two is palpable."

I place my hand on his arm. "It is? I can't let this ruin things."

"Why don't you just have sex with some rando?" Chris just doesn't get it.

"Don't you think I've tried? I'm every red-blooded straight males wet dream right now. As soon as I show up on a date it's all Seraphina this, or Seraphina that."

Chris eyes me up and down, as if he's thinking over my words, assessing them, making sure there's zero percent bullshit in them before he answers, "Girl, true that. I hear you." He chugs his cosmo down in one gulp and smiles. "What did you have in mind?"

Warren scoots over, wanting to hear my foolproof plan. Or at least what I hope is foolproof. It can work, right?

Of course it has to. I mean, I don't think I'll survive another minute without Emmett's hands all over me. I need the man, stat.

"Well," I lean in, "I was thinking if we could set up some sort of sexual rendezvous with Emmett, and tell him he'd be helping one woman fulfill her fantasy. But there's stipulations, no glasses, dark room, all that jazz."

Warren's brow rises like he's so not on board with my idea. "I don't think that'll work."

"Why not? From what I hear Emmett sleeps around. A lot. Why wouldn't he want a night of kink?" It's kinky, right? Sure, any man would go for this.

"How can he be sure he's not setting himself up for a bad press situation?" Chris orders another drink.

"Umm," I hadn't thought of this, "well, Warren will set it up. Make sure he can trust him. Make sure that Emmett is up for a fun night."

When in LA, sometimes you have to get adventurous, and maybe yes, I'm going to the extremes to get laid, but...you have no idea how long it's been.

You see a pretty movie star and think, wow, she can have anyone her little heart desires. Well, let me tell you...not anyone. Like, the way I want Emmett should be illegal. It should be a crime, and I should be punished.

But, the man I want to do the punishing would never jeopardize his career to give me an orgasm.

Hell, even I see all the flaws in my plan. I see that if Emmett were to discover who I truly am he'd fly out the door so fast you'd just see the imprint of his figure through the door, like in the cartoons. He'd cancel our contract, and I'd be out of an agent.

And, worse yet, I'd lose the Karl Devon movie.

But, if it works. My body alights with a fire just thinking about if I can pull this off. If the playboy of Hollywood can work me just right to multiple o's all night long. And I just know he can deliver.

I just know he'd like it dirty.

Ugh, I sound like a hussie. All I have are distant memories of lackluster sex.

Lots of lackluster sex.

I want to have the kind of sex you only read about in romance novels. That headboard bashing, girl screaming from the rafters type of sex. The kind that makes you feel sexy, devoured, and cherished all in the same breath.

That's what I want. And I want Emmett Garfield to deliver it.

Without knowing he's delivering it to me.

Is that so hard?

"We'll help. We're in." Both the boys say with a wink.

They laugh, then waggle their brows at me, and I dismiss myself to check my phone. There's a text from Emmett, "Wear that red dress tomorrow night."

I don't know why this one simple text makes me all giddy, but it does. Just knowing that Emmett is thinking about what I'll be wearing tomorrow night is hot. Even if he is just trying to get me to land a movie deal.

Maybe he found out more about the deal. The red dress isn't the sexiest dress I own, but it does present me in a more serious, sophisticated manner.

"Warren will you put the thought in his ear?"

Warren smiles, a devil-type of smile, one that means he's up to no good. One that means he's one-hundred percent on board.

This is gonna be so hot.

Chapter 4

Emmett

Let me just say one thing before we head on any further. I will *not* sleep with my sexy as fuck client. I just won't do it.

Even though she's wearing the exact red dress I asked her to. Now, I'm sure this temptress has a million red dresses, but she knew which one *I* wanted to see her in. It's like she has a direct link to my dick, and knows exactly what he wants.

But, this dress is special. And she knows it. It's the exact dress she wore when I plucked her from nothing and brought her up to fame. It was a quick journey for someone as talented as her. But, it was the dress that did it for me. I mean, don't get me wrong, she's gorgeous. But, the dress shows off every curve I know damn well she has.

I've seen her in her Seraphina outfit, and let me just say that image has supplied many of my fantasies for the past several months.

But this one, with Abby in the red dress. The dress she wore when she wasn't famous. Before she was *the* Abby

Carmichal, and was just Abby. This is the one that does it for me.

But, then again she was never *just* Abby to me.

I eye her from across the lobby of the swanky Lancaster Room. She gives me her best shy girl smile and it drives me fucking insane.

It's her real smile. Not her Hollywood, posing for the paparazzi smile.

Does she even know how perfect she is? She has to, I mean she's a famous movie star, and I know many men would be intimidated by her power, but I just find it sexy.

I raise my drink, calling her over and then I scan the room for the very tall, bald-headed Karl Devon. He's hard to miss, and thanks to Warren's top secret info, we should be early. I want to get a lay of the land. To feel the place out and figure a way to get my girl, I mean, my client in front of him.

It has to be super smooth. But, that's just how I operate.

I lift my drink to my lips, slowly. "Nice dress."

She runs her hands over it. "This ol' thing."

I move her quickly to a side table near the back, a table that will let me see every vantage point of the bar. "Drink?" I ask her.

"Diet cola."

Smart, no alcohol. Like I said, this girl thinks about her career first and everything else comes second. That's what makes her so goddamn good.

As the waitress passes, I order Abby's drink and sit back, scanning the club once more.

"So, what are we doing exactly?"

I smile. "We're acting like this is a normal night out for us. We're going to just accidentally bump into Karl Devon. And once we do, I'll do all the talking. Got it?"

She snaps her mouth shut and nods.

The waitress drops off her drink and I throw some bills

onto her tray. "And then after we meet Karl Devon, you're going to let me buy you dinner."

She stares at me like she has something more to say. Like the idea of dinner fascinates her and maybe she wants dessert too. There's a sparkle in her soft brown eyes. It makes me have to turn away or else I just might kiss her.

I'm gonna do like I normally do, have a nice dinner with her and then go home and jerk off to images of her in this simple red dress.

"I have a confession," she says, leaning over to tell me her secret and I hold my breath, waiting. "This dress isn't the same one."

I lean back, eyes wide. "Uh, yeah it is." Come on, I think I remember the dress. It's been the star of so many of my late-night fantasies it's not even funny.

She smiles conspiratorially. "I had a new one made when I had a mishap with the old one."

"Mishap?" I raise a brow. Now here's a story I want to hear.

She giggles and it fills my ears like music. "It was destroyed at a Hibachi restaurant." She sighs, and waves her hand like she doesn't think I'd be interested to hear anymore. "Long story."

Here's the thing. Most people would laugh it off, not wanting to be saddled down with a long story of how she ruined her dress, but not me. I find myself on the edge of my seat, wanting, no needing, more of this woman's stories. "I have to know."

She thinks about it for a second, placing a red-tipped nail to her mouth. Her lips. I wish she wouldn't keep my focus there. I love staring at her lips. Soft, pink, full. I can only imagine they're soft, but I'm pretty sure they are.

"Ok, well it was right after you discovered me. My family took me out to celebrate." She waggles her eyebrows. "I was going to be a huge movie star thanks to you."

"Thanks to me, you are."

She clinks her glass against mine in a cheers. "Well, the Hibachi chef was a little handsy, and asked me to come up and do a little trick. One thing led to another and the next thing I knew he had sliced my dress in half."

I grit my teeth just knowing someone else got handsy with this woman. "Like completely in half?"

"Yes, those knives they use are no joke."

"I believe it. So, what happened after that?"

"Well, my dress was hanging together by threads. And my father rushed me out of there, but not after fighting with the chef."

"Now that *is* something I would have liked to see."

She laughs, sipping her soda. "I was a small fry back then. You wouldn't have wanted to hang out with me."

I wish I could tell her how wrong she is. That I thought about her a lot after our first meeting. At the time, I was just getting out of a relationship with my long-time girlfriend, Cassie. I wasn't looking for anything but a bottle of whiskey to drown my sorrows in. Yeah, it was a bad breakup, and now I'm stronger and smarter from it.

But, I can't let Abby sit here and think I'm some sort of prick who only hangs out with people who are on the same level as me. "I would have hung out with you. And honestly, I'm offended I wasn't invited to the family soiree."

She full out laughs. And it's so cute. "Now that's something I would have liked to see."

I straighten my tie, my phone dinging in my pocket. "Why? You don't think I could have hung out with your family?" All I know of the Carmichaels is they weren't from a lot of money, and now that Abby has enough of it, she's paid off much of their debts and bought them a house in Malibu.

"I think you would have scared them off."

I lean in closer, but only to get my phone from my pocket

and nothing more. It isn't to sneak a peek down the front of her dress. No. It's not that.

She freezes, her glass halfway to her mouth.

"Do I scare you?"

She sucks in a breath, giving me my answer, but whispers a lie, "No, not at all." She sets her glass down and does this little giggle thing that sends a zing of energy straight down to my dick.

I don't mind her lying to me, because honestly I need to get this whole conversation on the fast track to deletion. We shouldn't be making googly eyes at one another in a darkened nightclub.

I check my phone. Warren. "I have to take this really quick. Keep your eyes peeled for our man."

She nods and I step away to answer the call.

"Warren, this better be good." He'd better not be telling me that Karl Devon thing isn't going to be here. Because if I have to set up another night of being tempted by Abby, I may just lose it.

No, this has to happen tonight.

"He'll still be there, but I need to talk to you about something. It's important, but you're busy." He brushes it under the rug, and I breathe in deep. I hate playing mind reader. "Tell me, Warren."

"I'll meet you at the Lancaster Room."

"This better be worth it." And I hang up.

"Warren's coming to meet us," I tell Abby when I sit back down. Whatever Warren has to tell me better be life or death type of importance, because Karl Devon just walked in.

And the whole club shifts.

It's game time.

"Follow my lead," I whisper in Abby's ear, taking a split-second to sniff the wild-berry shampoo smell from her hair. God, it's like a mother fucking aphrodisiac.

I steel my expression, making my way through the crowd

toward the big bald man on the other side of the club, with Abby following closely behind with the new old red dress. It makes me wonder why she felt the need to buy a new one. One exactly the same.

Did this dress hold as much importance for her as it did to me?

I hope so.

Warren must have been standing out-fucking-side because he shows up in minutes after we ended the call.

Warren rushes over, standing next to Abby and me. "Whatever you need to talk about has to wait," I tell Warren, grabbing Abby's hand in mine.

Which let me say right now, I've held her hand before. But right now, it feels so tiny. So delicate. And as I lead her through the club, I almost feel like she's mine. I have this protective vibe going on deep inside me, and I can't quite figure out why I'm feeling like this. It's driving me insane, and when other men look at her I want to rip their fucking heads off.

But it happens. I mean she's Abby Carmichael. I'm holding Seraphina's hand, and I need to make sure I get her right in front of Karl Devon. I need to make this happen for her.

"Karl Devon," I say with a grin. I've known Karl Devon for years. To say we're friends is pushing it. To say we know how to work together to get shit done is more like it. He knows I need him. He knows he has all the power in this room, but he also knows that I control the talent.

And I have a ton of talent on my roster.

So we play nice. We say hello and I introduce him to Abby.

"I've seen a few of your movies." Bonus, now I don't have to convince this oversized Mr. Clean to watch a few.

"They're great, aren't they?" I keep my grin steady, not really expecting an answer. "Let's get a drink together."

Karl Devon can very easily tell me to go fuck myself. He knows what I'm up to. He knows I know. And he knows I'm pushing Abby on him.

But the interesting thing about him not telling me to take a hike and never return means he *is* thinking about using her.

And that lights my eyes up.

Karl Devon gets tables pushed together with a snap of his fingers, and I'm pulling out Abby's chair in no time. It feels intimate but then, I remember the name of the game tonight and it's to charm the Versace pants off Karl Devon.

I order a round of cocktails, and while I'm speaking to the waiter, Karl Devon and Abby's conversation takes off. Seriously, there's nothing this girl can't do. I sit back and watch as she charms the fucking pants off this guy.

"Did you like Seraphina, when she was crying about the death of all the people across the world?" She gives him her best Hollywood smile. "Because I felt like that really opened up her character."

Karl nods. "I've been following your career closely."

Ah, this is good. Very good, but I feel a but coming on.

"But, I wanted to know how you are personally."

"What do you mean?"

Even I lean in, wanting to know exactly what Karl's speaking about.

He laughs. "I want to know what you're like when you're just being you."

She straightens in her chair, his question most likely throwing her completely off guard.

And it makes me wonder why.

Chapter 5

Abby

What am I like? I ponder this question entirely too long before blurting out, "I'm just an average girl." There really isn't anything majorly appealing about me.

Karl Devon eyes me for a moment, then laughs. "Oh believe me, there's nothing average about you."

I sneak a glance over at Emmett and his eyes eat me up. From head to toe. Like he's wondering if I'm average or not. And right now, I'm dying to know what he thinks. The whole world could melt away into a fiery inferno, and I would still want to know the answer if he thinks I'm average.

He takes a sip of his drink and then his eyes focus on Warren, waiting in the wings. "Excuse me a moment, I'll be back in a bit." He leaves the table and I'm left with Karl Devon.

I'm not nervous in any way, and I guess I should expand on the average thing. "What I meant by being average is I want what all women want, I guess."

Karl Devon is enamoured. "What is it that all women want?"

I chew on my bottom lip, then answer. "To be wanted."

He raises a brow, like a skeptic. "But you have millions of men who want you."

I smile, raising my glass to him. "Ah, they want the characters I play, but none of them really want me." I peek over at Emmett, who's talking to Warren.

Karl Devon follows my gaze. "Or maybe you want someone in particular to want you?"

He knows, and I blush hard. "Maybe." I take a sip of my drink, letting it cool me down. But then Emmett is back at our table, and my temperature quickly rises.

"What did I miss?" he asks, sitting back down in his chair.

Karl Devon smiles. "I want her for my movie," he tells Emmett.

My breath hitches and Emmett and I share a look of happiness between us.

"Really? That's great. I'll get everything set up," Emmett says, shaking Karl's hand.

And just like that I'm in a Karl Devon movie. I want to scream, or hug someone. Particularly, Emmett.

I smile at Karl Devon. "Thank you. I can't wait to make this movie with you."

He takes my tiny hand in his. "The pleasure will be all mine." And then he kisses it before walking away.

Emmett just sits back, smiling. "Wow it's a Christmas miracle. What did you say to him?"

I wink. "I was just my usual charming self."

Emmett gazes at me from over his drink, his brown eyes eating me up. "I believe that." He sets his drink down and leans closer. "Hey, that stuff you said about thinking you're average. Is that true?"

I pick at my drink's coaster along the table. "Yeah, sometimes."

He grabs my hand, sending a chill up my spine, and brings it closer to him. "You're anything but average."

I don't know if it's the timbre of his voice, or the intensity in his eyes as they stare at me, but chills skate across my skin.

My phone pings in my pocket and I glance down. "Everything's all set up," a text message reads from Warren.

I let go of Emmett's hand, knowing he just agreed to go and hook up with some stranger. My mood depresses. "I should probably head home," I tell him.

His eyes hold mine. "What about dinner?"

I wave a hand. "I'm not that hungry. Go on without me." I try to force a smile, but it's just not in me.

Walking away from the table, Warren gives me a thumb up and I try to smile again. I should be ecstatic. My plan is working. All the details can be worked out. But the main thing is Emmett is in. And he's about to be *in* me.

I should be jumping up and down. I should be dancing and high-fiving myself.

But, there's an emptiness that's settling deep inside, and I can't shake it.

I remind myself this exactly what I want as I rush to the valet. I toss him my keys as his eyes bulge.

"Sera...Sera...Seraphina. Right away," the young valet stutters through his words.

"Abby," Emmett's voice calls from behind me and I spin around.

"I'm a little overwhelmed. I just need to get home and let it process that I'll be in a Karl Devon film."

Emmett rests his hands on my shoulders. "Let me get some food in you."

I want to say yes more than anything because saying no to Emmett is becoming harder and harder to do, but I know if I go to dinner with him I'll put a move on him. Try to see if he might cancel his own plans with me. Oh my god, I'm jealous of myself. I push away the silly thoughts. "No really, it's ok."

Emmett leans back, dropping his hands. "I won't take no for an answer." He calls for the valet. "And I won't let you go home hungry." He turns his head. "Warren, take my car home."

Warren nods, and my Mercedes pulls up and the valet opens the driver's side door.

"Fine," I say, "but, I'm driving."

He laughs, moving around to the driver's side. "Not a fucking chance in hell." And he slides into the leather seat like he owns it.

Another valet appears, opening the passenger side door, helping me inside and shutting the door.

"I do know how to drive, ya know?" I tell him.

He smiles at me. "What kind of agent would I be if I didn't pamper you in every way possible." His eyes hold mine, and I feel like there's a hidden meaning in his words. Or maybe I'm hoping there is.

I turn away from him, clicking my seatbelt on. "Where are we going, anyway?"

Emmett slams his foot on the gas, peeling out of the club's valet drive. "You'll see." He pulls his phone to his ear. "Yes, two filets, med rare. Yes, Ok. Sure." And then he hangs up.

And at the sound of filet my stomach growls. "Ok, I guess I'm a little hungry."

Emmett smiles. "We need to celebrate the Karl Devon movie."

Now it's my turn to smile, and just be overall happy. It's every movie star's dream to land a Karl Devon movie. Seriously. And here I am. At twenty-four, starring in one of the top dogs of Hollywood's film. I'm almost speechless. "Whoever thought I'd make it this big, huh?"

Emmett slows down. "I did. Abby, it's why I signed you without another thought about it. I always knew you'd be a star."

My insides melt away, and I close my eyes, leaning my head back against the cool leather of my seat.

The sun has long set over the Pacific, and it's beautiful out. There's a huge array of stars, blanketing the night sky, and I feel like I'm so close I could almost touch one.

Emmett continues driving up into the mountains, and I know right away where he's taking me. To the Hollywood sign.

It's a place I first came to when all my dreams came true and I starred in my first role. It's the one place that makes this all feel like reality.

After a few more minutes, we're tucked away on a blanket at the Hollywood sign, looking over Los Angeles. We're drinking wine that Emmett had delivered along with our food.

"You must bring all the ladies here," I whisper over my red wine.

Emmett gazes out over the view. "I've never actually been here before."

My eyes widen. "You're kidding me."

He shakes his head, slowly, bringing his eyes to meet mine and I suck in a breath. "I'm a Hollywood sign virgin."

"Well, you must have some pretty big pull to have us shuttled here after everything has stopped running for the night."

He winks. "I have my ways."

"So, I guess for all your dates you probably fly them to New York for a Broadway musical."

Emmett laughs. "As if." He glances back out over the city below. "Actually, I haven't been on a date in a long time."

I take a sip of my wine. Of course he hasn't dated. No, he only hooks up. Why bother paying for a women's meal when he can skip all that and get down to the good stuff.

God, men really are pigs.

"Right, why date when you can just have a string of one-night stands."

He laughs again, but this time there's a vulnerability

behind it I find endearing. "Haven't hooked up in a long time."

"But I thought you…"

He cuts me off, "slept with all of Hollywood? Yeah, hardly."

My mind whirls around the new info I'm receiving. Why would the tabloids say he's dating many women if he's….nevermind. I'm not going to even finish that thought. Of course you can't believe anything you read in the gossip rags, and now I feel foolish for ever believing it. "Ah, so how long has it been then?"

He stares at my mouth, and my body heats up the longer he stares. "A long time."

I feel like telling him, no, it's been a long time for me. But, I don't say anything. Instead I try to wrap my head around the fact that Emmett definitely agreed to a one-night stand to help a woman out.

So, maybe it has been a long time for him, and maybe he does need to get laid.

I try not to think about the jealousy that creeps up my spine, and remember to myself that I asked for this. That this is my one true Christmas wish.

Chapter 6

Emmett

Have you ever been told something that makes your head explode? Well, maybe my head hasn't exploded...but it could. Very soon.

Warren rushed up to the club to interrupt my meeting with Karl Devon, and I remembered at the time I wanted to murder him for doing so.

But, what he had said to me made me stop in my tracks.

He told me about Abby asking him for a favor.

He told me about what Abby wanted from me. How she wanted my hands all over her.

How she didn't want me to know it was her.

How her crazy little plan made my dick harder than it had ever been in its life. I mean, it's a crazy plan, right?

Have one night of wild sex with her and pretend it never happened. She would never know I knew it was her.

I mean, what idiot would say no to this?

Not fucking me.

It never occurred to me in a million years how hard the limelight must be for Abby. Sure, I can walk into a grocery store and no one knows who I am. I can't even imagine what she must go through on a daily basis.

She sips her wine and I want to toss the glass against the rocks of Mount Lee and take her right here and now, but it would ruin our whole relationship. It would ruin everything we've both worked so hard on.

I also am old enough to know that she doesn't have time to be in a relationship with me where I could spoil her day in and day out. I'm also a big boy and know that she doesn't want that.

And why should she? She's at the top of her career. She's a mega-star and I can't even imagine what she must be going through.

So, when Warren asked me to take care of her, I almost sank to my knees to kiss his feet for even asking.

I'd do anything for her.

And no, it's not because she's my best client. Or one of the biggest money makers on my roster.

Or the fact that her hair smells like wild-berries right now and I want nothing more than to kiss her.

No, it's simple. I'd do anything for her because over the past four years since I've known her she's been slowly claiming a piece of my heart every day.

So, tomorrow night when I'm supposed to meet her in the Hollywood Historic penthouse suite, I'll be there. Without my glasses, ready to pleasure her in ways I've only ever dreamed of.

Talk about dreams coming true.

I'm going to make sure I savor every single part of her so I'll be able to rewind my mind over and over again to that night and live a full and happy life just knowing I was the lucky son-of-a-bitch who got to make her fantasies come true.

We spend another hour outside, talking about what all will

be expected of her for the Karl Devon movie. We also talk about her family, and she even gets me to open up about my asshole of a father who was once studio head at Paramount. It's how I got into the business.

The bastard is long gone now, but I haven't mentioned his name in years.

There's something about Abby that makes me want to open up to her.

By the end of the night, when I'm dropping her off at her house, with Warren waiting in my car to take me home, I almost want to kiss her.

I almost want to tell her I'll see her tomorrow.

But, instead I act like my normal self and say good night, and leave her as she takes the last remaining pieces of my heart.

⸻

BY THE TIME tomorrow evening comes around, I've gone over the plan a few times with Warren, making sure Abby truly wants this. I've gone over all the outcomes that can possibly go wrong with this whole hairbrained plan, and honestly I can't find any.

As long as Abby thinks I have no idea who she is, then the plan is solid. Nothing needs to change with our working relationship. You don't understand how hard my dick is just thinking about tonight.

Warren texts me, letting me know Abby's waiting for me in the suite. My heart hammers in my chest, wondering if this is the right thing to do.

Of course it is.

Abby's upstairs, waiting for me. It's like a dream come true. And I don't know what I did this Christmas to be put on the good boy's list, but I'm definitely getting everything I want this year.

I've wanted this for a long fucking time.

I push the button to the elevator, my nerves already way past the level of excitement anyone's nerves should be. Breathe.

I feel a little silly as I watch the floor numbers pass by on the way to the top. How am I supposed to pretend I don't know her?

How the hell am I supposed to pretend I haven't wanted Abby since the first moment I saw her?

The elevator doors ping open, and I step out into the hallway. I came right from work, and I loosen my tie, and step up to the door.

I knock and then remove my glasses.

I take a deep breath, hoping I can keep it together and not blurt out the fact that I know this woman.

The door opens, and I stall a moment. Sure, I don't have my glasses but I'm not fucking blind.

Abby stands before me, tight little black piece of scrap that passes as a dress clings to her body. Her hair is long, and brown like the first time I ever saw her, and god she looks fucking delicious.

"Fuck me," I say as she pulls me inside.

It's dark, just as she wanted, and I'm not really sure if I should just get straight down to business. I mean, staring at her right now, I'm shell-shocked.

I know she's drop dead gorgeous, but I wasn't expecting this. I can barely make out her face, but she walks around the room with an air of confidence.

"Want a drink?" she asks me in a different voice and accent.

Damn, she is good at what she does. "Sure," I say, not really wanting to rock the boat just yet.

I'm supposed to act like I don't know who she is. I'm supposed to act like I'm here for some random hookup with some chick.

"What's your name?" she asks me, keeping up the game.

"Emmett, you?"

She fiddles with a glass of some liquor, dropping a few ice cubes in with a clink. "Um, you don't need to call me anything." She steps closer, holding the glass out for me.

I take it, gulping it down in one swallow. "Sure thing, sweetheart. What are you drinking?"

She glances back at her glass along the bar. "I'm just having a diet cola."

Of course she is. Always the actress. And then I realize this is a role for her.

I set my glass down, no longer wanting to make small talk with this Hollywood bombshell I've wanted for entirely too long.

"Come here," I say to her, crooking my finger.

She hesitates before moving closer.

My hand is still in the air, and I touch her face, tracing down the soft line of her jaw. I fucking knew it. I knew her skin would be super soft, and silky and all the things that turn me on. Because that's what I am right now...turned the fuck on.

"You're beautiful."

She smiles and turns into my hand. "You can't even see me."

My chest tightens and I have to remember to breathe or I might not make it through the night. "I can see enough." I bring her lips to mine, wanting to finally get a taste of this sexy woman.

And it finally happens. Our lips meet and I swear there's fireworks. I trace my tongue over her bottom lip before stepping an inch closer to deepen the kiss. I've got this woman in my arms and my heart's racing like a jackrabbit. And there's nothing I can think about but getting closer.

Closer. Closer.

I need to be closer to her.

My hand sweeps up her body and into her long, silky hair. I can't believe this is happening.

She breaks the kiss. "Maybe this was a bad idea."

No. No. No, I can't let her leave me tonight. She knows who I am. I know who she is, but I'd never tell her that.

"Please don't go. I'm here to make your dreams come true." My hand's still in her hair, hoping more than anything she doesn't walk out the door.

It would devastate me.

"I just..." she doesn't finish her thought. She doesn't do anything, and I know now I need to take this moment and convince her to stay with me.

My mind can't come up with words quick enough so instead I kiss her, remembering what it's like to have her in my arms so I can remember this for the rest of my life. "Please don't leave me," I say when I break the kiss.

She shakes her head. "I won't leave. But, I've never done this before."

"I'll take care of you." I almost say Abby, but keep her name to myself. "I've got you." I lift her in my arms, making my way to the four-post bed in the middle of the room.

I lay her down, stepping up so I can catch a slight glimpse of her. I wish I could turn a light on, but it doesn't matter, I'll let my hands guide me tonight.

"Emmett, please touch me," she whispers, and I swear the accent is gone from her voice. It sounds like Abby. And it does something to me.

Something primal.

I step closer to the edge of the bed, loosening my tie all the way and slipping it over my head. My shirt is next to go, and as I slip it off, Abby squirms along the bed. My heart pounds throughout my body, deafening me with it's rhythm.

"I can't take it anymore," she whines.

Oh damn, neither can I.

Chapter 7

Abby

I can't believe I'm really here. I can't believe the way Emmett kissed me. It shook me all the way to my core. How a man can kiss like that and not spontaneously combust from having that much power is beyond me.

And I can't believe I haven't combusted into a million tiny pieces the moment he touched me for the first time.

I want him so much it hurts.

Right now, he's undressing just for me. And I can't peel my eyes away from him, even though the room is almost pitch black. There's a sliver of light creeping in from the hall and from the window.

There's a small part of me that wishes Emmett knew it was me behind the character I'm trying to play. I wish he knew it was Abby.

But, I can't ever let him know, so I get back into character, and remind myself that this is what I've wanted for so long.

And it's funny, how fantasies go, I'm about to fly off the

edge just having him here in the same room. His eyes burn holes in my facade, and I swear sometimes when he stares at me, it makes me think he really wants all of me.

Like this isn't just about sex for him.

"I want to make all your fantasies come true tonight," he says in a deep, gravelly voice. It's his bedroom voice, and I've only ever heard it in my dreams.

But the reality is so much better than any dream version I could have ever had.

Before I can say or do anything, he's climbing the bed, hovering over me.

"Tell me you want that." He leans close, his nose running along my neck. "Tell me."

"I want that."

His eyes meet mine, and for a split second I think he may recognize me, but he doesn't say anything, except, "Good."

He flips me over on the bed, and the next thing I know his hands are all over me, unzipping my dress, removing it from my body as his tongue drags along the skin of my neck. I don't even know how he's so in control right now.

I can barely move, let alone think.

"Leave the heels on," he tells me when I go to remove them.

I lean my head back, closing my eyes when he grabs my ankle, him kneeling right between my legs. He kisses my skin, dragging his tongue down my leg, moving closer and closer to the one spot I want him the most.

My fingers fly into his hair when he gets closer, and I move my body in time with his.

"I'm going to make you come a few times tonight. First with my tongue, then my fingers, and lastly with my hard cock."

I suck in a breath. "Yes. Yes."

He's a master in the bedroom when he spreads my legs apart and brings his mouth over me. I buck off the bed, not ready for how powerful his tongue is as it laps at my wetness. Oh my God. This. This is what I wanted.

His expert tongue finds all my pleasure spots and he grips my ass with both hands. "My dick is so hard eating you out," he says, and then returns back to his mission. His one true mission of getting me off.

And I'm so close. I'm right there, teetering on the edge, barely able to contain myself. Every nerve in my body is on fire. Every sense is alight with sparks. I'm this live-wire and I can't control how I'm feeling right now.

A small part of me wants to tell Emmett who he's kissing. Who he's touching. But, would he stop? Would he be upset?

Ugh. I can't think about any of this right now. I'm so close to coming undone all over Emmett's tongue. My heart slams inside my chest and I try to control my breathing.

I love the way he touches me. And I hate that this is only a one-time thing. He keeps working me over, and my body builds and builds.

And then, the stars all collide together, like some cataclysmic shift in the universe. My mouth opens and I string out one unintelligible word after another. My body hums as Emmett doesn't relent. He keeps touching me, kissing me, and nibbling all over my sensitive skin.

He moves up my body, his eyes drinking me in. It's dark, he can barely see me, but his hands…oh my…his hands are everywhere. Touching, feeling, memorizing every curve.

"Everything about you is perfect," he whispers against the shell of my ear.

He kisses me, full on the lips, like he's starving for my mouth.

His tongue roams over my tongue, and I taste myself.

It turns me on. "Don't stop," I tell him, losing my accent completely. I try to overcompensate. "Please, don't stop."

He props himself up on his elbows, staring down at me. "You have me as long as you want me."

Should I tell him I want him always? Do I want him always?

He kisses me again, and my thoughts are swept away by a painful amount of desire. The thoughts of forever fade away, but they don't disappear completely, because well let's face it, I think I kind of do want this man forever.

His hands are in my hair, and he sniffs deeply. "I've always loved the smell of your hair." Then his lips are roaming over me, trailing kisses along the column of my throat.

He's always loved the smell of my hair?

He doesn't know who I am.

Maybe he's lost in the moment and this is what he always says to women?

"I need to be inside you." He props up on one hand, holding his dick in the other, and he positions himself at my entrance, sliding a condom over himself before entering.

And then I hold my breath, thanking my lucky stars that all my dreams are about to come true as Emmett pushes deep inside me.

"God, you feel so good. So damn good," he breathes out, his body stilling just a bit before he begins rocking into me again.

"Don't stop," I whisper.

He kisses my lips, sucking my tongue into his mouth. "You feel too good to ever stop." He closes his eyes, moaning and groaning, and I can't believe this is really happening.

"Abby," he groans out, and I barely hear it.

But then, I sit up, pushing him back slightly. "What did you just call me?" I ask in my accent.

He blinks. "What did I say?"

"You called me Abby."

Chapter 8

Emmett

Fuck. I got too caught up in the feeling of it all. She felt so damn good. So much better than I ever expected her to feel. So much better than anyone I'd ever been with.

I closed my eyes, not wanting the feelings pouring over to stop. And I accidentally said her name.

Fuck.

I stare at her, trying my best to make out her eyes in the dark. "I didn't say Abby." I'm trying to play it off, like she's hearing things. But, she's not buying it.

She pushes me off her, and I grab the covers and wrap them around me. "You called me Abby. Do you know who I am?"

I run a hand through my hair, blowing out a deep breath. I don't want to lie to her anymore. I want her to know I know it's her. "Yes, I know it's you."

She stands, wrapping a robe from the hotel around her body, flipping on a light. "I can't believe this."

"Abby, I'm so sorry." I don't know what to say to make this better, but I have to say something. I can't let her walk out this door. "Abby, please," I hold her arm, moving her to sit down on the bed beside me, "I never meant for this to happen. Warren approached me about having sex with some random woman who needed help." I take a breath. "And I shot it down. Truth is, I haven't had sex in a long time. I'm not about that one-night stand life."

"So why did you say yes?" She crosses her arms over her chest, but it's not because she's mad, it's more like she's guarding her feelings. Guarding her heart.

"I explained to Warren that I was appalled he even asked me, and he blurted out it was for you."

She covers her mouth with her hand. "Oh my god."

"Wait, don't be mad at Warren. He wanted to help you out. I wanted to help you out too, Abby," I reach out to touch her hand, "I never knew dating was so hard for you. I figured you could have anyone you wanted."

She smiles, gazing at me from behind her long lashes. "Not anyone."

"Abby, baby…" I want to kiss her. Now that I've even tasted her I don't think I'll ever be able to walk away from her. "I wanted you. That's why I said yes. Because I wanted you more than anything. And when Warren told me what you wanted I couldn't possibly ever say no."

"You wanted me?"

Her eyes are innocent, and I've never seen her look so vulnerable in all her life. It makes me want to sweep her up in my arms and tell her yes over and over again. I almost do it, but I smile. "Abby, I've wanted you since the first moment I saw you. I know we have a good working relationship, but I can't stop thinking about you."

"I can't stop thinking about you either." She leans in and kisses me, and I take my chance to hold her close.

And then I can't stop kissing her. I tug at the string of her robe and when I release it, I get to see her body up close, and personal with the lights on. And I can't stop staring at her.

"I feel bad you don't have your glasses." She juts out her bottom lip and I suck it real quick.

I tap my temple. "Contacts." You think I'd go in blind to have sex with the one person I've wanted to have sex with in forever? I'm no dummy.

I pull her closer, kissing her laughter away.

"You're a very bad boy, Mr. Garfield."

"Oh, you don't know the half of it."

"Tell me then."

"I've had so many dirty thoughts about you, Abby. So many dirty things I've wanted to do to you." I move my hand over her naked body, feeling her heated skin, pulling her robe off.

This is it. The moment we've all been waiting for...or well, I have been. This is *that* moment. The one where all the seriousness of what's about to go down weighs heavily on us both.

"I don't want things to change between us," she whispers.

"They won't." And I kiss her lips. But, if I'm being honest here, I *want* things to change between us. I *want* to be able to do this each and every night. I *want* to be the one to hold her close every single fucking day.

And if we're getting technical, I want to be the *only* mother fucker who gets to touch her. No one else, but me. I want her to be mine.

And I hope she wants that too.

But, I'm not going to ruin my chances here to be with her for this one night only. I mean, if this is all I can get, I'll take it with a big ol' smile on my face. I'd be an idiot not to.

And I'm the luckiest fucker in the world right now. And I bet every other man in the world would agree.

"I just want you to see me," she whispers.

I prop up on my elbows, running my fingers through her

hair, staring into her bright eyes. "I've only ever seen you. Since the moment I first met you, it's only ever been you."

"Kiss me, Emmett." And her wish is my command.

I taste her lips, and I can't stop tasting her. I ease back into her, slowly at first, letting her get used to the size of me.

"You don't understand how long I've wanted this." I push deeper, holding her hands above her head with mine.

"I want to touch you," she whines.

I suck in a deep breath. "I've wanted this so long that if you touch me right now, I'll completely lose it." I need to get control of my body back before this whole show is over before it begins.

She doesn't fight against my hold on her hands, she only rocks her body beneath me, meeting me thrust for thrust. And it feels so fucking good.

Everything she's doing right now is perfect.

"Abby, I want things to change," I tell her, and I should really keep my mouth shut.

She kisses my neck, nipping along my skin. "You do?"

"Yes, I want to be with you. I know it's crazy, and you're at the height of your career, but I can't keep quiet anymore."

"I want you too." She stares at me. "I want all of that too."

And right now, she's made all my dreams come true.

THANK you so much for reading The Favor.

The Billionaire's Nanny

Chapter 1

Bree

"Take care of our boy," Smith says with a grin as he closes the door.

"Our boy," I whisper as my heart pounds in my chest.

Smith makes it impossible to know what he's thinking. One day he'll be sweet with small innocent touches which make my skin burn. The next day he'll all but ignore me. After months of being the nanny to his son, Carter, it gets confusing. I know my main priority is Carter, but I can't help the fact that when I leave, Smith is the one I'm thinking about.

"Bree, come look at my block building," Carter yells, breaking my train of thought.

"Wow, that's the best building I've ever seen," I say.

I sit down to play with him, but unfortunately, my mind isn't here. I'm thinking of last night. Smith once again worked late, and I had fallen asleep on the couch. I heard him come in the front door, but I stayed where I was, because there was a part of me that wanted to know what he'd do seeing me asleep on the couch. I may have even made sure the short sundress I had on rode up letting my panties show just a bit. He whispered my name and my heart picked up speed, but I didn't move. I don't know what he was thinking, but he sat down by my head and the only thing he said was 'fuck.' I'm not sure if it was because I was asleep or because he's having as hard a time as I am not ripping his clothes off. Either way, the only thing he did was cover me with a blanket and go to bed. I can't read him and I'm not sure if that is my inexperience or just him.

My phone rings and I rub Carter's little head while I stand to grab it.

"Hello?"

"Hey girl, what's your plans tonight?" Julia, my best friend asks in a hyper voice.

I know what she wants.

And I know people my age should be out experiencing life.

I don't answer right away, as I look around the penthouse. Apparently, a little too long for her.

"Bree, you need to stop playing mommy and come hang out with us," she says.

"I'm not playing house. I'm doing my job."

She sighs and I roll my eyes. "You know I wish I could believe that. I really do, Bree."

"What's up, Julia?" I ask, losing my patience.

"I was wondering if you wanted to act like the nineteen-year-old you are and do something fun tonight?"

"If Smith doesn't need to work late, sure," I say.

"Yeah, whatever. Give me a call."

She doesn't even wait for my reply and hangs up. I shake my head and put my phone down. She doesn't understand. This is my job. I need to be here when Smith can't be. She is right, though. I have avoided hanging out, especially if it means I get to spend some time with Smith. Right or wrong, it's how I feel.

I want to be here.

After making Carter his favorite dinner of chicken nuggets and french fries, I sit down to relax a minute while he eats. It's been a long day and it's far from over. Smith called and told me he needs to work late. It's no surprise. It happens all the time. I spend more time here with Carter, and sometimes Smith, than I do with my own family. A smile pulls at my mouth when I think of it. It's exactly where I want to be.

"All done," Carter says, pushing away the little bit of food left on his plate.

The night carries on with the routine, several stories, and snuggling on the couch until I need to get him in the bath. I always text Smith to let him know how the night is going. My texts are always about Carter, even though I want them to be about so much more. I don't think I can stop this want, this need. It's consuming me, in the best damn way.

Smith's mesmerizing eyes. The way the corner of his mouth pulls up on one side when he watches me. It turns me on in the most primal way. In a way I've never felt before. It's no big secret I have it bad for Smith, and I wonder if he somehow knows about it.

I think I keep the ogling to a minimum whenever he's around, which isn't much. Mainly, it's mere misses. When I get here in the mornings, he's usually rushing off to work. And by the time he shows up at night, it's always so late I leave so he can get some rest.

Most nights, he appears like he's been run through the wringer. And with his demanding job, I'm sure he has. Letting him know how I feel will never be an option. I need this job. I can't afford to lose it because I have the hots for my boss.

He'd probably laugh at me if he ever knew the truth. He's older. More sophisticated. I'm sure he has no need for a naive stupid girl who works for him.

Not that I'm stupid, but I'm sure Smith has tons of sophisticated women throwing themselves at him daily.

He is definitely the most gorgeous man I've ever seen. With big strong hands that I'd love to have wrapped all around me, keeping me safe, and turning me on in the most sensual of ways.

After Carter's bath, I take him upstairs to get him ready for bed, and I grab my phone, wondering what I should text Smith.

Wondering if I *should* even text him. It's harmless, really. I need to let him know everything is safe and sound here, so he doesn't worry.

Once I've convinced myself that's all I'm doing, I text him to let him know I'm getting Carter into bed.

Chapter 2

Smith

"All snuggled up."

It's innocent texts like these from Bree that get me all riled up. I shouldn't be getting turned on, but it's kind of hard not to, no pun intended, when the sender is a wet dream personified.

"All warm and cozy." Another text brightens my phone, and I try my hardest to kill the fantasies of Bree, snuggling up next to me, after she sucks my dick with her plump red lips.

What is wrong with me?

She's my son's nanny, for fuck's sake. And worse, she's nineteen.

But she's also gorgeous.

Roger Canton, Acquisitions VP, oblivious to what I'm really thinking about, drones on and on about an upcoming merger. It's more of a hostile takeover, but merger sounds more appealing. Especially, to the motherfucker whose company I'm taking right out from under his Ferragamo clad feet.

I'm trying to focus, but it's hard to concentrate when I have a hot-as-fuck nanny at home...snuggling.

"Victory!" she texts again. "You can tell me how great I am later."

Oh, I'd love to tell her a lot of things later. The texts coming in are that she's putting my son, Carter, to sleep, but for some reason, I can't stop my overworked mind from going in the sex direction with her. It's been like this for five months.

I never should've hired her. But, when my ex-wife flitted away to travel Europe with her new boyfriend, leaving our four-year-old with me, I needed to hire someone who could help me take care of him. I'd like to think my desperation clouded my judgement, and not the curves or clear blue eyes of the Lolita that showed up at the interview with a bewitching smile.

I'd fire her, just to remove the temptation, but she's fucking great with Carter. It's almost domesticated when I come home from work and they're sprawled out on the living room floor, laughing and playing a game.

I'd love some time off to play as well, but with my work schedule, it'll never happen. When your company is buying another company out, well, all dreams of fun and sunshine die in the corporate office I find myself imprisoned in.

My dick throbs with thoughts of her as I slide my phone in my pocket, and pretend to listen to Roger as he explains the contract that has kept me here late tonight.

"Is that the nanny?" Roger asks, lifting a brow.

"Her name is Bree."

"Her name is also a lawsuit waiting to happen."

He's not only my VP, he's also a long time friend, so he can be mildly intrusive. And annoying.

"I don't know what you mean," I reply, leaning back in my chair.

"What do you think I mean, Smith? You're a thirty-five year old billionaire, and you don't think she'd like a piece of that?"

I give him a hard stare. "I believe that concludes everything."

"There're thousands of women you can fuck." He pauses. "That one is trouble."

"I'll take your advice under consideration."

He's right, I have endless options. The ballerina with the new company that just opened up downtown was more than ready to slide my zipper down last night. Instead, I'm obsessing about the nanny.

She's intelligent, and I actually enjoy talking to her.

I just want one night. One night to fuck the hell out of her. My dick hasn't seen action since my divorce. It's been a long time. A really long time.

I glance at my watch, then push away from my desk and stand. "It's late. Have Morgan draw up the final contract."

"I see it on your face." He nods, and rises. "Maybe you should consider another nanny for Carter."

I cross to the wall of glass in my office and the only thing I see reflected on my face is day old scruff and annoyance in my brown eyes.

The city lights buzz with excitement, and I remember being out there, living in the moment. Those days are long gone. Running this company, coupled with father responsibilities, don't leave much time for anything else.

Carter is everything to me, and there is nothing I wouldn't do for my son. But a man has needs. And right now, I have a multitude. They all center around Bree.

Maybe she is too young, and I should sever all ties. I just can't bring myself to do it. I want her.

"Maybe you should keep your opinions to yourself," I advise, turning to face him. "Don't worry, my money is protected."

He taps his heart. "Is this?"

"Absolutely."

I can see it in his furrowed brows he wants to say more, but he wisely chooses not to. "See you tomorrow," he says, on his way out.

The night air is crisp and cool on my heated skin when I leave the office, and I drive home consumed with want and desire. My fingers tighten on the steering wheel in anticipation of what to expect when I get there. I've amassed more money than I can ever spend by being a ruthless bastard. Who knew a doe-eyed girl would be the one to slay me.

Maybe I should just get her out of my system.

My cock hardens with thoughts of Bree as I take the elevator up to my penthouse.

The lights are low when I enter the foyer, and I sidestep a Tonka toy truck in the center of the tile.

I drop my keys on the entry table before crossing the hardwoods to the living room.

And there she is, curled on the couch, in a pink t-shirt and short white skirt, looking very fuckable.

"Are you awake?"

"Yes, I'm awake." She sits up. "Just resting my eyes," she whispers.

"Sorry I'm home so late."

I move toward her, knowing I shouldn't. Knowing I should stay out of her seductive atmosphere.

I'm used to taking what I want, so I'm not used to this agonizing feeling washing over me.

"It's ok," she tells me, letting her eyes drift over my face. "What time is it?"

"Late. You can stay here tonight. That way you don't have to drive."

She smiles, and my heart damn near goes into cardiac arrest.

I yank my tie off and throw it across the armchair. "Coffee?"

"Sure." She stands, running her fingers through her tousled hair, smoothing it down to the tips.

Before I wrap it around my fist, I turn away and cross into the kitchen, flicking on the light.

She follows me like a good little girl. My dirty thoughts run a marathon in my head when she walks across the tiled floor and hops up onto the granite countertop. Her skirt rides up her thighs, and I catch myself staring at her tanned legs. I pick the caramel-flavored pod I know she likes and push it into the Keurig.

She crosses her ankles, palms flat on the counter, and leans forward. "Mm." She inhales deeply as the coffee percolates. "Smells good."

Ignoring the twitch in my dick, I pull two black mugs from the cabinet and ask her about Carter. She lets me know they had a great day, and he finally went to bed with no problems. For that, I'm glad.

It was rough at first when Carter came to live with me. My late hours were hard for him to deal with, so Bree has been a lifesaver.

As I wait for the coffee to finish, I undo my top button and crack my neck to the side, rubbing my hand along the tight muscles there.

"Are you tense?" she asks.

Fuck. She has no clue. "Yeah, a little."

"Come here." She holds her hands out, and against my better judgement, I turn around.

Her fingers work magic over my muscles, and I let out a slow hiss as my dick grows harder.

Fuck, this girl's hands will be my undoing.

She scoots closer to the edge, and her knees rest on either side of my hips. My cock pushes against the zipper of my slacks, and I roll my neck to the side, as she caresses my shoulders. The heat of her pussy burns into my back, and like an unanswered prayer, she places a tentative kiss against my thrumming pulse.

It's the spark that ignites the firestorm. I turn around and capture her mouth with mine. She grips my shoulders and moans. Her plump bottom lip tastes so sweet.

My heart thunders as I try not to take things too fast, but I can barely hang on. "You have no idea what you're doing to me," I husk against her mouth.

"I want you so much," she whispers between kisses.

I pull back. My eyes can't get enough of her. Her innocent smile. Her lust filled eyes. Her nipples trying to burst out of the tight shirt she's wearing.

It's a very bad idea, but my hand trails up her thighs to her sweet spot, and is met with purple-lace panties.

"Did you wear these for me?"

She blushes. "Yes."

I run my finger along the panel of her damp panties before pushing them aside to feel her slippery skin.

"Ever been licked by a man?"

She shakes her head no, and then places her hand atop mine, pressing it harder against her pussy. "I want you to be my first."

Fuck. She's definitely trouble. I'm a man who loves trouble, but should I walk away and do what's right?

I never claimed to be a good guy. All rational thought leaves me, and I remove her panties in a rush, and lift her tanned legs over my shoulders, diving in to suck her clit between my lips.

My dick grows, throbbing with want for this beautiful woman.

She's sweet, like a ripe peach. "You taste so good."

"Please, don't stop," she pants out, rubbing her pussy against my face.

"I won't stop, until you're screaming my name."

I lap at her wetness, holding onto her ass, eating her out on my kitchen counter, waiting for her orgasm to obliterate me. And it's coming. I can tell by the way she thrusts her hips. I can tell by the way she gets wetter by the second.

I can just fucking tell.

My finger slips inside her and I still, unable to wrap my mind around the fact I'm doing this with her tonight.

This should be forbidden. This should be wrong. And maybe it is. But, I no longer give a fuck.

"Your little pussy is clenched so tight. Relax for me, baby." I kiss her thigh and push my finger deeper, plunging further inside.

She eases her legs apart, and god, her pussy gleams with her wetness, and I groan as I slip another finger inside her.

She bucks, and I clamp one hand over her hip, trying to steady her in place as my face gets lost between her legs. She moans and twists, and my cock is painfully hard, wanting to fuck her.

Being inside her will be the highlight of my life. The fuck of all fucks. I can already tell, just by the way her tight cunt holds onto my finger like a vice.

She feels too good, and I can't even think about anything other than sticking my tongue as deep as I can inside her, letting the taste of her coat my tongue. So I do, removing my fingers, I swipe my tongue all over her, starting at her ass and ending at her clit.

He head falls back, her mouth opening to whisper the words I so badly want to hear, "I want you, Smith."

Fuck, I'm so turned on right now. I continue working her body with my tongue like she's mine. And I kind of wish she was.

My heart beats wildly like a mad man. My whole body is on fire, burning with a need so crazy I can't believe it's real.

Her fingers tug at my hair. "I've thought about you doing this."

I turn her on. That thought right there about does me in. "You've touched yourself thinking about me?"

She squeezes her thighs against my face. "Yes, so many times."

My cock is ready to go, it's harder than it's ever been. And I want nothing more than to fuck my need into her, let her know just how much I've thought about this too.

But first. I smile at her, and then place her legs back over my shoulders, running my finger along her seam. "I'm not going to stop eating your pussy until you're screaming my name."

She leans back, spreading her legs more and I hover my mouth over her opening. And then I drag my tongue through her wetness, loving the way she goes wild beneath me.

She's so close.

I can tell.

I slide my finger inside her, back and forth, over and over again as I suck her clit.

She loves it, squirming and moaning, bucking her hips as she digs her fingernails into the skin of my shoulders.

"Hold on, baby girl. I don't want you to come just yet," I hum along her wetness.

Her skin is hot. Her pussy clenches my fingers.

I push my finger deeper, letting her ride my hand.

My breathing picks up and my skin feels like lava. She turns me on in the worst of ways, and I realize something to myself as I continue to pump my fingers in and out of her. She always has.

Bree has turned me on since the first moment I laid eyes on her. When she came to interview for my son's nanny, she wore a red skirt, that went past her knees, and a silk-white blouse. She was like a dirtier Mary Poppins, and I wanted her even back then.

I was a goner, just biding the time until I couldn't hold off the attraction to her any longer.

"You have no idea what you're doing to me," I confess to her.

I return my head to my new favorite place of being nestled between her thighs, and keep swiping my tongue over her.

She lets out a moan and I keep going, reveling in the fact that I'm doing this to her. That I'm turning her on this much.

My heart beats frantically inside my chest. My skin heats up, and my cock grows larger than life.

I replace my tongue with a finger and stare into her eyes. And then I finger fuck her, letting her pussy ride out her orgasm on my hand. "That's right come all over my hand."

She doesn't stop thrusting her hips against my palm, and I kiss the corners of her mouth before sliding my tongue along hers.

"I'm coming," she cries out.

It's stunning.

"You have my dick so hard," I say after her body has calmed from her climax.

Her eyes glance down and I run a hand over the bulge in my pants. I take her hand and run it over my cock. "See, this is how bad I need you. There's so many things I've fantasized about doing to you," I tell her.

Her mouth hangs open a second before she licks her luscious pink lips. "Tell me."

My heart bangs hard against my sternum as I think about all the naughty things I've pictured late at night after Bree has gone home. "I want your pretty mouth wrapped around my cock."

She licks those pretty little lips again. "Mmm."

"I want you to take me deep down your throat and suck me off." I rub her hand over my pants and the outline of my dick.

"Tell me you want it."

Her big eyes stare up at me.

"Tell me you can't wait to taste my cock." I'm so fucking

turned on right now. And a bigger part of me can't believe this is happening.

Brave with courage, I stare into her eyes, waiting for her to say the words I so desperately need to hear.

The words I so need her to say.

Chapter 3

Bree

"I want to taste you," I say. I can't believe this is finally happening. In the kitchen, no less, but I had to make my move tonight or never get another chance. His chocolate-colored eyes drop to my mouth and I lick my lips.

"Oh, fuck." He grabs my hair in his fist, leaning my head to the side to gain better access to my neck where he plants his perfect lips, nibbling and sucking my tender skin.

His teeth are going to leave marks, and I hope they do. I want his brand on my body to never go away. I want him to mark me. To make me his.

I reach out for his zipper and his large hand clasps around my wrist. "Have you ever sucked a man's cock before?"

Part of me wants to lie and say yes, because I don't want him to think I'm a foolish, inexperienced girl, but I shake my head, my eyes never leaving his. "I want to suck your cock, Smith."

He runs a hand through his short dark hair, and for a

moment, I think he's going to put an end to this, but then his hand guides mine to his zipper.

His eyes close, his head falling back slightly, when I undo the button and unzip his pants. The hard outline of his oversized dick strains against his black boxer briefs. I've never done this before, but instinct has me dropping to my knees on the tile floor.

I peer up at him, and his eyes are fixed on me. His tongue peeks out to coat his bottom lip. He's so sexy. So masculine. I want to memorize every moment of my time with him.

When I free his cock, a drop of precum glistens on the tip. I stick my tongue out and take a swipe, licking it up.

The minute my hot mouth makes contact with his velvet skin, he groans. So growly. It's the best sound I've ever heard. His fingers twist in my hair, pulling and tugging me closer. I wrap a hand around his thickness to pump, matching the rhythm with my mouth as I take him as far down my throat as I can.

"Fuck, Bree," he murmurs, bracing a hand on the countertop as his hips buck, fucking my mouth. He takes control, and I open my lips wider, letting him thrust deep down my throat.

I love the feel of his skin inside my mouth. The taste of him. I'm so turned on. I need relief.

"I'm going to come," he tells me, before he tries to pull out. I dig my fingers into his ass, wanting it all from him. Hot liquid shoots down my throat, and I swallow as quickly as I can, milking his dick with the last of his release until his orgasm subsides. He pulls his cock from my mouth, and I wipe my bottom lip and rise to my feet. He startles me with a kiss. It's slow and sensual and much more than I deserve.

I pull away. "I have to go," I tell him, forcing the words out and rushing out the door.

Smith is much too fast. Traveling faster than the speed of light must be another perk of immense wealth.

"I should let you go," he says, clasping my wrist, "but I can't."

He can, and he will, but not right now. Not when he's looking at me like he wants to rip my clothes off.

I'm weak for him when he rubs his finger across my bottom lip. I'm also greedy and selfish; my body still aches, and I want him every way he wants me. I want him to remember me forever. I want him to give me everything he can.

Instead of leaving, I walk back inside. He follows me, and shuts the door behind him.

I've never been so brazen, but I've also never felt this type of insane sexual chemistry. I know where his bedroom is, so I cross the hardwoods to the staircase and make my way to his master suite, with him following me.

He locks the door behind him, and I move to the center of the room where I shed my skirt and T-shirt.

The scorching look in his eyes nearly sets the material of my bra and panties on fire.

I need release, so I run my finger to the center of my legs where I can't take it anymore and touch myself as he watches.

"Tell me how wet you are," he says.

"Very wet for you," I tell him as my finger makes contact with my slippery heat. I rub back and forth, toying with my clit. God, I need him inside me.

He steps closer and my heart pounds loud, the sound of it vibrating in my ears.

"Play with yourself for me." He stands at the foot of the bed, unbuttoning his shirt, as I finger myself, transfixed by his etched abs and lean muscles.

I touch myself, moaning as I do and he licks his lips, his eyes never leaving mine.

I am so wet. And it's all for Smith.

He removes the last of his clothing, and the sexy black boxers slide down his legs.

His dick is strong and proud and he grabs a hold of it.

"Is this what you want?" he asks, stroking his hand up and down his thick length.

My mouth salivates at the sight. "Yes, please."

"Bree, baby. You don't know what you're doing to me," he husks each word out as if each syllable burns on his tongue.

He sits on the edge of the bed and watches as I remove my bra and panties for him, groaning when my fingers trace over my hardened nipples. I cross to stand between his thighs.

He grabs a condom, and this is really happening.

I've dreamt about this so many times. And I hoped he felt the same, but really, I thought he'd push me out the door. He could have anyone. He doesn't need a nineteen-year-old messing up his life. So I'm going to take all I can get from him.

I straddle his thighs, and sink my pussy down over his length, slow at first. His fingers grip my hips, and once he's fully inside me, I rock back and forth in a steady tempo as he watches himself pump in and out of me.

"Fuck, yes." He moans. "Ride me."

"I've wanted you for so long," I whisper. "You're all I think about."

I've maybe even went as far as to picture it all with him.

He groans out as he keeps grinding me against him. "You like the way my cock fills you up?"

"Yes, yes." I moan as I ride him harder.

"You like the way I fuck your cunt?"

Ahh, I can't take much more of this. I'm so turned on. "Yes."

He bites his bottom lip as his hands reach around and grasp my ass, his fingers digging into each cheek, holding me in place as he moves inside me. Each rock of his hips drives me closer to exploding.

"Ride my cock you fucking dirty girl."

Thrust.

"Your pussy is so hot."

Thrust.

"So fucking good."

He squeezes my nipple between his fingers. "Play with them for me," he begs in a throaty whisper that is so damn hot it pushes me to the edge of an orgasm.

I reach both hands up, massaging my breasts as he watches. His eyes sear me as my fingers pinch my nipples, and he grows harder inside me. "Keep going."

His hands grip my hips as he watches, digging into the skin, bringing me down harder onto him.

He keeps thrusting, moving and fucking me until I barely know my own name.

"Smith," I cry out, as I feel my orgasm building low in my belly. I'm so close. It's so good.

I ride him, grinding my pussy down harder, bouncing with each move of his hips.

He reaches down to play with my clit, rubbing with just the right amount of pressure.

I've never felt anything this good. Sure, I've had sex, but never like this. This man is a sex god and knows just how to touch me. I'm close to coming undone, and it terrifies me and excites me all at the same time.

I feel that first pop of my orgasm like a firecracker throughout my system, spreading through every cell. And then I can't hold back any longer. He pulls me down and pushes up and I'm gone. Completely gone.

"That's right. Come all over my big cock," he says.

And I do.

Hard.

He presses his lips to mine as my orgasm crashes like a wave through me.

"I love your pussy," he says, breaking the kiss. "Oh, fuck, I'm gonna come."

His body rocks up into me, and I ride out the last of my climax as his teeth sink into my shoulder. "Damn, Bree, ahhh." And then he jerks a few more times before his eyes find mine.

And we just stare at each other. Our breathing comes out in quick bursts. I search for the regret in his hooded brown eyes. It's not there yet, but it's coming. I'm almost sure of it.

I feel too much. I need to think.

I climb off him, rushing to the en-suite bathroom to clean up.

This was...I don't know what this was. Well I do, I just don't want to admit it.

I find my clothes after I exit the restroom, and Smith waits for me in bed. Faster than I've ever dressed before, I slip out of this fantasy where we live happily ever after, and into what I was wearing before I removed it all. I'm as confused as he looks right now.

"Thank you for everything," I tell him. "But I quit."

And then I leave him behind.

Chapter 4

Smith

I haven't slept and when Carter comes running into my room, I know it's never going to happen.

"Pancakes, pancakes," he yells, jumping on my bed with his eager happiness.

No matter where my mind is, when it comes to Carter it doesn't matter. I grin as I scoop him off my bed. "Pancakes it is, little man."

I pour him a glass of milk while I get busy making his breakfast. His laughter as he watches TV floats through the house and warms my heart. He's truly the greatest thing to ever happen to me. When someone talks about true love, this is what they mean.

Once we finish breakfast and get dressed, I decide to take him to the park to play out some of his energy. I think a little fresh air will be good for the both of us. As much as I want to focus all my attention on him, I'd be lying if I said I haven't been thinking nonstop about Bree. About the look on her face when she walked out last night. It's not what I wanted. I care about this girl. But, I shouldn't be feeling anything toward her. She's my babysitter, and a damn good one. It's hard to find good help in the city.

And I hope I didn't just fuck this whole thing up.

I watch Carter run around and my confused mind takes over.

I think of last night with Bree. Fuck, it was more than I ever expected it to be. The things that girl made me feel and that I clearly made her feel. We may both be able to hide what we are feeling, but last night was real. The first real I've had in a long time.

It hits me like a punch to the gut. I'm falling for her. Not just wanting her in my bed, no, wanting her in my life. Not just for Carter, but for us both.

How can I make her see that I want more? It's difficult with a kid to think about. I have to put him first and not jeopardize anything with her job. I need her as my babysitter, but I need her with me more.

Fuck, I wish life were easy. That I could just say what I feel without having to worry about repercussions and everything turning to shit. Because, things usually do turn to shit. Sure, I could find another babysitter, no problem.

But, what about Carter? I can't be the type of man who traipses women in and out of his life. I don't want him to get attached to someone only to lose her later down the line. I won't do that to him.

All my thoughts center around what to do about Bree as I watch Carter go up and down the slide several times at the park. It's a great day here in the windy city of Chicago, and I want nothing more than to spend it with Bree by my side.

In the past, there had been many times I would meet the two of them at the park after a long day at work. She would smile, and Carter would beg for me to push him on the

Filthy Romance

swings. It was nice. It was something I want in my life. A family.

I think back to the last night. How willing she was to be with me. How everything in her eyes told me she needed me. Fuck me. I could fuck this girl forever. The sexual energy between the two of us is insane.

God, the more I think about it, the more I want her.

I'm done playing this game. I know what I want and I'm used to getting it. My eyes are on Carter as I grab my phone. I need to see her.

Chapter 5

Bree

I left in the middle of the night. Afraid to face Smith in the morning. Smith. Last night was beyond words. It was sensual and surreal. It was something I'd been wanting for some time.

Of course, I felt it was a teenage crush. Something he would never even think about. Or actively pursue. I'd seen the way he would stare at me late at night, but I never imagined it would ever happen.

I dreamed it would. Even fantasized by touching myself late at night in my bed. He is always the first thing on my mind when I wake up, and the last thing I think about when I lay my head down at night. He really is such a good man. The way he is with his son, well, it makes me swoon.

On my way home in the wee hours of the morning, I tried to talk myself out of the feelings beginning to take root deep inside me. I tried to make me forget about all the late night chats him and I would have discussing poetry, or pottery. We would discuss everything and anything.

This wasn't anything to him. It was one night, and I'm sure he's already regretting everything. I pull up to my tiny apartment complex and hop out of my two-door Sedan. Julia, my roommate and best friend, should be up and getting ready for school at this hour. My classes start a bit later, so I usually miss her in the mornings.

I walk inside, tossing my keys on the entryway table by the front door. I lean my body back against the white door, and scream a happy squeal. Julia rushes out of the bathroom, a red towel wrapped around her torso.

"Is everything alright?" she asks.

"Everything's perfect. Well, kind of. It happened." I smile, wide.

Her eyes grow huge, and she comes closer to me, stepping over all the books and magazines in the middle of the floor. Most likely left there from her late-night studying. "It it?"

"Yes. Smith and I had sex." My grin is so big, my face can barely contain it.

She covers her mouth, her towel slipping a little and she adjusts it higher. "Are you freaking kidding me? Oh, wow. How was it?"

"Insane," I say, kicking off the door and moving further into the apartment, tossing my purse on the purple couch we got at a thrift store.

Julia glances down at her towel. "Come to my room and tell me. I need to get dressed."

I follow her, recounting my whole night with Smith Prince. The way he held me close. His tender touch. His naughty words. Everything. I leave nothing out.

She hangs on my every word, and I can't believe it's all real either. She smiles as I tell her how I feel about him. It makes my chest heavy thinking about it. But, I'm an adult now. I need to act like one. Sleeping with my boss is something I should have never done, and I have to accept the consequences. I quit my job.

I love Carter. I love working for Smith. And I need the money. School and rent are expensive. I can not afford to be without a job right now, but I walked out. My resolve strengthens when I decide I will act like an adult and behave accordingly. Start looking for another job. And for God's sake, turn off my feelings for the gorgeous man with the dark hair and dark eyes that keep me company at night.

Julia leaves for school, and after a long, hot shower, I get ready to head off to class. I throw on my jeans and a white babydoll tee, tossing my hair into a ponytail and I head out the door.

Right when I step on campus, my phone chimes. Five words in a text from Smith stare back at me:

I need to see you.

I fire off a rapid message about being busy with school and send it off, worried I may be overreacting. I will have to eventually see him again to get my last paycheck.

Halfway through my first class, my mind is a mess of broken thoughts about Smith. I send another text:

When?

Within a few minutes, he answers.

My place tonight.

My chest heats, and a smile travels all over. As much as I want to push him away and pretend I don't care, I can't. It's obvious. But, then, I worry. What is this about?

The rest of my day is spent in misery with looming thoughts of Smith tossed aside. Not having money for bills, and possibly having to call my parents and beg for some money until I can get a new job.

The latter upsets me most. My parents never had much faith in me, and never thought I'd make it this far in school. They swore I'd come running home after my first semester.

Don't get me wrong, they love me. I'm sure somewhere they want to see me succeed, but they feel I need to lean on them every step of the way. Moving out on my own was a big deal to them, they didn't like it.

I guess they just want me to stay their little girl forever.

MY NERVES HEIGHTEN as I stand at Smith's front door. I chew on the tip of my thumb nail as I press the doorbell.

It isn't late enough where Carter should be sleeping, so I'm not afraid the loud bell will wake him.

Sure enough, Carter answers the door all happy and innocent. I bend over and wrap my arms around him, hugging him as hard as I can. "Hey you," I say with a smile on my face.

Smith comes up behind him, and my breath catches. He's so good looking. Sexy walk, complete with a swagger I find appealing. I glance up into his heated eyes. The same eyes that pierced through me as he sank himself deep inside me. He stalls a moment, unsure of what to say until he breathes a sexy, "Hey."

"Hi," I say back as Carter grabs my hand, pulling me further inside the condo.

"Carter, only for a little bit and then it's bedtime," Smith calls after us.

"Let's play." Carter takes me to the center of the living room and plops down on the floor, with his toy trucks by his side.

Smith sits on the couch, a file of papers in his hand with his black-rimmed glasses perched on his perfect nose. He reads a bit while Carter and I play and it's nice. It almost feels domesticated in a sense. But, I don't let the fairytale run away with me just yet. I remind myself who I am. The babysitter. That's it.

After half an hour, Smith announces it's time for Carter to

go to bed, and butterflies race inside me. I move to the couch as he tucks Carter in, waiting for whatever he has planned.

What if this is what that was? One last goodbye to Carter, playing with him one last time before I walk away forever.

I will myself to stay positive. I fidget with the hem of my blue dress as I wait for him to return.

"How about some coffee?" he asks in a sexy deep voice that startles me.

"Oh, ok." I get up from the couch and follow him into the kitchen. The same kitchen where last night he dined on me like I was his favorite meal. I gaze at the counter where I perched myself last night while he sucked me into his soft lips.

"Yeah, about last night," he starts as he grabs two mugs from the cabinet.

I cut in, "It was a mistake. I'm sorry."

He grabs my hands, leaning me back against the counter as he steps closer to me. "Don't say that, Bree. I don't think it was a mistake at all."

Completely stunned by his words, I stare at him with wide eyes. Until that nagging voice in my head says, "You quitting wasn't the mistake, you fool." I find courage I didn't know I had and cross my arms over myself. "Which part?"

He hands me my coffee and nods for me to follow him. Without question, I do. We sit down on the couch and I carefully sip the hot drink.

"I think I need to make myself clear," he begins. "Last night wasn't something I planned, but it's also not something I just want to forget. I'd like to forget the part of you walking out, but you were scared. I'm not scared, Bree. Everything in my life seems to have righted itself since you. Carter loves you and needs you. Just like I do. I want you, Bree. I want us to be together."

This can't be real...it has to be a dream. This sexy as hell, extremely wealthy, accomplished man wants me? Not only does he not think last night was a mistake, but he wants more.

Things like this don't happen to ordinary girls like me. I want it. I've longed for it. How is it all going to work?

"I want you too, Smith. So much," I begin. "But how?"

Our coffees are long forgotten on the small table as he pulls me on his lap. He cups his hands on my face, running his thumbs across my cheeks. I'm lost in his eyes, in his touch. "It will work however we want it to work."

With that, he presses his lips to mine and the second our tongues touch I no longer care. I don't care how it works. Or what people will think. All I care about is how he makes me feel. The burning flame that he makes larger than life, and then extinguishes. I don't need any more convincing, this is exactly where I want to be.

Chapter 6

Smith

This is heaven. Bree's soft lips against mine. Her sweet tongue on mine. Her sexy, tight body pressed against me. It's fucking everything. I can sense her worry, but right now I can't think about it. All I can think about is carrying her to my room and burying my cock deep inside her wet, tight pussy.

I break the kiss and see the want in her innocent eyes. Without a word, I lift her and carry her to my bed. I kick the door closed behind us and she slides down my body. "Undress for me," I demand.

She doesn't miss a beat as she begins to slowly unbutton her dress. My dick is so hard I need to rub it watching her. She notices and her cheeks flush with pink.

"Baby girl, you see what you do to me? That's nothing to be embarrassed about."

She bites her lip, giving me a small nod as she continues to unbutton her dress. I join in and pull off my T-shirt, tossing it to the floor. Her dress slides off her delicate shoulders and floats to the floor. Unsure what to do next, she stands still watching me.

"Come take off my pants," I say, holding my hand out to her.

She complies and looks up at me as her small hands work to unbuckle my belt and jeans. She pulls the zipper down and her hand barely touches my hard cock. But fuck, it's enough to make me close my eyes briefly. She continues, sliding my jeans down to the floor.

"Slide my boxers off and drop to your knees. I want your hot mouth wrapped around my cock," I say.

She obeys. Once on her knees, my cock is inches away from her mouth. I grab a fistful of her hair and pull her closer. Not enough to push my dick deep into her mouth, but enough that I grab my rock hard dick and pump it. "This is what you do to me, Bree. You make it impossible to think about anything but fucking you."

A moan escapes her when I push myself against her lips. She opens her mouth, and the second her lips wrap around me, I lose it. I pump my hips like I'm fucking her pussy and groan out when she takes all of me. She's young, but fuck, she knows how to get me off. I also know if I keep this up I'm going to come and I'm not ready to. Reluctantly, I pull my cock out and she lets out a small whimper.

I grab her arms and pull her off the floor. "I will come in that mouth, but right now I need to be buried deep inside you." I slam my mouth to hers and make quick work of getting off her bra and panties. I continue kissing her as I back her up to the bed. "Get on the bed," I order. When she does as I say, it makes this need I have for her even stronger.

I spend the next half hour worshipping her body. I kiss, suck, and lick every inch of her soft skin. All while avoiding her hard nipples and dripping cunt. I'm teasing her. Touching her in ways I hope no one else has, making her want me as much as I want her. I know she does. I see it in her eyes. In the way her body reacts to my touch. It's fucking hot.

As I kiss her inner thighs, she groans when I once again avoid her pussy. I glance up at her and grin. "You want something, baby girl?"

"Yes," she moans out.

My fingers inch closer to her wetness, as I continue to tease her. "Tell me."

"I want you," she whispers.

"You have me, Bree. I want you to tell me what you want me to do right now. Beg me for it," I demand.

It takes her a minute to find the confidence, but when she finally does, it's fucking perfect. "I want your mouth on my pussy before your cock slams into me."

I attack. I can't handle it anymore. My mouth works over her dripping cunt. I bite her clit, suck on her, and push my tongue inside. She's gripping the covers for dear life, her hips rocking against me. I reach up and pinch her hard nipples, evoking a scream from her. Fuck, I need to feel her wrapped around me.

Her clit gets one last long suck, before I climb up her body. My dick teases her opening. "You won't fucking leave this time. I want you here when I wake up."

"Oh, damn. I'm not leaving, I promise," she breathes out.

With that promise, I slam into her, making both of us moan in pleasure. I grab her hands, placing them on my chest while I fuck her. I thrust into her with uncontrollable force. It's like I've held back for too long and my body is in charge. The sight of her beneath me is everything. Her eyes closed, her mouth slightly open as she moans. The way her body rocks with such force when I push into her. Her tits bouncing, her nails scraping my skin, the sweat glistening on her body.

"Oh, Smith, yes," she moans.

I know she's close. I reach down and rub her clit, and she

nearly bucks off the bed. Fuck, it's sexy to watch her come undone. I'm so close too, it's getting harder to hold back.

"Look at me," I force out. Her eyes snap open and lock with mine. I pinch her clit and pound her over and over. "Come for me, baby girl. I need to feel you."

I watch her as she gives herself over to me completely. It's like a moment I can't explain. I see it in her eyes. Feel it in her body. She's mine. In the moment she became mine. Just like that, her orgasm rips through her and she shouts my name. I slam into her, making her pleasure last, before I come. It tears through me with a force I've never felt. She owns me.

"DADDY, DADDY," Carter yells, crashing through the door. "Bree?"

Shit.

She jumps up, holding the sheet against herself. "Hey, Carter buddy."

"Carter, why don't you go put cartoons on and we'll be right out to make pancakes?" I say, calmly.

He jumps off my bed and rushes to the living room.

"Oh my God. What are we going to do now?" Bree, asks holding the sheet tighter to her.

I chuckle and pull her back onto the bed. I climb on top of her and kiss her nose, resting my forehead to hers. "Now, we tell him that we're together. This is what I want, Bree. I want you here in my bed, in my house, every day."

"You want me here all the time?" she questions.

"Yes, I do."

"How? I have school and you have work. There's Carter and I need to find a job," she rushes out.

I laugh and kiss her soft lips. "You have a job."

"You know that makes me sound like a hooker, right?" she says, lifting her eyebrows.

"It's not perfect, but we'll figure it out. In the meanwhile, I would like you to move in with us. I'll take care of your schooling costs. I'll pay you to be with Carter, but only until you get your career going. I don't intend to pay my future wife to watch our son," I say, meaning every word.

"Wait, what?" she shouts.

Once again I laugh and climb off of her. "For now, just move in with me."

I get dressed, knowing in my heart, this is the beginning of the rest of my life.

Chapter 7

Bree

"Babe, I'm home," I say, dropping my keys on the console table.

"Bree," Carter yells, running toward me.

I scoop him up in my arms and hug him tight. "I missed you today. How was daycare?"

"I made a picture for you and Daddy," he says with a huge smile.

"I can't wait to see it." I put him down and he dashes off to his room. "Babe?"

I look around for Smith, but can't find him. I go into what is now our room and when I turn to leave, I feel his comforting arms wrap around me.

"Hey, looking for me?" he whispers against the shell of my ear, sending shockwaves straight to my core.

Immediately, I get chills and my heart starts to pound. The effect this man has on me still catches me by surprise. The last few months have been amazing and cruel. The first few times we went out, Smith got a lot of stares. We ignored them, but the first time he brought me to a company party, that was a different story. While he was off talking business, I was confronted by Roger. He all but told me that I should stop shaking my ass in front of Smith. That I was nothing but a distraction. An itch that Smith needed to scratch. He said there was no way a man of his intelligence, status, and wealth, could possibly have anything in common with someone as young as me. It felt as though someone reached in and ripped my heart out. I wanted to shout, to cry, to run away from the insults. But, I pushed it all down and gave him a smile. Words at that point failed me, but Smith had come back and heard it all. I don't know exactly what was said between them, since they left the room, but I do know that the next day Roger had one hell of a shiner.

This was something we encountered quite often in the beginning. The question of how could Smith possibly have anything in common with me? My parents all but disowned me. My friends told me I was crazy jumping all in with a man that had a built-in family. His friends watched me like I was going to need a bottle and burp. It was hard on me, but Smith didn't let it bother him at all. He's told everyone the same thing. "What we have is between us. You don't need to understand it. We do and that's all that fucking matters."

On the flip side of all the criticism, I've been swept off my feet. Smith has taken me places I've only dreamed of going. Restaurants, theaters, blacktie weddings. But, we've also been on picnics with Carter, sipped coffee at cafes, and eaten pizza in bed. He was determined to prove to me that not only were his feelings real, but that this would work. I've been convinced a hundred times over.

We became this family of three and I couldn't ask for more. He wants me to finish school, so I can begin my career in fashion. But, in order to do that we needed to put Carter in daycare. It broke my heart, but I know that in the long run it's for the best. I'll be doing what I love, and Carter will be used to being away from the both of us. He loves it, and I'm so glad. I can't wait to not only graduate and find my path in the fashion industry, but not rely so much on Smith. I want to feel like an equal partner, not a dependent. He's never made me feel like that, but having him pay for my schooling, our home, and anything I could need, it sometimes feels like it. I've got big plans though, I'm determined to have my own fashion line and I know I'll do it.

"Hey," Smith says, turning me to him. "Everything alright?"

I hug him tight and kiss his chest. "Everything's perfect."

And it is. I've never in my life had this feeling of being so complete in my life.

Carter busts through the door, holding a drawing he made of the three of us together. I'm in the middle, holding each of their hands, and when I see it my eyes well up with tears.

Never in my life did I ever think I could be this happy.

Chapter 8

Smith

Later in the evening, once Carter is put to bed, I grab the remote to the stereo and put on a soft tune.

"Would you like to dance?" I ask Bree.

She smiles, looking ever so beautiful in a long silk nightgown. "Of course," she says, staring up at me underneath those long lashes.

There's just something about this woman that makes me go weak in my knees. And I am *not* a weak man. I've never been known for being weak for anyone. Except her. She does something to me. Makes me go all primal beast on her or something.

I can't get enough. I don't think I'll ever be able to get enough either.

She has big ambitions, and it turns me on. She barely lets me help her succeed, and I could, so easily. But she wants to make a name for herself on her own. It turns me on. It made me fall in love when I thought I already was. But I was so wrong, because every day I'm finding I love her more and more.

I hold this woman in my arms, swaying her body to the beat of the music. "I love dancing with you."

She smiles up at me. "What else do you like doing with me?"

I audibly growl at her question. "You should know by now all the things I like doing with you."

She raises a thin eyebrow. "Maybe I need to be reminded."

Unable to take the pounding in my chest, I lean over and capture her lips with mine. "Then let me remind you every day for the rest of our lives." I continue kissing her, unable to get close enough.

She wraps her arms around my neck, tugging at the strands of my hair with her fingers.

I deepen the kiss, pulling her body snug against mine. I've never before in my life felt such passion for one person, but every day I find I'm feeling it more and more with Bree. "I need you," I tell her. "I need you on your hands and knees right now."

She stares up at me, dropping to her knees as slowly as possible. She licks her lips on the way down and I can barely contain myself. "Is this where you want me."

I nod, over and over, my cock growing three sizes bigger in the blink of an eye. "Yeah, baby. I want your mouth wrapped around my thick cock before I fuck your tight little pussy so good."

She tugs at my pajama pants, bringing them down my legs and I step out of them. She rubs her hand over my boxers and the ridge of my cock begging to be freed.

"You're such a naughty little thing."

She licks her lips again as she hooks her fingers into the

waistband of my boxers and begins to tug. "I am your naughty girl."

"Fuck yeah, you are. Show me how naughty you can be." I lean my head back and groan as she removes my boxers from me. "Fuck, Bree."

She gazes at my stiff hard on like it's the most glorious thing she's ever seen, and it turns me on even more. "Is this what you want?" She licks up one side of my dick and then back down the other.

"Naughtier." I want her doing things to me I can't even fathom right now. I just want her lips all over me. That wicked tongue she possesses works magic over my skin, making me come alive more than I ever thought possible.

She palms my dick in her fist and licks at the head. "I can be naughtier."

"Fucking show me," I tell her, running my fingers through her silky strands. "Show me how you can be my naughty girl."

She sucks on the tip of my dick, making my eyes roll back into my head.

I've never felt anything so good. "Yes, so naughty."

She continues to suck me off, making it her mission to get me to come as fast as she can. And if it's not her mission, it should be, because she's achieving it very well.

I stop her after a few minutes, and she pops off my dick, licking her lips as she gazes up at me. "I need to be deep inside you," I tell her, helping her up from the floor.

I carry her off to our bedroom, setting her on the bed. She smiles at me, knowing full well the things she does to me. How quickly she can turn me into a ravenous beast. How turned on she can make me.

When I first hired her, I knew she was beautiful, but I never planned on falling for her like I have. Sure, we've been through our ups and downs, and it's mainly brought on by others, but together we're so much stronger. It's true love. The kind of love you don't find every day.

Filthy Romance

THANK you so much for reading The Billionaire's Nanny

About the Author

Logan Chance is a *USA Today* and Top 20 Amazon Best Selling and Goodreads Choice Award nominated author with a quick wit and penchant for the simple things in life: Star Wars, music, and smart girls who love to read. His works can be classified as Dramedies (Drama+Comedies), featuring a ton of laughs and many swoon worthy, heartfelt moments.

Never miss an update, sign up for Logan's List: Join Here
Don't be shy, follow Logan on all platforms:

Also by Logan Chance

The Taken Series
TAKEN BY MY BEST FRIEND
MARRIED TO MY ENEMY (BOOK ONE)
MARRIED TO MY ENEMY (BOOK TWO)
STOLEN BY THE BOSS
ABDUCTED BY MY FATHER'S BEST FRIEND
CAPTURED BY THE CRIMINAL

Men Of Ruthless Corp.
SOLD TO THE HITMAN

Vampire Romance
Wicked Matrimony: A Vampire Romance

A Never Say Never Novel
NEVER KISS A STRANGER

The Playboy Series
PLAYBOY
HEARTBREAKER
STUCK
LOVE DOCTOR

The Me Series
DATE ME
STUDY ME

SAVE ME
BREAK ME

Sexy Standalones
WE ALL FALL DOWN
THE NEWLYFEDS
NAUGHTY OR NICE
The Billionaire's Nanny
The Favor
Holiday Hideout
Step-Santa
Ruin's Revenge
Hated By My Roommate

Steamy Duet
THE BOSS DUET

Box Sets
A VERY MERRY ALPHA CHRISTMAS
ME: THE COMPLETE SERIES
FAKE IT BABY ONE MORE TIME
THE TRIFECTA SERIES: COMPLETE BOX SET

Printed in Great Britain
by Amazon